TRACEY MARTIN

MISERY HAPPENS

MISS MISERY

BOOK FIVE

MISERY HAPPENS

TRACEY MARTIN

CITY OWL
PRESS

MISERY HAPPENS
Miss Misery, Book 5

CITY OWL PRESS
www.cityowlpress.com

Cover Design by MiblArt. All stock photos licensed appropriately.

Edited by Danielle DeVor.

For information on subsidiary rights, please contact the publisher at info@cityowlpress.com.

Print Edition ISBN: 978-1-64898-289-7

Digital Edition ISBN: 978-1-64898-290-3

Printed in the United States of America

PRAISE FOR TRACEY MARTIN

"The action in *Wicked Misery* was great, as was the suspense. Each character felt authentic, and the dialogue had me laughing. I definitely want to continue this series."
– *Bad Bird Reads*

"Readers of *Wicked Misery*…will surely be turned into fans, and will find themselves eager for the next installment."
– *RT Book Reviews*

"*Darkest Misery* is recommended for paranormal romance readers who enjoy a high-stakes story."
– *Library Journal*

"This world is rich, it has a lot of non-human, mystical elements in a human setting… I also loved the plot. A nice murder mystery with twist after twist."
– *Fangs for the Fantasy*

"Jess is finding out it's not so easy to let go of her past as she discovers the terrifying truth behind the Gryphons' treachery in this riveting urban fantasy romance, *Misery Loves Company*."
– *Evampire*

"The action was intense and the danger and mystery behind Jess's case brought along lots of drama and suspense in *Dirty Little Misery*."
– *Urban Fantasy Investigations*

For the ones who never stop fighting for a better future and the ones who have hung in here for all five books – the stubborn people, I guess.

THE MISS MISERY SERIES
BY TRACEY MARTIN

Wicked Misery

Dirty Little Misery

Misery Loves Company

Darkest Misery

Misery Happens

ONE

THE APOCALYPSE DIDN'T ARRIVE QUICKLY, NOR WITH THE ferocity of a punch to the face. Instead, it crept in quietly, a crimson sky oozing over the earth until it blanketed every continent.

Frankly, I'd have preferred a punch to the face. I knew what to do to people who were punching me. I did not know how to handle a world gone mad, bloodthirsty, and irrational. Especially when the real hell had yet to break loose.

"Seems to me that discretion might have been a better choice." Claudius wrinkled his nose at the airport's exhaust-filled terminal and waved a careless hand in the direction of the five Gryphons filing out of their SUVs. "Dezzi and I are the only ones who need to be here. And you, I suppose."

Behind Claudius's back, the long-suffering leader of Boston's satyr domus rolled her dark eyes. She did not, however, contradict him. Preds, regardless of their race, rarely showed their disagreements in front of Gryphons. Also, Claudius outranked her. It was more Dezzi's style to challenge his authority in subtle ways.

I bounced from foot to foot. I was wired on adrenaline and the human anxiety that permanently buzzed throughout the city, and trying to keep my distance from the satyrs' Upper Council member. Claudius had only been bumped from the top of my shitlist because a certain fury had murdered one of my friends. That said, I wouldn't put it past Claudius to reclaim his place at the top if given enough time. The arrogant, flowing-haired jackass had almost gotten *me* killed once already.

"Discretion failed us in Phoenix and Paris," I said, casting a wry glance at Gryphon Agent Tom Kassin. "The fury prison is open, the sky is bleeding, and the time for sneakiness is gone."

Tom nodded in agreement, which was almost as eerie as the crimson sky or the mostly deserted airport terminal. I could probably count the number of things Tom and I agreed on with one hand. Although, unlike with Claudius, I'd recently developed a grudging respect for the blond-haired, baby-faced Gryphon.

It was Tom's fraternity—*Le Confrérie de l'Aile* or the Brotherhood of the Wing—that I wasn't so certain about. Call me petty, but I couldn't entirely get over how they'd performed secret experiments on my teenage self that had turned me into a magical anomaly. Sure, their intentions had been good, but we all knew where good intentions led.

In our case, hell might be more literal than figurative. We'd begun referring to the creatures who had been locked in the magical prison—known as the Pit—as demons, and it was for more reasons than just ease of distinguishing them from the modern furies who'd freed them. Our ancestors had called them the same, and they scared the shit out of super-powerful preds like Claudius.

In the past three days, not only had the red sky spread from its origin above where the furies had opened the Pit, but the frequency of thunder had increased too. We had every reason to believe this was a sign that the Pit's inhabitants were moving about, gaining in power now that they could feed off the negativity and fear generated by the six billion humans on this planet.

Fear, which the preternaturally red sky obviously made worse.

People—be they human, magi, or pred—seemed to have had three types of reactions to the sky changing color. A few were trying to carry on as normal. Others were hunkering down, stocking up on gas, water, ammunition, and—weirdly enough—toilet paper, though not necessarily in that priority. Finally, the most annoying ones were taking to the streets in Boston and cities around the world. This third group was a scary mix of angry conspiracy theorists, religious fanatics, and a rapidly growing segment of the population who were known as anti-magers because they believed any use of magic by any race was evil and the cause of our current problems.

Claudius voiced his skepticism about the need for our Gryphon escort with a grunt. I took my cue from Dezzi and simply rolled my eyes as I wandered away. Ever since I'd had a magical collision with Raj, one of the fury ringleaders and the bastard at the top of my shitlist, my ability to get angry had been muted. I wasn't sure what that meant, but since furies fed on anger and fear, I suspected it wasn't good.

On the other hand, it probably was a boon to my blood pressure given how much time I'd had to spend in Claudius's company lately.

A lone cabbie drove by our spot in the passenger pick-up lot, and the taste of the driver's grapefruit-flavored fear shot over my tongue. It faded as he passed from my sight, but I pulled a stick of gum from my pocket anyway. Lately, I'd taken to chewing a lot of the stuff or munching on breath mints in order to deal with the constant sour taste of that particular emotion.

"You okay?" Lucen came up behind me.

I wanted to snark at him for asking such a ridiculous question, but I held my tongue because he meant well. He knew it wasn't just the situation with the Pit being open that had me on edge. It was being forced to deal with more satyrs from the Upper Council. Alas, Claudius, though a jackass of the highest order, had finally made himself useful and convinced the rest of the highest-ranking satyrs that they better help our tentative Boston-based alliance. That was why we were here. After intense political negotiations with the Gryphons, the satyrs had admitted that they held the fifth Vessel of Making.

We had the other four, which meant once we had the satyrs' Vessel too, we could unite all five and relock the Pit, preferably before the creatures inside escaped. Or that's how the theory went. How that would actually work, well, that was something we were struggling with.

I offered Lucen a stick of gum. "I'm fine." Then I wondered if that was a lie, and if so, could my misery-feeding boyfriend detect it?

Lucen declined the gum with an expression of comical distaste. "Sure you are."

"Hey, if you don't like my answers, why ask the question?"

"Habit?" He smiled impishly. The combination of the terminal's yellowish lighting and the ever-present red tinge from above gave everyone a creepy hue, but in that moment his blue-green eyes twinkled as bright as ever.

It was a good thing Lucen's appearance was only the third sexiest thing about him, following his sense of humor and protectiveness. Otherwise, I'd feel pretty shallow for the way I could lust after him no matter what the situation.

Even now, I longed to rest my head on his broad shoulder and breathe in deeply of his cinnamon-scented pheromones. The summer night was exceptionally humid, and imagining the taste of the thin layer of sweat on his skin was a tease. It wasn't even about sex. I just wanted him to hold me and lie to me and tell me everything was going to be okay. But this was neither the time nor the place. An unfortunate rule of the apocalypse was the more you craved comfort, the fewer opportunities you had for it.

"You're only asking out of habit?" I pretended to pout. "And here I thought you were genuinely concerned for my mental well-being."

Lucen took my arms in his hands and kissed my forehead. "Always, little siren."

Someone purposely scuffed their shoes against the asphalt as they came up behind us. Since I couldn't detect any emotions, it had to be Dezzi or Claudius. With my luck, the latter.

Indeed, my luck held. Claudius reached out with his power and lightly brushed my mind. Despite my unwillingness, my body reacted to the sensation, and I shivered. Lucen could sense my stronger arousal too, and he tightened his grip on my arms.

"You know it's impolite to eat in front of the rest of us." Claudius leered at me.

I clenched my jaw, and Lucen responded before I could. "She is a satyr. Lacking horns doesn't change her race."

"Stop it," I whispered to Lucen. Picking fights with Claudius was more dangerous for him than it was for Dezzi. Claudius already had it in for

Lucen, mostly because he thought Lucen was slumming it by being with me, and Lucen rose to the bait every time the topic arose. It was only because Lucen was currently Dezzi's acting lieutenant that he was here tonight. Usually, Dezzi tried to separate the two men.

"Being an abnormal human does not make her one of us. If I can feed on her emotions, if I can addict her"—Claudius's smirk broadened—"then how can she be?"

The memory of Claudius in my head, of how I'd hated him even as I was begging for his touch... It hit me all at once with a searing heat, like a salamander's bite to the brain. Suddenly, I was reliving that moment, the way I'd clung to Lucen's railing and spread my legs for the arrogant bastard in front of me.

All the rage I'd felt then exploded inside me. The unnatural calm I'd been experiencing was gone, replaced by a red-hot fire. Damn it, I might not be able to punch the apocalypse, but I could whale on a jackass of a satyr.

I spun around, slipping Misery from the sheath at my hip as I did so. The knife's black salamander fire-forged blade was beautiful in my grip and so easily lethal. Just a single nick would make Claudius bleed out. None of his power could save him from that, and while I held the weapon in my hand, I felt every bit as powerful as he must have when he'd lorded his control over me.

Claudius's eyes opened wide in surprise as I raised the blade toward his annoyingly handsome face. Oh, how I'd love to see it scarred.

Vaguely, I was aware of Lucen calling my name and the Gryphons pausing whatever they were doing and turning my way. But hot blood raced by my ears. I didn't care what they thought, just as I didn't care that threatening an extraordinarily powerful satyr whose help we needed was not a smart idea.

I didn't fucking care about anything except giving in to the fury boiling in my veins. The world had gone mad, bloodthirsty, and irrational, and at last, I'd gone with it.

"Back the hell off." My body was so tense it hurt my jaw to speak. "I don't care what you think I am or what you think of me. But if you ever invade my head that way again, I'm going to tie you up with your own intestines."

Hell, I didn't know why I shouldn't do it anyway. My hand trembled with the urge to drive my blade into Claudius's throat. No satyr healer could close that wound before he bled out, and wouldn't that be oh so satisfying.

Claudius could probably use his magic to force me to drop the knife, but maybe he didn't want to chance that I could move faster than he could mind-fuck me. He kept backing up, and he cast disdainful glances at Dezzi and the Gryphons as he did. "You need to learn to control her."

"Fuck you!" My vehemence echoed off the terminal's filthy concrete walls. "I'm not a satyr or a Gryphon. Nobody gets to claim me or control me, and you certainly don't get to define what I am."

Then I lunged at him.

TWO

LUCEN'S HANDS SHOT OUT AND SNAGGED MY WRISTS, AND HE wrestled me to the ground. I was still yelling irrationally at Claudius when Lucen's power crept over my senses, and I realized I was holding a deadly blade dangerously close to him.

As quickly as my outburst came on, my senseless rage broke. Panic overwhelmed me, and I dropped the knife. Lucen seized the opening and pinned my arms with his own, and I could feel his chest rising and falling against my back. Giving in to his body's rhythm, my own breathing slowed, and my emotions settled back to normal.

What the hell? I'd been ready to kill Claudius, and while goodness knew I owed him a solid kick to his ancient satyr jewels, I did not go around murdering people for being assholes. Even my bad temper had limits.

With a great expression of concern, Tom inched forward and picked up Misery. "Jessica, are you feeling all right?"

Claudius wiped invisible dirt from his silk shirt. "Clearly, she's not. She's lost her mind."

"I..." Dragon shit on toast. I hated agreeing with his Upper Council Asshole, but he wasn't entirely wrong. "Something like that. I don't know what came over me. I'm fine now."

Lucen released me, and I sighed. Being pressed up against him had been the lone bonus of my emotional breakdown, although I was aware that the Gryphons from *Le Confrérie* were looking at us funny, and it wasn't merely due to my irrational behavior. The Gryphons couldn't accept that Lucen and I had a relationship that was more than predator and prey, even though they were the ones who'd made me a quasi-satyr in the first place.

"It's this instability. The stress is getting to us all." Dezzi's silver watch gleamed against her dark skin as she made a show of checking the time. "The Council's flight landed twenty minutes ago. Where are they?"

Lucen ran his hands through his blond waves, his face filled with concern. "I hate to bring this up, but, Jess, I thought you and anger…"

Wetting my lips, I retrieved my knife from Tom. "I know. I don't understand it. Maybe it's like Dezzi said. Maybe it's been building inside me since we got back from Paris and the stress finally released it."

Maybe, but that explanation didn't stand up to scrutiny. In reality, Claudius's nastiness had been no worse than any dozen insinuations he'd made my way in the last few days. And it sure wasn't worse than the emotional trauma of attending Olef's funeral or standing over Devon's cursed, unconscious body. Yet another thing I wanted Raj's head for.

So why this? Why now? I didn't like it. My stomach twisted, and I spat my barely chewed gum into a tissue. I'd almost choked on it when I'd lost my shit, and after everything I'd been through, I'd be damned if it was a piece of peppermint gum that did me in.

"Jess, what's this about you and anger?" Tom asked.

Oops. With everything else going on, I must have forgotten to mention that particular aftereffect of having Raj invade my head. I didn't really want to discuss it now, not with Claudius eyeing me with great curiosity. As if I needed to give him another excuse to call me inferior.

"Ah, there they are." Dezzi quit tapping her foot as the terminal doors opened, and I was saved from responding by the arrival of the new Upper Council satyr. I should have been relieved, except I was about to have to deal with another satyr who would probably be as unpleasant as Claudius. And like Claudius, would hold me in particular disdain for being abnormal.

Nonetheless, I straightened my spine and did my part to appear professional, or at the very least, nonconfrontational. "About time," I muttered. "Let's get this package wrapped up and go home."

The three satyrs who'd exited the terminal building hadn't bothered hiding their horns, and they were accompanied by six badass-looking human lust addicts, all packing visible heat. I'd thought it was more evidence of their arrogance when I'd learned they'd be traveling by private jet, but apparently there were practical reasons as well. They weren't reckless enough to travel without heavy protections.

And Claudius had been arguing for discretion. Ha. At least his fellow Upper Council member was too smart to bother with that.

It was simple to pick out which of the three new satyrs was the Council member and which of the others were either assistants or bodyguards. For starters, only one of those satyrs gave off the telltale sign that she was wicked powerful.

In general, I was immune to pred magic unless the pred was touching me, but Claudius had proven to be an exception. The female satyr in the middle of the arrivals was too. I could sense her power before the group crossed the first lane of traffic, a scent I couldn't name but which made me think of warm spices, cool silks, and sand between my toes. As did her tan skin and waist-length black hair. Her suit was impeccably white and form-fitting, her heels high, and her face flawless in spite of the six-hour flight from Los Angeles.

I couldn't help but be jealous. Sure, while I didn't have to worry about hiding horns if I wanted to blend in, I wouldn't have minded inheriting half of whatever appearance-related mojo seemed to come naturally to all normal satyrs.

"Raia." Claudius stepped toward the crosswalk, for the first time smiling in such a genuine way that it didn't inspire fantasies of me decking him.

Given the constant background rumble of the airport traffic, I didn't know how she could have heard him say her name, but the female satyr smiled back. Intrigued by this almost friendly interaction, I didn't realize at first that the Gryphons' nervousness was on the rise.

Before I had a chance to figure out what was going on with Tom and the others, tires squealed and a large SUV raced around the corner. Eating its exhaust came five giant Harleys. The roar of their engines echoing off the terminal lot was deafening, and the curses their riders wielded—that was blinding. I saw the group of visiting satyrs scramble to get out of the lane of the speeding bikes, saw the Gryphons and Dezzi's satyr bodyguards rush forward with weapons drawn. Then the parking lot vanished.

Several people shouted, and I cursed. Instinctively, I dropped to a crouch and whipped out the special gun the Gryphons had given me. Even as I did, Tom was on top of the situation. I heard a pop among the noise, and a bright light flooded the area. Some kind of magical flare visibly pushed the unnatural darkness aside.

What I saw almost made me wish I were blind again. The furies on the bikes had apparently been protected against the temporary darkness, and they circled the new satyrs and their addicts, trying to keep them contained. In their upraised hands, they carried long, salamander fire-forged swords, and they swung them wildly but with obvious purpose, herding the group into a tighter formation. Meanwhile, the two non-Council satyrs and the addict guards had dropped their luggage and were starting to fight back with their own deadly blades and firepower.

A noose of fear wrapped around me. I wasn't sure where to aim or whether I should. I only had eight of the Gryphons' special, pred-killing rounds. Eight shots, and my aim was not the best. Plus, while Claudius and Dezzi held back, Lucen had run to join the fighting. I couldn't risk hitting him.

The Gryphons, naturally, didn't share my concern. Nor did the guards who were trapped by the furies. They were taking aim at the riders, and the shots were going everywhere.

Shit. I darted closer to the nearest car as the air filled with bullets, and not a moment too soon. The SUV's doors burst open, and four more furies poured out. I had a second to notice that one of them was Raj before they too began shooting at us.

Tom skidded next to me under a hail of fire. "Protect the package at all costs."

I knew he was right, knew that was our priority, but I feared for what that cost might be. I also didn't know where the Vessel of Making was. Presumably someone had stuffed it into one of the suitcases, but it was far too dangerous to dash into the melee when I had no idea which piece of luggage I needed to grab.

Through the haze of smoke, I saw that one of the furies had been knocked off his bike, and one of the addicts was down too. But beyond that, it was too dangerous to stick my head up for long. The noise bouncing off the walls and the stench of the gunpowder alone were almost incapacitating.

Bracing myself, I poked my head around the car's trunk long enough to fire in Raj's general direction, and I ducked back to safety as a couple bullets lodged themselves in the nearest taillight, shattering it. Sweat rolled down my back and made keeping my grip on the gun challenging. Something about this whole situation struck me as wrong. All this gunfire was unusual for preds.

While I coughed from the smoke, a shriek pierced the commotion and someone shouted, "Go!" Tom sprinted around the car. Adjusting my grip, I stood on shaky legs, ready to take another shot.

But as I searched for an opening so I wouldn't hit any of my allies, Raj caught my eye. At well over six feet, with red-and-black glyphs tattooed on his face, he was kind of attention-grabbing in a way that could give small children nightmares. But it wasn't his appearance that drew my awareness. He held my gaze with something far stronger.

The tightened sensation in my gut intensified until the chaos of the fighting drained from my consciousness. There was nothing else in the airport terminal but the two of us. Nothing in me except my rage. Just like I'd been craving Claudius's blood moments ago, bloodlust for a certain fury narrowed my world to a single thought.

Kill.

Whereas my reaction to Claudius had been irrational, this was not. More to the point, deep inside, I now understood the reason why I'd attacked Claudius. My temper had been set off by Raj being so close. He was in my head still.

I didn't understand how it was possible because I wasn't an addict.

Thanks to Claudius, I knew what it felt like to be one, and besides, my company would have noticed if I was. But there was also no denying that the feeling I got when I looked at Raj was the same feeling I had when I created an addict-like bond between myself and a human.

Something was wrong here. Very, very wrong, and there was only one way to handle it.

I was going to kill Raj.

A niggling voice in the back of my mind reminded me that wasn't my goal. I was supposed to be protecting something. But what that something was had vanished, and I bade the voice to go away. It had no ability to influence me. My focus was all-consuming. Anger was all I knew.

Blood. Kill. Fury.

I screamed, letting the emotion erupt from my chest, but in the confusion, I doubted anyone noticed. From the corner of my eye, I could tell there was commotion among the Gryphons and satyrs. Could tell the furies were gaining the upper hand.

Raj barked some kind of order to his people and grabbed one of the Harleys. He was going to get away. The evil bastard thought he was leaving. Like hell he was.

I'd ridden to this party myself, not wanting to be crammed into a vehicle with the Gryphons, or worse, trapped in a car with Claudius or any other Upper Council members on the drive home. My precious Dragon'sWing was parked several spots away, luckily out of the direction of the fighting. Taking a deep breath, I sprinted toward it.

For a moment, my back was exposed to the hailstorm of lead, and I could sense a bullet flying near my skull. Then I swung my legs around the motorcycle's familiar seat and started the engine.

The guttural thunder of the furies' bikes grew louder. Raj wasn't the only one making a getaway, but he was the only one who mattered. Even now, my sight homed in on him as I scanned the terminal. The magical rope that bound us was in place, yet if it functioned like my bond with humans, it would grow weaker the farther away he got. Eventually, it would snap.

I couldn't allow that. I might not get another chance. Besides, whatever that something was that I was supposed to be worried about, the same voice in the back of my head was convinced Raj would have it. Raj was the furies' Boston Dom, just as Raj was one of the ringleaders who'd set the demons free. Every direction led back to him.

Lucen shouted my name as I stuck my helmet on, but I ignored his voice. To my left, Raj was disappearing down the long terminal, and the magic connecting us was stretching. I couldn't see it, but feeling it was enough. I imagined it attaching me to him like some evil umbilical cord as I gunned my engine and took off.

Whoever designed airports had a cruel sense of humor. The lanes twisted and turned, sometimes sharply. Off ramps and on ramps circled the terminal buildings in a maze, and when combined with the usual airport traffic, staying on Raj's tail would have been damned near impossible if I had to rely on sight to keep up. The bond, however, didn't care if I had to stop abruptly for an airport shuttle or take a corner blindly. I could tell where he turned even if I couldn't always tell where I was going.

Raj's bike had the more powerful engine, but my Dragon'sWing was built for speed and maneuverability. Between my legs, the bike thrummed with my tension, urging me to go faster than the traffic would allow. If only Raj would pull onto a highway. I wanted to leave behind the humid, exhaust-choked air.

But more than that, I wanted to kill Raj. The chase would be fun, but catching him would be satisfying. Determination pulsed in my veins with my heartbeat. My vision rendered the world as red as the sky above.

I followed him until he plowed through a cheap metal fence that blocked off a closed parking lot. As the contraption went flying, skittering across the uneven and damaged asphalt, Raj spun his bike around.

Got you, I thought, but then I realized he was reaching for something. A gun. And I was heading straight toward him with no cover.

The next few seconds were a blur. Not even adrenaline could save me from the pain. Raj fired, I tried to duck, and in doing so, I couldn't avoid the patch of broken blacktop in front of me. My bike went careening out from beneath my legs. In the split second before I crashed into the pavement, amazement washed over me. So this would be how I died. Flayed and broken at the fucking airport.

So much for that magi prophecy of how I was supposed to save the world.

THREE

FRAGILE BONES AND DELICATE SKIN SLAMMED INTO THE gritty ground, not to mention the effect that impact had on my poor internal organs. Shoulders then legs, hands and head—I didn't know how the asphalt and I met. I just knew it fucking hurt.

My bike had vanished, and I was surprised my conscious awareness hadn't too. Honestly, I wish it had because every part of me felt broken. My tongue tasted blood. How could I not be dead? How could I be thinking semi-clearly?

I shifted my legs, and though my muscles shrieked, they moved. Whimpering to control the pain, I pulled my arms toward my chest, trying to maneuver into a position so I could sit. My head swam and so did the parking lot, and I managed to remove my helmet though I almost vomited from the intensity of the pain.

Yet through it all, my heart continued to beat. My lungs continued to fill. And the magic connecting me to Raj continued to override every other concern. The ground vibrated with the hum of his bike's engine, confirming he was as close as I sensed him. Bastard. I might be bleeding to death internally, but as long as I could move, I could take him with me.

I tossed my helmet aside and discovered my hands were covered in blood. No matter. If I could twitch a finger, I could press a trigger. But the gun turned out to be far more uncomfortable to hold than my helmet, requiring a far greater range of motion to grip. I inhaled sharply, causing additional searing pain in my rib cage.

Raj approached, a pair of kickass boots in my peripheral vision. My arm shook as I attempted to raise the gun, but I had no chance of shooting anything except his ankles. Even as I tried, I realized he must have been watching me struggle for a while. To confirm it, he snatched the gun from my hand, and I couldn't stop from screaming as the action further abraded my palm.

Raj kneeled next to me, and I hissed as he used the gun barrel to push hair out of my face. "You are something, soul swapper. Just look at you. Still fighting. Someone obviously covered you in some impressive charms for you to be moving and breathing, but being able to move is not half as fascinating as willing yourself to do it. There's so much anger in you that it must power you nearly as strongly as it does me." He made his point by inhaling deeply with an expression of disturbingly erotic satisfaction.

"Go to hell." My words were mushy. Shit. How many teeth had I lost?

Raj chuckled. "No need for that. We've brought hell to us. With your assistance, of course." He sighed theatrically. "I did warn you back in France that if you came with me, you'd be well treated, but if you refused, we'd get you one way or another and not as friendly-like. It's simply unfortunate that I can't take you with me this time. In your condition, throwing you over the back of my bike might kill you regardless of the charms holding you together, and if I wait for assistance, your friends might get here first. I have more important things to deal with than them."

Raj tossed my gun aside and to my surprise, pulled a handkerchief from his inner jacket pocket. While I tried scooting away unsuccessfully, he wiped blood from my face. It was almost gentle, but I understood why he did it, and it wasn't out of concern for me. The only reason Raj wanted to take me with him was for the unique magical properties I contained, some of which were in my blood.

He stuffed the handkerchief away and stood. "It'll be interesting to analyze this and see what it's useful for. Heal well, soul swapper. I know there are two others biologically similar to you, but there's no one half as fun. It'd be a shame if you died."

I considered cursing him again, but it took far too much energy to form words. All I could do was sit there, trembling with rage and sweating in agony, and let him walk away. Watch him climb on his damn Harley and listen to the engine roar before he disappeared.

A swarm of imps that had been dancing around a nearby streetlamp flew my way, attracted by the magic in my blood. Just what I needed on top of everything else—an imp attack. But the anti-imp charms I had, courtesy of Lucen, forced them to keep their distance. Finally, one small positive for the night. And yet as they hovered in an effervescent cloud above me, I couldn't help but think they looked like vultures guarding their carrion.

Praying my phone hadn't been damaged in the crash, I felt for it in my jeans. Thank dragons it was on the side of me that hadn't hit the ground at full force. Clenching my jaw against more pain, I reached into my pocket with my shredded fingers and retrieved it.

Lucen picked up on the second ring. "Are you okay?"

"Um, no." I expected to hear gunfire in the background, but his side of the line was quiet.

"Are you wearing your pendant? I'm coming for you."

I groped at my neck and touched the silver fox. The pendant he'd given me was both pretty and functional—a tracking charm. Although I'd resented the idea of being tagged, this was the second time Lucen's gift was coming in handy.

"Bring a doctor," I managed to say before my hand gave out and the phone slipped through my blood-slicked fingers.

LUCEN WOULDN'T SHARE ANYTHING ABOUT WHAT HAPPENED at the terminal after I left. He simply fussed over me and told me not to worry. For possibly the first time in my life, I was feeling crappy enough to take his suggestion, at least for a short while.

When the EMTs arrived, all anyone wanted to tell me was how lucky I was to be alive, and since no one else rode in the ambulance with me, I was further deprived of news. The Gryphons were too busy, though I had no idea with what, and Lucen didn't want to stay in such close proximity to the EMTs while they were treating me in case his power distracted them. I supposed that made sense, but it irked.

Worse than that, it meant I had to wait longer to get information about what happened with the satyrs and the furies. By the time I reached the hospital, the pain medications I'd been given had kicked in enough that I was no longer able to not worry.

Additionally, without Raj so close to me, my irrational anger faded until I could think straight. Now, however, I could detect him in my head, and I suspected he'd been in there the whole time. I simply hadn't been aware of the thin bond connecting us. With effort, I might even be able to follow it again. It was a hopeful thought, although that sort of concentration was currently beyond me.

I flopped against the sturdy hospital pillow as the ER doctor finished reviewing my injuries. "So when you say 'miraculous,' does this mean I can go?"

The doctor frowned. "Under the circumstances, it might be wise for you to stay for more tests. We don't know yet whether—"

"She'll be fine." Lucen appeared around the sheet that separated my narrow section of the room. "You said nothing's broken."

The doctor took a step back. Lucen had his horns disguised, but she must have detected something was off about him. Most likely, she was feeling flustered by an intense arousal that would have seemed to come from nowhere. "Nothing appears broken, but with the extent of bruising—"

"She'll be fine," Lucen said more firmly. He smiled, and I understood he was purposely working his mojo on the doctor to gain her compliance. "Why don't you draw up the release paperwork or whatever you need to do so she can leave?"

"If that's what you want?" The doctor turned her concerned face toward me.

It was what I wanted. Since Raj was no longer distracting me from our plans, I needed to get back to them. To find out what happened after I lost it and went chasing him and to see what I could do to help if what happened was bad.

On the other hand, I sure didn't feel up to walking out of here yet, and what if there was internal bleeding? Trust Lucen, I told myself. If my normally overly protective satyr was pushing for my release, my condition couldn't be that bad.

I nodded at the doctor, who didn't appear entirely convinced. However, she pressed her lips thin and left. After she did, Lucen pulled a chair up to the edge of my bed, and another satyr followed him into the pseudo-room.

"Azria?" So this was why Lucen was insistent that I'd be fine. He'd brought one of the satyrs' own magical medics.

Like Lucen, Azria had her horns hidden. She tucked her pink-dyed curls behind her ears and began retrieving several items from the bag she carried. The first one she handed me was a pain-relief charm, which I took gratefully. The hospital had offered me potent painkillers, but I'd refused everything except the extra-strength Tylenol. I didn't need my head getting cloudy again. Alas, Tylenol had only taken the edge off.

Lucen squeezed my hand as I draped the charm around my neck. "Kassin wanted to send a Gryphon healer in to tend you, but I convinced him to let us have a go at it first."

"Um." I bit my lip, not wanting to offend Azria's healing skills but feeling it necessary to point out the obvious. "Will your medical charms work since I'm not a normal satyr? Ouch."

Azria had taken a sample of my blood while I was looking at Lucen. The satyr medic stuck the drops in a bowl and added what appeared to be some pre-mixed spell ingredients to them. "Lucen tells me that when you were turned, your eyesight corrected itself. To his knowledge, you haven't even come down with a cold in the last ten years, and you've healed very quickly from prior injuries."

"And to top it off," Lucen added, "the protective glyphs we gave you did far more than they should have if you were human. You don't have so much as a concussion or a broken rib from your accident."

"To be fair, I'm covered in the glyphs you gave me and the ones the Gryphons gave me. I'm wrapped in magical Teflon. I'm surprised I didn't bounce off the pavement."

After fighting with the furies in the Alps, Dezzi had insisted the satyrs add their own spells to the many the Gryphons had already covered me in. I didn't know what all of them did, but I was pretty sure there were tattoo artists out there who were covered in less ink. Except my glyphs weren't permanent. Once the magic was used up, they'd disappear.

On that thought, I inspected my arms, unsurprised to learn the marks on them were noticeably lighter. Definitely some of that power had been burned.

"Little siren, as far as I can tell, you went flying off your motorcycle at high speed. The fact that you're in one piece is a testament to those charms, yes, but also to the fact that you're physically a lot tougher than any human. More like one of us. I thought you were okay with that."

"I am." I took the vaguely acidic-smelling concoction Azria handed me and drank up as she indicated. It was hardly the foulest-tasting thing I'd ever had in my mouth, and with a wrinkled nose, I returned her cup. "I'm just not sure what it means."

Azria was busy mixing up something new, and she didn't glance at me as she answered. "It means magical remedies are likely to work more effectively on you than human ones. Now show me where the worst of your bruising is."

"That would be my whole body." Moaning, I lifted the scratchy blanket covering my hospital gown. While Azria spread some cooling paste on my thighs, I turned to Lucen again. "Speaking of my bike, where is it? And is the you-know-what safe? And how's Tom and Dezzi and everyone else? For that matter, why hasn't Tom checked in with me yet?"

"First, how about you tell me what you were thinking taking after Raj by yourself?"

In spite of the drugs and charms, I winced as Azria smeared yet a third remedy on my abraded wrists. "Later. Can we focus on what's important?"

Lucen leaned back in his chair, looking weary. "All right. Least bad news first—your bike has been carted away."

"What do you mean by carted away?"

Lucen smiled sadly. "Let's just say it's far more damaged than you are. I expect it's totaled."

"What?" I jerked forward, almost knocking the bowl from Azria's hands, my heart sinking. "No. No, no, no—not my Dragon'sWing. Come on. I love that bike. I will never be able to afford to replace it with something half so nice."

"Sorry, little siren. The bike is a wreck."

Whimpering, I flopped back, though I was aware how ridiculous I was being. *It's a bike, Jess. Not the end of the world. The real end of the world should be your concern.*

Damn it. I forced myself to put aside my misplaced angst. "You said that was the least of the bad news. This doesn't make me hopeful."

Lucen rubbed the day-old scruff on his cheeks. "Yeah, about that. We lost the Vessel."

I gaped at him, too horrified to speak. A hole opened in my gut, and I thought I might be sick yet again. "The furies got it? Oh, shit." An unhappy silence followed, broken only by the sound of Azria packing away her supplies and a couple nurses talking down the hall.

Lucen cleared his throat. "After you took off, the fighting died down. Most of the furies got away, but we did manage to take one alive. The Gryphons took him to their headquarters for questioning. Meanwhile, they're blocking off the city."

"Blocking it off?" I flexed my fingers, which weren't nearly as stiff as they'd been a few minutes ago. Azria's spells must be working. Thank dragons. I was not sitting out the rest of this fight. "How long can they do that for?"

"I'm not sure, but as long as we know the Vessel in is the city, we have a chance to track it. If Raj smuggles it out, we might lose it for good."

I closed my eyes and searched for that thin thread connecting me to the fury Dom. It was there, for whatever good it would do. The Vessel could be anywhere already, and there was no sense in going after Raj if the Gryphons had a lackey in their possession who we could question.

"I want to talk to this fury," I said. "I have a suspicion. Something about being ambushed tonight stunk."

Lucen dumped my torn and bloody clothes on my bed. "Yeah, it did. That's why I was able to convince Kassin to let us tend to you, even though he's suspicious of our magic. He wants you on your feet ASAP.

He's holding a strategy meeting at the damn Gryphon building in..." Lucen checked his phone, "...thirty minutes."

Warily, I slid out of the bed and tested my legs. They held, and I sighed with relief. "Let's go then before this night gets any worse."

"Can it?" murmured Azria as she hitched her bag over her shoulder.

I shook out my abraded denim, hoping there was enough fabric left to keep my jeans on. "It can always get worse. There's been no zombie sightings yet. Right?"

Lucen cringed, and I shrugged. Whatever. There was a reason I didn't do optimism.

———

MY BODY STILL ACHED BY THE TIME WE REACHED headquarters, but Azria's spells were working. The scabs and skin flecks that decorated my hands were disappearing, and I assumed the rest of my injuries were too. I had survived this much. As for the rest of the night's events, well, that remained to be determined.

Headquarters was a madhouse. The Gryphons were mobilizing every resource at their disposal and calling in every one of their agents, charm specialists, or healers they could drag off their normal jobs and put to work. The National Guard helicopters that had been circling overhead since the sky reddened, and their constant thump-thump, had been augmented to include two of the Gryphons' own.

Olivia Lee, Director of the Boston office, must be spitting salamander fire. She was already less than thrilled that the Brotherhood had moved many of their resources to her building, and with no wonder. They were a secretive, high-ranking bunch, which was enough to annoy anyone. Plus, they were using up a lot of Boston's conference rooms and lab space, and undoubtedly drinking coffee that came from the Boston office's budget. That they were now poaching her agents for their projects had to smart.

Of course, it wasn't just the Gryphons who were alarmed. Gunthra, the goblins' Dom, was at headquarters, along with Dezzi and the Upper Council satyrs, and they were all trying to figure out how to help. In a way, it was inspiring. I only wished it had taken something less than the potential end of the world for this sort of cooperation. In fact, if everyone had been cooperating a couple weeks ago, we might not have been in this situation at all.

"Jessica." Tom pounced on me the moment I limped through the door of the conference room. "We need to talk."

I collapsed on a chair to give my legs a rest. "I'm fine by the way, thanks for asking. How did *you* survive the shootout?"

He ignored my sarcasm, but judging by the dark lines etched into his face, he hadn't fared well mentally. "You're up and moving, and that tells me what I need to know. We have bigger problems than social etiquette."

"Fair enough. How's the fury hunt going?" Although Lucen had rushed to get us here, we'd missed the briefing Tom had called. As Tom had explained to me over the phone during the drive, there was no time to waste talking.

Tom shut the conference room door and ran his fingers through his hair. It was just the two of us and piles of notes, books, and photographs spread over the table. Rather ominous. "I've convinced the others to nominally bring in Director Lee. We need her assistance—and this office's assistance—to canvas and blockade the city."

"I don't disagree that the director should have a clue what's going on, nor that she's very competent. But given what happened, bringing more people on board seems risky."

"You're referring to our leak problem."

My eyebrows shot up. That was exactly what I was referring to, but I hadn't expected Tom to suggest it. I'd made the case that a leak existed weeks ago when we were ambushed in Phoenix, and Tom and the rest of the Brotherhood had been in denial. "Excellent. They say the first step is admitting we have a problem. And before you start accusing the satyrs, I strongly suspect the person is a Gryphon."

"I'm aware."

Right. I'd made my case for that too. "Yeah, well, I consider tonight to be more evidence that I'm right."

Tom regarded me curiously. "Why is that?"

I'd had a lot of time to think about what bothered me during the fighting at the terminal, so I laid it out. "The furies came armed with regular guns, which is really unusual. Preds almost never fight each other like that since the bullets aren't lethal. That tells me they were expecting Gryphons to be there when we met the new satyrs, and that suggests to me the leak was a Gryphon. The satyrs weren't aware you were planning on providing extra security until right before we left."

Tom nodded slowly, swirling the remains of a mostly empty coffee cup around. "Well reasoned."

I gazed longingly at the coffee dregs. It had been a long night, and it was far from over. Feeling like I'd been hit by a tractor trailer didn't help. "Was that a compliment? I'll take it. If that wasn't your logic, though, then what changed your mind?"

"The fury we captured."

I cursed silently, annoyed to have missed the interrogation. "What did he say?"

"That they got their information from the Gryphons." Grimacing, Tom pushed away the cup and stretched his arms. "Normally, I wouldn't put much faith in anything a fury said, but we had some strong lie-detecting charms on him. Plus, after what's happened before, it adds up. I don't like admitting it, but I'm not unreasonable."

I bit my lip and refrained from making a joke. When I'd first met Tom, I'd thought he was a zealot, putting his infuriating organization ahead of people—including innocent children like I'd been—and ignoring the consequences. But it wasn't *Le Confrérie de l'Aile* he cared about. It was his mission, and I could respect that, although it would take a swarm of imps to make me admit it.

"So what are we doing about it?" I asked. "It has to be someone who was involved in the Phoenix plans since we were ratted out there too. There's only, what, maybe ten people who knew about tonight and who had also been part of that mission?"

Tom motioned to the closed door. "Which is why I'm only sharing this information with you. We will find out who it is, but for the moment, we don't have the time to go searching for our leak. Every resource has to be put toward finding the Vessel."

I gritted my teeth. Much as I wanted to find this leak—the person who'd gotten me kidnapped and almost killed on more than one occasion now—Tom was right. "Did the fury tell you anything else that might help?"

"No. He seems clueless. He doesn't know who the leak is, and he doesn't know where Raj is taking the Vessel." Tom got up as the conference room door opened.

In strutted the Upper Council satyr who'd arrived tonight. Her white leather suit was smudged with dirt, but she'd otherwise put herself back together. No mutilated jeans, bloodstains, or a dirty face for her. Seriously, how did she do it?

She clasped her hands together. "My understanding is that the Gryphons are trying to find the Vessel before the furies can destroy it. In that case, I have more information about this Vessel that you obviously need to know."

FOUR

"What information?" Tom asked.

The Upper Council satyr's head snapped his way, and only then did I realize she'd been addressing her comment to me. She raised a well-plucked eyebrow in Tom's direction then returned her gaze to me. "Somehow the furies were able to ambush my arrival. Rumor has it there is a leak in Boston. Do you trust this man?"

Next to her, Tom's face turned as red as the sky outside, and in spite of everything, I had to repress a giggle. I was so used to being bossed around by the Brotherhood and ignored by Claudius that there was something incredibly funny about the situation.

I struggled to my feet and held out a hand toward the satyr. "Yes, Agent Kassin is one of the only Gryphons at the moment I'm willing to trust. Claudius said your name is Raia, right?"

"Yes, it is. A pleasure, Jessica." She pressed her hand lightly against mine, once more filling my imagination with a teasing sense of warm spice. Then Raia motioned her head toward Tom. "I detected no reason to suspect your friend, but one can't be too sure under the circumstances."

I refrained from disclaiming Tom as my friend since I could already taste his annoyance.

Scowling, he shut the door, but the blood was draining from his face as his regained control of himself. "Information about the Vessel should be shared with Agent Blecher, as well."

"Ingrid Blecher is the Gryphon in charge of this mission," I explained to Raia. "She's probably not the leak either."

Raia took a seat next to me, arranging her thick, black hair artfully over her shoulders. "That may be, but it is you, I understand, who is acting as the liaison between my people and the Gryphons. I will liaise with you, and you may pass the information on to whomever you believe is appropriate."

I caught Tom eyeing me, torn between amusement and insult, but I couldn't respond without Raia noticing. So I sat back down and folded my hands. "Okay, so let's liaise. What do we need to know?"

"Both good news and bad news." She cast her dark eyes in Tom's direction as he joined us at the table. "Your concern about the furies destroying the Vessel is ill-founded. The Vessel cannot be destroyed."

"Is that the good news or the bad news?"

Raia tapped her fingers together. "I consider it both. You need not be concerned about losing the Vessel for good, but nor will you be able to prevent others from using it in the future if that is your hope."

"I'm assuming your people have attempted to destroy the Vessel then."

"On numerous occasions, specifically to prevent the possibility of it being reused. All attempts proved unsuccessful." Raia's phone vibrated on the table, but rather than answer, she drew a light pink nail down its length. The phone fell silent, as though soothed by the gesture. "When Claudius informed us what was happening here, more recent attempts were also made. Again, they were unsuccessful."

Interesting, but satyrs weren't furies. The former excelled in seduction; the latter in destruction.

I studied Raia a moment longer, contemplating how to tactfully question the satyr's magical qualifications in this regard. She was clearly as powerful as Claudius and possibly older. So far, she also seemed far more reasonable than him, but seeing as I'd only spoken with her for a couple minutes, I wasn't counting on my impression lasting. Since she wasn't being overtly rude, however, I preferred to remain on her good side.

I took a deep breath. "Don't take this the wrong way because I'm sure your people were thorough in their attempts, but furies excel at this kind of thing. I don't think we can count on them failing."

Raia smiled in a way I found difficult to discern. "I take no offense at being told I'm not as destructive as a fury, but I think you'll find I'm quite right about this. Attempts to neutralize the Vessel's threat were not the work of a moment. We have tried for centuries."

"I hope so." I rubbed at my itchy, healing arms. "Tom, if Raj has to keep this thing away from us and he can't destroy it, then he'll have to hide it. That should give us more time, shouldn't it?"

Tom shrugged. "It might. We'll need to involve more people in brainstorming about where he might hide it. Even with our agents scouring the city using detection charms, this search could take days that we don't have."

"Then all things considered, I suggest we omit your pals in the Brotherhood from the discussion. We need people who we know aren't the leak and who know the city."

He nodded but was clearly not pleased. "Gather your friends. In light of the leak most likely being a Gryphon, I'm going to restructure the teams I have doing the search to make sure all *Le Confrérie* members are paired with a local Gryphon. No one is tipping off Raj again. You have ten minutes."

Damn it. While I understood the need to hurry, that was barely enough time to grab a cup of coffee.

RAIA BOWED OUT OF FURTHER DISCUSSIONS WITH POLITE excuses, and it was just as well. Her expertise lay elsewhere. While I shuffled my way to the break room for caffeine, I texted Lucen, telling him to gather Dezzi and whoever else he thought would be appropriate.

Ten minutes later, with coffee obtained, I returned to the conference room to find Tom along with Ingrid, Lucen, Dezzi, Gunthra, and another goblin. None of them appeared happy to be there, but personally, I was relieved. Claudius was nowhere in sight.

To my surprise, Olivia Lee was also there. Her neat, dark hair was tucked behind her ears, and her lips were thin with distaste for the company, but I sensed she wasn't as unhappy to be called upon as the others. She had good reasons to want to be involved.

"I decided Director Blecher should be kept informed," Tom said, "since she's in charge of this mission. And Director Lee since she's providing resources and presumably is very familiar with Boston's magical community."

"Fine with me." As I told Tom earlier, I couldn't imagine Ingrid was the leak, and I was certain it couldn't be Olivia.

"I should be kept informed of what?" Ingrid asked in her German accent.

This was not the time to bring up the leak, so I evaded that part of the answer as best as I could. After filling everyone in on what Raia had shared, I added, "We need people who know Boston well to suggest where Raj might successfully hide the Vessel."

Olivia bristled. "His success is not guaranteed. The teams have only been searching for an hour, and the detection charms don't have a long range. We need more time."

"I'm sure your charms are strong enough to get wind of it eventually," Lucen said, "but time is something we don't have a lot of. If I were Raj, I'd simply throw the thing in the Bay. We can't possibly keep a watch on the entire coast, and if he did that, it would take ages for anyone to find it even if the charms pointed us in the right general area."

"Not as long as all that, I'd hope." Ingrid studied the city map someone had tacked to the wall. "The agents searching the city are using very powerful magic-detecting charms, as Director Lee said. The satyrs haven't disguised the Vessel's magical signature the way our people once did. It would stand out, even deep under the water."

"For now," Dezzi pointed out. "But if Raj and company do choose to use similar spells, we have a limited search window. The sort of magic involved would be time consuming, but they might have begun the process before tonight. We still need to hurry."

I was getting sick of being told we had a limited window. We'd been racing the clock for so long I'd forgotten what it felt like to stand still.

"Then if I were Raj, I'd temporarily hide the Vessel somewhere that would make it hard for it to stand out while I got to work. Somewhere it was surrounded by lots of powerful magic, like a charm shop in Shadowtown."

I rested my head in my hands while everyone debated this idea and tossed out more of their own. The caffeine wasn't doing much to help me wake up physically, but as my body continued to heal, I felt mentally stronger. But would it be enough to do what I was considering? There was only one way to find out.

"What if I can track Raj?" I suggested as the conversation came to a lull. "It's not as ideal as tracking the Vessel itself, but he's the most likely person to have it."

Seven heads swiveled my way, and Lucen frowned. "Is this a reference to what happened at the airport?"

I fortified myself with another swallow of coffee. "In a way. Raj is in my head, or I'm in his. Ever since what he did to me in Europe, there's some kind of connection between us. I used it to track him when he left the terminal tonight. Maybe I can use it again."

Tom and Ingrid exchanged unreadable glances. "But he was close by earlier," Tom said. "He could be anywhere at the moment."

"He's somewhere in Boston," Olivia added quietly.

Tom sighed. "Jessica, you didn't think to mention this before?"

"I didn't realize what was going on before. Look, I know Raj could be anywhere, but since I've become aware of the connection, I can sense it. If I concentrate on it, I might be able to use it."

The room was silent, then Dezzi nodded. "Then I say it's worth the attempt. The rest of us can continue prioritizing where we should search, and Jessica can try her method."

"I agree." Olivia couldn't hide her dislike of agreeing with the satyrs, so she didn't bother. "The more options, the better. Jessica, what do you need to do this?"

Good question. I thought a minute, trying to imagine anything that would be useful, but as I'd never attempted anything like it, I hadn't a clue. "Just a quiet room."

Tom volunteered his office for me, and I left the Gryphon-to-Gryphon and Gryphon-to-pred tension behind, gladly. Shutting Tom's door, I chose a clear spot on his cluttered floor to sit. Then I closed my eyes and breathed deeply a couple times.

This was not going to be easy. My nerves were rattled, and the air was practically electrified with the city's tension. This very same buzz had kept me up at nights when the red sky first hit the East Coast. While exhaustion had finally enabled me to sleep, my blood continued to tingle with the emotions.

Come on, Jess, and focus.

Although I was aware of the connection between Raj and myself, I was unable to clarify it. With my eyes closed, visualizing the bond as a rope was usually easy. It always appeared the same too—a glowing cord. Yet not tonight. Tonight there was no magical glow. No easy-to-define rope. Behind my eyelids, there was only blackness that disappeared into more blackness. There was a heaviness to that nothingness too, a purpose or a presence. An awareness.

My heart beat faster with fear as I became more and more convinced the darkness hid Raj's black eyes. That somehow, on the other end of our connection, he was sensing me.

Ridiculous, I reminded myself. *It's just the fear and anxiety surrounding me playing havoc on my senses.* Yet I couldn't shake the sensation, and more things that shouldn't be possible were happening too. The bond stretched and tightened as though Raj was moving farther away. But surely Raj was already far enough away that if he was moving, noticing the motion would be impossible. This motion wasn't smooth either, but jerking. It was almost as if he was tugging on the bond.

My fingers curled around the loose fabric of my jeans. Was this purposeful? Had Raj sensed me as well?

The cautious side of me urged me to open my eyes and give up, but I ignored it. While the idea that Raj was staring back at me through our connection creeped me out, if he was, ignoring his ability to do so did no good. Bonds between addicts and preds went both ways, and I suspected this bond was just a strange version of one. That meant open eyes wouldn't save me. Only finding Raj and killing him or forcing him to cut the connection would.

That opened up a whole new conundrum. If I'd somehow made Raj aware of our connection, and he did cut the rope too soon, I'd lose my chance not just to find the Vessel but to find him. Although the Vessel was my larger goal, this was also personal. I owed Raj some salamander steel to the heart.

Focus. My mind was drifting again, fear obscuring my ability to sense the bond.

The trouble was, the more I struggled to sense the bond's direction, the harder it became to notice it at all. I grasped at it with my mental fingers, and the rope turned to smoke. Frustration built in me, overpowering the fear. I had to relax.

"All magic works on the same principles," Lucen once explained during the few lessons he'd given me. "With a little experience, you'll notice you use the same tricks over and over again."

And what was the hardest trick of all to learn? That there was a difference between focus and effort. Sensing magical energies required concentration. But magical energy hated to give itself up to people searching for it. If you tried too hard, the power retreated into the shadows.

That was my problem. I had to let go of the idea of searching for the bond, of wanting to will it into the shape I needed. I had to maintain my awareness, but let it show itself to me.

I swore there was nothing more difficult than trying not to try, especially as I felt Raj's dark eyes staring at me and my forehead tingled with the sensation. As my anxiety over the Vessel poked at my brain, letting go of my desperation became ever more challenging.

When I finally succeeded, however, everything snapped into place at once. I couldn't form an image of the bond, but all the power was clearly defined in my gut. I jumped to my feet and spun around in Tom's office, identifying the direction.

Relief would have to wait. Hoping I could hold on to the sensation, I shuffled back to the conference room like a sleepwalker—eyes open but otherwise dead to the outside world and fearful of any more distractions. Director Lee and the goblins had left the conference room, and conversation broke off as I entered. I stood at the head of the table, barely conscious of everyone staring at me, and pointed. "That way. Raj is in this direction. Someone needs to drive me."

"That way is Shadowtown," Lucen said, breaking the surprised silence. "Makes sense."

Tom put down the pen he'd been using to mark up the map. "Are you sure?"

"Positive." Far from getting weaker with distractions, the longer I stood here, the stronger the sensation was becoming. I was getting better at grasping it.

Ingrid pulled out her phone. "It will be difficult to put together a large enough team to lead a raid into Shadowtown. I don't like taking people off search duty when we have no guarantee this fury has the Vessel."

"Then don't," Dezzi said. "Shadowtown is already highly agitated. What with the rash of attacks on our people by human vigilantes, the HELP Act likely passing in Congress tomorrow, and us here, working with you—it is too much. If you lead an army of Gryphons into our neighborhood, the people who care nothing for Raj and know nothing of what's going on will pour into the streets anyway."

I swallowed. I didn't know what in the world the HELP Act was, but everything else Dezzi pointed out was true. I couldn't sense the anxiety in Shadowtown, but it was evident in the way the preds were acting. "Dezzi's right. We don't need to spawn more fighting. I'll track down Raj on my own."

That went over about as well as a sprite at a pool party. Everyone yelled at me at once.

I raised my hands in frustration. "Then what do you want? I understand not wanting to take people from search duty, but I'm your best lead."

Dezzi stood, and she did that weird thing where she could radiate her power and authority. "Lucen will take you to Shadowtown. At The Lair, you'll meet a team of my people who will accompany you both in your search."

Ingrid shook her head. "A single Gryphon at—"

"Cannot be spared," Dezzi said. "As you pointed out. Shadowtown is our territory. We handle our own problems, and Raj is a shared one. Humans will only be vulnerable."

Tom opened his mouth, probably to protest that I was human, but none of these people were stupid. We couldn't risk the leak discovering our plan, and in case Raj didn't have the Vessel, the Gryphons were better off following their current course.

And I was better off with a satyr army than a Gryphon one. The satyrs wouldn't disapprove of me killing Raj to avenge Olef. That was just pred justice.

A delicate shiver ran down my back. Sometimes, with every new misery I faced, I wondered if my humanity was finally slipping away.

FIVE

LUCEN DROVE, AND THE CLOSER WE GOT TO SHADOWTOWN, the closer I could sense Raj was. By the time Lucen parked behind his building and let us into his darkened bar, I knew I had a problem. My gut was registering all Raj, all the time. I had no sense of his direction.

Lucen flipped on the lights, and I took down one of the stacked chairs.

"Everything okay?" He unlocked the main door to let in the posse Dezzi had called.

Sitting down, I closed my eyes. "The sensation is too strong here. I need to recalibrate or something."

Because my eyes were shut, I didn't see who Dezzi had sent as the satyrs filed in. But I heard a voice that sounded like Gi's comment that it had been too long since The Lair was open normal hours. Sad, but true. Damn, I missed normal.

Perhaps sensing that my mind was wandering, Lucen shushed everyone. "Jess needs to concentrate."

The noise of clunking feet and squeaking chairs dimmed, and voices fell to a whisper. Fortunately, reorienting myself was easier than what I'd needed to do at headquarters, and I accomplished it in what seemed like only a few minutes. With the sensation clearly in my mind, I opened my eyes and circled the chair, paying attention for changes in strength. It was like being stuck in a twisted game of Marco Polo, the one minus the friends, the swimming pool, and the fun.

"I think I've got it. He's that way." I gestured behind the bar area, which coincidentally was also deeper into the neighborhood and away from the T station.

At some point during my find-Raj meditation, Lucen must have run up to his apartment because he'd changed out of the dressier clothes he'd worn to the airport. He stood in the bar's kitchen doorway, pulling a T-shirt on. "That was too fast, little siren. You didn't give us time for a round of beers."

I agreed with the idea of changing, so I took apart my sloppy ponytail and redid my hair into a tight, no-nonsense braid. But the rest? "You want a beer before a fight?"

"I'm powered by alcohol. You asked once how I could drink so much while staying in shape? Now you know."

Gi winked. "We get all the good vices."

I snorted, not wanting to admit that I wasn't entirely sure if they were joking. These days, nothing would surprise me. "Yeah, well, I'm powered by the desire to cut the smirk off Raj's face and to close the Pit. So less drinking and more fighting."

Lucen slipped his leather jacket on over his shoulder holster. "You heard the woman. This apocalypse sucks the fun out of everything. Let's get moving."

After a moment I realized they were all waiting for me to lead the way, so I headed out the door. Halfway up the stairs to the street, I glanced behind while Lucen relocked the bar. Dezzi had sent five satyrs to accompany us. Besides Gi, I recognized them all, though I didn't know everyone's names. Over the last couple months, every one of these brawny men had been enlisted to protect me from one threat or another.

And they were all brawny men, Lucen included. I'd thought perhaps Dezzi would send Melissa, another satyr who'd acted as my bodyguard before, but clearly not. It made sense, I supposed. Furies were huge themselves and nearly all male, and it stood to reason that Raj would probably have his own posse with him for protection.

I would have to assume, too, that the satyrs were well-armed besides looking capable of throwing one hell of a punch. Lucen had his gun, and several carried visible blades, but we might need curse grenades and who knew what else.

On that thought, I held out my hand. "Anything you guys want to share with me?"

One of the satyrs dropped two tiny, spherical grenades into my hand, and Gi handed me a much larger one. Feeling better, I added the curses to my pockets and continued to street level.

Then I followed the pull of the bond. At each intersection, I had to pause and reassess the situation, making guesses about which way to turn in order to stay on course.

Shadowtown was a weirdly shaped, crooked neighborhood, far longer than it was wide. I'd explored most of it, but I hadn't wandered down many of the streets for a while. My trips tended to take me in the same directions, most of which were on the main drags. I passed the bakery where I liked to buy croissants, passed the goblin-owned bookstore that led toward Gunthra's house, and finally I ended up at a five-way intersection.

The streets came together at odd angles. Down one on my left was the drycleaner's shop where sylphs had attacked me and several Gryphons a few weeks ago. Parts of the area had been heavily damaged in the fighting that followed, but there were few traces of it here. I couldn't tell if the fighting hadn't extended so far in this intersection or if the normally fastidious preds had already cleaned up the damage.

All the ornate but slightly sinisterly styled buildings were commercial on the ground floor and apartments above. Except for one on the opposite side of the intersection. That building came to a sharp angle at the corner, and it held a bank on the bottom and law offices on the higher levels. It was where the connection was tugging me, as strong as it had been when I faced Raj at the airport.

"There." I motioned toward the building. "I'd bet Raj is there. Do you think he'd stuff the Vessel in a bank vault or something?"

Lucen frowned. "The bank's been closed for repairs since the fighting the other week. I doubt it."

So did I, but I had no better ideas. "That's where I sense him."

"Then that's where we go."

We took off across the intersection way too easily. The inhabitants of Shadowtown were as on edge as everyone else, and traffic—vehicle and foot—were both light. The bar on one corner was open, but the restaurant next to it was closed. Same with the charm shop at the other end of the five-way.

Gi tried opening the bank's door, and to my surprise, it wasn't locked. The reason, however, was obvious. The other side was a rubble pile, extending upward beyond the opening. Chunks of stone and concrete were all I could see, and yet the heavy glass door in front of it appeared pristine.

I blinked at it. "I guess we're not going in that way."

Lucen drew a finger down the carved stone on the side of the doorway. "I wondered why this place hadn't reopened when it appeared to have been fixed up so quickly. It's a disguise charm."

"You can disguise a whole building?"

"With sufficient work, you can disguise anything. Didn't you used to put a disguise charm on your bike to keep people away?"

I took a step back down the sidewalk, searching for another entrance. "I used a distraction charm. But thanks for reminding me that Raj is responsible for destroying my bike too."

"Sorry, little siren. It's the same principle though."

I jumped as part of the building blew up. Swearing, I hunched over, sweaty hands on my thighs as one of the satyrs waved away the smoke. He'd blown the lock off the door that gave access to the upper stories. "A little warning next time before you set off explosives?"

"So much for the chance to go in quietly," Lucen muttered.

I shrugged. There was no quiet, a fact we'd discussed on the way here. Based on what had happened at headquarters, I had a strong suspicion that Raj could use our connection the same way I did. Which meant he knew we were here and we could be walking into a trap. As I often did, I fervently wished I could sense pred emotions. Needing to rely solely on my human senses could be damn inconvenient.

"Looks like we can get in this way." A satyr stood in the newly opened doorway and switched on a flashlight.

I had no flashlight myself, but I did have a reloaded gun. I pulled that out and immediately stuck it back in the holster when my phone began to play "Highway to Hell." A couple of the satyrs laughed.

Lucen had been messing with my ringtone on a daily basis, starting with the obligatory R.E.M. offering. It wasn't as though we had time for this joking around, but I knew why he was doing it—to keep my spirits up. Admittedly, this was no easy task he'd set himself. Also admittedly, the sexiest thing about Lucen wasn't his abs but his sense of humor. It didn't always work on me lately, but I appreciated it more than ever.

Alas, I did not expect good news on the other end of the line. It was Tom. "We think we've found the Vessel."

"You do? You have it?" The laughter around me died away as the satyrs listened in.

"Not in hand, but one of the teams has reported finding an unusually strong magical signal. They're tracking it down. Hold on."

I gritted my teeth, waiting for Tom to return. "They think they've found the damn thing," I whispered to Lucen.

Lucen produced a detection charm from his pocket. "Are they sure? There's some very strong magic in this building too."

"Still there?" Tom's voice was back in my ear.

I sighed in exasperation. "Yes, I'm here. I've found Raj. Are you sure the Vessel isn't with him? We're detecting strong magic here too."

"I'm not sure of anything anymore." He sounded exhausted. "Another team just called in because they've also picked up signs of hefty power, but on the opposite side of the city."

"Peachy. So this is Raj's plan for hiding it. Lead us on wild-dragon chases." I glanced up and down the intersection, expecting to see violent furies closing in any moment as Raj sprang his trap, but all remained calm. The quiet was enough to make the hairs on my neck stand up. "We're going in then."

"Be careful. Let the satyrs do the fighting."

Of course. Tom believed I had a larger role to play in this war. I hung up, wondering why he thought I'd start being careful at this late a date.

I signaled to the satyr with the flashlight and retrieved my gun. "Let's do this."

Four satyrs entered the building in front of me, and two—including Lucen—went behind. The light switch in the stairwell refused to cough up any light, but I could see the damage all around in the tepid glow of several flashlights. Gouges had been cut in the plaster walls, and the heavy wainscoting bore blackened curse scars and possibly signs of fire damage. The satyr at the head of the line called, "Be careful" as we reached the second-floor landing. A step near the top had a chunk blown out.

"Where to?" Lucen asked, deftly stepping over the missing stair.

I closed my eyes, but any ability to be more precise was gone. Trapped in such a small area with the men, some of whom were forced by simple physics to be in contact with me, was interfering with my ability to focus. My body stirred with faint but noticeable lust, and I had no sense of Raj's direction. He could have been right on top of me.

That thought gave me pause, and I looked up. The building was only three stories, but I didn't relish the thought of climbing higher. All that rubble on the bottom floor must have fallen from somewhere, and this landing didn't scream stable. If I bounced on my toes, the dusty wood squeaked and moved with me.

"I can't tell anymore," I admitted. "He's too close."

"We should start at the top then." Gi pointed his light and gun up the last flight of stairs.

"It might be faster if we split up," said the satyr who'd blown open the door.

Lucen kicked aside rubble that had settled on the next step. "We stay together. Protect Jess and keep your eyes open. There's got to be a trap."

I wasn't sure if I was glad or not that I wasn't the only one thinking it. The same way we'd climbed the first set of stairs, we took off up the second. These were in even worse condition. Once, the satyrs had to skip several steps, a tense moment when we weren't sure if the wood would hold their weight. But it did, and I found myself being passed from Lucen to Gi since my legs wouldn't reach across the same distance. It would have been uncomfortable and awkward enough without the bonus arousal.

I readjusted my shirt on the landing and stood back to allow Gi room to kick down the stairwell door. Two more satyrs rushed forward, weapons drawn. A dark hallway greeted them, but no furies.

"What a shithole," one of them commented. He tossed what looked like a curse grenade down the hallway, and it lit up the area like a floodlight. The sounds of many scurrying feet followed.

Great. Whether dragons or rats, it all sucked.

"We couldn't have tried that earlier?" I asked, blinking as my eyes adjusted.

"The light wouldn't have worked as well on the steps," the satyr said. "So do we start knocking down doors or what?"

"I don't have a better plan. If something changes, I'll let you know."

There weren't as many offices up here as it would have appeared from street level, though in part that was due to several walls having disintegrated. More plaster chunks, shards of glass and remnants of things that might once have been office equipment crunched underfoot. The floor was definitely of questionable utility in some places, and it wasn't always easy to see where. Everything was coated in a thick layer of plaster dust. Spiders, dragons, and other creatures had made quick work of claiming the space for themselves as was evident in the many cobwebs and the piles of dung in the corners.

"Look." Lucen pointed toward a set of footprints in the dust. "Pretty recent."

"I told you, he's here." Somewhere. The building wasn't huge, and we were halfway down the hall. Much as I didn't want to walk into a trap, the fact that we hadn't yet encountered anyone was even more disturbing.

Keeping my back to a crumbling wall, I wet my lips and neared the next corner. The room around the doorway was dark, cast in shadow by most of the magical glow. I inched closer, and someone poked me in the shoulder.

Cursing, I spun around and backed myself against the opposite wall. A long, bent nail stuck out of the splintery molding. A fucking nail. I took a deep breath, my heart pounding in my throat, then I sneezed from the nasty air I'd inhaled.

"Jess, you okay?" Lucen was at my side before I could regain my wits.

"Fine. I'm fine. Hey, what's that?" He'd been using a flashlight to peer into the darker room, and its beam had briefly illuminated a strange shadow on the floor.

The other week in Europe, I'd been pushed into a trap Raj had made. He'd used my blood to create a magical cage, a feat accomplished by drawing glyphs on the ground. The memory of it had me shuffling back another foot until I could figure out what I'd seen on the floor.

Lucen signaled for Gi, and the other satyr nudged the light down the hallway with his boot. It didn't brighten the room much, but the strange shadows morphed into focus.

"Just more debris." Lucen pointed the flashlight along the far wall. "We've reached the end of the floor."

Under the ghostly light, it appeared as though someone had blackened the windows in the room. They hadn't done a perfect job, and the glow of the streetlights peeked through cracks in the paint.

"Still sense him nearby?" Lucen asked.

I nodded but winced. It was as though Raj was everywhere, and yet there was no sign of his presence. "Time to go down, I guess."

"You hear that?" Gi asked.

I'd heard nothing, but in a flash I was as alert as everyone else. I raised my gun in the direction of the stairwell, and the satyrs did the same with their weapons. For a couple of seconds, I held my breath, straining for signs of a threat. An eerie stillness enveloped the area as we stood motionless. Then all at once, the hallway erupted with a boom.

The noise shook the fragile structure. I ducked low as the ceiling crumbled onto my head. Any second I expected the whole building would crash down with us in it, but that was obviously not Raj's intent. The blast was only a distraction. Three furies burst through the stairwell door before we could climb to our feet, and the next thing I knew I was pelted with something wet.

I dropped my gun as my world was pulled out from beneath me. A disorientation curse. Dragon shit on toast. Of course, it would be. Raj wanted me alive.

"Jess, stay low!" Lucen yelled, as if I could do anything else. I was in absolutely no shape to join the fighting.

Somewhere, someone was shooting, but I didn't dare turn and look. A few feet over my head, a bullet collided with the wood, and splinters rained on me. Lifting my gaze a couple inches, I could see the edge of the doorframe into the blacked-out room. Filthy floorboard by filthy floorboard, I wormed my way on my stomach toward the doorway. Behind me, I could hear shouting and bodies and steel slamming together. Clearly, not everyone had been hit by the curse.

Thrilled to finally see some cover ahead, I moved a little too quickly, and my stomach lurched. The floor seemed to roll away beneath me. Up became down, down became sideways. I pressed my lips together so I wouldn't vomit, but the sensation of falling was overwhelming.

"Behind you, little siren." Lucen didn't sound so good himself. Since he'd been right next to me, some of the curse must have hit him too.

I wiggled deeper into the room to allow him cover, my head too fuzzy to worry about the splinters and broken glass that were digging into my thin shirt and exposed stomach. The debris in the center was several feet away. If I could get behind it and use it as a shield... I was almost there, and I shut my eyes to fend off my nausea.

But as I reached out to push myself along, something unexpected happened. When I felt the floor drop out from beneath me, it wasn't the curse. The floor simply wasn't there. My arms met with nothing but air where floor should have been.

Another disguise charm, I thought, and that was all I had time to think. Too much of my weight hovered over the nothingness. Without any way of maintaining my balance, and already suffering from severe vertigo, I couldn't figure out how to pull myself backward.

So I slipped forward instead, and screaming, disappeared down the hole.

SIX

I WAS STILL SCREAMING WHEN I SLAMMED INTO...MORE AIR?
Groaning, I peered through the stray hairs that had fallen into my face, but
my world was a blur of faintly glowing color that told me nothing.
Confusion made me dizzier. I couldn't focus, so I shut my eyes one more
time. All I could tell was that the pain I'd been expecting never arrived.
My limbs dangled over nothing, yet an invisible cushion supported me.

Then that vanished with a distinct popping noise. Even if my brain had
been fully functioning, I had no time to ponder what was going on. The
floor and I met at last, and I was pretty sure it had the upper hand. The
only thing I couldn't figure out was why it hadn't attacked me sooner.

I rolled over, willing the vomit down my throat. High over my head,
Lucen was yelling my name and I could hear more sounds of struggle, but
I had no ability to respond. I feared if I opened my mouth, I'd puke. Plus,
all of my energy should be saved for getting to my feet and figuring out
where I was. But my body was having none of that idea, however sensible,
and I curled into the fetal position instead.

"Get her out of there."

Vaguely, I recognized Raj's voice. Figured. If only I'd interpreted the
sensation that he was right above me correctly—that he was actually right
below me—this mess might have been avoided.

Fear pumped my blood faster, but it did nothing to help me dispel the curse's effects. All I could do was swear to myself. Rough hands grabbed me under the shoulders, and I was dragged from wherever I'd landed.

Now would be a nice time to hurl, I told my stomach, but it stubbornly refused. My damn freakish body had a mind of its own. The curse must be slowly subsiding, but not vomiting was just a start. Being able to fight off an attack was something else entirely, and I didn't trust the curse's effects would disappear fast enough for that.

Whoever had moved me let go, and my upper back smacked into the floor. I barely managed to protect my head. At last, I pried open my eyes a crack. Raj was telling someone to hurry, and heavy feet stomped behind me. As the room swam into focus, I watched a fury slam closed some kind of metal gate. A second later, an object crashed into the concrete behind it and swore. I blinked again, testing my ability to sit. Lucen. Shit. That object looked like Lucen.

Sure enough, he pushed himself upright. In the dim light, he appeared as groggy as I did, and blood trickled down his head. I opened my mouth to call out his name, but an unpleasantly familiar pair of motorcycle boots landed in my line of sight. Was it really only a few hours ago that I'd stared at Raj's shoes? I so did not enjoy being in this position.

"We need to stop running into each other this way, soul swapper." Raj's voice told me he was grinning, but lifting my head high enough to confirm it was asking for trouble.

Rather than waste my limited brainpower thinking of a witty comeback, I simply raised a middle finger.

Chuckling, Raj pressed it back down, and his touch made my skin crawl. The anger I'd been nurturing this evening spiked, and the bond connecting us flared as though it was strengthened through the physical contact.

"The good news is that we don't have to *keep* meeting like this," Raj said. "You're coming with me this time. You see? I made sure you didn't even get hurt when you fell, so there'd be no excuse. Of course, I can't say the same for your boyfriend."

"Jess?" Lucen's voice was weak.

I tried looking around Raj's large legs, but the fury completely blocked my view. "I'm okay," I told Lucen, though that was probably a lie.

Raj lifted my chin so I was forced to see his scarily tattooed face. "Oh, yes. She's fine. We'll take good care of her."

His goons laughed, but Raj was on to something. Our bond was stronger than ever when he touched me. I could visualize it once more—a thick, darkly powerful rope. Only not a rope. A circuit.

I'd never figured out what exactly Raj had done to me in France when he'd used me to channel power and open the Pit. But whatever it was, he'd used the bond to feed me power too. That must mean I could use it to take from him.

Bracing myself mentally, I grasped our connection and yanked on Raj's magic. It came at once, eagerly, flooding my senses with a hot, dazzling burst of sheer energy. The effects of the disorientation curse flew away, blasted right out of me. Alas, next came the disturbing rush I'd been waiting for. My every nerve lit up, and my head became too light. I shuddered from the impact and tried to force the energy hit down, grounding myself. As I did, the long-simmering rage in my blood began to heat up.

To my surprise, Raj laughed. "Yes, there does appear to be some residual connection between us. I'm no more certain of what it is than you are. I could detect your unease and confusion when you were attempting to locate me."

Peachy. As I'd suspected. Sometimes being right wasn't worth it.

Shakily, I climbed to my feet. I was sick of staring at Raj's boots, and my muscles buzzed with power. One more pull on the bond and I'd be ready to take on the world, or feel like it anyway.

My head wasn't entirely sure that was a good idea though. Raj had fed me so much power last time that it had hurt. My brain had felt like it was being split in two, and my body—far from being strengthened by the hit— had been hard to control. Right up until the moment I'd passed out. In some ways, it wasn't as bad as what had happened when Claudius had addicted me, but it wasn't a situation I wished to repeat. Under the circumstances, however, I didn't see what other options I had.

"Can you break the connection?" I spoke casually, but it would be good to know if Raj could cut me off if I got too greedy with his power.

Although Raj was over a head taller than me, now that I was standing, I could see more of the space. We were on the ground floor, and the ruined area was part of the bank. Smashed and charred desks had been pushed aside, and the teller counter was covered in chunks of the ceiling. A moldy-smelling carpet runner had been rolled into a corner.

Then there was Lucen, locked behind a fancy iron-gated door. He'd pulled himself to his knees, and his hands were wrapped around the bars. With a determined expression, he shook his head at me. Was he telling me to stop drawing power from Raj, or warning me not to goad Raj into breaking the connection? Or was it something else entirely?

Raj noticed my furrowed brow and glanced in Lucen's direction. "Anything that can be made can be unmade. Don't fret. But until I have you safely tucked away, our connection is too useful to remove. What if you ran again? How could I draw you to me?"

He gestured behind me, and two ugly furies approached Lucen. One of them held a salamander fire-forged knife with a wicked, curved blade. Lucen saw it too. He inched away from the gate, but the second fury was unlocking it. He was trapped.

Fear froze my mind, but not for long. The ice in my veins warmed to anger, and that awoke my courage. Fed by the rage Raj induced, my resolve strengthened with every breath. As for my own magic, whether my power was fueled by the bond with Raj or whether it was simply adrenaline, I had no clue. But my senses felt like they were expanding. My entire being, body and soul, swelled. I yanked on the bond and sucked in every fiery drop of power I could pull from Raj. Although my head began to throb, the energy didn't bowl me over. I absorbed it, my skin tingling from head to toes to fingers.

The effect reminded me of stretching a muscle. The deeper you forced yourself to stretch, over time the deeper you could stretch with ease. And the last time I'd done this, Raj had blown me apart. Over the ensuing days, my magical muscle had contracted, but apparently it had been ready and waiting to be stretched again under the right conditions.

There were no conditions more right than this. Losing my

Dragon'sWing was a shame but not a tragedy. Losing Olef was a tragedy, but it couldn't be undone. Losing Lucen? That was a giant fucking *hell, no.* To protect him, I would let forth a torrent of blind rage so strong it would make the rest of these so-called creatures of anger jealous.

On that thought, I pulled harder on the bond. Nerves shrieked, and my head pounded with a warning to stop, but the smirk on Raj's face slipped ever so slightly. It was working, and that was all the encouragement I needed.

I strained with the effort of hoarding more power, and a red veil settled over my vision. At the same time, my eyesight sharpened. The magic powered every sense. I could hear the footsteps high above on the third floor. I could smell mildew lurking in the rubble, the dragon droppings decaying in the corners, and the hint of heated metal in the lamps that lined the room. And I was ready to taste blood.

Raj staggered back. His smirk vanished entirely, and his eyes filled with an emotion I'd never seen before on a fury. Fear was too strong a word for it, but it was definitely concern. I had to act quickly. If he could break the bond, he might decide it was worth it after all.

"Get. Away. From him." Even my voice sounded deeper.

Raj cocked his head to the side, examining me. "That's enough, Jessica."

I jerked forward, feet sliding on the dust. Raj was reclaiming his power, reversing the pull of the bond. I could feel the energy draining from me. My world was becoming duller again, my vision clearing.

His minions had paused to gape at us, but now that the universe seemed in order once more, they returned to unlocking the gate. Lucen had crept farther into the room, and at his side, his fingers had curled into a loose fist. He met my eye and winked, moving one finger minutely to show me the curse grenade he held.

Thank dragons. I should have known he had something, and that reminded me of the ones I'd stuffed in my pockets and the knife at my hip. The furies hadn't bothered to disarm me yet, probably because I was supposed to have been reeling from the disorientation curse. It was a mistake I intended to make them pay for. Just as Raj's unwillingness to break our bond was too.

I grasped at the connection, but Raj was ready. Instead of an influx of power, all I managed to ensnare were dregs. Raj held tight. I attempted it again and stumbled, and Raj crossed his arms smugly. Shit. Even if I could take the power from him, he was still far stronger than most preds.

The iron gate swung open with a great creak, and the fury with the knife barged in. Lucen raised his hand, and in the second before the grenade exploded, I darted out of the way. The area filled with the green smoke of anti-magic. There was no way Lucen hadn't been hit himself given the tight quarters.

I could tell Raj hadn't been expecting it because the bond jerked as surprise caused him to loosen his grasp. I didn't bother to pull on it though. Not yet. In the split second I had before Raj recovered, I retrieved the large grenade Gi had given me, spun around and hurled it at the two additional furies in the room.

I had no idea what was in the curse, but it blasted open the front wall, leaving a fabulous seven-pointed curse scar behind on the bits that remained. The two furies were thrown back and piled in a heap by the teller counter.

Raj's eyes opened wide as he took in the carnage, and I seized my opening. Grabbing my knife, I charged. But Raj must have been able to read me via the bond better than I could read him. He was still a pred, after all. My negative emotions couldn't be hidden from him, and anger was the force driving me.

He snatched my upraised arm with a painfully strong grip and wrestled me toward the floor. With my arm twisted behind my back, I had no choice but to release the knife. It clattered to the hardwood beams, taking my hopes with it.

At least two hundred pounds of solid, fury muscle pressed down on me as I screamed in frustration. Every attempt I made to break Raj's hold was easily countered. He was far bigger and stronger, and while those things could normally be overcome by training, he was in my damn head, anticipating my moves.

He pressed my arms into my torso, wrapping one of his own arms around me. With the other, he picked up Misery. Then he hauled me to my feet. "I did tell you I'd enjoy this far more if you struggled, didn't I? And you struggle so well. It makes it so much more fun than a normal human would." His face pressed against the side of my head, and he inhaled audibly.

I started to swear at him then I remembered that amused him more. *He likes the struggle. Don't struggle, you dipshit. It only makes him stronger, and it turns him on.* I shuddered mentally at the memory.

It only took Raj one arm to drag me toward the blown-open section of wall. "Thanks for this, soul swapper. It's a lot easier than climbing out the rock pile in the back."

Fuck you, I thought and sucked in a long draw on the bond. Power radiated throughout me. Raj didn't respond, but I didn't get the sense it was because he hadn't noticed. He was lifting me over the bodies of his fallen minions, and his grip around me slackened.

To get us both out of here, he'd have to carry me over the loose debris and through the wall. It would require concentration, and it was not a time he could engage in a literal power struggle with me.

So I tugged on the bond again as Raj put the first foot on the rubble pile. The chunks of plaster were strewn precariously, and the pile shifted beneath us. Raj tensed, collecting his balance, and he had to adjust his grip. I gained a little more wiggle room.

Up another step, and another. Raj was clearly aware of the battle of the bond, but he wasn't taking it seriously. I was sure it was partially because he had to pay attention to his footing, but mostly because he didn't take me seriously as a threat. That had been all too evident since our meeting in France.

It was his mistake. I didn't need to be as powerful as he was to be a threat. From the corner of my eye, I could see Misery's hilt. Raj had taken my sheath when he'd pinned me to the floor, and he held the whole contraption in a loose grip in his left hand.

Don't think about Olef, I told myself as dust dribbled onto my head. *Don't think about the prison being open. Don't worry about the Vessels. Just focus on Lucen and Steph and Devon. Concentrate on the things that make you happy. The reasons you're fighting, those that aren't about revenge.*

It was hard, so hard, while touching Raj to ignore the fear and rage he induced. His shirt was mildly sweaty, and I swore I could smell the effect of his pheromones when I breathed. But rather than picture the bond in my mind when I pulled on it, I pictured Lucen, and I didn't pull with a heart full of vengeance but of love.

Raj couldn't anticipate those emotions because they didn't register with him. When I snatched at the bond, he wasn't ready. The pure, uncontested hit of power burst through me like a shock wave. I gasped with pain, magical nerves ablaze, and Raj faltered.

This was it. Fueled by all the magic, my hand shot out faster than should have been possible. The speed charms drawn on me be damned—I didn't need them in this instant. My fingers closed around Misery's hilt, and I cried out just to release some of the power.

Raj dropped me, but he was an instant too slow. As I collapsed to the heap, I drew my blade down Raj's torso. Now was he was the one yelling.

It was odd. I'd carried the knife around with me for months, but I'd never used it. The ease with which the blade sliced through Raj's shirt and carved a red line down his stomach shocked me—it had to be part of the magic of the salamander fire. I stared up in relief and horror as Raj clutched his upper body, his eyes wide with shock. Blood poured from between his fingers.

I felt ill all over again, and the knife slipped from my grip as Raj stumbled out of my line of sight. My lips were dry, and I was still lying motionless when I heard a crash. Then the extra burst of power running through my blood, the anger and fear Raj's presence riled up, was gone. Poofed out of existence.

I clasped a hand over my mouth, emotions numb. It could only mean that Raj was dead at last.

SEVEN

I KICKED A PARTIALLY MELTED STAPLER ACROSS THE FLOOR IN frustration. Using the magic-detecting charm Lucen had brought, I'd been over every reachable inch of this husk of a building. The only thing I'd found besides more dragon droppings was Raj's decoy. It appeared to be some sort of curse grenade that was giving off shit-tons of magic, but it definitely wasn't the Vessel. I was going to have to call the Gryphons' equivalent of the bomb squad to dispose of it safely.

As for Lucen, once I'd freed him from the vault, he'd returned to the upper floors to assist in the fighting, but there hadn't been much left. The remaining furies had either fled or were injured or dead. Alas, they weren't the only ones. Gi was mostly unscathed, but a couple other satyrs were badly hurt. Lucen had gotten Azria on the phone, and she was on her way to help with the healing.

Miraculously, my phone hadn't been damaged, and I got it out, debating whether to first call Tom about the Vessel problem or the emergency line about the curse grenade. Lucen stepped through the busted front wall before I decided, and I lowered my phone. "How's it going up there?"

He pushed his sweaty hair out of his face and sighed. "I think everyone will survive. How are you doing?"

"Me?" I waved my arms in circles. "All healed up from earlier. Fine."

"That's not what I meant."

I turned my back to him, careful to avoid glancing at where Raj lay in a bloody heap. There was so much blood that if I concentrated, I swore I could detect its coppery tang in the air.

"Little siren?"

My phone burst to life, and "Highway to Hell" seemed more appropriate than ever. I held up a finger in Lucen's direction as I answered. Tom had made my decision for me.

"We have it."

I tripped over a loose floorboard in surprise. "You're talking about what I think you're talking about?"

"Yes. I'll fill you in when you get here, but it's safe for the moment." Tom paused, and I could hear voices in the background. "We have to deal with that other issue now. You've claimed you're more accurate than a lie detector. If that's true, it might be helpful."

Tom had to be referring to the leak. "I'll be there as soon as I can. Oh, and Raj is dead."

A brief pause on the other end suggested I'd caught Tom by surprise with the information. "Good. This evening's been salvageable after all." He hung up.

Good. The word summed up exactly what I was feeling. I should have been ecstatic that we had the final Vessel, but I couldn't summon the emotion. All I could do was good. It had to be exhaustion. The only thing I felt with any intensity was tired.

"What was that about?" Lucen asked as I tucked my phone away.

"The Gryphons have the Vessel." I forced a smile because damn it—it was the least I could do when I should have been dancing with joy.

Lucen's eyes widened then his whole body sagged with relief. "Best news I've heard in a while."

"Yeah. Are you okay dealing with the mess here? Tom needs me at headquarters to deal with something else."

Shadows darkened his face as he scanned the room. "I can handle this, but does he need you this instant?"

Headlights appeared down the street behind Lucen, and a car parked along the rubble. Azria and Raf—another satyr who acted as a medic for the domus—got out.

"It's the leak thing, so yes." I waved to Azria. "The Vessel isn't safe yet."

Lucen scowled. "Neither are you. Be careful."

"I will." I stretched to kiss his cheek, and he brought me into a deeper embrace. Wrapping my arms around him, I tried to relax and failed. Much as I wished I could sink into him and claim the comfort he was offering, my mind raced. I needed to keep moving in spite of my exhaustion.

Lucen must have been able to tell what I was thinking. "Go, but we need to talk later."

I wondered about what but didn't hang around to ask. My blood compelled me forward as though I would lose momentum if I paused, and I couldn't afford that. The night's checklist was two-thirds completed. Raj was dead. The Vessel was obtained. All I had left to do was find the leak.

Well, that and then figure out how to use the Vessels to close the Pit, but that was on the checklist for tomorrow. As intent on accomplishing tasks as I was, even I realized there was only so much that could be done before I collapsed.

WHEN I'D LEFT GRYPHON HEADQUARTERS TWO HOURS AGO, IT was mostly dead. When I returned, it was bustling. Many of the Gryphons who'd been sent out to search for the Vessel or assist with the blockades were returning. Somehow, amidst the chaos, Tom found me immediately.

"Where is it? Is it safe?" I accosted him with questions before he could get a word in. "Have you started the investigation yet?"

Tom yawned and motioned for me to follow him into his office. "It's locked up and under heavy protection. And no, I was waiting for the Brotherhood's members to all return before I started asking questions. I don't want to give away our hand yet."

"Give away what hand?" I moved aside a couple books and sat on Tom's desk. It took less effort than clearing a chair.

Tom ripped open an unmarked manila envelope that was sitting by his computer. "There are ways to get around lie detectors. But if no one knows we're going to question them, then no one has a chance to try to counteract this." From the package, he took out a vial filled with blue liquid.

"Is that some kind of lie-detecting charm?" Polygraphs were useless on preds and magi, so the Gryphons had developed magical means of encouraging truth telling.

"Basically." Tom handed it to me to inspect. "It's no more foolproof than a standard polygraph, but it helps. I had someone in the Boston lab make it while we were searching for the Vessel. Then I remembered your claim. Between this and you, I figure catching the leak should be simple."

"You should know better than to believe anything around here is ever simple."

Tom's smile was grim but not without humor. "It's all relative. Compared to closing the Pit, this had better be."

"Stop it. Your optimism is giving me a rash."

"Is it feeding off others' misery that makes you so negative?" Tom took the vial from me and stuck it in a pocket. "We just scored an important victory. Step one in closing the Pit. It's not time to throw a party, but perhaps we can afford a bit of optimism."

I crossed my arms and slid off the desk. "Last I knew, you were accusing me of not taking the situation seriously enough. Also, last I knew, the Pit is still open, and we don't know how to close it or if we have all the pieces. I don't see what there is to be cheery about if I'm being serious."

"That's true, but one thing I've learned since joining the Gryphons is that it's important to celebrate the little victories, otherwise you become overwhelmed." Tom pressed a couple buttons on his phone, and mine vibrated with the arrival of his text. "Let's go accomplish another one."

He headed past me, and I followed him out of the office. I could taste the anger simmering under his calm, optimistic surface. Tom was furious that his precious fraternity could have a leak, and I understood that. He felt betrayed by someone in it, much like I felt betrayed by everyone in it. I hoped victory in this would be more satisfying for him than killing Raj had been for me.

I shivered, uncomfortably aware of what I'd just thought. Not liking the implications, I pushed the memory of Raj from my head and focused on the task ahead.

"So how are we going to—?" Fear shot through me, potently lime like a frozen margarita, and the jolt of energy that came with it was intense. But frozen margaritas sounded good. This, I could tell from experience, was not.

I grasped the conference room door, attempting to locate the general direction of the emotion's source. *Le Confrérie de l'Aile* members were decked out in charms that dampened their emotions, making it harder for preds to prey on them. But from dealing with Tom, I knew the charms were only so successful with strong feelings. "We don't need this meeting. I've found your leak."

Tom had seen me in action enough that he didn't question how I knew. Well, not much. "You can't be positive what you're sensing is from a fraternity member, can you?"

"No, but someone is panicking with the intention to run minutes after you request a meeting with the Brotherhood? It can't be a coincidence."

Tom's blue eyes darted between me and the vial he'd taken out of his pocket. "No one should know what this meeting is about. But all right, check it out. If you're wrong, I have this and everyone assembled."

I didn't wait around for any additional instructions. Someone with the intent to flee wasn't going to do me any favors and leave a note about where they went. I barreled through the hall and burst into the stairwell, almost skidding down the steps in my haste.

Tracing the emotion's source was an awful lot like using my bond with Raj to seek him out. But whereas that had felt unnatural and new, picking out emotions was second nature to me. I'd been doing it for ten years whether I wanted to or not.

Headquarters' current state made it easy too. Most of the people here were tired. If they felt anything besides that, it was the same generic anxiety that permeated the city. In some cases, the anxiety was mixed with a mild annoyance at having to work an extra shift.

Almost to the ground floor, my feet thudded against the concrete steps. Only when I hit the landing did I discover my error—the emotion's taste was getting weaker again. Damn it. The person I was searching for hadn't gotten this far yet.

My magical buzz and determination were all that kept me moving. My muscles whined at me as I forced my legs up the previous flight, and my lungs weren't much more pleased. Sweat broke out on my neck. It occurred to me that after everything I'd been through tonight, I probably didn't smell so sweet.

Oh well. I shoved the stairwell door open and ran right into someone on the other side. He visibly shook off the impact, and I swore in surprise.

Apologizing, I assessed the obstacle in my way. The other Gryphon was a member of *Le Confrérie*, an Indian man who'd introduced himself as Kevin, though I was ninety-nine percent certain that wasn't his real name. I was also ninety-nine percent certain that he wasn't the source of the panic I was sensing.

"Sorry," I muttered again, this time to atone for my language since I'd never heard the man swear. "Did you see any other members of the Brotherhood go that way?" I motioned down the hall.

"Just Theo's down there. He said he had to gather things to bring to Tom."

Theo. Of course. I could have slapped myself for not figuring it out.

Theo was on my short list of possible suspects because he was one of the eleven Gryphons who had been given access to all the leaked information. Plus, Theo was the fraternity's charm-making expert. He spent more time in the labs than anywhere else. Tom hadn't been careless enough to ask a *Le Confrérie* member to make his truth serum, but if Theo had seen a Boston Gryphon working on it and had asked why…

"See you upstairs," I called to Kevin as I willed my feet to move.

Unfortunately, surprise was not entirely on my side. Theo couldn't sense me coming, but he was quite capable of hearing my pounding feet approach and putting the facts together, and he didn't wait around to confirm his suspicion.

He must not have bothered to change out of his uniform before running because a streak of black and gold disappeared around a line of cubicles. He was heading toward the lab area, a bad choice but not one I'd begrudge him since I was chasing.

Although Theo knew the lab section better than I did, I had three advantages. One, I carried nothing, and he had a pack of belongings on his back. Two, the adrenaline boost his fear provided him was nothing compared to the magical hit it gave me. And three, while we were both charmed out the ass for additional speed—ironically from glyphs drawn by him—I had bonus magic that the satyrs had given me.

I caught up to him as he rounded the next corner. My fingers brushed his sleeve, and as he turned, his hand closed around some curse he undoubtedly intended to aim my way. The only weapon I carried was my knife, and that wouldn't be much help. Luckily, looking at me to aim meant Theo wasn't looking where he was going. He banged his shoulder into a doorframe.

He faltered from the impact, giving me the additional second I needed. I tackled him, knocking the curse out of his grip and forcing him to the linoleum. Theo was no slouch in hand-to-hand combat, and we struggled on the floor, neither gaining the upper hand but both of us definitely earning plenty of bruises.

Finally, I swiped the curse container from his reach. Theo slammed an arm into my stomach, but his angle diminished the blow's force. I grunted with pain, but my fingers grasped the trigger on the curse container and pulled.

The magical spray hit him in the chest. Instantly, his body went limp, and his eyes closed. Body aching and my lip bleeding from where he'd decked me, I climbed out from beneath him. Theo's breaths came long and steady, suggesting the curse was some kind of sleeping charm.

Lovely. I was the one busting my ass, and it was the traitor who got to nap.

HALF AN HOUR LATER THEO'S HANDS WERE BOUND, AND TOM dosed him with the counter-curse. Theo darted awake, swiveling around in his chair and taking in his handcuffs and the interrogation room's beige walls. Resignation weighed down his face, and fear was no longer his predominant emotion. It was sweet, vanilla sadness. Odd.

In my experience, two emotions tended to prevail in people who were discovered to be lying or deceiving. Anger was the main one, probably at either the person who called them out on their lies or at themselves for getting caught. Running beneath that was almost always a salty-flavored embarrassment. Sadness was new to me.

Theo's gaze moved from Tom to Ingrid and settled on me. Again, where I'd have expected anger aimed at me for capturing him, I picked up on a mild fear instead.

"Your abilities are impressive." It was probably the longest string of words Theo had put together in my presence.

I neglected to thank him, letting his other two interrogators handle this. I'd caught him, and I'd serve as a living lie detector, but this wasn't my show.

Ingrid's hair was falling out of its messy bun, and her voice was as weary as she looked. "Why, Agent Stephanopoulos?"

Theo folded his hands together, at last turning his attention from me to his boss. "Because I have a family, and they need to be protected."

"That is what we're trying to do." Ingrid leaned over the back of an empty chair, and her reading glasses bobbed against her chest. "That is the mission you interfered with."

"That is the mission you're going to fail." Theo cocked his head toward me. "Her abilities are unusual, but you have no idea how they might actually help. You're relying on interpretations and translations of a very old text that said an *other* was required to save the world. You don't know for sure if she's what was meant. Come on, the furies used her and one of the others like her for their own interests. How can they be useful against the original furies if they can't defeat a modern one?"

Thanks for the vote of confidence, I thought, but I was too stunned by the length of Theo's speech to bother with my own words. Besides, it wasn't as if he were voicing thoughts I hadn't had myself. My stomach turned, acknowledging that, in many ways, I agreed with him.

Tom slammed a hand onto the metal table. His face was red, and his rage simmered hot beneath the surface, unblockable by the charms he wore. "You passed on information to the furies long before what happened in France. You had no idea whether Jessica and Mitchell could handle them."

"I had an idea. We've read the same prophecies, Kassin. Our interpretations differ. The furies knew what would happen with her power. They know far more about what they're doing than we do."

"So they approached you, and you made a deal with them?" Ingrid crossed her arms. She was clearly furious too, but she had a much tighter grip on her feelings.

Theo shrugged. "I have a family to protect. I don't want the furies to get away with what they've done, but they will. They have. We don't know how to close the Pit, and we don't have any weapons strong enough to fight the demons when they emerge. I don't want to lose, but I don't see how we can win. So yes, for my family's sake, I threw my lot in with the likely victors. I was promised my wife and children would be protected."

Tom laughed bitterly. "You can't trust we might defeat them, but you will trust a fury's promise?"

"Of course not. I'm not the one here willing to believe in miracles." Again, his gaze flickered in my direction. "I have a magically binding contract."

Behind my back, I dug my nails into my palms. The hyper-focused state I'd been in since Raj's death, the momentum that had pushed me through my tiredness, was evaporating. Along with it came the physical pain of my new cuts, bruises, and strained muscles. But worse was the emotional assault.

It would be one thing if I could have been angry with Theo, but any anger I harbored was cool and distant. Rather, it was the same, sickening resignation I sensed in Theo that had also taken residence in me. More than fear, it was dread. While Tom and Ingrid fumed that Theo had made their chances more dire, my pessimistic heart whispered that he'd only done the smart thing under the circumstances.

How could I be angry when he made valid points? How could I call Theo a coward when I considered Tom a fanatic for believing the opposite of him? Where was my middle ground?

And mostly, how could I claim Theo was wrong when I hadn't been able to defeat Raj? Or when killing Raj had left me... I dug my nails in deeper, driving away the images of Raj's blood coating my knife.

Theo spread his hands in a gesture of contrition. "I am sorry I made everyone's life more dangerous, but I'd do it again. Who do you think the demons are going to target first when they leave the Pit? It's going to be a massacre, and we and our families will be first in line for the slaughter."

EIGHT

I COULDN'T GET THEO'S WORDS OUT OF MY HEAD AS I MADE MY way to Shadowtown. *I don't want the furies to win, but they will. Our families will be first in line for the slaughter.* The first statement hadn't been carved in stone yet, but the second struck me as all too likely if they did.

We—mostly Tom—had spent another hour grilling Theo for any new information he might be able to provide. But while Theo willingly coughed up what he knew, it wasn't much. We got the names of who he assumed were the five ringleaders among the furies, for what that was worth. Technically, they were down to four ringleaders without Raj.

Rather than lock up Theo, Tom and Ingrid decided to keep him nearby in case he could be of use later. He'd be outfitted with both an ankle monitor and a tracking charm, much like mine but not removable, and left in his hotel room under guard. It was the Gryphon's equivalent of house arrest.

My presence wasn't necessary to see any of that through, so I finally got to leave. The T system had shut down for the night, and I'd had to call a ride for the drive home. My driver was listening to NPR, and although part of me didn't want to hear unpleasantness, my ears nonetheless perked up when I heard the words HELP Act. Dezzi had mentioned something about that earlier.

"Representative Mark O'Donnell of Massachusetts' First Congressional District joined colleagues from across the nation today in cosponsoring a bipartisan bill known as the Human Empowerment and Liberty Protection Act or the HELP Act," the NPR reporter was saying in her perfect diction. "The bill grants humans the right to protect themselves from perceived threats of a magical nature. Supporters claim the bill is merely an extension of current self-defense laws, particularly those known as 'stand your ground' laws. Representative O'Donnell had this to say about the proposed bill."

My Uber driver merely tapped his fingers against the wheel, but I leaned forward to hear the radio better. The audio changed to a male voice, presumably O'Donnell's. "Humans have been forced to accept living in close quarters with those who would prey on them for too long. In light of recent events, it's become clear that the laws which were supposed to protect humanity from the alleged 'pred' races are archaic failures. Everyone has the right to protect themselves from those who would threaten them with bodily harm. We should have the same right to protect ourselves from those who threaten our souls with harm. If you wouldn't hesitate to shoot a bear that's attacking you, why should we have to lie down and die if a pred attacks?"

The station switched back to the female reporter. "Critics of the bill stress that the language is too broadly worded, essentially giving humans the right to attack any nonhuman they encounter without fear of legal consequences. The HELP Act is a response to the mass shooting of several satyrs and harpies by a group of humans in Miami two days ago. While none of the injuries were fatal, the incident has spurred more violence and rioting as the debate grows over whether such actions are justified under the circumstances."

My driver grunted, whether in agreement or disgust I couldn't tell. "World is going to hell."

"Yeah, it is," I said, too tired to get sucked into a conversation.

Shit. No wonder Dezzi was concerned about the HELP Act. It sounded like a plan for disaster. There were ways to confirm whether someone had been magically attacked, and therefore if self-defense was justifiable under this law, but those traces of magic in the blood didn't last long. Ultimately, this law was giving humans the right to attack at will. After all, just standing near a pred was enough to leave magical traces on people.

The sad thing was, though I'd like to blame the hysteria and recent increases in violence on the Pit opening, I strongly suspected this was simply human nature at work. History was full of examples of fearful people committing atrocities. The only difference was that these days all their fear was feeding some ancient demons.

You fed them too, Jess. You had to have your revenge on Raj. You gave into your rage, full of self-righteous fury.

I gritted my teeth and bade the voice in my head to shut up. Raj had attacked me. It was self-defense.

It was a moment you'd been yearning for. A moment you relished.

Except I hadn't. I'd wanted to, but the blood. So much blood everywhere. I could see Raj's surprised face. I could...

"You can let me out here." I needed to move, to burn off the memory with exercise. Exactly what I'd been doing all night.

The car slowed, and the driver frowned at the quiet street. "You sure?"

"Yeah, I'm good."

We were a block away from where I'd asked to be dropped off, which was a block away from the edge of Shadowtown. Humans never liked going into that neighborhood, and when they did, they typically added a surcharge to their fare. But these days, even the surcharge wasn't enough for most of them. Not at night.

My ride sped off, and I turned toward home. Concentrating on the wail of police sirens in the distance, the aches in my muscles, and the eerie deadness all around, I was able to distract myself for several minutes. Imps danced about by the streetlamps, but aside from the lights glowing behind closed curtains, they were the most obvious signs of life. The few businesses that were open seemed to be trying to hide that fact.

A stab of pain pierced my heart as I passed by The Lair. Though it had been closed hours ago, the bar's neon signs currently lit up a small patch of the street. But it too had opened quietly. The bar's outdoor seating remained stacked and piled in a corner of the patio. Any patrons were hidden away inside.

Lucen didn't have much time to manage the place given his other responsibilities lately, but he was trying to keep it open as often as possible. The satyrs liked to congregate there, and it provided a defiant sense of normality that was desperately needed.

Although I was too tired to drink, I was half tempted to pop in myself, but I doubted Lucen was around. What happened with the furies earlier was probably keeping him busy. I hadn't gotten a reply from him to the text I sent about Theo other than *good*.

Good. It was apparently the word of the night. So why didn't I feel it? I had no answer to that question, and I didn't particularly want to dwell on it. Picking up my pace, I swatted at a curious imp and kept going.

About ten feet past The Lair's entrance, Lucen called out to me. "Little siren."

He didn't need to yell to be heard these days, and I spun around. "I wasn't expecting to see you there."

Lucen had changed into his third outfit of the day, and the only reminder of our earlier fights was the small dab of white goo on his left cheek. That was the magical bandage preds used to heal skin broken by salamander fire blades.

Lucen stepped past a stack of chairs, holding out a hand to me. "Dezzi wanted to meet about what happened, and since I was going to be here, I figured I might as well open for a few hours." He gestured to me with the open hand.

"I'm tired. I should sleep. Tomorrow's not going to be any easier."

"Yeah, yeah, I know. No rest for the wicked lately. But we should talk."

The light changed down the street and a couple cars blew by, tossing hair in my face with their wind. I started to ask what we were supposed to talk about, but Lucen's stare was getting to me. Whether talk, sleep, or none of the above, I'd prefer being around him for it.

"Damn you and your persuasiveness," I told him, clomping down the steps.

He held open the door. "How come it was never so easy before?"

"Yet another question I can't answer. How did you know I was out there?"

"Because I've always been able to tell when you're nearby." Instead of slipping behind the bar, he took my arm and walked to the far side of the room with me. "These days it's easier to notice because there aren't any humans hanging around to cloud the air."

"So you're saying I stand out? Peachy."

"You've always stood out, little siren."

I grimaced. Though Lucen meant it as a good thing, it rarely had felt that way to me. More than ever, it was likely to be a bad thing. *We and our families will be first in line for the slaughter.*

Lucen seemed reluctant to let go of me as I took my preferred seat at the end of the bar. In the mirror that faced me, I scanned the room. Dezzi must have left, but a handful of satyrs remained, talking in low voices. At any moment, I expected the door to open and Devon to breeze through, but of course that wasn't happening. As glad as I was that Lucen was attempting to keep some semblance of normality, it was depressing when the normality was all wrong.

He rubbed a warm hand across my back, and I might have melted into the furniture. "What's wrong?"

"Nothing really. Was thinking about Devon. Any change?" Raj had cursed Devon unconscious when the satyrs and Gryphons had tried rescuing me in the Alps, and none of the usual counter-curses had revived him. It was one of the many reasons killing Raj should have been a fist-pumping triumph.

Lucen's hand tensed then resumed its motion. "Not yet. Azria mentioned earlier that she's working on a new counter-curse. He needs to stop being so lazy and wake the hell up. This isn't a good time to leave me with his responsibilities on top of my own."

Lucen's tone couldn't rise to the occasion to match his words, and his attempt at humor fell flat, which was unusual but unsurprising. Devon had been his good friend for ages. However furious I was at Raj, and however upset I was about Devon's situation, it had to be far worse for Lucen.

"This isn't just about Devon," Lucen said, and I didn't need to read his emotions to tell he wanted to change the topic. "Talk to me."

Yawning, I forced myself to sit up straighter. Barstools made slouching dangerous. "About what? I'm tired, like I said. It's been a long night."

"But a productive one." His left hand joined the right, and he began massaging my shoulders. "You should be happy, and instead you're sad."

"Everything here is right and yet wrong." Briefly, I shared what I'd been thinking, not only about Devon but about the fake normality.

Lucen let me go, and while I spoke, he went behind the bar. "We'll get it back to being right soon enough."

Would we? Theo didn't think so.

When I said nothing in response, Lucen set an empty mug in front of me. "Coffee?"

I shook my head. "It'll keep me up, and I really do need sleep."

Lucen poured a mug for himself, another reminder that the world had gone mad. This time of the night—make that early morning—he typically drank beer if he was drinking. He noted my raised eyebrow with a shrug. "I don't like you being sad, little siren, but I am glad you're back to normal yourself."

I narrowed my eyes at him. "What does that mean?"

"After what happened with Raj..." He paused to sip his coffee, and I got the sense he was waiting for me to jump in. I declined, not wanting to talk about Raj. Alas, that was apparently Lucen's point. "You're doing it again since I mentioned his name."

"Doing what?" Getting irritated?

"Shutting down. Going numb. All that nearly manic energy you were—"

"Manic? I wasn't manic. I was focused. I was excited to be making progress. I had momentum."

Lucen pressed my twitchy hands into the wood. "You were making yourself move so fast because if you paused to breathe, you would have to deal with what you did."

I sucked on my lip. "I did what I had to do. It wasn't anything more than Raj deserved."

"I wouldn't claim otherwise." He released his death grip on my hands and placed a shot glass in front of me. "You've never killed anyone before, have you?" It was a statement masquerading as a question.

I hadn't, not to my knowledge. I'd gotten into fights, tossed curse grenades at people, hit Gryphons with chairs. I'd shot at preds, but they'd lived. Hell, I'd nearly killed a fury once and had beaten the magic out of his serial killer addict. Yet despite that, all of which had been done in self-defense or defense of others, my kill tally was zero.

Funny how I'd never even thought about having a kill tally until tonight.

My silence spoke for me as Lucen poured some top-shelf bourbon into the shot glass. "Drink it."

"I don't need—"

"Just do it. Believe me, I'm not recommending you make a habit of treating your moral conflicts with alcohol, but you're not going to sleep tonight without some help. I've seen enough people go through what you're dealing with."

I sighed and sipped the bourbon. Lucen had killed people before. He was old enough to have lived through more brutal times, and pred-on-pred violence remained a depressingly regular part of life in Shadowtown and similar communities. Each domus operated like its own little mob competing for addicts and power, and most humans were blissfully unaware of what went on. The façade of peace preds maintained was a shallow one. It existed primarily because they despised the Gryphons and magi more than each other.

That Lucen had risen to his position in such a society was indicative of his intelligence, his ability to snag useful addicts, and undoubtedly a willingness to do the nasty things that had to be done for survival. It didn't make him a bad person exactly, no more so than any other pred, but there was no question that he'd had to have nurtured a hard exterior to protect the generally kind person who lurked within.

In fact, now that my memory was going down this route, it wasn't too long ago that I'd seen Lucen decapitate a magi who was attacking us in bird form. It hadn't seemed to bother him, although I hadn't known Lucen as well then. Maybe he had gone home and drank afterward. Maybe he did know that of which he spoke.

Regardless, I wasn't about to let good bourbon go to waste.

"I wanted Raj dead. I wanted to be the one who killed him. But watching him bleed out..." I closed my eyes, seeing red everywhere, then took another sip. "It wasn't the satisfaction I expected. And I don't get it. After everything he did, it shouldn't bother me. So why does it?"

Lucen's smile was entirely sympathetic, and he gave my wrist a squeeze. "Because you're a decent person, Jess. That's what separates you from Raj. Killing others should never be pleasant. Fortunately, or unfortunately, it gets easier, just like most things the more you do them."

"There is going to be more, isn't there?" I examined the cuts and calluses on my hands. I was going to have a lovely scar on the back of my right one from when I'd hit the asphalt at the airport. Tough skin. That was what I needed—literally and figuratively—if I was going to survive.

"Before this is over, it seems inevitable."

I downed the last drop of bourbon. "Do you think we really can succeed?"

Lucen poured a second shot, drank half of it, then refilled the glass and pushed it toward me. "I have to believe it, little siren. I have to."

NINE

At his insistence, I spent the night at Lucen's, though to be honest, he didn't need to insist very hard. While he closed The Lair, I went up to his apartment and crashed. In spite of his fear that I wouldn't be able to sleep, I didn't even notice him climbing into bed. Either he'd been completely wrong about my conscience, or he'd snuck a sleeping charm into the bourbon. I wouldn't have put the latter past him.

Lucen and others were due at Gryphon headquarters later the next day to discuss plans, but I had to be there a few hours earlier to continue my magical training. I left Lucen in bed, went home to shower, change, and eat, then prepared to head out. When I opened my door to leave, I discovered two satyrs standing there.

Gi had his hand raised, poised to knock. Melissa was behind him. They were both decked out in their full bodyguard gear, looking like a couple of leather-clad badasses.

Human ones. They were both wearing disguise charms to hide their horns as well.

"Um, hi?"

Gi stepped out of the way as I exited the apartment. He didn't appear badly injured from last night, or if he was, his clothing hid the extent of it. "Forget we were coming by?"

"That would suggest I'd ever known to expect you."

Melissa had a smirk on her face as she headed down the stairs, as if my reaction had been anticipated. "Dezzi and Lucen thought there might be retaliation after what went down last night. They want you protected."

"Of course they do, and naturally they didn't tell me." I locked the apartment, not bothering to resist. We'd been through this drill before, and it was easiest on everyone just to roll with it.

Gi took up the rear. "It's for the best. You've heard about what's going on at the Gryphon building?"

I paused, my gut tightening with worry, then I opened the door onto the street. "Um, no. What's going on at the Gryphon building?"

Gi's voice was grim. "You'll see."

YOU'LL SEE. IF THAT WAS ONLY THE EXTENT OF IT. REALITY WAS more like you'll see, hear, and be swallowed up by it.

Half an hour later, sweat beaded on my neck, courtesy of my anxiety and the extreme heat that continued to strangle the city. Several dozen protestors had gathered in front of Gryphon headquarters, waving signs and chanting words I couldn't make out. The Boston PD had set up barricades to provide a safe aisle for people like us to walk down on our way toward the building, but not everyone was respecting boundaries. Without even knowing who we were, a couple people shouted anti-magic slurs at us.

I rolled my eyes and pressed on, and apparently that infuriated one of the demonstrators even more. She ducked under a barricade, but to do what, I never found out. Melissa jumped in front of me, and the woman's hand snagged the disguise charm my bodyguard wore around her neck, exposing her horns.

The woman's face turned white, and she shrieked. "Satyrs!"

Shit. I couldn't imagine how anyone heard her over the noise, but the people nearby did and they repeated her cry. The word and the ensuing panic spread throughout the crowd faster than we could beat it the hell out of there.

Gi wrapped an arm around me, and I swore as the barricades on either side of us came crashing down. On my left, a man about my age grabbed at my shirt collar. I was pretty sure he'd mistaken my pendant for a disguise charm and intended to rip it off, but this was hardly the time to explain that it was actually a tracking charm. The finer nuances of magic— and well, everything else logical—were lost on these people.

Angry mobs weren't known for their interest in reasoned discussions.

What they did do, however, was provide me with one hell of a hit of magical energy. I smacked the guy's arm away and shoved him into the swarming crowd with more force than I'd intended. His peppery anger surged as he fell, and a potent lemon fear rose to the surface. Then the particular taste of this one man's emotions dissolved into the wretched blend of the couple hundred others I had to contend with.

Some people fought to get to us, apparently in an attempt to rip us limb from limb, while others ran away. Gi tried to block my body with his as we continued pushing our way through, but he was in as much trouble as I was. Normally, most humans wouldn't mess with as imposingly built a guy as Gi, particularly once they knew he was a satyr. But as I'd discussed with Lucen last night, these were not normal times. Angry, frightened people clawed at my bodyguard, tearing off his hat and threatening to expose more of his sun-phobic skin to the afternoon light.

I love humanity, I reminded myself. *I used to want to be a part of it, and I want to save these people.*

Well, maybe not these people in particular.

Somewhere in the crowd, these people in particular were starting a new chant. I couldn't make out most of the words, but "kill" definitely caught my attention. Peachy. I did not like the sound of that. If this was the appetizer stage of the apocalypse, I wanted to be drunk off my ass by the time the main course was unleashed.

Alas, drinking my way to the end of the world wasn't an option for me. Just as it wasn't supposed to be an option for me to go around punching all the hate-spewing, frightened people who were adding to my stress levels. I was supposed to be playing nice in the hope that it would prevent further violence, but the louder the chanting got, the less inclined I was to hold my fists. The next person who touched me was becoming my stand-in for the apocalypse and getting decked with the full power of my frustration.

"Almost there," Gi said as I tripped over a fallen police barricade.

I had to take his word on that since I was too short to see above the crowd. Our march through this melee felt like it was taking forever. For every step I got closer to the building, I was shoved two backward.

The police had been keeping people off the building's massive steps. I was counting on them remaining clear, but I was also beginning to think that was unrealistically optimistic.

"Jess!" Somewhere straight ahead, a familiar voice called out my name. My heart beat faster as I strained to see who it was. When I opened my mouth to yell back, one of the demonstrators whacked me in the back with her sign.

That was it. I was done. Enough with this woman and the sour orange taste of her fear, enough with the reek of two hundred sweaty bodies, and enough with playing nice.

I spun around and snatched the woman's sign. Cardboard tore in my hands. But instead of trying to hold on, the woman unexpectedly let go of her end, and I stumbled backward into Gi. His body braced me as I swore and fought for balance.

Strangely, the woman who just a moment ago had tried to beat me with a stick ignored me when I glared at her, and she wasn't the only one. People pointed up, toward Gryphon headquarters. Craning my neck, I searched for whatever had distracted them, and was shocked to see the sky turning blue. Not blue as in the color the sky was supposed to be, but blue as in someone was spraying down the crowd with sweet-scented blue gas. Dragon shit on toast. Wasn't this getting better and better?

Fearing the worst, I put one hand over my mouth and used my stolen sign as a bludgeon, swinging it wildly to clear a path toward the building. Only belatedly did I realize I probably should have been running in the opposite direction if the cops were gassing people.

"Jess!" The same familiar male voice yelled my name, and a tan hand reached out to me.

"Andre?"

Agent Andre Pagan helped me up the first couple granite stairs in front of the stately building. Gi was right behind me, and I lowered the sign as the crowd settled back behind us.

"Hang on," Andre said. He picked up a small canister by his feet, aimed the hose on the end of it toward the crowded sidewalk, and doused the air in more of the blue gas.

Blinking, I glanced around and discovered two other Gryphons with similar contraptions doing the same thing. None of them wore gas masks, and I slowly lowered my hand from my mouth. Whatever they were spraying didn't seem to have an effect on me either, other than making my nose burn with the powerful scent of gardenias.

"You okay?" Gi asked. His clothes were disheveled, and his sunglasses were missing.

"Yeah, I'm good."

Melissa burst through the crowd a second later, her red lips set in a scowl. Without a word, she adjusted my shirt for me and fixed my necklace. "Can't risk Lucen seeing you look abused. Some bodyguard I am if I'm the one causing trouble."

"You didn't cause it," I told her. "They did."

For the first time, I noticed a faint, cherry-like scent from Melissa's pheromones as she fussed with me. My skin tingled with magically induced lust near her fingers, and it hit me fully how a pred's magic was as much for defense as offense. Yes, we called them preds because they were predators, but they could still be prey. With their power, a pred could subdue one, maybe two, human opponents. But an angry mob? Not so much.

I combed my fingers through my hair and assessed the crowd. Things had quieted to a murmur. A few people had fled, but most were backing up politely while the PD reset their barricades. It was all far less boisterous than it had been before Melissa had been outed as a satyr. "What happened, and what is that blue stuff?"

Andre signaled to a cop and started up the steps. "This? This is my new best friend. I call it kumbaya gas."

"Some kind of magical tranq?"

I could sense Andre's apprehension at talking with satyrs nearby, but he nodded as though everything was totally normal. "Yup. We've recently been authorized to use it. It won't work on preds, and we're covered in glyphs that protect us from it, but it's better than valium on a regular human. Personally, if this insanity keeps up, I'm pushing to have a liquid version of it pumped into the municipal water system."

"If this keeps up," I repeated Andre's words, my stomach sick with dread.

Realizing I still carried the stolen sign, I tossed it to the granite steps. MAGIC IS UNNATURAL was written on it in bright green letters. The sentiment was as uninformed and ridiculous as what was on some of the other signs, but at least the person who'd created it knew how to spell.

"What is with the mob out front?" I asked. "I thought the demonstrations were being held at the Common?"

Gi opened the main door, and we filed into the safety of headquarters. The four of us paused in the busy lobby, and Andre set down his canister to wipe sweat from his brow.

"People are not happy with the Gryphons today," he said.

"Why? Most humans practically worship you, especially under the circumstances. They're counting on you to save the world."

Andre shook his head. "Gryphon U.S.A. Headquarters issued a statement this morning, specifically not lending their support to the HELP Act. That's what's got those people outside riled up."

After showing Gi and Melissa to the back door so they didn't have to face the mob again, I went up to the labs. Mitch Johnson and Grace Park were already there. We were the three surviving members of *Le Confrérie de l'Aile's* experiments, the three Tom and the others were counting on to somehow save the world. *Somehow* being the keyword.

I was no badass warrior or magical proficient. That I was alive today was due just as much to the massive amounts of help I'd received from Lucen and others as it was due to some innate cleverness or skill on my part. And while I was learning, and eager to learn more, I was depressingly far ahead of where Mitch was. More depressing yet, Mitch was far ahead of Grace.

All the years I'd spent cursing my allegedly rogue gift were years I'd nonetheless engaged with it, used it, and honed it. Mitch had tried to ignore his and used it only to assist in his work as a psychiatric nurse. Grace, on the other hand, had done her best to suppress hers altogether.

"Here's to the hero of last night." Mitch raised a beaker filled with some murky concoction. "I'd offer you a drink, but I don't recommend actually downing this stuff because I'm pretty sure I messed it up."

I set my bag down in a corner and took out my copy of the basic charm-making book I'd been given. "What's it supposed to be?"

"Some kind of pain-relief charm, but I don't think it was supposed to turn cloudy. Too many dragon scales or something." Mitch flipped a page in his book. "Not sure why we're bothering with these lessons. Last night, Grace and I were getting our beauty sleep, being useless, and you were kicking ass. Seems to me that's what the Gryphons need us for."

"You wanted to be out there?"

"Hell, no. I was merely making a point. I don't need any more mental or physical scars."

Mitch rubbed his arms as if subconsciously touching one. With everything else going on while we escaped from the furies in Europe, neither of us had noticed at the time that he'd gotten badly cut. The scar was hard to see because of his dark skin, but I knew that particular scar was merely the physical manifestation of wounds that bothered him more. He'd been hurt worse in other ways by how the furies had used the two of us to channel magic.

I grabbed a magic-resistant smock from a hook. "Please, that's nothing compared to what I went through last night." I parroted what the ER doctor had told me, trying to make light of my ordeal, but Grace blanched nonetheless.

"I heard about everything that happened," Mitch said. "Kassin made sure to give us a rundown as soon as we got here. My first impression of you, when you told me you hung out with satyrs, was that you were a crazy woman. You're only confirming that."

"Ouch. Coming from someone who works in a psych ward, that smarts."

Mitch peered into his beaker dubiously. "My patients weren't crazy. They were ill and in need of help. You are out of your damned mind. It's an important distinction."

Grace, who'd been slouching at the other end of the room, stopped staring at her nails and glanced over. "You hung out with satyrs? Why would you do that?"

Unlike Mitch, who appeared worse for the wear since being recruited by the Gryphons, Grace looked far better. She'd been in rehab when we found her, a result of a decade spent using alcohol and other drugs to numb her misery-sucking power. Under the supervision of Gryphon healers, her health was improving.

"They taught me a lot," I said. "It made things easier to have someone who I could talk to about my weirdness."

"I've heard you've become particularly close with a couple of them." Mitch threw me a what-the-fuck sort of expression before dumping the beaker's contents down a drain.

Damn Tom. My relationship with Lucen had, unfortunately, become common enough gossip fodder around here. But Mitch had specifically said a couple, suggesting Tom hadn't kept quiet about discovering I had a thing with Devon too.

When I didn't respond to Mitch's comment, he took the hint and went back to his concoction. "Again, I ask—is there really any point to this?"

I turned my back on Grace's scandalized stare, but I couldn't block the taste of her disgust. "The only way to get better at sensing magical energy is to practice sensing magical energy. I've had to essentially pick a magical lock before, and it would have been handy if I'd been more experienced at knowing how to choose the right anti-magic. I can see that situation coming up."

"Fair enough." One by one, Mitch set out the ingredients so he could try the charm a second time. "Do you think you could have outed the Gryphons' traitor sooner if you'd been more skilled?"

"Unlikely." I grimaced because having discovered Theo's duplicity earlier could have saved both Mitch and me from a lot of pain. Noticing that Grace hadn't even cracked open her spell book, I turned to her. "Do you need help?"

Grace's fingers curled around the cuffs of her long sleeves. "No. I get you're both okay with all of this, and I want to help, but I just don't like it. I've never used magic for anything before, and now I'm stuck here because of some court order, and people are drawing glyphs on my skin and giving me these magical tonics. They make me feel better, but I'd never have taken them if I didn't have to. And I can't ignore the way I can sense other people now either. It's like hundreds of cats constantly scratching at my soul. I hate it." Abruptly, she slammed her lips together and pulled even harder on her sleeves.

Despite any emotion-muting charms the Gryphons might have given her, Grace's unhappiness and anxiety flooded my system. I felt sorry for her, but I didn't know what to do to alleviate her fears. For her safety, she was better off here.

It wasn't simply a matter of training her to fight. Not anymore. Since Raj had made it clear last week, and again last night, that he was interested in harvesting bits and pieces of me for spells, we had to assume he wasn't the only fury with that idea. Likewise, I wasn't the only "rare creature"—to use Raj's words—that would be considered for the task. Mitch and Grace would suffice as well.

"You don't have to take any of those healing potions they offer you," Mitch said while I was composing my response. "They're only trying to help."

Grace slumped against the wall, shoving her book away. "I know, but I also know those special Brotherhood agents really want me to. I feel pressured because I can feel what they're feeling, but I'd rather be on the other side of these walls than in here."

"With those anti-magers?" I wrinkled my nose. "I understand not enjoying being a misery junkie, but those people are scary in their own way. The HELP Act is terrifying, and I nearly got torn apart trying to enter the building today."

Grace stiffened her shoulders. "There are some good points to the HELP Act, and the anti-magers make some good points too. I don't approve of the ones who are getting violent and looking for fights, but magic does cause lots of problems."

"Cars cause lots of problems," Mitch said. "Traffic jams and accidents. But they're also damn useful."

"Cars don't turn people into addicts and ghouls. They don't curse people."

I bit my lip to keep from frowning. "No, but they can kill people, accidentally or on purpose. Just like magic."

The more I listened to Grace, the more concerned I became. Since she'd arrived in Boston a couple weeks ago, I'd been struck by her fear, but I'd assumed it would lessen over time. I believed, as had Tom, that if she learned more about what she was and how to control her power, it would help her anxiety. But so far, Grace had shied away from learning, and she only endured the help the Gryphons offered. Instead of being empowered and her fear decreasing, she was withdrawing more than ever, and her fear grew stronger. If it weren't for those charms she wore, the magical hit I got off her would likely be quite potent.

"It's not the same for you," Grace said, jolting me back to the present. "None of it bothers you the same way. You don't mind being a pred. You chose to spend time with them."

I cringed. "I wouldn't say I don't mind. I mean, I did. It bothered me a lot when I first found out. But they're not all evil. I've had to accept that. It's thanks to one satyr specifically that I'm not bothered by what I am or what I can do. He helped me when he didn't have to, many times. He taught me how to control my abilities better, supported me when I tried to use them for a good purpose. He showed me they aren't all bad."

I swallowed past a lump in my throat, wondering when I'd started getting all emotional while thinking about Lucen. Then I realized it was because I was living with the constant worry that each time I saw him it would be the last. One second there, one second gone. Just like Devon had been taken from me.

Mitch had heard my how-I-met-Lucen story, and he grinned. "Probably didn't hurt that you were this cute, seemingly harmless girl in a Gryphon Academy uniform at the time you met. Probably tipped some satyr fantasy."

I flipped him off, though I was certain Mitch was right to an extent. "It might have helped, but I'm sure it was my freakish gift that interested him the most."

"So you admit the only reason this do-gooder satyr helped you was because he thought you were an interesting specimen or something?"

Grace had given up all pretense of practicing and was playing with her phone. "It's not because he actually cared about you."

"Maybe not at first. But who genuinely cares deeply about anyone when they first meet? That's the sort of thing that has to build over time. No one is friends with anyone else instantly. No one falls in love at first sight, no matter what the stories say. Those things take trust."

If Grace was any more dubious, her eyebrows might have flown off her head. "You really trust a satyr?"

"I love him."

Oh. Oh, shit. Had I just let the L-word slip in public? Judging from the shock emanating from Mitch, and Grace's potent horror, it would appear I had.

Mitch scratched his scruffy black beard. "You know, when Kassin said you were friendly with a couple satyrs, I didn't exactly take things that far. I thought, well, maybe Jess is braver than I am, and she's determined to discover if what they say about satyrs in bed is true. But even still, that's not what I was expecting by friendly."

My cheeks warmed, and I fought the urge to pull my hair down and cover up the visible signs of my embarrassment since it would do me no good. Besides, the end of the world was upon us. I might as well own up to everything. Right?

"We are satyrs. And we are human. Whether I'm in a relationship with a guy who can feed on my unhappiness, or whether you're in a relationship with a human who feeds you with unhappiness, what's the difference? You've seen the news—humans hunting down preds, preds draining their addicts to ghouls. We're all predators, and we're all prey. It just depends on the situation. So if you find someone who has your back, regardless of the danger, then who cares what they are?"

Since I'd shocked the room into silence, I figured why not keep going? "Lucen has had my back for ten years. That's more than I can say for most other people I've known. How can you not care about someone who does that for you? So, yeah. I love a satyr. And for the record, everything they say about them in bed is true."

Although the taste of Mitch and Grace's icy shock lingered in my mouth, Mitch burst out laughing. I knew I liked that guy.

TEN

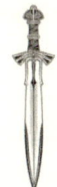

BOSTON'S HEADQUARTERS DID NOT HAVE A CONFERENCE ROOM large enough to hold everyone who gathered for today's meeting. Director Lee had sacrificed the biggest room in the building—possibly on the condition that she got to attend—and we were still cramped. Though, to be fair, that was partially because each group insisted on leaving space between themselves and the other groups.

It was like being back at a middle school dance, with the boys hanging out at one of the end of the gym and the girls at the other. Of course, at a middle school dance the boys and girls were less prone to killing each other.

After Ingrid provided everyone with a recap of last night's events, Claudius stepped to the front of the room along with Raia. Although stepped didn't quite capture his all-domineering posture and the expression of thinly disguised disdain on his face. Sweeping his long hair over his shoulders, he eyed me lasciviously. Whether it was to provoke me or Lucen, I couldn't tell. His magic lightly brushed my mind, caressing me with soft fingers, but despite the sensation being disturbingly pleasant, I was not amused. I was even less amused that his casual way of toying with me suggested he was unfazed by how I'd attacked him last night at the airport.

While Claudius chuckled to himself over my silent reaction, I turned my attention to Raia. She hadn't exactly been friendly to me, but she'd been reasonable, and so far, she hadn't tried to invade my head. When it came to preds, that stuck her firmly in the inoffensive column. But then again, I set a low bar for that column when preds were involved. Not messing with my soul or otherwise trying to harm me was all it took.

Fortunately, it was Raia who addressed the group. She wasn't haughty, as I imagined Claudius would have been, but direct. I let my mind wander while she spoke about the importance of the mixed alliance and how the satyrs' Upper Council had agreed to share their information.

I was getting jittery from all the tension when Raia finally got to the good part. "Now that we have collected all five Vessels of Making in one place, I know the question that continues to haunt us is: what is the next step? How do we use these Vessels to close the Pit and prevent the original demons from escaping? We might be able to help with that too."

The surprise that rippled around the room knocked me from my stupor. I glanced at Lucen and then Tom, but they both appeared as taken aback by Raia's announcement as I was. Even Dezzi's dark eyes opened wider.

But amidst the excited murmurs came the sound of voices that were less than thrilled, and a magi with the red plumage of a falcon shifter stood in the far corner. "We've been piecing that information together already."

Ugh, Xander. The only other person I disliked almost as much as Claudius. The room was packed, and since I couldn't sense magi emotions, I hadn't noticed the small contingent of them who had staked out a spot in the back.

Not content to stay there, Xander pushed his way forward. "One of our own was quite busy researching that very information, and for his trouble, he was murdered by one of your own."

"Not by one of our own," Dezzi said, facing Xander. "By Raj."

Xander's feathers fluffed. To him, as with most magi and humans, preds were preds. Once, I'd thought the same, but I'd had the sense to learn. Xander, though much older than me, probably wasn't interested in that. "The point is, our people are already working on gathering the necessary information. If you'd like us to compare your notes with our own, we can discuss."

The point really was, as it became clear in the ensuing minutes, that Xander—if not all the magi—resented the idea that their contribution to the alliance might be usurped by a bunch of satyrs. The satyrs, in turn, resented being associated with the furies and having their work and intelligence discounted. The discussion degenerated predictably from there.

Dragon shit on toast, I was stuck in a room filled with wannabe heroes, each hoping to out-hero the others. With chagrin, I realized I'd been guilty of the same thing earlier when I'd been annoyed at Ingrid for overlooking my showdown with Raj. Part of me had wanted to be credited for that despite most of me still not wanting to relive the moment.

"Think Andre's got any more of that kumbaya gas lying around?" I muttered.

"Got any what?" Mitch asked.

"Never mind." I tried to get Tom's attention, but he was deep in some internal discussion with Ingrid. Peachy. It wasn't fair to expect Mitch to jump in when he didn't know these people as well as I did, and I hadn't seen Grace show up at all. Therefore, it was going to have to be me taking control. Time to put my freak warrior status to use.

I stood on my chair and waved arms. "Hey, excuse me. It doesn't matter who has the intel. If we can't cooperate long enough to use it, we're all dead anyway. Everyone can write their own version of history if we win."

Could and undoubtedly would.

Xander's golden eyes bore into me, and I could tell from his fluffing head feathers that I'd totally affronted him by interrupting. Good.

"You," he said, and the one syllable summed up his feelings aptly.

I stepped down, crossing my arms. "Me." *You damn Hitchcockian nightmare.*

Claudius, for his part, silently stared me down.

I wasn't sure my plea for peace and harmony succeeded on its own, but Xander and Claudius apparently discovered they had one thing in common

—a dislike of me. I tolerated being chastised for my rudeness because it got the conversation back on track.

Alas, once Raia and Xander got around to sharing what they'd discovered about how to use the Vessels, any fleeting hope I'd nourished for a quick end to the meeting was crushed. There were timing issues to consider and more items had to be collected or prepared for use. The ritual would be every bit as complicated—or rather more so—than what I'd seen the furies do to open the Pit.

Naturally. As Tom had pointed out not so long ago, destroying things was always easier than creating them. In this case, we weren't creating the prison again from nothing, but we were building up magical walls the furies had torn down.

"It sounds like it would be simpler to build a new prison from scratch than rebuild the old one," Lucen said.

One of the magi shook her head. "In some ways, yes. In others, no. We have no blueprints for how to begin. If we use what our ancestors already created, we have a guide. Making our own could take years. I think we'd all prefer to avoid that."

Then Raia said one more thing I didn't want to hear. "There is also one more item we will need. Someone will have to obtain the key to relock it."

JESS USE KEY

Never mind the emotion-dampening charms I had, I was positive every pred in the room noticed how my blood had just turned cold.

JESS USE KEY

Those words had been scratched onto Olef's apartment wall with his own blood. His last message, a directive to me. I swallowed. "The key was supposedly left inside the prison. How are we going to obtain it?"

Raia's face was expressionless as she considered me. "Someone will have to enter the prison and bring it out, obviously."

I laughed, or tried to. The sound was ugly and didn't suggest amusement. "Go inside? What's that proverb about letting slumbering demons lie? Why can't we make a new key? That's got to be easier than making a whole new prison."

Was it my imagination, or did Raia not look particularly pleased about this development herself? "Presumably the key fits this magical lock. If we started anew, we would have a new key. If we're rebuilding from the old prison's magical bones, we need the old key."

I swore under my breath, and I wasn't the only one. Several of the *Le Confrérie* members in attendance turned a bit green. Like me, they must have been imagining themselves being volunteered for this mission.

Tom put his pen down, his face strained. "Do we have any idea what we might find inside the Pit?"

The Gryphons looked at the magi, who looked at the satyrs, who looked at the goblins, who looked right back at Tom.

"No," said the same magi who'd spoken earlier. "There are no records of it for obvious reasons. All we can do is speculate. We can't even say for certain what the key will look like."

"You've got to be kidding me," I whispered into the heavy silence.

Tom dropped his pen. "What?"

Oops. "I said, how do we possibly prepare for this sort of thing, and how can we possibly decide who has the skills to go in and search?"

Claudius cleared his throat, and the asshole smiled at me. "How many people we send in will have to be determined, but the last question is simple. You are supposed to have the skills. The Gryphons might not have realized it at the time, but this is certainly why you were created. You and your half-breed friends must go in."

A couple feet away, Lucen's hand crushed his paper coffee cup, and next to me, Mitch's fear burst in my mouth like lemon sherbet. I could almost hear them both silently yelling and protesting. Of course, so was I.

Instead of showing my fear, however, I let my annoyance seep into my voice. I matched Claudius's fake smile with one of my own. "You would say that. Any reason to get rid of us *half-breeds* you find so offensive."

Tom waited for the room to settle down. "According to the prophecies, only warriors who are unlike the typical races might be able to defeat the originals—the demons."

"The others," I said dryly. "Half-breeds. Abominations. Rare subspecies. I've been called them all, but I've never been called a warrior. That could be a problem."

Raia turned my way. "This will not be about how well you can wield a sword, though that might help. This will be about how well you can manage your gift. How much power you can channel and control. I've been made aware of your kind's unique abilities, and I am in agreement with Agent Blecher." She nodded toward Ingrid. "The three of you might be the only ones on Earth who can keep the demons out of your heads long enough to accomplish what must be done."

"Wait, you can't? Preds can't addict other preds."

Claudius scowled, but Raia answered my question despite his disapproval. "That is true, but by now you must have noticed that furies are different from the rest of us. It is far more difficult for them to bind even the least powerful of us than it is for them to bind a human, but it can happen. And the demons trapped in the Pit are incredibly more powerful than your average fury."

Well, shit. So that explained a good deal about why Gunthra and all these powerful satyrs, goblins, and more were willing to expose their secrets and stores of information with the Gryphons. They were as scared shitless as the rest of us.

The stunned silence in the room was so loud that I almost missed hearing Claudius say he was going to train me.

ELEVEN

I DIDN'T HAVE MUCH MORE TO SAY AFTER THAT.

Okay, that wasn't entirely true. I had a lot more to say after the news that I'd need to work with Claudius and that I'd need to be the one to face down an army of fury-like demons. It was just that most of what I wanted to say was incoherent babbling. By the end of the night, I might yet end up rocking back and forth in a corner, sucking my thumb.

The meeting dissolved about half an hour after my wits fled. Between the Brotherhood's research, plus what the magi and the satyrs shared, it turned out we knew a lot more than I thought we did. But knowing things was only helpful in the theoretical sense. The more we knew, the more work we knew had to be done.

None of the work involved me anymore, nor Mitch or Grace. Until further notice, our training regime had changed. We were to focus predominantly on drawing power, the behavior I thought of as reversing the pred-addict bond. The two terms meant essentially the same thing to the preds, but it didn't matter what anyone called it. It was going to suck, especially the part about working with Claudius.

While everyone split up to get back to work, I returned to Shadowtown with Lucen. Grace was refusing to participate, and Mitch was overwhelmed, so we'd begin our sessions with Claudius tomorrow. That way, Mitch and I would be better rested, and maybe Grace would be more cooperative.

Lucen didn't say much on the ride back to The Lair. From the set of his jaw, he was no more excited about me and Claudius sharing space—never mind a bond—than I was. What Claudius had done last time was all too fresh for both of us.

Paulius, one of Lucen's bartenders, had already opened The Lair by the time we arrived, and a surprising number of patrons had crowded inside. It only took me a minute of overheard conversations to figure out why. Satyrs and harpies had gathered to fume over the HELP Act. A few goblins had also joined the crowd, suggesting their preferred hangout was closed.

"I should go home," I said, ignoring my better judgment and taking a seat at the bar.

Lucen tossed off his jacket and grabbed us beers. "No, you shouldn't. It's not safe. You should stay here tonight."

"It's not safe to sleep alone? Talk about your end-of-the-world pick-up lines."

Lucen popped the cap off my bottle and handed it to me. "I wasn't going there, but you're right. Damn, I excel at these sorts of things, don't I?"

"And you're ever so humble to boot."

"Please. Humility is just a consolation prize for people who are lacking in awesome."

I choked on my beer as he grinned. "I've seen your awesome, and I don't think the health department would approve of you flaunting it around foodstuffs."

"This is why I love you, little siren."

After the kind of day I'd had, I didn't understand how Lucen could make me laugh and relax, but damn. I was stressed as hell, but my muscles loosened, and I was genuinely smiling. "Yeah, I know. Speaking of which, I might have accidentally let something about us slip in front of Mitch and Grace today. One might even say I ranted a touch."

"Do go on."

I gave Lucen a summary of the conversation while he poured drinks for a couple harpies. His cheesy grin had somehow managed to expand by the time I finished.

"You truly are maturing," he said. "First, you stop being ashamed of our relationship. Next, you let yourself be scolded by Xander and Claudius for the good of humanity at the meeting. I'm impressed. You wouldn't have tolerated that not so long ago. Maybe you are destined to be humanity's savior."

"Bah. The relationship stuff came out by accident, and their reactions put me on the defensive. Not to mention I cursed at Claudius and Xander way too much in my head to be considered anyone's savior."

"But you loosed your tongue in one situation and held it in the other. Appropriately, I might add. It's progress."

I tossed a peanut at his head. "I've never been ashamed of our relationship, just so you know. It's dealing with everyone else's reactions that bug me."

"Don't give in to the haters. Besides, most people are probably just jealous."

"Because you're awesome?"

"Exactly."

I snorted into my beer bottle. "Either your ego is getting out of control, or you're doing a very good job of not letting me think about what was discussed at the meeting."

The smile slid from Lucen's face. "Not that good obviously since you brought it up." He leaned over the bar toward me, lowering his voice. "I'm not any more excited about what happened than you are, but I'm afraid Claudius and the magi are right. You, and maybe Mitch, might be the only ones who can keep the demons out of your heads long enough to get your hands on the key. But I promise you won't have to try it alone."

My stomach squirmed uncomfortably with the thought of Lucen risking his life next to mine in some creepy magical prison. This wasn't the time to bring it up though. If he insisted on coming with me, I wouldn't—and couldn't—stop him. I'd learned my lesson in France.

"I'm not happy about Claudius being the one to work with you either," Lucen said. "I'm not sure why he's more qualified than anyone else, but he'd better deal with the idea of me being present. There's no way I'm leaving you alone with him."

"Thank you."

Lucen straightened and signaled to someone over my shoulder. "Wow, no glaring at me for my overprotectiveness?"

"Huh, you're right. Guess I really have matured. Or it could be that I'm simply determined to make you suffer his Supreme Upper Assholeness with me."

"Is that what you've been calling him?" Dezzi's voice had me spinning around on my stool. Luckily, the only person with her was Sonya, the newest addition to Dezzi's inner triad—aka, her top three advisors.

I settled back and pretended the Dom hadn't startled the crap out of me. "I admit nothing."

"No one of reason would hold it against you if you did," Sonya said. The black-haired satyr was usually even quieter than Dezzi, and she rarely spoke to me at all. I was unsure whether she liked me, and while I didn't exactly care if she didn't, it was nice to hear something that sounded like approval from her.

True to her style, Sonya pointed to something behind the bar rather than ask for a drink. I had no clue what it was, but Lucen apparently understood.

He set a glass down in front of Sonya and got to work. "Dez, why can't someone else work with Jess?"

Dezzi brushed her braids over her shoulder. "Because if Jessica is to have a chance of holding her own against the demons, she must first be able to handle Claudius. That said, she is not ready to take him on yet."

I grimaced into my beer. "Thanks for the vote of confidence, but if I can't, there's no way Mitch can." I didn't bother mentioning Grace since that was obvious.

"No, he cannot either. Which is why, after you left, I proposed that you do not begin practicing with Claudius. Tomorrow, you'll work with me. Mitch will work with Lucen. When the two of you are ready, then Claudius gets his turn. Raia agrees with me, as does Agent Kassin."

Lucen banged the wine bottle he'd opened for Dezzi against the bar in surprise. "That actually makes sense."

Dezzi made a noise like he'd wounded her. "Of course it does. It was my idea."

"Yes, Mother." He bowed as best he could with the bar between them, and Dezzi sighed.

"Mitch is too jittery to enter Shadowtown," she said, "so we will meet at the Gryphon building tomorrow. It's not my preferred arrangement, but it will do for now. Mitch needs to concentrate, not be distracted by additional anxiety."

I blamed it on the temporary relief Dezzi had given me, but I laughed. "There you go being damned reasonable again. Why aren't you on the Upper Council instead of Claudius?"

Dezzi's face pinched, and for a second I worried I'd hit a nerve. Then she took a long, blissful sip from the wine Lucen had poured her. "Why would I want to be? Here I am in charge, and normally, the Upper Council ignores us because we are a well-behaved domus. If I were on the Upper Council, my power would be split. My decisions would have to be approved by committee, and I would have to deal with more people like Claudius. Besides, look at my face. Do I look old enough to be considered an elder?" Winking at Lucen, she grabbed her glass and strolled over to a table of satyrs.

Sonya left a few minutes later as well, and I twirled my mostly empty beer bottle around on the condensation. "I like Dezzi. I'm not sure I want her in my head, but I guess I'd rather it be her than Claudius. Is she going to have to drop an addict to make this work?"

"I doubt it." Lucen swiped my bottle from me. "Dezzi likely has a bit of reserved power. Not enough to hold you as an addict indefinitely, but temporarily she should be fine. Speaking of which, if Claudius gets to bond with you, and Dezzi gets to bond with you, I'm starting to feel left out."

"Tell me you're joking. I've had furies and sylphs in my head too, you know. It's not a gift I grant people."

"But it would be a gift if you let me in. Since you're staying here tonight, maybe we should practice so you can impress everyone tomorrow."

I rested my head in my hands. Nope. I still couldn't tell if he was joking. "I'm not sure I need more practice."

Lucen wore a faint smile, but his eyes were serious. "You've cast out people of average ability, or less than average. You struggled with Raj. We can't say how you'll fare against Dezzi. Practice wouldn't hurt seeing as we don't have a lot of time for you to become proficient at this."

I peered up at him through my fingers. "You're totally serious, aren't you? This isn't an excuse to rope me into some mental bondage just for kicks."

"Oh, it might be fun, but yes. I'm serious. Consider me a step up between the fury you subdued once and Dezzi."

"You know this for sure?"

"I know who the members of Raj's council are, or were at the time of the event. And those sylphs who attacked you—Assym wouldn't have sent them to do grunt work if they were more important. So yeah, it's a safe bet."

Groaning, I pointed at a clean shot glass. "You disappoint me. I was assuming your reasoning would lead back to how awesome you are. If I'm going to willingly let you torment me, I need another drink."

Proving how well he got me, Lucen placed the bottle of Jameson next to a glass. "Don't worry, little siren. You will become well acquainted with how awesome I am later."

LUCEN WAS RIGHT, NOT JUST ABOUT BEING AWESOME, BUT also about how he would prove to be more of a challenge than the fury and the sylph I'd mentally wrestled with in the past. Nonetheless, it didn't take too many tries before I could reverse our bond with ease.

Since our relationship wasn't hostile, and since I was a kind of satyr myself, I'd thought the experience of reversing a bond with him might be different than it had been with others. As usual, I was wrong.

Certainly, having him addict me was a different experience. Magically induced lust for a guy I already lusted after was, in some ways, better than being filled with magically induced rage or self-doubt. Unfortunately, in other ways, it reminded me too much of what it had been like the one time I'd been cursed and drugged with F, an illegal aphrodisiac. My sexual tension couldn't be sated until I managed to reverse the bond with Lucen.

While the experience didn't fill me with sexual ecstasy or even joy, it did make me a touch more confident about what was to come. I got up the next day around noon and prepared a giant breakfast while Lucen showered. If I was going to face down Dezzi and possibly Claudius later, I needed my nourishment.

My phone began playing "Bad Moon Rising" as I cracked a fourth egg into a frying pan, suggesting Lucen had changed my ringtone yet again while I was sleeping. Wiping my hands on my jeans, I answered it without checking the ID, assuming it was the Gryphons. "Yeah?"

"Jess! Seriously, this is how you answer your phone these days? 'Yeah'?" Steph's voice crackled with amusement. "Are you that important now?"

"Duh." I grabbed a spatula and began stirring up the eggs. "How are you holding up?"

Steph groaned. "Been better, but I haven't lost my shit like everyone else is doing. Speaking of which, did you read about those people in Texas yet? All the members of some church poisoned themselves and their families last night because they believed it's the end times."

Closing my eyes, I inhaled deeply of the scent of scrambled eggs cooking in bacon grease. Suicide cults or pacts. Wonderful. The juxtaposition between my role and current activities versus the rest of the world's increasingly erratic behavior had never felt starker.

"I'll spare myself the details and take your word for it." I consoled myself by taking a bite from one of the bacon strips.

"The details aren't that exciting anyway. The reason I called was to see if you could spare an hour this afternoon for your best friend."

I switched off the burner and put a lid on the pan to keep the eggs warm. The Gryphons would tell me I shouldn't spare an hour today, tomorrow, or any time until our mission was complete. Yet my common sense warned me I might be dead by then, and Steph was my best friend. Along with Lucen, she was the only person I knew who'd had my back for ten years. She'd never failed to help me when I needed it, and if I explained what was going on and why I couldn't give her an hour later today, she'd understand. The seriousness of what we faced was evident.

I'd also hate myself though. The Gryphons and satyrs might balk, but I could take a single hour off practicing. Worst-case scenario, I'd stay up an hour later to make up for it.

"Yes, totally," I said before I could change my mind. "What's up?"

"Oh, good. I was thinking it might not be a bad idea to buy some charms. Protections for me and Jim."

I waved a couple fingers at Lucen as he strode into the kitchen. "It can't hurt."

"That was my reasoning, but a lot of people are thinking the same thing. I've heard prices have shot way up, and I haven't bought a charm of any sort in years. I have no idea which shops to trust or what's a fair price. I did some research online, but it's not that useful. Most of the stuff I've found is only about staying away from pred shops."

And yet some of the best charm makers I'd met were preds. I wasn't about to drag Steph into Shadowtown though, nor would she want to go. For the types of charms she was interested in, a magi would do just as well.

"Do you want to meet around five at the hospital?" The hospital she worked at was near The Feathers, and Steph would be getting off from work around then. I'd probably be ready for a break too.

"Five thirty?"

"Done. See you then." I hung up as Lucen was divvying up the eggs, bacon, and toast onto two plates. "I'll need to take a break this afternoon."

He carried the plates to the table, and I joined him with the coffee. "So I heard. What's going on with Steph? That was Steph, wasn't it?"

"Yup." We talked and ate and were in the middle of cleaning up when both our phones received a text within seconds of each other. I dropped my dishtowel. "Tom."

"Dezzi."

Weird, and I hoped it was a coincidence. I read the message, which was short and demanding, even for Tom. *news now xander*

"Xander's holding a press conference," Lucen said, explaining. Dezzi must have provided more details.

We both dashed into the living room, and Lucen flipped to a local station. The press conference had just started, and Xander was already in the middle of speaking. Behind him I could make out the façade of what appeared to be city hall, plus his bodyguards and a few magi I didn't recognize. In front of him was a sizable contingent of the press, both local and national.

Lucen put a protective hand on my arm, no doubt sensing—as I did— that for Xander to have drawn this large a crowd, he must have enticed the press with something juicy. Granted, he was a city councilor and a well-known name in Massachusetts politics, but his reach didn't typically extend beyond the greater Boston area.

Xander's four-fingered hands adjusted the paper he was reading from, and the mics picked up on the noise. "There has been much anger and understandable frustration expressed lately with how the current situation is being handled. Of course, we all expect politicians to bungle a crisis, and Congress and the President have not let us down."

He paused for polite laughter. "But our representatives and the President can be held accountable for their actions. There is another group, however, which lacks that sort of oversight. I'm speaking of the Angelic Order of the Gryphon."

Lucen let out a low whistle, and my jaw might have dropped an inch. There was no way Xander was going there. The magi had allied themselves with the Gryphons for centuries. Legend had it that it was, in fact, the magi who'd originally given humans the gift of magic so they could protect themselves from preds.

"It is said Gryphons are born, not made," Xander continued. "That fewer than one-hundredth of one percent of humans carry what the Gryphons refer to as a gift. If you have it, you are one of them. If you do not, you can never be one of them. But the Gryphons would be quick to point out that with their gift comes a great responsibility. They protect the rest of humanity from preds and magic-related crimes. But what happens when the Gryphons fail to do that? Or, perhaps more accurately in this case, what happens when they choose not to?"

He was going there. He was totally going there. I didn't believe this.

Lucen snatched the remote and turned up the volume.

"Let us consider," said a louder Xander. "In these past couple weeks, even before the sky turned red, Gryphons from Boston and around the world were forming an alliance with the very preds they are supposed to protect us from. Purportedly, these meetings were held to prevent the catastrophes that have struck as late—here, Atlanta, Sydney, Buenos Aires. And do I need to point out the sky above?" Xander turned his face upward. The backs of several reporters' heads suggested they were doing the same.

"The Gryphons failed. But has that stopped them from conferring with preds? No, it hasn't. Do we expect better from them? Of course, we do. But why should we? Any human can be born with a so-called gift. It does not make them a better, smarter, or braver person. Take, for example, Victor Aubrey. The serial killer who recently terrorized Boston and who confessed to killing at least ten people—he had a gift."

The crowd murmured. I swore, and so did Lucen.

Victor's gifted status had been carefully hidden from the public for good reasons. Also, Victor had not actually been a Gryphon. Like me, he'd been kicked out of the trainee program, something Xander conveniently didn't bother to mention. Although, it was true enough that Victor *hadn't* been kicked out because he was a sick bastard. He'd been booted for the same reason Mitch and Grace and I had been—the Gryphons didn't think our gifts had developed.

"Or take another example," Xander continued. "You might have heard the name Jessica Moore mentioned in connection with Aubrey. You might recognize her as the woman who was supposed to testify against Aubrey in court."

My stomach dropped right to the floor, and I involuntarily covered my mouth with a hand. Oh, shit. Lucen took my other hand, but the set of his jaw made it clear that he wasn't in the mood for comforting me. More like killing a certain red-feathered magi. That made two of us.

Xander glanced up from his notes, and I could have sworn his golden eyes met mine through the signal connecting us. "What the Gryphons never told you is that Moore also has a gift. Moore is a vigilante, known by some in this city as the Soul Swapper. She used her power to steal people's blood and traded their souls to preds for monetary compensation. And how did she gain the trust of preds to do this? She accomplished that because her gift goes beyond the traditional; she has powers like a satyr. She can seduce people into doing whatever she needs. If that's not scary enough, you should know it was the Gryphons who gave her that ability. And the Gryphons have been willing to overlook her crimes to get her to cooperate with them."

In the kitchen, my cell rang. What would no doubt be the first of hundreds of calls. I silently screamed a million curses at Xander.

"Lately, some people have been saying that magic is the problem in our world. Magic has caused the devastation we're seeing. I say no." Xander lowered his notes and stared right into the cameras. He must have practiced his poses. "Magic itself is not the culprit. It's the misuse of magic. It's putting magic in the hands of a select few who, for no meritorious reasons, have the ability to wield it. That is the problem. Perhaps it is time humanity reconsider the role the Angelic Order of the Gryphon plays in our society. Perhaps it's time to clip their wings before it's too late."

Xander nodded a confirmation that he was finished, and the scene erupted with shouting. Reporters practically burst open with questions that Xander refused to answer. Finally, his bodyguards caught up to him and escorted him away against the noisy backdrop. The TV station switched over to an anchor for the recap, and Lucen hit the off button.

My whole body was cold as I sank to the floor. "I... I... He just said all that, didn't he? I'm not having some weird, waking nightmare?"

"I'm going to pluck every feather from his damn body. I'm going to find an oven big enough to roast him like a chicken. Jess." Lucen knelt next to me and pulled hair out of my face. "Jess?"

"He... I... Fuck."

"It's going to be..." Lucen sighed. "Never mind. It's not going to be okay, but we can deal. We've dealt with worse."

I dug my fingers into his arms. "My mother doesn't even know half the things Xander just told reporters. He exposed... Gah." Speaking was challenging when you couldn't breathe, and it wasn't merely my lungs failing me. It was my brain.

Lucen pried my fingers off him and squeezed my shoulder. Both of our phones were going crazy. "It's not only you, little siren. Xander threw the entire Gryphon organization under the proverbial bus. The feather-brained idiot proved himself to be more arrogant than Claudius. There is going to be hell to pay for him."

I swallowed. "Possibly, but what's said can't be unsaid. Not when all the major news channels are covering it. Shit. Even *my mother* didn't know."

Lucen stood, dragging me off the floor with him. "Then it might be time to call her before she finds out another way."

Nodding, I picked up my phone from the kitchen table and had to resist the urge to smash it when it rang again. "What is Xander thinking? He can't possibly be this pissed off because Raia shared information his people had been holding on to. Is this really retaliation for not getting his share of the glory?"

"No idea." Lucen opened the fridge and got out Sweetpea's breakfast of raw meat. "Despite what I just called him, Xander can't be a complete fool. I imagine he's trying to do two things. He wants to protect himself and the magi from becoming shooting targets thanks to the HELP Act, and he's positioning himself politically. People aren't happy. He doesn't want that unhappiness associated with him."

Sadly, I could understand it if fear for himself and the magi were part of Xander's reasoning. I hated the HELP Act too. Almost as much as I hated Xander. But fear was no excuse for throwing other people into the line of fire for you.

If this was how the day was starting off, I needed more caffeine. I wandered back into the kitchen to refill my mug. "Is it too early to start putting whiskey in my coffee?"

TWELVE

Lucen left not long after the press conference ended, ostensibly to go check on how Azria was doing with Devon, but mostly—I suspected—to meet Dezzi face-to-face to discuss the Xander situation. He could have done it over the phone, but he wanted to give me privacy to speak with my mother.

I'd turned the volume off on my phone while I tried to calm down, and it sat on the kitchen table, taunting me. A snake poised to bite if I got too close. It was a shame I didn't have voice control with it. I wished I could tell it to dial my mother's number without needing to touch it. That way I wouldn't risk seeing how many calls and texts I'd missed.

Since I had no such luck, I braced myself and checked. I had texts from Steph and Tom, and I'd been included in a bunch of group messages sent by various members of the Brotherhood. Those things I could handle. The missed-call log, however, was more annoying. Reporters, more reporters if I had to guess, and possibly reporters from as far away as the UK. It was kind of hard to tell since I deleted all the messages mostly unheard. Some of them were from people I hadn't spoken to in years.

I also had a message from my mother. Dragon shit on toast. I'd huddled on the sofa pretending to calm down for too long, and she'd gotten the news elsewhere. Her message wasn't long, simply: "Jess, call me." She sounded worried.

Taking my not-spiked second cup of coffee into the living room, I returned to my spot on the sofa and called her back before my phone burst into song yet again.

She picked up before I heard a ring. "Sweetie, is there something you've been meaning to tell me?"

"Nice, Mom. Way to lay on the guilt when I'm already a mess." I dropped my head to my knees. It would be easier if she was angry with me. Then I could get defensive.

Every parent needs to have that talk with their children, the one that's potentially awkward for the kid and possibly sad for the parent as they realize the cute baby they held in their arms has developed into an entirely different sort of creature—a hormonal adolescent. My conversation with my mother was basically the same deal, only the kid was the one doing the explaining and the different creature was more literal than not.

Was it any wonder I hadn't wanted to have this discussion? Initially, I'd refrained from telling her about my misery-feeding abilities because it would freak her out. Not to mention I didn't understand them and feared I'd be banished from human society for them.

Then I didn't tell her how I'd turned those abilities into assets, using them to alleviate my guilt by helping others. And when I found out what had really happened to me and what I really was, telling my mother the truth became more difficult. My mother feared preds, as did most sensible humans. Because I loved her, it killed me to imagine how much the news would hurt her.

Unfortunately, I had no choice now but to confess it all. Xander had robbed me of the possibility of finding a gentle way to break the news.

She was very calm on the other end, very quiet when I finished pouring my guts out. "Is that everything?"

Yes, it's everything. It's more than everything. More than enough.

I took a deep breath, thankful I couldn't sense her emotions over the phone. Normally, that inability frustrated me because I was so used to relying on my ability. But not today. Today, I'd never been more thankful for Alexander Graham Bell and his crazy invention.

I traced a finger around the seam on Lucen's blue sofa cushion, listening to Sweetpea scratch at his cage. "There are a few more things."

"Well, I'm already sitting down, and I have an open bottle of wine in the fridge, so you might as well go ahead."

"Sorry."

"Don't be sorry. Be honest."

Being sorry would be easier, but there was no way I could let her discover more about my freakish life by accident. I gathered my courage and spit out the words. "I'm kind of in a relationship, and the guy is kind of not human."

Before she could interject, I told her about Lucen, doing my best to explain how I got involved with him. It sounded as if she whimpered a couple times while I spoke, but when I finished, she held it together long enough to request a photo so she could determine for herself if Lucen was attractive. The lighthearted comment sounded a touch forced, but she was making an effort.

That said, I refrained from mentioning Devon. One satyr in my life was plenty for her to accept. Two would be pushing my luck. The idea that monogamy simply wasn't possible for them might break her. I wasn't sure how well she was holding it together as it was.

A clinking noise in the background made me guess she'd broken out the wine. "So the Gryphons turned you into an unusual type of satyr, you've been hiding your gift from me for a decade, working for the Gryphons, almost getting yourself killed, and you're dating a satyr. Do I have everything straight?"

"Pretty much. I'm sorry I didn't tell you, but I didn't want to worry you."

"I'm in a bit of shock, I admit, but I can handle more than you think. After all, half your genes come from me."

Okay, she might not be freaking out, but this calm guilt trip was worse. She knew I'd always identified more with my father. He'd been the Gryphon, and when my gift had started appearing, I'd latched on to him. Ever since I was young enough to understand, I'd wanted to follow in his footsteps.

You may yet. He died in the line duty, and so could you.

I made a mental note to finally sign the formal agreement with the Gryphons that Tom had given me last week. It would make me an official member of the organization, rather than the consultant I was currently labeled as. I'd been putting it off, not wanting to take the step. I was still too bitter at the Gryphons for everything that had happened to me and unsure what signing would mean for my future. But the Gryphons took care of the families of those who died in their service. If there was anything left of the organization and my family in the future, I liked the idea that they would get compensated for my loss.

The roar of a truck on the street outside jolted me from my morose thoughts. I needed to stop picking at the seam on the couch, or I was going to rub a hole through the fabric. "Mom, there's no way I can forget where my genes come from. You stare back at me every time I look in a mirror. I just wanted to protect you. I was hurting, and I didn't want you hurt too."

"I'm positive you meant well, sweetie, and I'm not mad at you. I promise. I'm not entirely horrified either. No matter what you can do, I will never question that you are a good person who has tried to do good."

I sat up abruptly, uncomfortably aware that my eyes were burning and my throat tight. "Thank you."

"I'm not sure how I feel about you being romantically involved with a satyr, although I suppose I can get used to many things. Eventually. Very eventually."

"He'll grow on you. He has that effect on people."

"It's his effect on people that disturbs me. Give me time, Jess. We need to talk in person soon."

Time. The one thing that we didn't have much of. On that thought, I checked the clock. I had to get moving to Gryphon headquarters and fast.

Guilt, and the genuine need to make sure my mother truly was dealing as well as she purported to be, kept me on the phone longer than I should. After hanging up, I hurriedly ran through my texts from Tom to make sure nothing had changed because of Xander. There was a whole lot of discussion about Xander going on, but nothing from Tom—nor Lucen, nor Dezzi—indicating a revision to our plans.

When I rushed out the door, my only concern was remembering to enter headquarters via the employees-only back door. This would involve calling Tom or anyone else inside and being let in since I didn't have that kind of access as a mere consultant.

The afternoon rush hadn't hit yet, so the trains were mostly empty, which was a relief. The entire subway ride over I felt horribly conspicuous, as if I were wearing one of those *Hello My Name Is* stickers on my chest. Except my sticker was enormous and someone had drawn satyr horns over my last name. For the first time, I wouldn't have minded having Melissa or Gi with me. No one had mentioned anything about sending over my usual bodyguards, and because of everything that had happened today, the thought had slipped my mind too.

A mob continued to swarm around the Gryphons' steps, as did a faint blue haze. The haze was barely noticeable given how the high afternoon sun bleached the red sky, but I could see it if I squinted. Andre must have been hitting the kumbaya gas again.

More disturbing than the continued presence of the peace-loving anti-magers was the news vans. Three had set up shop as close to the protesters as they could get, and more people mingled around on the opposite side of the street, all giving off the vibe of being too curious for my comfort. Even if only half were journalists, it was too many for me.

Heart beating faster, I cut over a block early and approached via the back door. Tom had gotten my text that I was arriving, and he opened it. "You're late."

"Don't. It's been a rough day, and I was afraid the people out front would want to tear me open and see what color my insides were if they recognized me."

"It might not only be the people outside you need to worry about."

I stuck my sunglasses back on. "Great. Think these will help?"

"I think you'll walk into walls."

I shoved the sunglasses in my bag, doing my best to ignore the stares from the Gryphons we passed. "What's happening with Xander?"

Tom punched the elevator button with brutal force, and his voice picked up that odd accent it always got when he was stressed. "You were copied on the texts, right? He betrayed everyone in this organization and revealed confidential information. He must be trusting we're too busy with other concerns that there won't be fallout from his pathetic display."

"Will there be? Did he actually break any laws?"

"The Gryphons' legal council is considering that part. He's definitely not going to be working with us again though. The other magi in our coalition have been calling and trying to distance themselves from him. Are you going to be okay?"

I shrugged. "I had an interesting phone conversation with my mother earlier, but I'll deal with the rest once I'm convinced I'll live long enough to have reason to worry."

Keeping my head down, I followed Tom into a conference room on the third floor. Mitch and Grace were already there, huddled uneasily on the opposite side of the room from Lucen and Dezzi. Dezzi was all business as usual, but Lucen seemed amused by their discomfort. I punched him lightly in the arm for it.

"How is this going to work?" Tom asked, shutting the door.

The conference room table had been pushed against a wall, and Dezzi moved a couple chairs into the open space in the center. "It is simple. Lucen and I will gain entry into the others' heads. Once we do that, they try using their gifts to take control of the bond. It will not be exciting to watch. It's all a battle of mental and magical wills."

Mitch raised a tentative hand. "Um, my understanding is that it takes a bit of work on your part to break us down, so to speak. It sure did when those furies addicted me the other week. Not to come across like a prude or anything, but wouldn't that involve physical contact?" He gave Lucen a wary expression, which naturally brought the smirk right back to Lucen's face.

I punched him again. "It takes work for a pred to do this sort of thing normally because normally you'd be fighting them. In this case, you won't be. When you feel Lucen's magic knocking on your brain, you'll let him in. You could be on opposite sides of the room if you wanted."

"Yes, but that wouldn't be half as much fun." Lucen stepped away before I could land a third blow.

Dezzi smacked him instead. "This situation is serious. Please try to act like it."

"So there's not going to be any weirdness going on here? Because..." Mitch stuck his hands in his pockets, and I could detect a distinct salty embarrassment running beneath his anxiety.

Grace, on the other hand, radiated pure fear. She'd pressed herself against the corner, but I sensed she wanted to dash for the door.

"There's only weirdness if you want there to be." Lucen smiled, doing just enough to keep his amusement in check that I had no excuse to slap him for it.

Tom pulled a chair over to the door. "I'll stay here for a while to keep an eye on everyone. I have to leave in an hour, but if it will make you more comfortable, I can have another Gryphon replace me." He spoke primarily to Grace, though she didn't acknowledge him.

I bit my tongue. It would not make me more comfortable to have Tom here. I trusted Dezzi and Lucen, and I knew Dezzi was right that no physical contact was necessary. But regardless, there was no question that this training was going to be physically arousing, even as it was magically and mentally taxing. And heaven help me if Claudius was brought in to test me soon. I didn't care for the idea of Tom seeing me writhing in heat.

I wasn't sure if Mitch had thought things through to this extent, or if he had and would prefer knowing a Gryphon with a lethal weapon was on hand to keep control regardless. For his sake and Grace's, I held in my objection. Maturity sucked.

Dezzi shrugged to indicate that Tom staying was a waste of time, but she didn't argue. "Since we know Jessica has experience, I'm going to start working with her, and Lucen will work with the others."

"No." Grace extricated herself from the corner. "I'm not doing this. I'm not letting any of you into my soul. I'll watch if you force me to, but I refuse to participate."

The mischievous gleam on Lucen's face dimmed, and his voice became serious. "No one is going to hurt you, I swear. You heard Agent Kassin. I understand this might not be comfortable, but if you can learn how to do it, you'll be safer."

"It's soul self-defense," I added. "It's the same as learning any self-defense technique or martial art. It might hurt to learn, but it's a skill that can save your life."

Grace wrapped her arms around her small frame, shaking her head violently. "I'm not interested. I'll take my chances."

"Grace, we talked about this," Tom said.

"I changed my mind."

That was an understatement. Her fear was so strong it was making my extremities quiver with the energy hit. I bounced from foot to foot as Tom and Dezzi attempted to assuage her rising panic. Mitch chimed in too, promising her that he wasn't excited about the idea either, but it was necessary.

None of their approaches worked. I sensed that Grace was more on edge than ever, and everyone's combined pressure was working her into an awful state. Fear predominated in her heart, but her guilt was also growing. The combination made for a terrible one-two punch to her head.

"Guys." I held up my hands. "We don't need to force her into this. Let Mitch and I practice first. Grace can watch and see that nothing bad happens."

Grace wasn't as grateful for my defense as I thought she would be. "I don't want to watch either. I just need space. I have to leave." Before we could say anything else, she ran out of the room.

Tom jumped up to follow her, and I put a restraining hand on his arm. "Let her go. She doesn't like magic, and this is all hard on her. As long as she's in the building, she's safe."

Tom scowled and took out his phone, presumably to notify others to make sure Grace didn't try to sneak outside without a guard. "She needs to learn these things. We're counting on her."

"Not everyone is cut out to be a warrior," Lucen said. "What you're expecting of people isn't easy."

"I'm not a warrior," Mitch muttered.

I grabbed one of the bottles of water Tom had arranged on the table. "You're here and you're trying. I think that makes you one. And who knows? Grace could come around still. She might just not have found the strength yet."

"That almost sounds like optimism," Lucen whispered to me.

I flipped him off. "Can we get started? I have to meet a friend in The Feathers in a few hours."

Tom wasn't thrilled by my pronouncement, but Dezzi agreed that we might want a break by then. So we got to work.

Thank dragons Lucen had suggested I practice with him last night. It made the ordeal less uncomfortable since I knew what to expect. But it was no easier. Initially, I was distracted by Tom's increasing boredom as he watched us, as well as Mitch's anxiety. Then by my own nerves. I was too aware of the hundreds of Gryphons in the building, all of whom now knew my secrets.

I couldn't sense anyone else's emotions when Dezzi was in my head, so the problem then wasn't their turmoil but my own. My lack of control. Because I was distracted with worry, my will was weakened, and I lost the ability to focus on our bond. After a second time of not getting too far, Dezzi broke our connection, and I crumpled to the floor. My head was splitting, and my body quivered with unfulfilled lust. I ran a hand over my hard nipples as I curled in on myself. I wasn't sure which pain was stronger, but I was certain I felt like an idiot.

Dezzi dropped onto a chair near me. "You're not paying attention. Your mind is..." She twirled her hands around in the air.

"It's been a long day." Out of the corner of my eye, I could see Lucen's back, and I forced myself to turn away. He had his own task, and he certainly wouldn't help mine. "I'm ready. Let's try again."

The third time, I succeeded. On my knees on the conference room floor, sweating with need and straining to keep my hands PG in front of my audience, I did it. When the direction of Dezzi's power changed and the full force of it slammed into me, stars formed in front of my eyes. My cells felt like they were exploding, but I laughed and raised my arms skyward with elation. Dezzi's magic healed my headache instantly and lifted my mood into the stratosphere. I could have flown into The Feathers.

Then she cut the connection, and I crashed into reality.

"Good." Dezzi grabbed a cookie from the tray on the table and took a bite as though starved by the exertion. "Faster this next time."

We did it again and again. When I could reliably reverse the bond fast enough that I didn't do anything embarrassing first, Dezzi had me practice controlling my response to the magic hit. Euphoria was great and all, but if I couldn't control my emotions while buzzing with so much power, I wouldn't be able to strategize or fight effectively.

The effort should have left me exhausted, but feeding on powerful magic negated the tiredness. I actually felt pretty damn great when I next checked the time. "I have to get going. My muscles are telling me I could sprint the whole way to The Feathers, but somehow I doubt that's the truth."

Dezzi snorted. "You might as well try. This time of day, you might be able to walk there faster than the T can take you."

I doubted that too, although Dezzi had a point. I didn't look forward to fighting the rush hour crowd on the train, especially when I might be recognized.

"I will check in with Lucen and Mitch," Dezzi said as I got out my phone. "I am curious whether Lucen is experiencing the same side effect of this bonding as I did."

"Side effect? What do you mean?"

Dezzi tapped a finger against her lips in contemplation. "I expected your ability to reverse the bond would drain me of energy, and it did. But it also drained away some of my own uniquely satyr emotions. It was more than just what I give to you with a normal addict bond."

Uniquely satyr emotions? It took me a second to understand what she meant. "The lust?"

"Yes. It was lessened. I assumed it was flowing into you along with the power."

I nearly dropped my phone as I realized something I'd never thought about before. "It does, er, did. Reversing the bond helps me control the feeling, but it doesn't make it totally go away. When I reversed the bond on that fury the first time, I was filled with anger. I thought it was because of the situation I was in, but it must have been partly his magic coursing through me. The same thing happened when I did it with the sylph the other week. When I pull from you, I'm pulling more of everything."

"You take the good and the bad. It is an interesting phenomena," Dezzi agreed. "And I'm sorry to say that you are ready to begin work with Claudius later."

"Peachy." I crept out of the room so I wouldn't disturb the men and texted Steph to assure her we were on in spite of the day's events. As I stuck my phone away, my hand grazed a familiar glass jar at the bottom of my bag. Grinning with relief, I pulled out a half-empty container of glamour. It must have been lying around in there for weeks.

I practically skipped into the nearest bathroom and used the spell to rearrange my face. Although I was probably paranoid about being recognized beyond the walls of this building, I saw no need to take chances. Besides, I couldn't easily take my satyr bodyguards into The Feathers with me. They wouldn't want to go, and the magi wouldn't want them there. With a fake face, I wouldn't have to. I'd be free of dangerous humans and any furies who wanted revenge or pieces of my flesh for other reasons.

The subway was every bit the nightmare I expected it to be, but Steph was ready and waiting near the hospital's main entrance when I got there. I sent her a fake-me selfie so she'd know what I looked like.

She lowered her sunglasses as I approached. "Your artistic skills need practice. Or were you going for a disguise that says 'I broke my nose and it was never set properly'?"

"Bite me. It's been a long day." Ugh. How many times had I said that today? I needed a better excuse. Though true, I was getting sick of it.

Steph crushed her cigarette, and we started walking. "Yeah, that clip of Xander is everywhere. Shit, I'm getting bugged by people who know that I know you."

"Hence why my phone has been turned off most of the day."

"I am so sorry. Do you want to grab a beer after this and vent?"

I sighed and pushed my magically straight, red hair out of my face. "I'd love to, but I have more work to do later."

"It pisses me off that you and those Gryphons are doing so much to stop whatever's coming, and some jackass of a magi—"

I hushed her. We'd passed beneath the colorful archway at the edge of The Feathers, and magi outnumbered the human population around us. "Not here."

Steph made a noise of disapproval but nodded. "So where are you taking me?"

"We're first going to a shop owned by a crow shifter named Vekta. She specializes in defensive kinds of charms, mainly. Next, if you want some general good luck, which is never a bad idea, I'll take you to another place. Luck is pricey though, and that was before the world went to hell."

Steph kicked an empty soda bottle out of our path and wrinkled her nose at the stench emanating from a restaurant on the right. "I'll see how much money I have left after the first shop."

Haggling with Vekta took forever, but the magi didn't recognize me, which was a relief. Steph could make fun of my disguise all she wanted. It worked. Although Vekta side-eyed me a couple times, as though something about my manner or voice was familiar, she never tried to guess my name.

"To luck or not to luck?" I asked when we left.

Steph clutched her purse and the shopping bag closer to her side. "Maybe. Depends on what kind of price I can get."

We paused at a busy intersection beneath a brown flag bearing the form of an owl, and I checked the time. I had no great incentive to return to headquarters. It might be necessary, but facing down Claudius was at the bottom of my list of fun ways to spend an evening. "Let's go find out about some luck then."

The shop I was taking Steph to was situated just off the central intersection in The Feathers. The intersection—not the shop—was a terribly designed piece of real estate. Rather than traffic lights on each street, the roads met in a roundabout, the center island of which showcased the statue of some famous magi who'd played a heroic role in the American Revolution.

That magi had probably never anticipated that Boston's traffic would ever reach such horrific levels. The cars, the bicycles, and the pedestrians made for dangerous street crossings. Even with the reduced traffic these days, it was ugly.

Probably because everyone needed to concentrate on their personal surrounding to avoid ending up a street pancake, no one paid attention to the two humans standing in the center of it all by the statue. As my feet touched safer ground on the opposite side of the street, my gift picked up a familiar and most unwelcome emotion. An oily taste, reminiscent of stale French fry grease, filled my mouth.

I associated that flavor with evil intentions, people about to do terrible things. Sometimes, I could get a sense of what those things were, but that wasn't necessary today. I spun wildly in the direction of the emotion, just in time to see the two humans fling a sign that said NO MAGIC atop the statue.

I screamed at Steph to run. Screamed at the humans to stop. But my voice was garbled to my own ears. My speed charms had activated, and the world slowed down as I searched for an opening in traffic, a path to the center of the roundabout.

Even with charms I wasn't fast enough. One of the humans pulled a colorful sphere out of his bag. No question, it was some kind of container, probably a type of curse grenade. I dropped to the street, yanking Steph down with me.

My charms stayed activated long enough that I saw the statue, the humans, and more explode in slow motion.

THIRTEEN

LIKE FIREWORKS, CURSE GRENADES DIDN'T HAVE TO MAKE noise. Most people who made them added the boom, not merely for the effect but to let the person using it know the device had released its contents.

The curse grenade these anti-magers set off didn't make a sound, but the device exploded anyway and in completely surreal fashion because of it. A silent, golden flash blasted the statue and a good chunk of the traffic island into millions of granite pebbles and a few boulders. And there began the noise.

The debris stormed down on the intersection, smashing car windshields and bodies, and crashing into the asphalt. Horns honked and people screamed. Screeching metal and shattering glass followed and followed, a series of never-ending echoes as cars continued to collide and alarms wailed.

Down on the ground, I'd covered my head with my arms so I didn't see it, but I could hear and imagine it. Some of it I felt, a hailstorm of unknown objects pelting me in the back.

The blast itself was over in seconds, and then the grenade went off again. I'd raised my head, coughing from the dust that landed on me, and so I saw the encore. Green sparks shot off in all directions from the rubble. Swearing in shock, I barely darted out of the path of one as it streaked by my head. It punched a hole into the building behind me, and a second flash of light—also green this time—followed. A horrendous shriek and explosive rumble came from inside the building.

And still, the original sparks kept flying in a beautifully deadly starburst pattern until they hit a target. Booms and the sound of things breaking reverberated in all directions. Buildings and the ground trembled.

I blinked a couple times, my eyes feeling like they were coated in dust. "Steph, you okay?"

She was huddled next to me, her arms wrapped around her purse and shopping bag, her hands on the sticky, gross concrete. Coughing, she lifted her head. "What the hell?"

"Come on." I climbed to my feet, dismayed to see how close I'd been to get hitting by a car that had been rear-ended. "We need to get away from the street."

A haze of golden dust hung over the intersection, and the air smelled toxic. In the distance, sirens announced the arrival of some sort of authority, but it wasn't the Gryphons. Their sirens had a distinctive sound. Whoever it was, I couldn't see how they were going to make it through this clusterfuck in their cars. Yet somehow they had to. People were screaming and their fear was increasing, warning me that there were serious injuries nearby.

Steph coughed again, her breathing wheezy. I helped her to sit by a pile of concrete bricks that once been part of a building. "Can you walk?" I asked. "Can you leave without me and get back to the hospital?"

"Without you?" Steph covered her mouth with her hand. "Where are you going?"

I wasn't sure. I was used to chasing after the bad guys, fighting to stop them. But in this case, the bad guys were already dead. It was the good ones who needed attention.

Rising panic surrounded me, pulling me in all directions. I couldn't sense physical pain or magi emotions at all, but the mental anguish of the terrified and dying humans reverberated in my bones. It was both chilling and energizing, and for once, it was useful that these awful emotions juiced me. I could help a few people, I hoped. My problem was I didn't know where to start. Nor did I have anything helpful on me.

"Get on your phone. Call the Gryphons. I'm sure someone already has, but do it anyway just in case." I assessed the former building behind Steph, fairly certain someone was trapped under the rubble. "And keep your head down."

Steph coughed in reply as I climbed through the ruined façade, tracking the trail of fear. What was left of the building's frame creaked and swayed around me. Shit. I had to be fast, and I had to get Steph farther away from this deathtrap.

Sunlight beat down through the broken windows, illuminating a collapsed staircase. Keyboards lay on the ground, some with keys jutting out at odd angle and others simply broken in two. Guitars had been smashed to pieces, and books of sheet music had blown over the clutter. Remnants of other instruments littered the floor.

The rubble shifted under my feet as I maneuvered closer to the person I could sense. Catching my balance, I barely distinguished a white feather among the broken wood. "Anyone there?"

Two voices answered my question. One of them had to belong to a human, a young one from the sound of it.

"Hold on. I'm going to dig you out." My strength charms activated, burning like brands on my skin as I tossed aside heavy bits of wood and plaster. Nails tore at my jeans, and glass fragments burrowed into my palms. As I worked, more charms heated up. Endurance, pain relief, speed. I didn't have a clue what some of them were.

The remains of the staircase shook, and I hauled away more crap. I was making what was left of it more unstable, but if there was a better way to do this, I hadn't any idea what it was. My only equipment was my hands, so I'd simply have to work faster.

The magi came free first, a burly owl shifter who flung the last piece of rubble off himself with my help. He had one arm wrapped around a young human boy, clearly having tried to shelter the child with his body.

"I got you. We'll get him next." I held out my scratched and bleeding hand.

The magi grabbed it and tumbled out of the gap in the rubble. He was stooped over, feathers crushed and likely sporting broken bones. Blood stained The Beatles T-shirt he wore. "Jonah, the boy—his leg is trapped."

"I'll get him. Get outside if you can. This building isn't stable."

The magi didn't leave though. He hovered around me, doing what he could to help, including continuously speaking in a calm voice to the boy, for which I was grateful. Every time I got more rubble cleared, the boy tried to move and ended up yelling in pain. Tears glistened in his eyes, but he didn't cry even as plaster dust drizzled on his head.

At last, I shoved the final chuck of drywall away, revealing his bloody leg. I was going to have to carry him out of here.

"Come on." I knelt to his level and held out my arms, all the while hoping my back or my charms didn't give out.

He winced as I lifted him, and his voice trembled. "Where's my mom?"

Mom? I glanced at the magi, and his face filled with worry. Shit. Focusing my gift in the immediate area told me nothing good. I couldn't sense another human in the rubble.

Breathe, I told myself. His mother might simply be unconscious.

"We'll find her," I said.

"That's right. We will." The magi stroked the boy's head. "You need to keep being brave."

Didn't we all.

A wood beam crashed to the floor as I adjusted my grip on Jonah, mere inches from where he'd been trapped. I jumped, barely repressing a curse, and he tightened his grip around my neck. More dust rained down, and the building moaned.

"That's it, we're out. Come on." Caution warred with my need to hurry as I navigated the treacherous floor. With the magi's help, I managed not to lose my footing, but it was close. I nearly twisted my ankle when a brown blur caught my eye and distracted me. A dragon was my first thought, but no. Dragons never got that dark a shade. It was probably more falling debris.

Outside, chaos continued to rule. The helicopters that had been circling the city were above us, and a couple of cops had appeared but with no sign of their vehicles. The dozens of cars and trucks involved in the massive pileups had emptied of their passengers, at least those not seriously injured. Humans and magi roamed the streets, dazed, frantic, and more often than not, bleeding.

Searching for a safe spot to set down the boy, I finally came to the conclusion that none existed. I left him with the magi at a fair distance from the building by a totaled minivan.

"The Gryphons are already on their way. But, Jess?" Steph swayed on her feet, tugging on my arm. "Purple smoke—that's salamanders."

"What? Where?" I saw it as I asked. It was behind the building I'd emerged from. There wasn't a lot yet, only a simple purple wisp. But after a few salamanders had burned part of the city not so long ago, no one in Boston was ignorant of how quickly they could grow. Or how much they could destroy. "Shit."

Steph grabbed the hood of the nearest car for support and sat on it. Its owner was too busy gazing around in dismay to notice, and Steph pulled out a cigarette with a shaky hand. "Can you catch it?"

I laughed without humor. "Maybe if I had a spelled net or some sprites, but catching salamanders is a bit outside my experience, and I don't have those things." I didn't wish to face it down either. Been there, done that once. Had nearly had my skin seared off.

If I didn't do anything though, there was no telling how much damage the creature could do. For that matter, there was no telling how many there were. A chill crept over me as I realized what sorts of establishments might have been destroyed in the secondary blast. Charm makers would naturally have salamander eggs for their work, and if one had hatched a salamander before the explosion, it could easily have gotten loose.

This was the busiest intersection in The Feathers. A very commercial area. There were more charm makers per square foot in this vicinity than in the rest of the city. Who knew how many salamanders I could be dealing with? Not to mention what else. Every city had its imp issues and dragons in the sewers, but we could be talking sprites slipping into the city water supply or half-finished charms and curses seeping into the ground.

And miniature trolls.

My head snapped to the right as the flash of brown reappeared. Damn.

So that's what that brown shadow I'd seen was—a building-chewing, two-footed termite.

The mini troll popped its knobby head out from the rubble. It was only about four inches tall, full grown. Its beady black eyes scoured the area, its jaw working furiously as it chewed on a section of the blown-out window frame.

Some cultures considered mini trolls delicacies, and many spells used them in various ways. Hell, some people kept mini trolls as pets. While they were certainly cuter than their regular-sized counterparts, they could be every bit as damaging. There was a reason most municipalities banned them for noncommercial keeping. A single mini troll on the loose could chew through a house's wood frame in a couple weeks.

Most reports put their intelligence somewhere on par with dragons—well above most magical creatures—and I swore this one kept its gaze fixed on me, as if it knew I was contemplating how to catch it. Unlike a salamander, I had a chance. Assuming, that was, I could grasp its tiny body before it attempted to bite me with its impressive teeth.

A disturbingly loud rumble ensnared my attention while I contemplated the troll. At first, I thought it was more of the ubiquitous thunder I'd been hearing for the past week, but my ears sorted it out. It had come from the direction of the salamander smoke. More raised voices emanated from that direction too. My pulse quickened. A building had collapsed. From the fire? Was the smoke getting thicker?

I tapped Steph on the arm. "Help me."

"Catch a salamander? Are you kidding me?"

"Catch a troll. Come on." I snatched an empty plastic shopping bag that littered the street.

Steph coughed, saving me the trouble of pointing out that smoking when the air was already plenty full of toxic dust might not be the best idea. "What do you need me to do?"

I picked up a piece of attractive wood that I suspected had once belonged to some sort of musical instrument. "You hold this out to it with one hand, and when it gets close, you throw the bag over it. But watch out for its teeth. Hold it by the body and tempt it with the wood. It'll calm down."

"I know how to care for trolls." Warily, she crushed her cigarette and took the wood and bag from me. "My grandparents had one when we were kids. But why aren't you helping?"

"Because I'm going after the salamander."

"I thought you didn't have supplies for that?"

I tied my hair back. "I don't, but any of these charm or supply shops should have some."

"The Gryphons are coming. Let them handle it." Her fear registered more clearly to me than the general fear I sensed all around. It was a bright lemonade that made me crave a cool drink.

"I am a Gryphon." Whether I wanted to be or not. Just like I was a satyr. Both those designations came with certain responsibilities.

Jaw set, I took one more scan of the area. The worst of the noise had died down. The yelling had muted to upset voices, and the crunch of concrete and plaster crumbling was less powerful. Car alarms still shrieked and unseen sirens blared, mixing with the thump of the helicopters. Fear and a touch of anger were heavy in the air along with the dust. But I couldn't see anyone in the immediate vicinity I could help. It didn't mean there weren't any, but my best chance for saving lives at this point was to go after the salamander. Catch it before it devoured too much.

"Don't spend too much time with the troll," I added. "If you can catch it, great, but it's not the biggest problem. Getting to the hospital is more important."

Assuming the salamander, and any of its brothers and sisters, was reined in before it got to the hospital.

"I'm starting to become nostalgic for the days when you only hunted bad guys," Steph said. "I trusted you could subdue those with your gift."

Me too. Life had been simpler then, or perhaps it had just seemed that way. I sure didn't miss worrying about finding my share of the rent money or mourning my nonexistent love life. On the other hand, I'd gone from waitress to warrior a bit more quickly—and without as much preparation —as I'd like.

I covered my mouth with my hoodie sleeve as I wove through the jungle of cars and rubble. The air had taken on a particularly sharp twang, the odor of sulfur mixed with burning plastic and untold other horrors. As I turned the corner, the press of people moving in the opposite direction thickened. A magi grabbed my arm, yelling "Salamander" at me as she fled.

Yup, salamander, run away. What are you doing, Jess? This is no time to try proving to yourself that you can handle whatever the Gryphons need you to do.

Aha. So that was why I was doing this. Nice of my survival instinct to kick in at last and inform me, but I paid it no mind and kept moving toward the smoke.

I wasn't far from the original explosion here, yet this street was mostly untouched except for the accidents. That, and the one wrecked building that was burning. No question this was the structure that had been hit in the secondary explosion, and most likely it was the one the salamander had escaped from. Its windows had been blown out on two stories, and the wood door and trim were heavily charred. Black and purple smoke poured from gaping openings.

I glanced past the wreckage in the middle of the street and into the fronts of the surrounding buildings. Apartments. Cafes. A post office branch.

Finally, a charm shop. That was what I needed. I dashed over, but the door was locked. A bell over it jingled as I tugged on the handle, and I swore. Backing up, I peered through the window, searching for whether it contained a net.

I couldn't be sure, but it did contain a magi. He waved me away frantically. I pointed at the burning building. In the distance, the sound of Gryphon sirens was a delight to my ears.

"Get away! Shoo!" the magi yelled at me through the glass door.

"There's a salamander—"

He held up a giant canister with a nozzle. Through the clear plastic, I could see sprites circling. "I'm aware. So get out."

You had to be kidding me. This guy had what I needed, and he was hoarding it. "Can I borrow that?"

"Are you crazy? This is in case it gets close. Go away and wait for the Gryphons."

"I am a Gryphon."

He drew his brown, feathery eyebrows together. "Oh. Badge?"

Grunting in frustration, I pulled out my badge and pressed it against the door.

The magi frowned at it. "This says you're only a consultant. Wait, it also says Jessica Moore. You're that woman Xander was talking about. Go away! The real Gryphons are coming. I hear the sirens."

"Oh, for the love of…" I was so furious I actually stamped my foot. The sirens continued to wail, but they didn't seem to be getting any closer. There were no charms to magically part cars in the case of traffic jams, after all.

Wetting my lips, I searched the street for another charm or supply shop, but the burning building was probably the only other one in the immediate area. Figured.

I was running out of options. I could be sensible and wait for the Gryphons to arrive with their sprite-water and nets, or I could be stupid and try to staunch the damage. The smoke was increasing and the temperature rising. Already, the purple flames had spread to nearby buildings.

I spun around at the sound of a door opening behind me. The magi tossed a charmed net at my head and slammed his door once more.

Grimacing, I pulled it off my face. "Thanks!" Jerk.

I wrapped my fingers around the silky fine fabric, feeling foolish. It was one thing to be reckless and charge into danger when I had an excuse to back out. Now, I was armed. The only thing to do was go forward and hope I didn't turn into crispy-fried Jessica while I played the hero.

I'll just take a quick check inside the shop, I told myself. *If I can't see anything, I'll scamper along with everyone else.* Maybe I'd run into the salamander on my way back to Steph.

Before I could change my mind and do something sensible, my feet carried me across the street. Most of the smoke was streaming from the upper stories, but it was the ground floor that was ablaze. Going inside would be suicide if I could do it. The heat was scorching. Flames licked across every surface, burning in an array of colors that suggested they'd found interesting tidbits to devour. Even the air smelled hot—a deep, disturbing scent that singed my nose. Probably it was some kind of chemical or charm ingredient burning.

Then I saw it. A tiny salamander, about the length of my hand from wrist to fingertip, scurried out from between a burning counter and the wall. It paused for a second, then the blazing yellow-and-gold body pranced across the shop's tile floor, swishing its tail.

I let out a breath. It was too young to be super hot and small enough that I might have a chance of catching it yet. How it could have done such damage was surprising, but it had been given plenty of time to attempt it.

All right. I could do this. Facing down a baby salamander couldn't be any less unpleasant than facing down Claudius. Right? And the salamander was less likely to molest me.

I readied my net, wishing I had a pair of dragonhide gloves on me. "Hey, you!"

I hardly had enough experience with salamanders to know if they responded to voices, but this one didn't. It ignored me to chomp on any interesting and flammable piece of debris it found. Not good. I didn't need it getting any larger.

Someone had lost a flip-flop while running, and I gingerly picked it up with a single finger and flung it at the creature. That worked. The shoe passed right through it, but the salamander's head snapped up, and a pair of glowing eyes assessed me.

"Come on." I kicked a piece of debris toward it.

It came on, streaking out of the shop, right by me and down a narrow alley before I could grab it. Peachy.

I charged after it and skidded to a halt. We were on safer ground here. The walls on either side were brick, the trash cans were metal, and the ground was asphalt. The alley reeked of substances best left unsaid, but most were unlikely to be flammable. The salamander realized this too, and it scampered from wall to wall, searching for a source to feed its hungry flames. It was almost cute.

And almost fast enough to get by me a second time. Its tail whipped the edge of the net as I lifted it off the ground, and searing heat shot through my littlest finger. Teeth clenched, I made sure the entire beast was contained before I dropped the net and gave in to my pain. Clutching my hand, I bounced around on my feet, doubled over until the agony dissolved into something merely excruciating. Sweat beaded on my neck. Just that one brief touch and my entire body was flush with heat of the not-so-good sort.

It was time to get out of here and seek medical attention of my own. Fanning my neck with my ponytail, I grabbed the net. In the distance, the Gryphon sirens had died down, and the roar of motorcycles approached. By the engine noise, I could tell these were built for speed and maneuverability, like my poor, beloved Dragon'sWing. It had to be the Gryphons, having at last ditched their regular vehicles. About damn time someone figured it out.

I turned around, ready to flag someone down for salamander disposal, and discovered I wasn't alone. So that was how my baby captive had caused so much damage—he'd had company. Three medium-sized salamanders glared at me, blocking the alley entrance.

I was so toast.

FOURTEEN

A BEAD OF SWEAT ROLLED DOWN MY CHEEK. THIS WOULD ALSO explain why I was so warm.

"I don't suppose you guys negotiate, huh? Prisoner exchange? I give you back your young, you let me pass?" I held up the net. Inside, the tiny salamander chewed on the spelled fibers, but with no fuel, he was already shrinking.

The larger ones didn't appear impressed. Nope, salamanders didn't negotiate. Salamanders probably didn't understand what negotiate meant, or any of those other words I'd used.

"Okay, flames-for-brains, we will...um..." Suddenly the alley's barrenness was not a point in its favor. There was nothing here I could even pretend to use as a weapon, and no structures tall enough for me to climb and make an escape.

Engines roared by and faded in the distance. "Hey, come back!"

I dropped the net and reached for my phone. The odds of anyone getting to me before the salamanders decided Jess flambé was the only thing worth eating were not in my favor, but I had no ideas beyond calling for help.

Sizzling spit fell from the salamanders' mouths and sputtered on the pavement. Slowly, they crept forward, and slowly I stepped closer to the wall I couldn't climb. The emergency line rang and rang. The switchboard had to be overwhelmed because of the attack.

Meanwhile, the heat from these three beasts was growing unbearable. I swore my skin was cracking already. I hurt right down to my brain as though suffering from sunstroke.

I gave up on the emergency line and scrolled through my contacts for Andre's number. If I could get through to someone...

Or not. The salamander in the center got bored of toying with me and charged. I dropped my phone, racing back to the wall, as if by some miracle I'd develop the ability to scale bricks. My heart beat so fast, and I was so high on my own fear and adrenaline, I actually thought it might be possible. Almost there.

A horrible screech from behind made me stumble. Water shot me in the back. My hands smacked into the bricks, and I fumbled around as a Gryphon blasted the last of the three salamanders with sprite-water. The creature sizzled and screamed in fury, fighting the sprites, but sprite always won. In seconds, there was only another innocuous puddle on the ground.

Bridget Nelson—the only friend I'd known longer than Steph—lowered the hose. "Jess? What are you doing here?"

<hr />

TEN MINUTES LATER I WAS EFFECTIVELY GROUNDED BY THE Gryphon healers. I sat in the lobby of a boutique hotel that had been given over to the Gryphons to operate out of. A couple humans and a few magi were also there being treated for magical injuries. People with normal ones, such as smoke inhalation or broken bones, were being taken to the hospital where Steph worked.

"Your face is looking better," one of the healers said. "You no longer share a passing resemblance with a tomato."

"I'm half Irish. It doesn't take much more than a little exertion for me to share a resemblance with a tomato."

I was glad to hear I was healing though. When I thought my skin had been cracking, I hadn't been entirely incorrect. The heat from the salamander had burned off the remaining glamour I wore, which explained not only the painful crackling sensation but also how Bridget had recognized me.

The healer examined my burned finger and nodded in satisfaction. "You should be fine. Agent Nelson says you were trying to catch the salamanders with just a small net."

"I was trying to catch *a* salamander with a net. A tiny one. It was the best I could do. We didn't need a repeat of the last time salamanders got loose."

"No, we don't." She smiled and rewrapped my finger. Because the salamander had actually touched me there, the damage was far worse. The cooling salve the healer had given me meant my face was no longer in pain. My finger, on the other hand, ached like that time I'd run into my mother's hot iron when I was a kid. "So we've got a pred working with us. The world truly has gone crazy."

I tensed, assessing the woman's emotional state. All I detected was a general spearmint anxiety. Nothing out of the ordinary. "I'm not a pred."

"I don't really care what you are. If you're on our side, it's all good. That's what most of us think, so you know." She handed me a white tube. "Put more of that cream on your face and finger tonight and tomorrow morning. If your finger still hurts, use it tomorrow night too."

"Got it. Thanks."

Bridget had refused any more offers of help from me because of my injuries, but at my insistence, she'd checked up on the boy the magi and I had pulled from the rubble. Rescue workers had located his mother, seriously injured but alive, and they'd both been taken to the hospital.

Relieved for the small blessing, I found a relatively quiet corner of the lobby and called Steph. She'd texted me about fifteen minutes ago to let me know she'd arrived at the ER.

"Are you okay?" she asked in greeting.

I lightly rubbed an orchid blossom between my fingers, checking if it was real. It wasn't. "Only mildly toasted."

"Seriously?"

I filled her in quickly, skimming over the bits that made me sound the most reckless. "I could use a night off after this. A glass of wine, a game of pool. I've been in touch with Dezzi, and she's given me permission to recuperate. So I wouldn't have to feel guilty about blowing off my training and going to Fitzpatrick's with you."

"That's not going to work for two reasons. The doctor wants me to keep off my feet and rest. I hurt my ankle worse than I thought. I sprained it. It's swelling up like a grapefruit."

I hadn't realized her ankle had been what was bothering her. "Well, that's what you get for wearing those ridiculous heels."

"Bitch. You wish you had my fashion sense. Oh, and second reason we can't go drinking tonight?"

I guessed before she could answer her own question. "Fitzpatrick's is closed because of the red sky?"

"Are you kidding? My family's more Irish than yours. If it's the end of the world, we're going to go out drinking as it burns. No. The other reason is that you need to get your ass whipped into shape so this shit doesn't happen again. Go kill things for me."

I took a long swallow from the water bottle I'd been provided with. "That's not exactly what I'm training to do."

"You can explain the details later. Just go do it for me."

ALAS, AFTER MY CALL WITH STEPH, THERE WAS NO WAY I couldn't feel guilty if I slacked off tonight, so I called back Dezzi and told her I wanted to train more. She didn't sound surprised that I'd changed my mind.

I swung by my apartment first, escorted once more by Melissa, who joked that I shouldn't be allowed to go anywhere by myself these days. She waited in my living room, reading one of my books while I showered and changed into clean, less smoke-scented clothes.

From there, it was off to Purgatory. Headquarters was already short on space because of *Le Confrérie* taking up residence, and after the attack in The Feathers, they needed more room for their agents to work. Dezzi had volunteered Devon's club for us to use. As a Dom, I guessed she could do that.

Before he'd been cursed into a coma, Devon had hired a new executive manager to replace his old co-owner who'd been arrested. But the club had reduced its hours lately without him. It struck me as unfortunate since Purgatory's clientele was exactly the sort who'd dance away the apocalypse, probably while listening to angsty music about it. But without Devon around, perhaps I wasn't the only one who thought the club wouldn't be the same.

Dezzi had a key, and she opened the back door for me. Since there was no need for Melissa to hang around, she took off, and I followed Dezzi into the main area of the club where Mitch and Claudius were staring at each other uneasily.

Well, Mitch was uneasy. Claudius seemed amused while he helped himself to some scotch.

"You will be compensating the owner of this place for drinking his stock. Right?" I leaned against the chrome railing that separated the bar from the dance floor.

Claudius swished the amber liquid around in a glass. "It remains to be seen whether the owner of this club will ever learn of its loss."

My hands curled into fists. If it wasn't for Dezzi placing a cool, restraining hand on my arm, I'd have lunged at Claudius with my knife a second time.

The Upper Council satyr chuckled. "So I'm not wrong that you have feelings for that one too. What an interesting threesome you must make."

"Go to hell." Damn it, now I needed some of Devon's booze myself. Unlike Claudius, however, I wasn't going to steal it. Also, unlike him, I was going to need a clear head for what was in store. "Where's Lucen?"

"Mitch will be working with me," Dezzi said. "He successfully managed the bond with Lucen earlier. When it didn't appear that you would be training tonight, he made other plans."

I bit my lip. Yeah, but Lucen had said he'd be present when I had to work with Claudius.

The voice in my head sounded whiny. Maybe I should have texted Lucen and let him know the training was on, but how could I have known he'd be called away so quickly? I considered texting him now. Dezzi was fine and technically more powerful than him, but I'd feel safer with Lucen around.

"Your boyfriend—the conscious one—is busy keeping his addicts well fed tonight." Claudius tipped back his drink, his brown eyes filled with mirth at my expense. He was enjoying my anxiety.

Dezzi sensed my unease too, and certainly the surge of anger that coursed through me at Claudius's taunt. "You two need to work together. It would be helpful to us all if you tried not to antagonize the other."

I gritted my teeth. "I didn't start this."

"Didn't start what?" asked a vaguely familiar voice.

Raia appeared a moment later, walking down from the balcony. My hand, which had rested against my knife for support, dropped to my side as an idea came to me. Raia's power had to be on par with Claudius's. If she was here, perhaps that meant she was willing to work with me instead.

But my hope was ill-founded. Plans hadn't changed, and Raia was only present to observe. She took a seat at the bar while Dezzi and Mitch retreated to a separate room so we couldn't distract each other.

"So." Claudius set his glass down. "If I recall what happened last time, this should be fun."

I wrapped my fingers around the railing and gripped it hard. Every muscle was tense. I was getting a headache just thinking about what to expect.

Just brace yourself. You're stronger than you were last time. You can—

Claudius didn't give me time to finish my internal pep talk. His power blew over me like a warm, summer breeze, carrying the deep, woodsy scent of an ancient forest. My head swelled with the sensations it brought. And the ideas. My nerves lit up, waves of pure heat traveling down my body and pooling between my legs. My nipples puckered, and I closed my eyes, my lips falling open as I succumbed to the desire.

Out! Block him out! My survival instincts kicked in. A very real fear struggling against the lust.

"You can't practice if you fight me," Claudius said, pointing out the obvious.

My eyes stayed closed, but I could sense he was standing closer. The air on my body warmed, and my grip on the railing loosened. *Yes, that's right. Don't fight him. Let him in. Let every part of him in.*

I wet my lips, wondering if he got turned on by using his power. I was fairly sure he wasn't actually touching me, yet I could feel him anyway—a hot, silky presence sliding between my legs. My body throbbed, and I squirmed from the waist down.

"Now." His warm breath was on my face.

I gasped, sensing the bond between us form. My body screamed in fear and delight, and it was only by some miracle I didn't come right there because the pleasure was so intense. Through the bond, I thought I could detect a touch of disappointment from Claudius about that. Then the ghost of an emotion vanished.

Reverse the bond now, Jess. You can do this. Visualize it and grab hold.

I tried. I really did. For a second, I had it and gave it a promising tug, but nothing happened. Then my visualization faded. Though I could feel the bond like a satin cord around my waist, I could no longer see it. Instead, I saw myself naked, standing in a lush, gorgeous forest. A steamy breeze lifted my hair, tickling my back and brushing like fingers at my thighs.

"It's not going to be that easy," Claudius said.

I jumped, spinning in circles, but his voice was real and this was my imagination. I willed my body to open my eyes, but my eyelids were too heavy. What the hell? I wrapped my arms around myself in fear.

"I don't have to get in your head this way to addict you." Claudius was closer still. The real me was vaguely aware of his torso pressed into mine. His hands were on my hips, and his erection grazed my stomach. Imaginary me, or real, or both, moaned. "But if I can do this, the demons can do worse. And what they can do probably won't be as enjoyable."

He materialized in the forest with me. Brilliantly naked, with the golden glow of the sunlight adorning every ridge of muscle and the sweeping line of a glorious erection. He glowed like a god, and my knees quivered with the urge to kneel before him. My body ached more than ever.

Find the bond again! You do not want imaginary sex with Claudius.

Oh, but I did. I wanted it with the worst sort of need. A craving even

Lucen had never aroused from me before. I was an alcoholic begging for a drink, and Claudius was the bottle of whiskey tempting me.

An addict. That's exactly what I was.

I shivered, and in my imagination, I turned and ran. I couldn't attempt to find the bond—never mind reverse it—with Claudius distracting me this way.

I could hear him laughing somewhere. The forest quivered with the sensual amusement. The trees were strangely phallic, their branches reaching out for me and their leaves falling, caressing my skin. My feet sank into dark, rich dirt that slipped between my toes and massaged my soles.

Claudius was chasing me, so I ran faster. I had to think of the bond, the goddamned bond. That was how he could follow me in my own head.

Pausing by a large, unidentifiable tree, I placed my hands on my waist. The cord materialized around me as fine, golden threads. Good enough. I stared harder at the threads, picturing them as magical conductors. Power in. Power out.

I searched for my power and pulled on the outgoing threads. Nothing happened. I was fighting myself. Some part of me—no question which part —didn't want to end this. I wanted Claudius to catch up to me, push me against this tree and shove himself inside me until I screamed with ecstasy. Then I wanted him to pin me down and take more of what my rational self refused to give him. I'd hate myself later but would love every second of it while it happened.

Stupid fucking hormones. I willed the thoughts away. I was not going to be controlled by the bits between my legs.

My anger brought on more power, and I smiled. Hell, yes. This was what I'd been missing. This was what I needed. Just like when I'd grappled with Raj, I needed to find some counter-emotion. With Raj, it had given me the ability to surprise him. With Claudius, it fueled my power in a way he couldn't so easily steal.

I grasped the bond again and yanked. It worked but not enough. Claudius's power slammed into me. My nerves screamed and not in delight this time. Harder then. I could take more than I had that day he'd done this to me in Lucen's apartment. I pulled, sensing Claudius's surprise. But oh, gods. The second pull sent me to my knees. My real ones.

My eyes flew open, the visualization gone, and I collapsed to the floor. So much pain. Hot and sharp and electric, it raked at my nerves. For the second time today, I was frying. No salamanders required.

Clutching my head, I floundered for more power, and the agony intensified. My head was going to burst, and yet the power I was sucking in was not enough to kill the headache. I simply couldn't hold it well enough for that. I couldn't control it on any level. Black dots formed in front of my eyes.

Then the worst of the pain vanished.

Groaning, I slumped farther and rested my head on my knees. "I was making progress."

"Yes," said Claudius. "At giving yourself a migraine."

I clenched my jaw, making the pulsing headache worse. "I beat your stupid game. I could have finished."

"You were close to blacking out." That was Raia, and my head snapped up. "Claudius is one of the oldest satyrs on the Upper Council. Yet he is far younger than the creatures in the Pit. You have a lot of practicing to do, so there is no sense in wearing yourself out right away."

If Claudius were the one speaking to me, I would have protested on principle. But since it was Raia, I simply rubbed my temples and acknowledged her point.

Claudius handed me an engraved silver flask. "Take one sip. It will help."

"What is it?" There was no way I was about to drink something just because he told me to.

"It's a concoction we had made for you. It will numb the pain, relax your headache, and restore your energy. It's potent, and it will only work on you because you have sufficient satyr magic in your blood."

"It's safe," Raia assured me. "I've seen your blood analysis, so it will work, though not as well as it should. It used to be given to warriors to help them fight longer and better in battle." She glanced at Claudius. "I can't tell what you were doing to her, but her resistance is better than you led me to believe."

His expression was distasteful. "But not good enough."

I scowled because I agreed with him. Cautiously, I took a sip from the flask and almost choked. "You're messing with me again, aren't you? This tastes like alcohol."

"It requires an alcohol base." Claudius capped the flask. "Give it a minute to work, and we'll start again."

I sighed. Swell.

FIFTEEN

THE NEXT MORNING WAS SATURDAY, AND I HEADED OVER TO
Steph's bearing gifts. Her boyfriend Jim was a nurse, and he was stuck
pulling a double shift, so I'd told her I'd stop by to make her breakfast and
catch up after yesterday.

Steph was the sort who stayed up late Friday and Saturday nights, so
breakfast didn't require me forgoing more than the usual amount of sleep.
It was half past eleven when I got there, and my stomach was rumbling,
which I took as a good sign. I couldn't be too messed up from yesterday's
Claudius session if I was starving. But while my head was better than
expected, I still felt run down. Climbing the steps to Steph's apartment
made me want to crawl back into bed.

To my surprise, when I knocked on the door, it was her cousin who
answered. Eric Marshall was an internationally bestselling thriller author
who, like many well-known people in the arts, had increased his chances
of hitting it big by trading his soul to a pred.

I didn't judge. Over the years I'd soul swapped, I'd met too many
actors, musicians, athletes, students, and more with sob stories about
trying to break in to an industry, a profession, or simply the right school
where the competition was brutal. I understood how hard it could be, and
I also understood how luck charms worked. I wasn't certain that most of

my clients did. A luck charm could ensure you didn't flub an audition or that you snagged an interview, but if you sucked regardless, it wouldn't land you a role or a job.

That said, I'd never found out exactly what Eric's deal had been for. He had enough talent to produce good books. Would they have earned him as much money and fame without the charm? I hadn't a clue, though odds were against it.

Besides, Eric had paid for his success far more than he'd anticipated. The goblin he'd bargained with had broken their contract and stolen his soul all at once, leaving Eric a ghoul. At Steph's request, I'd worked with the Gryphons to find the goblin and get it back before it was too late.

Looking at him today, you'd never know he'd been reduced to a barely conscious blob not quite a month ago. His eyes were bright and lively once more, and the smile that greeted me was pleasingly genuine. Then again, Eric had very good reasons to like me.

"Jessica, it's great to see you again." He reached for my hand, then realized I couldn't shake while holding a pastry box, so he took the box from me instead.

"You too. You look recovered."

"Honestly, I've never felt better. Not having that contract hanging over my head is the greatest feeling." Eric set the box on the table where Steph was sitting. "If my next book tanks because of it, oh well. Lesson learned."

Steph rolled her eyes behind Eric's back and inspected what I'd brought. "And if the world ends in a reign of fire tomorrow, you'll never know how it might have done. Ooh, are those sticky buns?"

"Sticky buns for you, chocolate croissants for me, and some other sugar-laden carbohydrate goodness just because. If the world ends in fire, it doesn't matter if my pants continue to fit."

"Amen to that." Eric went back to Steph's kitchen and got out the eggs. "Coffee is ready."

"Eric saw what happened yesterday on the news, and he came down here to help me out because..." Steph lifted her leg. Her ankle was wrapped in some sort of brace, similar to the one I'd had when I sprained my wrist back in June. "So how did it go last night? Did you kick ass and take names?"

I brought us both over mugs of coffee. "Not exactly."

I wasn't too keen on relaying what I was doing in front of Eric, but he listened with the rapt attention of a storyteller committing all the details to memory for later use. Like probably half the world at this point, he'd also heard about Xander's speech. While he pressed me for more information a couple times, it was clear he already must have bugged Steph for the more basic points.

There wasn't much either Steph or Eric could offer in way of advice, and I wasn't expecting any. I got my chance to vent, and over eggs, baked goods, and coffee, the conversation drifted to other topics. I was thankful not to be the focus of it right until the moment when Eric reversed direction and we ended up close to where we'd started.

"So how did you actually get the idea to trade souls?" he asked. "It's one hell of a hobby to have taken up."

I broke apart my last piece of croissant and shrugged. "I didn't do it expecting it to be a good time. I saw this girl about my age who needed help, and it seemed like something I could do."

Steph cleared her throat in dramatic fashion. "It was a bit more complicated than that."

"It was?" I raised an eyebrow.

"Yes, it was." She set down her mug and faced Eric. "When I met Jess, her gift was going rogue. She thought she was turning from this good little Gryphon wannabe into some evil, misery-sucking pred wannabe. I had suggested she embrace her newly discovered evil side, and I convinced her to buy the clothes to match. But even with a hot pair of leather pants, she couldn't let go."

I choked on my coffee.

Steph made a stop sign in my direction. "Jess may have made some questionable choices over the years—and I'm not just talking about her fashion preferences—but basically, she's a good person. So what does a good person with an evil ability do? She gives it an outlet. Jess channeled that terrible power into a good cause, so her conscience was clear."

"You make me sound far more..." I paused, not hearing what Eric was saying in response. Channel the power. That's what Raj was using me for when he forced me to help open the Pit. He'd pushed so much magic through me that I hadn't been able to hold it, and somehow, in a reaction that was way beyond my understanding of magical theory, that power had helped blow open the locking spell.

"Jess, you okay?"

I blinked. "Steph, you might be a genius. I think you just gave me an idea for how to do that ass kicking."

She clucked her tongue at me. "Might be? Please. There should be no question about that."

I WASN'T EXACTLY EAGER TO FACE OFF AGAINST CLAUDIUS FOR a second day, but I was interested in testing out my idea. An idea that, when I slowed my racing brain to ponder it more thoroughly, I wasn't sure how to actually put into practice.

Le Confrérie de l'Aile had called for a meeting this afternoon because they apparently had some updates, but it wasn't for a few hours. I went to headquarters early and immediately hit their library. I could really have used a tutor on magical theory, but Lucen was sleeping, Tom was busy, and I didn't want to bug Dezzi. If only Olef were alive, he'd have been the perfect person to ask, but I had fucking Raj to thank for murdering him. At least Raj was dead too.

She's a good person, I heard Steph say, and I sighed. Killing Raj might have been for a good cause, but it had been just as much for vengeance. Every day though it became easier to deal with what I'd done. Did that make me a bad person or simply normal? Or was the emotional fallout merely waiting for me to have a moment to deal with it?

Whichever, I didn't have the moment yet. In the library I found what books the Gryphons kept about magical theory and got reading. Anything that could help me understand what I'd done and how to do it with control—those were the only topics I had room for in my brain.

My nose was buried in my third book when I sensed someone hovering nearby. I dropped the book and found Tom standing in the doorway.

"Someone told me you were in here. You'll be late for the meeting."

I rubbed my tired eyes. "Do you need me? I'm learning useful stuff."

"Take the book then. Yes, we need you. Decisions have to be made, and your opinion will be crucial."

That intrigued me, and I marked the page in the book. "My opinion finally counts for something around here? Never thought that day would come."

Tom answered my sarcasm with an expression indicating he wasn't amused, and he walked away.

"Have you heard from Grace lately?" I asked, jogging to catch up. Despite the Gryphons' best efforts to keep an eye on her, she'd successfully managed to sneak out of headquarters the other day. Grace might hate her gift, but I couldn't believe she'd have managed to do that without it. When attempting to avoid people, it helped being able to sense where they were.

"No, but Mitch said she texted him last night when he asked if she was ready to return." Tom held open the door for me. "The answer was no."

"Shocker."

So much for being late—we were among the first people to arrive. Over the next several minutes, Lucen and the other satyrs filed in, along with the magi, goblins, and harpies. As usual, it was crowded in the conference room, and the groups self-segregated.

Mitch leaned against a wall next to me, more relaxed than I'd seen him before. I'd been informed he made good progress yesterday with Dezzi, so his confidence must be increasing. I was happy for us both. Grace was an unfortunate dead end. The best I could hope for her was that she learned to deal with her anxiety. Since that left only two of us who could potentially withstand the demons' powers, I wanted us both to be as strong as we could.

"We have much to discuss," Ingrid said, drawing my attention to the matter at hand. "Let's get started. I want to bring everyone up to date on what we've learned since the last meeting and hear how Mitchell and Jessica are doing with their training. Then we must consider everything and make a decision."

My fingers tapped the borrowed book's cover as I listened. Although I knew I should pay attention, I was eager to get back to my studying. The topics that Ingrid and the magi discussed didn't involve me much. Mainly, they talked about what they'd learned would be needed to perform the spell that would close the Pit.

Gunthra and the goblins had been busy working on that part too, and they also spoke. Everyone but Mitch and I had been busy gathering supplies as well as information and making plans about who would need to do what part. Closing the prison would continue to require the coalition to work together.

It was when the issue of timing was brought up that I understood the decision Tom and Ingrid had mentioned.

"The spell to close the Pit must be performed under a waning moon," Ingrid explained.

A few preds and Gryphons exchanged tense glances. They were obviously the ones who were used to making charms. A lot of complicated magic depended on different lunar and solar phases, so they would track those things.

"We can't possibly be ready by then," one of the goblins said. "The moon is already in a waning cycle. By the time we're ready to implement—"

"We have approximately seven more days." Ingrid looked at me and Mitch, then turned to the satyrs. "We might be able to have everything prepared by then. Will you be ready?"

Claudius reclined in his chair, crossing his arms. "Doubtful."

I narrowed my eyes at him. "We have to be. We can't put things off another month. The thunder is becoming more frequent, and people are becoming more panicky. All the chaos has got to be fueling the demons. Another month might be too late."

"Tomorrow could be too late," a magi said. "We have no ability to say when the demons will emerge."

"All the more reason to hurry."

Claudius cocked his obnoxiously perfect head to the side, meeting my glare. "Don't get angry at me. You two are the holdups. If this group had taken my advice and killed you and the others when I'd suggested it, the furies could never have opened the Pit in the first place."

My arm twitched. I was ready to throw the library book at him, but I took a deep breath instead. "We'll be ready."

Mitch mumbled something I couldn't make out, but I could be fairly sure it was along the lines of "Yeah, right." Even Lucen regarded me with concern. Apparently, no one believed I'd be able to take down Claudius in the next few days.

I fumed silently, feeling ridiculous. I doubted myself too, but I preferred it when everyone else claimed they believed in me.

"If we're moving ahead then," Tom said, "we need to discuss the team that's going to accompany Jessica and Mitchell into the Pit."

Claudius dragged his gaze away from me. "That would be a job for your organization, wouldn't it?"

Obviously, Claudius didn't intend to offer himself up as a volunteer. I searched the nonhuman faces in the room, wondering if he was going to be the only one to refuse.

"We don't know what we'll find in the Pit," Tom pointed out. "For this reason, we think that a diverse group would be best."

The magi who'd spoken earlier cleared her throat. "Odds are, in their attempts to escape over the years, the demons would have molded the prison with their magic. A group of trained fighters with many talents and skills does make the most sense."

"And a convenient one," said Gunthra. "Seeing as the magi boast no soldiers or warriors."

The many-colored feathers on the various magi ruffled. Gunthra knew as well as the rest of us that magi could be terrifying fighters when in their bird forms. But for the magi to defend themselves that way was akin to them bragging of the reasons why they should volunteer. No doubt that was Gunthra's intention. The silence that followed suggested the magi preferred to endure the slight rather than sign their people up for certain death.

Lucen broke the heavy lull. "Well, I volunteer."

My stomach sank. Of course he would volunteer. And later, I would not try to talk him out of it because it was his choice and it would be futile anyway. I'd simply lie in bed tonight, sick with worry.

Dezzi stood. The hard lines of her mouth made me believe she was about to chastise Lucen for not consulting her, but I was wrong. "I do as well, and I will find two more recruits among my people. Some of us are not cowards."

I couldn't tell if that comment was aimed at the magi, the goblins, Claudius, or all of the above, but Gunthra's ears flattened and Claudius bristled as though he'd sat on a pin. I gaped in shock, wondering if Dezzi intended to go through with her decision. I'd pegged her for a badass a while ago, but in a politically savvy, leadership way. Then again, as I'd reminded myself many times lately, preds didn't rise to her position without being able to prove themselves mentally, physically, or magically.

But whether Dezzi did or did not intend to enter the Pit with me, her public declaration shamed the room into offering up volunteers. The goblins grudgingly said they would come up with two or three candidates, and the harpies did as well. The magi made noise about searching for appropriate people.

Tom planned to head up the team for the Gryphons, and as the discussion descended into the minutiae of what sorts of skills he needed and when and where and how and a thousand other issues that had to be addressed, I shivered. Clasping my book against my chest, I stared at the side of Lucen's head. This was getting very real, very fast. And despite my bravado, or whatever the outcome of my go with Claudius later, I wasn't at all sure I'd ever truly be ready.

SIXTEEN

LUCEN TUCKED PURGATORY'S KEY IN HIS POCKET AND SHUT the club's door behind him.

"Does everyone on your council have a key to this place?" I asked, returning his coffee.

He smiled mysteriously but retrieved his cup without an answer, so I took that to mean no.

Between the sugar in my large café mocha and my nerves, I was wired. I was also relieved that Lucen was here today. As per our unspoken agreement, I didn't ask whether Claudius had been telling the truth about Lucen meeting with addicts during our training session. When Lucen had found out it had happened without him, he'd told me I should have called and he'd have been right over. I believed him, and it was enough.

Mitch hesitated at the threshold of the club's main room. "Do you think it'll work—this idea Jess was researching?"

Mitch hadn't gotten over his anxiety around preds, and he rarely addressed any of them without some provocation. But recently I'd begun noticing a change in the way he carried himself. An increase in his self-confidence. I hoped working one-on-one with Lucen and Dezzi was helping him become more comfortable with what he could do.

Lucen took a deep breath. "Honestly, I have no idea, and I consider myself well-read. I'm not going to throw the love of my life into danger often, but in this case, you might want to let her try this idea first."

"Wow, that's chivalry." I rolled my eyes.

"Little siren, if I were wearing a cloak, I'd let you step on it rather than sully your boots on this questionable floor. Would that be better?"

I made a show of sniffing his coffee. "What secret ingredient did you put in here?"

Mitch laughed. "You know, I was horrified when Jess told me about the two of you, but you're actually good together. And trust me, that disturbs me almost as much as what I'm about to do."

"Jess apparently has a way with all the satyrs in Boston," Claudius called out. He was lounging around the bar and must have been listening in.

My smile turned sarcastic. "Not all of them. Not as long as you're in town."

Claudius had his feet propped up on a table, and he let them fall to the floor with a thud. "No, this evening, I get to have my way with you again. Lucky for you, I brought more of this to heal your tender soul when it's over." He slapped the flask on the table.

My smile got stuck, and Lucen placed a reassuring hand on the small of my back.

Raia wasn't here tonight, so Dezzi and Mitch returned to wherever they'd gone the day before, and Lucen and I made our way to the bar. Claudius somehow had gotten hold of a remote to change the lights. He dimmed the bright ones overhead and cranked up the red spotlights.

I finished my coffee, unpleasantly aware of my heart beating. "Do we really need the mood lighting?"

"I'm simulating the great outdoors. Not that you'll notice, seeing as your eyes will be closed in ecstasy the whole time."

"Agony, you mean."

"For some people, there's a fine line between them."

I took up the same position I had yesterday, resting against the balcony. As much as I wanted to touch Lucen for support, I didn't think that was a good idea. I'd likely crush him in frustration. "Trust me, when you're in my head, it's not a good pain."

"You sure? You enjoyed it yesterday." Grinning suggestively, Claudius grabbed a chair and sat in front of me.

I let my simmering rage answer for me since he could understand it quite well.

My first attempt to thwart Claudius yesterday had, sadly, been my best. I blamed it on a deep-rooted exhaustion of my gift that even the satyrs' alcoholic concoction couldn't ameliorate, but regardless, I had not been pleased by my failure.

Nor what failing in this situation had entailed. It wasn't stripping in front of Claudius and Raia that bothered me so much. Hanging around satyrs had cured me of most of my modesty, and I was comfortable enough in my skin not to care if other people judged me for having less than newly shaven legs or extra padding on my butt.

What bugged me—no, what pissed the ever-loving shit out of me—was that I'd had sex with an imaginary Claudius. Not once but twice.

Thank dragons, this weird hallucinogenic sex did not equate to actual real-life sex, but it was horrible enough to have experienced it in any form. I'd failed to get a grip on the bond between us, failed to draw on his power, and in both those situations eventually failed to care. I'd given in and let fake him do exactly what he wanted to me.

I suspected the only reason the real him hadn't attempted the same stunt was because Raia and Dezzi were at hand to remind him that I needed to be willing to continue our training. It didn't matter if he could claim that I'd wanted his attention in the moment. If he'd overpowered my will and touched me in real life, I would have been out of there faster than anyone could say "acquaintance rape."

As it was, the whole ordeal still felt violating, but mostly I was just pissed off. I'd told Lucen about it, and I was quite certain there would be blood if Claudius pushed me harder today. Already, the muscles in Lucen's arms were taut as he stared down the back of his superior's head.

Claudius was awaiting my response, so I chose not to give him one. I focused on my breathing instead, finding a source of calm inside me. Claudius would not catch me unawares with his power this time. Besides, I had a plan. I simply had to remember to implement it.

"Let's begin then," he said.

As soon as the words left his mouth, I could detect tendrils of his power grazing me. Wisps of magic lightly brushed my face, and I sensed his body on mine without him moving. A gentle finger traced my lips, and I tingled. A slow stream of pleasure trickled down my core, between my breasts, over my stomach. It slipped between my legs, and I tensed, my breaths coming faster.

"Look at me, Jess," Claudius commanded. "Not at Lucen."

My brain begged me to resist, but Claudius's voice couldn't be denied. I wet my lips, heat rushing to face and my chest as I obeyed. The bond hadn't formed yet, but he was working on it. As usual, my subconscious was fighting it.

Claudius stood and stepped closer. His rich, woodsy scent washed over me, increasing the sensitivity of my skin. My fingers relaxed on the railing, and the memories of what he'd had me imagine yesterday flooded my mind. The way his teeth had grazed my throat, his hands firmly cupping my breasts, the pure heat of him as he'd thrust into me.

I realized my eyes had closed, and I opened them. Claudius's dark ones locked on my gaze. I was breathing hard, and my hands had given up on the railing, eager to find something else to touch.

"You're resisting less today," Claudius said. "Good. That makes things go so much faster."

I was mentally with it enough to scowl at him even as my body was crying out in need.

Claudius chuckled. "But still resisting. I want you to take your shirt off for me. Let me see how your skin looks in this light."

If his voice had demanded to be obeyed before, his commands were simply my will at this point. There was no fighting it, no consideration. I knew he'd pushed me to the breaking point at last. Do what he said and the bond would be formed.

My fingers curled around my shirt's hem, and I pulled it off. The cool air brushed against my exposed skin like a kiss. Grasping the railing once more, I tossed my head back and moaned in anticipation.

The bond—I could feel the bond. I was supposed to do something with it too, but the only thing I wanted to do was the satyr in front of me. I had to get it together. I had to focus. But oh, my clothes chafed, and my body ached. I needed a release before I could focus, only there wasn't going to be one, was there? Such was the agony of addicts.

Claudius dragged a finger along my bra's lace edge, setting my skin on fire. His voice sounded far away, which meant he wasn't talking to me but to Lucen. "Which one of you has the taste for lacy undergarments? Jess doesn't strike me as the sort, so is it you or the unconscious one?"

"If you touch her unnecessarily again, I'm willing to shoot you."

I gasped. Lucen's voice brought me some additional clarity. Lucen was here, and I was supposed to be testing my new theory.

Find the bond. Grab the bond.

I closed my eyes, searching for the threads. When I tried visualizing them, I wasn't surprised to find myself transported to the same forest as yesterday. Claudius had returned me here for each attempt. He must have liked my underwear more today because I wasn't naked this time.

He was though, leaning against a large oak. The branches behind him framed his head like a pair of antlers, and with the myriad glyphs covering his legs and his blatantly large erection, all he needed was a set of wooden pipes to have stepped out of some classical myth.

That erection. My eyes were drawn to it like an imp to a streetlamp. I wouldn't have thought it was possible to get any wetter but seeing Claudius in all his glory proved me wrong. My body was awash in heat of all sorts, and I rubbed my bare skin.

"That's it," he said as my fingers slid under the trim of my underwear. "Take them off. This is better than what you were trying to imagine, isn't it?"

Yes. Yes, it was. But the command in his voice resonated in my gut, a reminder of the bond. With a pang of regret, I lifted my fingers and concentrated.

There it was now, more greenish gold than last night, but there all the same. Before Claudius could distract me, I envisioned the energy flow and yanked on the power. Searing-hot pain slammed into me, and a low scream escaped my mouth.

Fake Claudius crossed his arms, watching me with an amused expression. His smugness made me angry, and I tried again. My nerves shrieked, and my brain began to pound on my skull. If I continued to pull, I'd come close to blacking out. Claudius would drop the connection.

Like hell. I wasn't suffering through this any more times than I had to. I was going to get this right on the first attempt.

Against the tree, Claudius winked at me, and I felt him give a gentle tug on the bond. Some of my pain vanished. "You're going to push yourself too hard, too fast. Come here, and at least enjoy the experience before you bring on a migraine." He wrapped a hand around his cock as if offering it to me.

"Fuck you." I pulled again, using the burst of power to will my eyes open.

Catching my breath, I discovered I was on the floor. So predictable. The real Claudius continued to hover nearby, but he wasn't touching me any longer.

Once more, I told myself. Breathe it in and breathe it out.

I grabbed at the power, keeping the visualization firmly in front of my open eyes. My nerves wailed, but this time when I drew on the bond, I imagined the power coming through the rope, into me, down the nerves and out of my fingers.

For a second, the pain overwhelmed me, and I thought my body might burst, then it subsided ever so slightly. My fingertips tingled as though zapped by electricity. Something deep inside my chest, however, expanded. I could take more energy next time. I was positive.

In again. My head felt like it was going to explode, but with this attempt, when the pain passed, it left the rush behind. Power spread across the cracks in my soul, filling them in and smoothing me out. I was dancing. I was floating. And even better, I was doing what I intended.

Again. I was vaguely aware that Lucen had jumped off the table where he'd been sitting, and Claudius's smug expression had lost some of its smarminess. My limbs were light, and I no longer ached. My pain had lifted with my mood. The magic was restoring me instead of breaking me.

One more time. I sucked hard on the power, hearing myself cry out as I drew it in. The bond flared, its golden color fading to a dull yellow then to orange then to a brilliant scarlet. Too much power threatened to tear me apart, and I flung the excess out through my fingers.

It flew across the seating area, past Claudius and Lucen, and slammed into the bar. Glasses exploded, and shards spun off in all directions. Liquor bottles burst, their contents showering the floor and us with potent sticky, sweet alcohol. Lucen swore, and I think I laughed.

No, I knew I laughed; I simply didn't feel like myself. I was drunk on Claudius's power and high from breathing the fumes. I was invincible and glowing. I was a god, and that meant for this very brief time, I outranked and out-powered His Supreme Upper Asshole.

So while Claudius gaped, I did the one thing I'd been meaning to do for weeks. I leapt forward and kicked him in the groin.

"Eat." Lucen shoved a bag of pretzels across the table. We were sitting around the one farthest away from the bar and therefore one of the few not covered in glass fragments or liquor.

My hands struggled to open the bag without sending the contents flying. Apparently, channeling so much power had its downsides. I couldn't stop moving, and the concept of doing anything gently was not one my body would tolerate. I had a bad case of what my mother used to call "the fidgets."

"I can't believe Devon's going to be thrilled about you raiding his inventory."

Sensing an imminent pretzel explosion, Lucen took the bag back and opened it for me. "Worry more about his opinion of you doing a few thousand dollars' worth of damage to his club."

I wasn't a huge fan of pretzels, but I took a bite, assessing the destruction. The area reeked of alcohol, and while I no longer felt drunk on the fumes, odds were good that we all were inhaling quite a bit of it. Dezzi had called the new manager and informed him that he might want to send in the custodial team.

"He's going to take the cost of this out of my ass, isn't he?"

"Assuming you both live." Claudius glowered several tables away. Our relationship hadn't exactly improved by me attacking his junk with a steel-toed boot.

I refused to feel sorry about it, and Claudius—to his credit, barely—had continued to work with me once he got over threatening to kill me in a variety of gruesome ways. Just figuring out how to channel the excess power clearly wasn't enough. I couldn't keep going around blasting the hell out of what was around me. Claudius insisted, as did the stuff I read in the Gryphons' books, that I needed to learn how to properly discharge the power.

I was having a difficult time of it. My second attempt at discharging had resulted in a couple cracked floor tiles, and by my third attempt, Lucen had retreated to the second-floor balcony just in case. Mitch and Dezzi had stood watch with him. Since I'd wrecked the bar, everyone had wanted to observe.

After the third attempt ended with me flying backward and colliding with the railing, we decided it was break time. I'd never managed to shake all the accumulated power, and my extremities trembled as a result. Dezzi had suggested eating something because the food would absorb some of the magic.

"Feeling better?" she asked as I crunched into my fifth pretzel.

I nodded. Better wasn't precisely the right word because buzzing with excess magic was euphoric. But I did feel more normal. More capable, say, of opening a bag of pretzels without casting its contents to the winds.

Dezzi waved a hand in front of her nose. "We are going to need to find a new place to train before we end up drunk."

"Anywhere but The Lair." Lucen helped himself to a handful of pretzels. "I just finished repairing the bar. I don't need Jess turning it into another war zone."

"Hey!" I stuck my tongue out at him. "It was trashed by sylphs last time, not me."

"Perhaps a padded cell would be appropriate?" Claudius suggested.

I flipped him off, and Dezzi took out her phone. "I'll figure out something," she said. "Meanwhile, this would be a good time for Jessica to explain what she did to Mitchell."

I washed down my last pretzel, wondering how to do that when I barely understood it myself. But Mitch didn't need much theory. Mainly, he needed steps.

"So basically, magic theorists describe power as consisting of emotional energy, physical energy, and magical energy," I began. "A person's soul is the source of all those things, and the ability to hold them can grow over time."

As I rambled, Dezzi's phone rang. My voice trailed off as I watched her expression change from concern to delight by whatever news she was receiving. "This is wonderful. I will be over shortly." She hung up and rejoined us. "That was Azria. Devon is awake."

OUR SHORT TRAINING BREAK BECAME A LONGER BREAK. MITCH had no reason to want to visit Devon, and Dezzi figured he and Claudius might as well begin working together. Since we needed to leave Purgatory anyway, and anyone with half a brain could tell Mitch wasn't excited to be getting the Claudius treatment, they returned to Gryphon headquarters to begin. That way someone could be there to supervise if necessary. The rest of us hurried to Shadowtown.

Dezzi seemed pleased but calm, as if she'd always expected Azria would find the right counter-curse. Lucen seemed relieved—Devon was his closest friend, after all—but he also expressed this feelings in a quiet way. I attributed that to being a man thing.

That left me as the only one of the three of us who was an emotional mess. Aside from my freakout when Raj had cursed Devon, I'd had little time to fret. The problems pressing down on my shoulders were far heavier than one unconscious satyr. Even one I cared about. My fears had to be saved for those middle-of-the-night fits when I woke up alone, my eyes wet and my heart convinced all was hopeless.

Even now, I didn't trust myself to be entirely happy. I'd proved I could handle Claudius's bond, and with Devon waking up, it all felt like too much good news. We'd experienced so little of that lately that I feared it being swept away as soon as I allowed myself to enjoy it.

Lucen wrapped an arm around me as we waited to be buzzed into Devon's apartment building, and I sank into him for support. He smelled of his usual cinnamon goodness mixed with the faintest hint of alcohol, which was—no doubt—my fault. The thought of cinnamon schnapps made me want to gag, but on Lucen, pretty much anything smelled good.

That reminded me of the additional complication caused by Devon waking up. Days before the fighting in the Alps, Devon had suggested he was interested in making more of our relationship. I wasn't sure what to do about that. My confusion had nothing to do with my feelings for Devon and everything to do with my thoughts about relationships in general. Having spent most of my last decade unhappily dateless, the idea of two men in my life made my head spin and uprooted my entire idealized version of my life. It was almost as wild as discovering I wasn't human.

Of course, contemplating the complications of an abnormal love life was a luxury I shouldn't bother to indulge in yet. So I hadn't ended up seeing stars while curled in the fetal position after today's bout with Claudius—that didn't mean we would succeed.

Azria met us at the door, and we found Devon propped up on his black sofa. A fuzzy orange blanket, which was completely out of place, had been thrown over him. For that matter, Devon appeared just as incongruous with his surroundings.

Devon liked the sleek, the modern, and the expensive. His large, top-floor apartment was decorated with tasteful leather seating, white rugs, glass, and marble. Maroon throw pillows and watercolors of scarlet poppies provided the accent. Everything was airy and modern, and everything probably cost more than I could contemplate. Everything except for the orange blanket.

As for the satyr who considered himself underdressed if he loosened his designer tie, he looked more like the blanket than his room. His curly black hair was in need of a more thorough brushing, and he sported quite the full beard. His displeasure at being discovered in such a state was evident when Lucen's first reaction was to take a photo. Devon struggled to raise an arm, and he pointed at the door. "Out."

Lucen grinned. "Get off that sofa and make me, you lazy ass."

Devon's arm flopped back to his side, and he gazed wearily at Dezzi. "Tell me I still outrank him and he has to listen to me." His voice was raspy and barely audible.

"Stop stressing him," Azria said to Lucen. She opened the water bottle on the living room table, refilled Devon's glass and handed it to him. "It's bad enough that he insisted on moving into this room before he'd let company over."

Devon winced as he drank. "She put this hideous blanket over me as punishment."

Azria tossed her pink hair over her shoulders. "You haven't eaten real food in ten days, your vitals are weak, I practically had to carry you in here, and I still don't know exactly what sort of curse I've been dealing with. I don't care if you outrank me. Don't give me more grief or I'll hit you with a sleeping potion."

Devon sighed dramatically. "I don't suppose Raj is hanging around Boston these days so we can ask him what he did?"

"Raj is dead," Dezzi said, sitting on a chair across from Devon. "Jessica killed him."

Devon's blue eyes flickered with a trace of his old humor. "My hero. Jess, where are you? I can sense you, but I can't see you. Why are you hiding?"

I'd been hanging back, feeling like an intruder. Dezzi and Lucen had known Devon far longer and better than I had. Much as I wanted to run over and wrap him in a hug—a gesture that would normally be as out of place between us as the ugly blanket—it didn't seem right.

Awkwardly, I stepped forward. "I aim to please."

"I know you do." He held up his hand ever so slightly. "Closer. I'm so low on energy."

"So you want to feed off me, is that it?" I knelt next to the sofa. "I didn't realize I came here to be your buffet."

I took his hand, letting his clove scent settle in my lungs. It was fainter than usual, but the effect of his skin against mine was not. Wisps of his magic swirled around my wrist, climbing my arm and caressing me in all the right places. My body reveled in the heat he brought, and unlike my battles with Claudius's power, I welcomed it.

Devon did as well. He closed his eyes and laid his head against the pillow, smiling. "That's better."

"Go easy on him," Azria said. "He could use some human contact to speed his recovery, but he needs rest and regular food too."

"Don't listen to her." Devon squeezed my hand. "This is what I need. And maybe some beer."

Dezzi tsked him. "You will listen to Azria. I expect you to get better quickly. Our plans are progressing, and I will need your help."

Devon's face turned unusually serious. "Understood. I have a few furies I'd like a word with myself."

"And a club in need of some repairs." Lucen flopped on a chair, his face impishly delighted. "Jess can fill you in on that."

SEVENTEEN

IN ORDER TO MAINTAIN THEIR BONDS, EVERY SO OFTEN PREDS
had to feed their addicts, essentially giving them the one thing the bond
forced them to crave above all else. For a goblin, the exchange might be as
simple as a gift from master to addict. For a sylph, it could be a
compliment. For a satyr, it wasn't something that could be exchanged in
public without causing a lot of trouble and possibly traffic accidents. I
hadn't thought much about it before, but this was a disadvantage the
other pred races didn't need to deal with.

Devon wasn't the sort of satyr who allowed his addicts access to his
personal space. But since taking him to Purgatory—which was where he
normally met them—was out of the question for the time being, he had a
problem.

I'd been recruited to solve it. Naturally.

"You truly are my hero." Devon gazed up at me from his sofa, doing his
best to adopt an innocent face that he couldn't quite pull off.

"You mean I'm your dinner."

He trailed a finger along the back of my hand, sending sensual shivers
down my back. "I was trying to put a positive spin on it. You ruined my
club. It's a gift that I'm allowing you to pay off your debt this way."

"Doesn't your insurance policy cover acts of magic?"

That earned me a derisive snort and some choice words about insurance, crooks, and anti-pred discrimination.

I considered his irritation a good sign, and honestly, I wasn't sorry to be hanging around, playing nurse. My head could use a rest after my repeated sessions with Claudius earlier, and Devon had missed an awful lot of news. I was in a good position to fill him in on everything.

Dezzi had left half an hour ago, and Lucen shortly thereafter to restock Devon's kitchen. While Lucen was gone, I'd helped Devon shower and shave, and I'd explained everything he'd missed. Azria had left behind a small bottle of some sort of charm that smelled a lot like the potion Claudius had given me to drink. Whatever it was, between that and my presence, Devon seemed more like his old self. A gaunter, weaker, crankier self, but it was an improvement.

The door opened, and Lucen entered carrying several shopping bags. "Finding basic supplies is getting harder and harder. Half the shelves were empty."

I closed the door behind him, and Lucen emptied the contents on Devon's counter. The news had warned as much about the latest run on food, water, and survival gear. Yesterday's attack in The Feathers wasn't an isolated incident. Over a dozen major cities around the U.S. and in Europe had experienced similar attacks, leading to a whole new level of panic.

"I want steak," Devon called out from the sofa. "And wine. There's a bottle of merlot on the wine rack that—"

Lucen slapped a can of chicken broth on the polished wood dining table where Devon could see it. "Azria said you need soft, easily digestible foods. So do you want broth or eggs?"

Devon winced. "Oh, come on. I thought she was referring to Jess."

Sneering, I snatched the can from Lucen and returned to the kitchen. "He gets the broth."

"Eggs! I want eggs." He muttered a curse then raised his voice. "I want my nurse back too."

Lucen was snickering silently, and he nudged me out of the kitchen. "Go to him. I'm the cook in this relationship."

"Yeah, yeah. And I'm the food. You both suck." Hands on my hips, I returned to Devon's side, but my phone rang before I could sit down. "Finally. Tom."

I'd left him a voicemail on the way to Devon's to let him know about my breakthrough with Claudius and that I was taking a much-needed rest. Given the importance of the news, I'd been expecting to hear back sooner.

"Jessica, this is fantastic," he said in way of greeting. "I didn't doubt you'd be able to channel so much power eventually, but I have to admit I was skeptical of your timeline."

I pushed aside the blinds covering Devon's picture window. Shadowtown and the rest of Boston glittered below in the darkness, but clouds had blown in during the afternoon and a light rain fell. I couldn't find any trace of the moon. "Just doing as the prophecy ordered."

"That's not how prophecies or visions work."

I let the blinds drop back into place, very aware of that fact. The magi's prophecy only hinted that someone like me would be necessary to avert the demons from taking over. It said nothing about whether we'd actually be successful if we tried. "I was kidding."

"Of course, sorry. I'm tired. We're having a busy day on this end too. Are you going to resume your training with Claudius tonight?"

Suppressing a groan, I sank onto the sofa next to Devon. The thought of picking back up where we left off made me weary. "It's only been an hour or so. Mitch needs time to catch up."

"Then we'll have to find additional recruits to help. It's very important that you learn how to control the power in order to take possession of the key."

Right. We'd been over this. The only new information the magi had been able to provide about the Pit's mysterious key was that it had to be charged with power in order to lock the prison. No one could explain exactly what that entailed, but I suspected—as Tom apparently did too—that channeling power was part of it.

It remained to be determined whether part was enough. My stomach revolted at the thought of all the unknowns, and Devon placed a reassuring hand on my leg. At least he was getting to magically chew on my displeasure.

"When will everything be ready to go on your end?" I asked. It wasn't that I wanted to stall, not exactly, but I did legitimately fear wearing myself out by pushing too hard. Not to mention pushing Mitch the same way.

"We can be ready in twenty-four hours," Tom said. "We've gathered almost all the supplies we need. The last crucial pieces are getting the teams together and prepped."

Twenty-four hours. Though I'd known our time was limited and getting shorter, hearing that I could be heading to my death in only a day made the situation so much worse. My heartbeat spiked, genuine fear replacing the anxiety I'd gotten used to living with. Lucen popped his head into the living room, sensing my emotions, and I forced a thin smile.

"I'll coordinate more time with Mitch and Claudius. We'll be as ready as we can be." I hung up and set the phone on the table. "I need some of that wine."

"You just turned several shades paler," Lucen said. "What did Kassin say?"

I swallowed. "I could be en route in a day."

Lucen shook his head. "Not likely. The Gryphons might be ready then, but our people will keep them waiting for recruits. Kassin doesn't realize the negotiating and politics of deciding who goes."

"Are you kidding? We don't have time to waste on power struggles." Power struggles that would most likely be useless anyway.

"And yet you will." Devon fought to sit up. "Once everyone's assembled, each group will want to be in charge, and they'll argue over plans. It'll be two days minimum before anyone deploys."

I retrieved my phone so I could check in with Mitch. "One day, two days. Whatever. It's coming up fast."

"Not a moment too soon," Lucen said from the kitchen. "We have to get moving."

Yeah, we did, but accepting it didn't halt the wave of nausea that came with hearing Lucen say we. I could resign myself to my fate. I could not be so sanguine about him, especially not when we'd gotten Devon back only hours ago.

Against Azria's orders, Lucen opened the wine. Normally, alcohol made me chatty, but I let the men take over the conversation, listening to them talk about the future as if our success at locking the Pit was guaranteed. I played along, not feeling nearly as optimistic as they sounded. I wondered if the two of them had always been good actors or if they genuinely believed we would all survive this ordeal.

In his weakened state, Devon was a total lightweight, and he fell asleep soon after eating. I paced the living room while Lucen made sure Devon had everything he'd need for tomorrow in case he wasn't feeling better.

When Lucen emerged from the bedroom, I was staring at a miniature portrait I'd found tucked in the corner of a bookshelf. The painting was no taller than my thumb and not much wider, and the colors had faded. The hairstyle and dress of the woman in it suggested early eighteen hundreds, possibly older. As it was the only item of Devon's I'd ever seen that wasn't modern, I assumed it had to have major personal value.

I showed it to Lucen. "Do you know who this is?"

"Nope, and don't think I haven't asked. Devon doesn't talk about his past."

I returned the portrait to the shelf with a sardonic laugh. "Gee, sounds familiar."

Lucen wrapped his arms around me from behind. "We've been over your issues with the past. I'm more interested in the future."

"Uh-huh. Speaking of, I don't suppose I can talk you out of a trip to prison with me in the future?" The words fell off my tongue before I could stop them, and I mentally kicked myself for asking after swearing I wouldn't.

"There is no way in hell I'm letting you enter that place without me at your side. We're a team. We're not going to argue about this, are we?"

Touching the pendant slash tracking charm he'd given me, I sighed and settled against him. "No. I've learned my lesson, and I'm resigned to the inevitable. I promised myself I wouldn't ask either. It's just I'm scared of anything happening to you."

Lucen pulled my hair back so he could rest his cheek against mine. "I've noticed, and I can't say I don't worry about the same thing. But I think we need to be—no, we should be—cautiously optimistic here. Look at the progress you've made today."

"Being able to draw on Claudius's power guarantees nothing."

"No, but it's a start." Lucen released me and leaned against the table. "Keep in mind what we're dealing with. These creatures create and feed on fear. They are the original misery-inducing monsters. The more afraid we are, the stronger they become. Simply the unhappier we are, the easier they can get into our heads. Maybe not yours, but the rest of us."

I sucked on my lip, acknowledging his point. It was the same logic I'd used in my struggle with Raj. Fear. Anger. Negativity. I needed to shake these things to fight with a clear head. Even if I could eventually channel whatever badass juju these demons launched at me, there was no reason to give them extra weapons. I wasn't about to become Miss Positivity anytime soon, but if I could let go of the issues that weighed on my soul, it could only help.

If I could be more like Lucen and let go of my past.

Theoretically, it shouldn't be too hard. I'd already faced my biggest issues head-on. I'd accepted I wasn't human. I'd finally achieved my dream of becoming a Gryphon, even if it wasn't how I'd envisioned it. And my darkest secrets had been exposed, and so far the important people in my world hadn't shunned me.

The only issue I hadn't entirely dealt with was standing nearby. But I'd had an epiphany about my relationship with Lucen while I was in Grenoble, hadn't I? I was never going to have anything resembling a normal relationship, but I'd decided I didn't need normal. A craving for normal was just the crutch I'd been using to prevent myself from fully jumping on the crazy train that was my life. Normal was a way to hide my insecurities about who and what I was. In the end, the only thing that mattered was I'd found someone who loved me as much as I loved him and who had my back no matter what. With that at our core, we could make anything work.

As long as I confessed the one point that had been nagging at my conscience for a while.

"Little siren, you lost in your head?" Lucen picked up his keys. "We should get going."

"When I was in the Gryphon archives in France, I went searching for information on how to turn preds back into humans."

Lucen set the keys down. "Okay. You're telling me this now—why?"

I resumed my pacing, hands opening and closing at my sides in agitation. "Because of what you said about letting go of negativity. I needed to get that off my chest so it's not an issue anymore. I mean, it's not an issue anymore anyway, but it felt wrong to not tell you what I'd done."

He took my hands and pulled me onto the sofa with him. "You went looking for a way to make me human."

I nodded, unable to meet his eyes. "It wasn't my best idea, and I'm sorry for wishing I could change you."

To my surprise, Lucen laughed. "You do realize you can't do that."

"What I realize is that I shouldn't want to do that. You're perfect the way you are, and it was selfish of me."

He put a finger over my lips. "Jess, it's not selfish to want something the way you want it. I know this isn't how you planned out your life."

"None of this is how I'd planned out my life, but I've had an easier time accepting the rest. I wanted to change you, not considering what you might want."

"And if you'd found a spell that could do it, would you have used it on me without asking?"

"No! I..." I tried imagining what I would have done. Turning Lucen human without his consent would have been every bit as violating as what Claudius had done to me over the bond. More so really because none of that had been real. But would I have actually broached the idea with Lucen? What if he had said no? I couldn't imagine him saying yes. Then what? "I'm not sure if I'd even have told you. I probably would have let it eat away at me, always wanting what I can't have."

"Which is for me to be human."

I flopped against the cushions. Confessing was supposed to lighten my conscience, but I wasn't feeling better. "Not that specifically. I just want you all to myself. I told you—selfish."

"There are things I wish I could change about you too, little siren. I think this speaks to your favorite word—normal."

I frowned. "What do you want to change about me?"

"To begin? This notion of yours that you can only be happy if we have an idealized relationship that I can't give you."

"But that's the thing—I've accepted it. I don't even want a house with a white picket fence, and two point two kids and a dog, and whatever else I always believed was normal. I'm not normal. I'm ready to embrace not being normal. I love you in spite of those things I don't like and can't change, and at some point, Devon..." I was at a loss as for what to say about him.

Devon certainly did not fit into my idea of a perfect relationship, yet somehow he'd wormed his way into my reality. I couldn't say I loved him. That all-consuming emotion was reserved for Lucen. Yet when I remembered worrying about him never recovering from Raj's curse, I was sickened. When I considered what I'd have risked to try to save him, I couldn't say where I'd have drawn a line. I couldn't give him up.

"That's not normal either," I said pathetically. "I wasn't supposed to form an emotional attachment to him." The plan had been the opposite. Devon was supposed to help me separate sex from emotions.

"No, but is it so horrible to care about other people?" Lucen's expression was as sarcastic as his tone. "I'm the one who's supposed to have a heart of stone here."

I smacked him in the chest. "Go ahead and make fun of me when I'm trying to have a moment of truth."

"I would never make fun of you for having a moment of truth. I'm merely pointing out that I don't understand how your brain works." Lucen reached over and flipped me back onto the sofa, raising himself above me. "Normal is an illusion that makes people miserable. The most important thing is doing what makes you happy. Are you happy?"

"Happy as I can be under the circumstances. Are you?"

"Nothing makes me happier than you being happy for a change. Except maybe knowing two of the people I care about the most also care about each other."

I slid my arms around Lucen, pressing myself tighter against his body. It was amazing how the simple act of holding him could bring me such peace and security when I knew how little of either of those things existed. "So you're not upset with me?"

"For thinking me less than perfect? No. Those of us who aren't perfect are allowed to make mistakes." He brushed my throat with his lips and slipped one hand down my side.

It occurred to me to respond to the insinuation that he was perfect, but his almost perfect fingers gently probed at the gap between my shirt and my jeans, and my interest in trading barbs vanished under his touch. Gasping, I arched my back to give him better access to my body. Desire burned away the last traces of my guilty conscience, and the heat of Lucen's skin spread along my stomach. I raised my head to find his mouth, wishing I could bury myself in him.

The need I'd had to repress for too long had awakened. Though I wanted to savor the moment since I might not have many more, my body urged me to go faster. It was funny how I'd once only thought of Lucen as a creature of lust; we'd had so little time to indulge in it lately. *What's important between us isn't sex*, he'd told me once, and I understood that. After all we'd been through and all that was to come, I could give up his touch if I had to. But oh, how I'd miss it.

I grasped the hem of Lucen's shirt, and a noise startled me. Glancing up, I discovered Devon standing in the doorway, rubbing his tired eyes.

"You are not going to ruin my sofa." He pointed toward the bedroom. "In here with me or somewhere else entirely. Have some pity."

I fell back against the cushions, overcome by a fit of silent laughter. No, this was not what I'd imagined my normal relationship would be like, but there was something hilariously mundane about it anyway.

EIGHTEEN

I JOLTED AWAKE TO THE SOUND OF PRINCE SINGING HE WAS going to party like it was 1999. Disoriented, it took me a couple seconds to figure out I was in Lucen's bed and that the owner of said bed had changed my ringtone yet again after I fell asleep.

Certain the noise had woken him up along with me, I made a point to kick him as I lunged for the phone. "Yeah?"

"Do you always answer your phone with yeah?" It was Mitch's voice on the other end.

Yawning, I checked the clock and was dismayed to discover it was only ten in the morning. "You're not the first person to ask me that. I thought you were Tom. Not many people are cruel enough to call me at this hour."

"The sun's been up for hours."

I forced myself upright, ignoring Lucen's death glare. "I'm on pred time. Weren't you up late working with Claudius?"

"Not that late. What were you doing at that satyr's apartment all night? Hold on, never mind. I'd rather not know."

"For the record, I was nursing a sick friend." Technically, that was true. Lucen shoved me toward the edge of the bed, and I grudgingly got up and went into the hallway. "I assume there's a reason you called before noon."

"Grace is flying back to Chicago today."

This information startled me so that I banged my toe on the edge of the railing. Grace had continued to refuse all training, and it certainly made sense that the Gryphons wouldn't want to put her up in Boston forever. But I'd never considered what would happen to her—or to any one of us—when our mission was over. Assuming we survived.

Still, if we really were going wheels up, as Tom liked to call it, in the next twenty-four to forty-eight hours, Grace might as well go home. She was of no use here and being stuck in Boston probably only increased her misery.

Wincing from the pain, I sat on the top step. "I guess it makes sense. What does this have to do with me?"

"I thought we could do something nice for her. Take her out for lunch or something before her flight."

This time when I winced it had nothing to do with my throbbing toe. "It's a kind gesture, but I think she'd appreciate it more if I didn't come along."

While Mitch had maintained some degree of contact with Grace since she stormed out of our training, my attempts to talk to her had been rebuffed. She'd never answered so much as a single text I'd sent. I wasn't sure if it was because she and Mitch shared a more similar story and had spent more time together than she and I had, or if my involvement with Lucen and the other satyrs had been too much for her to handle. Echoes of my conversation with Lucen last night played through my mind because I suspected it was the latter. I also suspected Grace would not be the first human for whom I was too not normal to accept.

I explained as much to Mitch.

He made a sound that suggested he didn't disagree. "Baby steps. This is why it's important for you to come with us to lunch. She's afraid of magic, including her own, and she was tossed into a shitstorm of it. As a result, she's retreating inward, becoming more set in her fear. This was the wrong way to make her comfortable with magic. She needs a more traditional desensitization approach where she's slowly introduced to the feared object and allowed to see it's not going to harm her."

"Are you going all psychiatric professional on me? I'm not sure I can deal before coffee."

"I may not have the M.D. or Ph.D. after my name, but I have worked with a number of patients who experience phobias, as well as other anxiety issues." Mitch sounded amused. "Magiophobia, fear of magic, is a real issue for some people. So are you in?"

I stretched my legs, mulling it over. I was already awake, and though I was dubious whether my presence would amount to anything besides making Grace uncomfortable, I'd need to go to headquarters eventually. "I'm in."

RATHER THAN BOTHER MY SATYR BODYGUARDS AT SUCH AN early hour, I used a simple disguise charm to change my hair color and stuck a large pair of sunglasses on. It wasn't as good as either using my remaining glamour or being flanked by two badass preds, but it was a whole lot easier, and I didn't consider myself in mortal danger anymore.

Notwithstanding being caught in the wrong place at the wrong time in The Feathers, no one had made any attacks on my life recently. The sylphs might hate me, but they were fretting over bigger issues along with most of the world. And without Raj wanting to pick my bones for magic use, the rest of the furies hadn't shown much interest in me.

If I had reason to fear anything, it was reporters. The Gryphons and I continued to be harassed by journalists, both legitimate and ridiculous. Just yesterday evening I'd learned a major, nationwide morning talk show had called the Boston office's PR person wanting to book me for a segment. When she'd informed me of it, Director Lee's tone had made it clear that her newly positive regard for me was rapidly fading under my notoriety.

Although I'd assured Olivia I had no interest in being gawked at on TV, it appeared TV was determined to pursue me anyway. Stepping into headquarters right before noon, I was dismayed to discover one of the famous faces on that particular morning show standing in a corner of the lobby. The host was surrounded by various young people all dressed in similar attire, all drinking coffee. Interns. I'd come to recognize the type.

Keeping my back to the group, I casually slumped against the farthest wall and sent a panicked get down here text to Mitch. Then I began making a list on my phone while I waited.

On my way over, I'd discovered an email from *Le Confrérie* with news about our departure plans. Devon and Lucen had been right. It was going to be at least another day before we left, and I'd spent the last hour pondering all the things I wanted to take care of before then. You know, just in case the world went on without me. Doing my best to keep Lucen's optimism theory in mind, I didn't think of it as a bucket list but rather a list of useful things to do before taking a long trip. It included stuff like call my mother, have a beer with Steph, finish my newest book, and pack a jacket.

As I typed, I debated the ethics of using my magic on the talk show people to persuade them to go away in case they recognized me and approached. I was coming down on the side of Screw Ethics when someone came up behind me and tapped me on the shoulder.

"Tip from a guy who's done far too many stakeouts," said Andre. "Wearing sunglasses indoors means you're either a giant douchebag or you're hiding from someone."

"I am. Hiding, I mean. Is that Monica Reeves over there?"

Andre glanced over his shoulder toward the blonde woman and her entourage. "Yes, I believe it is, and she's not nearly as hot in real life as she is on screen. Pity."

"That show she's on called here yesterday, trying to get to me."

"Looks like her employer thought sending her here might be more persuasive. Have you considered hiring an agent?"

I lowered my sunglasses so I could appropriately raise an eyebrow at Andre. "Are you serious?"

"Completely. You get someone to handle all the calls and nuisance for you, and they negotiate their cut out of the thousands you get for selling your story. What's to lose?"

I started to say "my anonymity" before realizing that was already lost. Hence my issue. "If I survive the next few days, I'll consider it."

I could sense Andre's anxiety rising over my words, but he had the sense not to offer false cheer. I wondered how much he knew. "Rumor has it you and those foreign Gryphons are going to be heading out soon."

"Tomorrow night, allegedly. You haven't been recruited to go?"

"Nope. One of the guys on the p-squad is going, but no one else from our office to my knowledge."

The p-squad—short for pred squad, which was short for their official name—was the Gryphons' equivalent of a SWAT. They were the men and women who performed the role that the population inaccurately attributed to Gryphons in general—that of kickass warrior.

Most Gryphons were magical detectives like Andre, or they were analysts or charm makers or healers. But the p-squad was the small subset of Gryphons who were the first line of offense when dealing with hostile preds. All Gryphons were trained to fight, but fighting magically and physically superior opponents was the p-squad's primary duty. It made perfect sense that *Le Confrérie de l'Aile's* team would be drawn from their ranks, whether in Boston or abroad.

"I need to take you out for a beer before you leave," Andre said. "If you're not going to sell your life story to the highest bidder, I need to hear more of it. You working late?"

"As usual." The elevator doors opened, and Mitch and Grace stepped into the lobby. Struck by an idea, I turned to Andre. "Want to go to lunch instead? I might not have time tomorrow."

If Mitch's theory was right and Grace needed baby steps to help her become less fearful of magic, I couldn't think of a better person to talk to her than Andre. He was funny, an upstanding Gryphon, and a totally normal human who happened to be magically adept. It probably also didn't hurt that he was attractive.

I filled Andre in on my lunch plans, leaving out the bit about how I considered him the perfect Gryphon spokesperson. He agreed, and the four of us ventured out past the peaceful crowd of demonstrators who clung to the building's front steps like a particularly stubborn imp swarm. Their numbers had dwindled since the attack in The Feathers, but the faithful few continued to hold up their signs. Grace's eyes were drawn to them as we strolled by, and I got the sense that she'd rather forgo our company for theirs. She didn't leave though, and while she kept as far from me as politeness would allow, we ended up seated at a nearby pizza place with less discomfort than I'd anticipated.

Despite needing to steer the conversation away from the topic Andre wanted to discuss, lunch went pretty well. But as I bit into my second slice of pizza, three slightly punk men entered the restaurant and caught my eye. On the surface, their appearance wasn't too unusual. Two of them wore leather jackets that identified them as belonging to a motorcycle club that had been participating in the anti-mager protests. Bright green NO MAGIC buttons stuck to their collars.

At the risk of alarming Grace, I lowered my voice. "See those protesters over there?"

Andre immediately picked up on what I was about to say, and he set down his food, frowning. "Why are fury addicts protesting magic? That doesn't make sense."

"All the more reason they shouldn't trust magic if they're addicts," Grace said.

"Maybe." I was about to let the strangeness of it go, believing my paranoia was getting the best of me after my almost run-in with the media at headquarters. Then one of the addicts nudged his friends.

I couldn't read an addict's emotions, and relying on that ability had made me a lousy judge of body language. But I knew I didn't like that nudge, nor the way the guy appraised me. As if he recognized my face and wasn't merely out for an interview.

Andre, on the other hand, had years of law enforcement experience to hone his people-reading skills. So when the men raised their hands toward their chests in unison, and Andre yelled at us to get down, I didn't hesitate. Feeling my speed charms kick in, I dropped to the floor next to him. My chair went flying out behind me, and my knees smacked into the hard, red-tiled floor as an earsplitting noise tore apart the restaurant.

Another anti-mager attack was my first thought, but I rejected it almost as quickly. That wasn't the sound of a curse grenade, and that stench wasn't magic. It was gunpowder. We were being shot at. What the hell? It took my brain another second to process the situation because it was so unexpected.

Andre shoved our chairs between us and the addicts as flimsy cover. I shifted position in my crouch, trying to push over our table, but it was too heavy. Mitch was yelling something, but the other patrons' screams and the breaking dishes made it too loud to understand him.

The storm of bullets paused, and Andre went charging. Using a chair as a shield, he dove straight into the nearest addict and tackled him to the floor in a blur of motion. Without Andre's back blocking me, I could see clearly at last. The restaurant was in chaos. Everyone had dived for cover by now, and the only faces in sight were those of the two remaining addicts. One was reloading. The other had his gun trained on Andre and was searching for an opening to shoot.

"Forget him," the second addict shouted as he changed clips. "Get those damned Gryphons."

It was ironic since Andre was the only one of us who was a real Gryphon by my estimation, but Andre wasn't in uniform, and we were clearly the targets. Without Raj to want us alive, someone must have put out an order to kill us.

From the corner of my eye, I could see Mitch trying to protect Grace, drawing them both closer to the window. My breaths were ragged, and I could smell blood. I had no curse grenades on me, no weapons except for my knife and a body that was hyped up on charms. No doubt it was those charms that had saved me so far. I called on the one for speed to assist me again, and I followed Andre's example.

Praying for my opening to hold, I burst out from under the table and crashed into the second addict. Before he could fire another shot, we slammed into the floor. Pain roared through my knees, and his gun went flying. I rolled to the side and knocked it farther from his grip. Swearing, the addict threw all his force against me, pushing me into the filthy tiles and pounding my arm. My bones screamed in pain. This guy's fury master was likely feeding him power, but he hadn't decked him out in charms. Thanks to mine and the fear fueling me, we were a fair match in spite of the guy's size.

More crashing noises echoed above, and the promise of distant sirens wailed, but my attention was focused on the single guy grappling with me. I reached for his gun, and he banged my head against the linoleum. I bit down on my tongue, blood filling my mouth. The gun slid farther away.

Mitch yelled my name as I tried worming out from under the addict's grip, and I dodged just before I taking a slash to the face. The addict had snatched a broken plate, and he wielded it above my face like a knife. If I could free a hand, I could grab Misery, but that wasn't happening. The jagged ceramic edge inched closer. Desperate, I aimed my knee at the addict's stomach, but he was suddenly thrown off me.

Gasping for breath, I shot up in time to see Mitch wrangle the addict to the floor. In the confusion following the fighting, a couple of other people had gotten involved. The man of the pair dashed out the door on the heels of the third addict who was fleeing, and the woman with him expertly helped Mitch bind the wrists of the guy who I'd fought. Andre had already subdued the first addict.

Gingerly, I climbed to my feet and wiped away my blood. "Grace!"

She was lying on her side, and the red soaking through her shirt sleeve was most definitely not tomato sauce. I knelt next to her, searching for the source of the bleeding. She was alive but almost catatonic from pain or fear, and she didn't move as I tried to help her.

"He got her arm," Mitch said.

The sirens outside grew louder, and flashing lights were becoming visible down the street. The woman who'd helped Mitch appeared at my side with a bunch of linens that she pressed into Grace's arm to deal with the bleeding.

For the second time this past week, I soon found myself sipping coffee and giving a statement to both the Gryphons and the police. Since the two patrons who'd helped out were off-duty cops, and Andre was already involved for the Gryphons, the process went a bit smoother than The Feathers' incident. Plus, this time we had caught two of the perpetrators alive. Not that there was any great mystery as to their motive.

Grace had been whisked away to the closest hospital, but since neither my injuries nor Mitch's were serious, we were escorted back to headquarters. There was no question of being recognized by the media when we arrived. My disguise charm had been ripped off during the struggle, and thanks to cameras everywhere, the firefight had already hit the news. As we were ushered across the lobby, I heard unfamiliar voices shouting my name. Fortunately, due to security and a seriously on-edge group of Gryphons, no one got near me except Tom.

"This is going to change things." He punched the button for the fourth floor.

I swished coffee around my mouth, still tasting blood. "How so and how's Grace?"

"She's stable. Agent Pagan tells me the speed charms you, Mitch, and he were wearing are probably what enabled you to duck in time. Grace never finished having the glyphs drawn on her before she refused our help." The elevator doors opened, and Tom led the way to a packed conference room. "The addicts who attacked you got their orders from the furies."

"That's not exactly a revelation," Mitch said.

"No," Tom said, "but the point is that someone among the furies knows the three of you pose a significant threat to their plans."

I repressed a swear. Theo must have told the furies about the prophecy before we caught him. While Raj had been alive, we were considered more useful in that state ourselves. But without Raj to argue against killing us, someone had taken the initiative to remove our threat.

"Peachy. So now what?" I took one of the empty chairs along the wall.

There were no preds in the room, only Gryphons and a couple magi. Ingrid turned my way from where she sat at the head of the table. "Now we move up the timetable. We can't risk another attack on you and Mitchell, so we leave for the prison gates immediately."

NINETEEN

SO MUCH FOR MY NOT-REALLY-A-BUCKET-LIST LIST. I'D BEEN
given an hour—an hour!—to pull my belongings together and return to
headquarters. Ingrid had also stated that I couldn't leave without a
disguise and preferably a couple guards, a restriction that would usually
have made me gnash my teeth but which I couldn't really argue about
anymore.

The timing though, that sucked. It wasn't so bad for Mitch, who only
had to grab the suitcase he'd been living out of, but packing aside, I wasn't
ready for this.

"Wait." I chased after Ingrid when the meeting broke up. "What about
the magi and pred volunteers?"

Ingrid kept a brisk pace. She was going along too, and no doubt had
her own preparations to make. "The magi recruits will be meeting us in
France. They are not Americans. As for the preds, we're not waiting. The
local Doms and council members have been informed of the change in
plans. They have had ample opportunity to choose their recruits. If they
want to be a part of this, those people will show up by the deadline.
Otherwise, they can provide people who are local to where we are going,
like the magi."

Well, that was that. I didn't know whether to be relieved that Lucen likely wouldn't be able to leave on such short notice or sad that I'd be without his company. Some part of me had wanted him by my side in spite of the risks. I mentally slapped that part for being so selfish.

Still, I intended to see him before I left. That was one thing that was nonnegotiable.

I paused by my desk to text him that I was stopping by my apartment, but he rang first. "Little siren, do not leave the building. I heard about what happened, and I do not want you stepping foot into Shadowtown. We have people keeping an eye on your apartment, and the furies are waiting for you. I'm bringing your overnight bag to headquarters. It's almost packed."

I dropped to my chair, amused and impressed that he was so far ahead of me. "You'd better have packed me practical underwear this time. I remember what you did the last time you brought me clothes."

"If you're referring to when the Gryphons were staking out your old place during the Victor Aubrey fiasco, I think this situation calls for something sturdier than lace."

Being hunted for a murder I hadn't committed should have called for more than the thongs he'd picked out too, but this wasn't the time get bogged down in butt floss. "Practical is the word of the day. What about you?"

"I'm being very practical and not bothering with superfluous clothing such as underwear."

"So you're coming with?"

Lucen must have stepped outside because the traffic noise in the background got louder. "That was the plan, and that much hasn't changed. I've got your bag packed with your spare clothes from my place, some supplies, and a few presents. I'll be over shortly."

My head was spinning, and my heart was torn between being happy to be with him and disappointed that he wasn't being left behind. The rest of me felt vaguely ill. "Presents?"

"Don't worry about it. Call your mom, call Steph. Do whatever you need to do. I've got the rest. See you soon."

He hung up, and I swallowed and stared into space for a couple minutes until my brain reminded me that was a waste of time. Lucen was right. I was boarding a plane sooner than I'd like so I'd better get on with it. There might be no time for beer, but there sure was for a few phone calls.

I WAS FRETTING OVER LUCEN'S ARRIVAL WHEN I GOT A TEXT that he was downstairs. I'd just gotten off the phone with my mother, and I didn't bother waiting for the elevator, taking the steps at a dangerous speed instead.

The Gryphons were gathering everyone near the interrogation rooms. When I burst into the one Tom pointed at, I discovered Lucen wasn't alone. Devon and Gi were with him. Three small travel bags sat by their feet, one of which was mine.

"You're not all going, are you?" I asked.

Lucen gestured to himself and Gi. "We are. Devon's not well enough yet, and Dezzi was going to go, but she can't leave on such short notice."

"I'm taking her place," Gi said. "I'm still your bodyguard."

"I'm glad to have you." I meant it. Turning to Devon, I added, "Should you be here?"

He shrugged nonchalantly, but behind his unconcerned attitude I could sense a tension in his stance. He looked worlds better than he had yesterday, but his clothes hung off him and his eyes lacked their sparkle. That might have said more about his state of mind, however, than his health. "I had to see you both off."

"Are these the presents you mentioned?" I asked Lucen, referring to Devon and Gi.

"He's one of them." Lucen poked Devon. "The other one is in your bag. It's from Angelia."

"Angelia?" Angelia was a sweet, dangerously sexy satyr who Dezzi had accepted into her domus when Angelia's old Dom had tossed her out for being blinded. She was also the satyrs' reigning drug queen. She made an illegal charm called F, but she was—supposedly—devoted to working on making it safer to use. We'd hung out a couple times, but our friendship was tenuous given my position with the Gryphons.

Surprised and curious, I opened my backpack and found a small charm vial on top of my clothes. The contents were peachy orange and odorless, and I had no idea what it was. Nor, for that matter, why Angelia would give me a gift.

"Angelia called it a kiss," Lucen said, seemingly as perplexed as I was. "She said it's meant to be drunk, and you should save it for when you need one."

"Okay then." If anything, that explanation was more confusing than enlightening, and I tucked the vial deeper into my bag. I didn't expect the Gryphons to search me for illegal charms, and I didn't know if this was actually illegal, but better safe than sorry. Particularly when one of Boston's most wanted satyrs was involved.

Out in the hallway, I could hear Ingrid had arrived and orders were being passed around. It sounded as though we'd be leaving for the airport soon. Devon must have had the same thought because he said his goodbyes to the men, then dragged me with him into a relatively quiet corner in the hallway, away from Lucen and the Gryphons.

It was obvious when he moved how much he still needed to recover. His usual cocky swagger was gone, and I wondered if his health was part of the reason Dezzi had opted to stay in Boston after all. Devon was her backup, and if not Devon, Lucen. Much as she might want to join the fight, she shouldn't leave without one of them being available and at full strength.

He took my hands, pressing me against the wall. "I've already threatened Lucen that if he doesn't bring you back safely, I'm feeding what's left of his prized three-hundred-dollar bottle of scotch to Sweetpea."

I smiled, shaking my head. "He's leaving while there's some of that left?"

"I have it in my custody for safekeeping. So now..." Devon let go of my hand and cupped my cheek, lifting my chin so I was gazing into his eyes. "You remember that outstanding favor you owe me?"

"You mean the thing about how I owe you for destroying Purgatory?"

Devon cringed. "No, but thank you for reminding me of that. I'm talking about the three favors you owed me for spying on you-know-who before our last adventure in France."

You-know-who, aka Claudius, chose that moment to show up, which explained Devon's word choice. Raia had arrived too, along with two of her addict bodyguards, whom I hadn't seen in a while.

I turned away from Claudius's ever-disapproving gaze and recalled the incident Devon was referring to. "I paid off those favors. One that very night, and the other our first night in Grenoble when, if you recall, you were in rather dire straits."

Devon had flown to France without much preparation, including no addicts. As a result, he'd been more wound up with sexual tension than your average teenage boy. In spite of my exhaustion, I'd spent considerable time helping him alleviate his distress that night.

The memory got me wondering—how were Lucen and Gi going to survive this trip without addicts?

"You paid off two of your debts." Devon smiled endearingly. "For your last one, I want you to pay it off by bringing Lucen back alive."

I swallowed, touched by the sweetness of the sentiment and overwhelmed once more by the fear that I could lose Lucen. "You know I'm going to try. I wish he wasn't coming."

Devon rested his forehead against mine. "I do know, and I know there's no way he'd let you go without him. I can't say I wish I was going too, but having to hang back and watch you both risk your lives this way isn't what I'd have chosen."

"I believe it."

"We're heading out in five minutes," one of the Gryphons called.

I tensed, and Devon leaned forward and kissed me. The warmth of his lips soothed my muscles, and I relaxed into him, pulling him closer. *This could be it. This might be the last time...* I shut up the horrible voice by kissing Devon harder, not caring which of the Gryphons saw.

Silently sobbing inside, I watched Devon leave a minute later, still feeling his arms wrapped around me and the final, chaste kiss he'd planted on my cheek. Forcing myself to focus, I returned to Lucen and Gi. Raia and her addicts had joined them, and I noticed the addicts carried three overnight bags. One of them was clearly hers.

Two other addicts, one man and one woman, had gathered with the group as well. The man I recognized as one of Lucen's, and I tried not to dwell on that, going so far as to nod a polite greeting his way. He probably didn't know who I was—and I didn't know his name—but this was our lives. I wasn't going to be a jealous bitch about it. Not anymore.

I assumed the other addict was one of Gi's, and since they both had bags as well, this answered the question that had occurred to me in the hallway. It was Raia's presence that surprised me the most. "I didn't realize you were going."

"I had not planned to," she said, accepting a cup of coffee from one of her men. "But I had anticipated providing you, Mitchell, and the other satyrs with some additional charms before leaving. I will do that on the plane."

"Sounds good." Unlike the addicts, I welcomed more magic.

CONSIDERING THE KIND OF DAY IT HAD BEEN, WE MADE IT TO the airport and across the Atlantic with a shocking lack of drama, particularly given the makeup of our group. Besides the Gryphons and satyrs, Gunthra had come through and supplied us with two fierce-looking goblin warriors. The Gryphons had one of their own jets waiting for us at Logan Airport, and it wasn't quite large enough to comfortably hold everyone, plus the preds' addicts. The task awaiting us, however, was enough to smooth over the weirdest aspects of this alliance.

As promised, Raia added to and enhanced several of my glyphs, as well as Mitch's, Lucen's, Gi's, and any Gryphon who was brave enough to let her help. Otherwise, she refrained from participating in the preparations, which were many. The strategizing that should have taken place before we left was held in the air while the six addicts, who had no clue what was going on, hung out unhappily in the back of the plane. I felt badly for them but didn't know what to suggest to improve their situation, and I didn't have much energy to ponder it since I was bogged down in the planning.

Without enough sleep the night before, I was groggy when we landed in an airport much closer to Grenoble than the one I'd flown into last time. I had a feeling Tom and Ingrid would have pressed on to our final destination if it weren't for a few practical matters that needed tending. We had to wait for the magi to arrive, and the members of World's p-squad to be brought into the loop. While those things happened, I got some sleep at last.

But hardly enough. Before I knew it, I was armed, and our caravan was heading toward the site where the furies had opened the Pit a couple weeks ago. Although neither Raia nor any of the addicts came along, we were a sizable group, and we filled several vehicles with ourselves and supplies.

Since the time I'd been drugged and brought there against my will, the Gryphons had taken over the grounds surrounding the Pit's opening. The house I'd been held at was actually a castle nestled in the Alps and used as a private residence. The closest town was twenty minutes away on narrow, winding roads that were surrounded by countryside. I was assured by the Grenoble-based Gryphons that during the winter, the town was hopping with skiers. But this time of year, the quaint hotels and decorative shops saw fewer tourists.

The castle had been the ideal location for the furies to set up their work—secluded but with easy access to civilization should they need it. A decaying chapel on the old grounds had served as the perfect location for the elaborate spell the furies had needed to cast as well.

Our plan thus far was simple. The Gryphons on site had already been sent the five Vessels of Making, and they'd begun as much of the Pit's relocking spell as could be accomplished ahead of time. Once we arrived, we would attempt one last prep session, then the Gryphons and magi would get to work on the final piece of it. A small group, including me, would then enter the Pit to search for the key. It sounded so simple, but I expected it to be anything but.

Nerves had kept me from sleeping well, and my eyes were closing involuntarily as our cars sped along the quiet roads. At first, I fought sleep, believing I should remain alert, but the battle was futile. I was just drifting off when Mitch whispered my name. Yawning, I stretched my cramped legs and tried to figure out what was going on. Something was definitely up, as evidenced by the Gryphons' rising anxiety.

"Something's going on," Mitch murmured unhelpfully.

We were tucked in the back of a long van, and we strained to see out our respective windows, but the landscape provided no clues. Members of the p-squad shifted uneasily, and I could hear Tom speaking rapidly in a low voice up front.

Lucen and the other preds were stuck in a different vehicle, and I didn't think he was driving, so I shot him a text. *Is something wrong?*

He responded quickly. *Must be, but don't know what.*

I took that to mean being able to see better wouldn't help, so I asked the closest Gryphon and hoped he spoke English. He did but was of no more assistance. Frustrated and growing anxious myself, I settled back and hoped Tom would share the news soon.

I got my wish about ten minutes later. Our caravan slowed as we neared the outskirts of the town and countryside turned to civilization. After a couple turns down the narrow streets, one thing became obvious— the town was deserted or close to it. A few of the buildings we passed had boarded-up windows. The window boxes, which a couple weeks ago had been bursting with colorful flowers, had gone neglected. Other less fortunate buildings had been reduced to burned-out husks. I didn't see a single bicyclist, pedestrian, or other car on the roads until we stopped.

Tom got off the phone, and we followed his lead and climbed out. Not that I'd had any doubts about what I'd seen so far, but standing in the main square at this time of day made it clear how empty the area was. There wasn't a single other soul in sight, although if I stretched out my gift, I could detect a few people who weren't part of our group nearby. Their fear predominated, and I got the sense they were hiding.

Mitch swore and tugged at my sleeve. A mountain ridge rose to the west, and plumes of scarlet smoke drifted above the peaks before disappearing into the blood-colored sky.

"What makes smoke like that?" Mitch asked.

I shook my head and turned to Lucen, who had joined us. He and the other preds shrugged.

Ingrid signaled for everyone to pay attention, and we gathered around the head of the line of parked vehicles. Along with tension, I detected an undercurrent of sadness in her that didn't bode well.

"This past hour," she said, "we received word from the unit stationed at the entrance that something was happening in the Pit."

"What does that mean?" one of the magi asked.

Ingrid clasped her hands together nervously. "We don't know. They seemed to believe something might be emerging. We stopped receiving updates half an hour ago. No one there is responding any longer."

My vision of the town blurred for a moment as I struggled to control my nerves as well as the head rush of the collective spike in fear around me. Steadying myself against the nearest SUV, I took a deep breath. Okay, so one of the demons had emerged. Therefore, I no longer had a reason to worry about that possibility. I simply had to deal with the consequences.

Don't be afraid. Don't feed the demons. I'd been repeating the mantra to myself since Lucen had brought it up, but it had been a lot easier to follow that advice when there was an ocean separating me from the Pit.

"Did the team on site finish their end of the preparations?" I asked.

Ingrid seemed relieved for a question she could answer. "They said they had, but we can't know whether more recent events have caused issues. We need to be prepared for Scenario S when we arrive. I want to review it."

Scenario S—for setup—wasn't so much of a backup plan as it was a few extra steps added to the original. In case the Gryphon team hadn't been able to prepare for our arrival, we'd each been tasked with one or more of the steps they were supposed to have finished. The goal was to get the site ready as quickly as possible if there was trouble.

It sure sounded like there was trouble. As we recited the painstakingly detailed process we each had to implement, a howl echoed off the mountains. A deep, rumbling sort of thunder followed, chilling my blood. It sounded angry, if thunder could be called that. A few seconds later, snow on the highest peak tumbled down the mountain's side, sending a puff of white into the air.

Everyone gaped in the mountain's direction for a second, then Lucen took my hand and we returned to business. We'd finished reviewing not only Scenario S but a variety of plans, and we were heading back to the vehicles when the door of the nearest shop opened and the sound of barking dogs filled the square. A middle-aged man tentatively stepped out, holding the leashes on three large dogs of indeterminate breed.

"Gryphons?" He spoke in French too quickly for me to catch the rest of his words.

Tom and some others had a brief conversation with him, then the man scurried back into the building with his dogs and slammed the door. Exchanging a glance with Lucen, I climbed back into my van.

Tom got in the front passenger's seat, and he twisted around to talk to us as we drove off. "According to the local who spoke to us, there are creatures in the mountains."

"What kind of creatures?" I asked.

"The demons," one of the Gryphons answered in a voice that suggested I was a being a dipshit.

I glared at him because *he* was the dumbass, then I turned my attention back toward Tom. "There are lots of different descriptions of what the original furies looked like."

"Winged," Tom said. "He described the one he saw as looking like a dinosaur or a large dragon."

"Swell." Mitch tapped his fists against his legs.

I grimaced. None of the descriptions I'd read had mentioned dinosaurs as a comparison, but then, no one who had seen one of these creatures firsthand would have known about dinosaurs. And it made sense. Dragons or wyverns were common comparisons in the histories, and I could see how someone could make the connection. The wings though—I'd really been hoping the drawings of demons with wings on them had been mistakes.

"He also said," Tom continued, "that everyone has been acting unnaturally aggressive. Those who hadn't fled have apparently been starting fights and wantonly destroying things. The charms you've all been provided with should help protect you from negative influences, but be prepared and conscious of your emotional states."

"Like that will help if one of them gets in our heads," muttered the same Gryphon who'd made the snide comment earlier.

Ignoring him, I swallowed and retreated inwardly to focus on my tasks.

But the Gryphon's voice niggled at the back of my mind. And just what if one of them did get in my head? Would I be able to handle its power? Triumphing over Claudius no longer seemed like such a victory.

In silence, we bounced along roads that were increasingly poorly maintained. Tree branches and other debris lay scattered along the shoulders and sometimes popped up in the middle of the lane, requiring evasive driving. Once, our caravan paused while several Gryphons had to clear a path. I couldn't shake the sensation that the small tree in the way had been left there purposely. Tucked in the valley, with the mountain's imposing walls on either side, we were juicy targets. Eventually though, the Gryphons got the tree removed, and we were on our way without incident.

The strange noises I'd heard in town continued erratically, frequently raising the hairs on the back of my neck. And was it my imagination, or was it getting dark way too early?

It's just the shadows, I told myself. *Nothing unusual. The mountains cast the entire valley in them, darkening the roads and blackening the trees.*

At last, we turned down the long drive toward the castle. About twenty feet in, the roadblock the Gryphons had set up was in place, and we had to stop a second time for it to be moved. A bright yellow sign with its ominous *Keep Out* was written in English, French, and German.

"Good advice," Mitch whispered to me. "Too bad we can't follow it."

I vaguely remembered that the driveway was long, but it wasn't much comfort as we left the trappings of civilization behind. The grounds around here gave me the creeps. There was too much isolation and too much nature. I was such a city girl. But when the trees seemed to sway with the next howl, I forgave myself for feeling chilled. It was fucking creepy, and that didn't include the very real monsters roaming nearby.

Our van rolled to a stop in the driveway, and we piled out of the vehicles, everyone on alert. Bracing myself, I spun around, searching for signs of danger. The p-squad fanned out over the driveway, securing the immediate area, at the ground level anyway. What good their salamander-forged blades would do against an actual demon remained to be seen. The texts suggested they would work, but they also suggested getting close enough to harm one was a rare feat.

Then again, the people who wrote those texts hadn't had bullets or curse grenades. I knew Tom and the other Gryphons were counting on modern technology to even the battlefield.

Ingrid was on the phone again, trying to contact whomever was supposed to be inside and not having any success based on the sound of things. Meanwhile, the remaining Gryphons and magi were retrieving their magical gear. Fidgety and useless, I joined Lucen and Gi who were conferring quietly by the Gryphon cars that had been here when we arrived.

Without a word, Lucen pointed toward a spot on the ground by the driver's side door of one of them. A partial dirty handprint stuck out against the black paint. Flecks of a reddish-brown substance intermingled with the dirt. As if I needed confirmation it was blood, a quick check of the ground provided it. The driveway consisted mostly of gravel, and more red splotches glared at me from the tan and gray stones.

I swore. "Guess we know why Ingrid's not getting a response."

"Possibly." Lucen stepped onto the grass, following a trampled trail leading toward the enormous stone structure. "I'm sensing someone alive inside, but they could be injured."

"There should be multiple someones." I stretched out with my gift as well, but I wasn't nearly as adept at this sort of thing as he was. The rising fear from all the close-by humans interfered with my ability to sense anyone farther away.

I joined Lucen on the lawn, not thinking about where I was walking until a cold sensation swept over me. My head swam with a vision of this very spot. Of Raj hurling a curse grenade at Lucen and Devon as they raced across the lawn to my rescue. The grenade exploded in black smoke, knocking them both to the ground. I ran toward them, screaming, and tripped on the grass while Raj laughed. They didn't get up. They hadn't gotten up. I was shaking Devon's lifeless body, crying and yelling, and Raj was laughing like a maniac. This was going to be how it ended—with everyone I loved dying. With my heart loaded with grief and my head filled with impotent rage.

"No!" I shrieked out loud, and all at once the vision exploded in my mind. My sight cleared, and I realized I was kneeling on the grass.

Trembling, I climbed to my feet and circled around. My heart was pounding, and I reminded myself over and over that Lucen and Devon had survived. We were here. We were going to put an end to this.

But in the meantime, we were being fucked with. So much was obvious because I wasn't the only one who seemed to have lost her grip on reality.

Lucen raced over and gathered me in his arms. "You okay?"

I nodded, watching Tom and Ingrid confer in low voices. He ran what must have been a sweaty hand through his hair, causing it to stand up in blond spikes.

"You?" I asked Lucen, dragging my gaze away from the jittery Gryphons.

"Not bad." He released me with a grimace. "I just felt this horrible fear come over me."

I laughed unsteadily. "Oh, that's it?" Quickly, I explained what had happened to me.

It wasn't surprising that if the demons were getting into our heads, whether intentionally or not, that it wasn't affecting Lucen or the other preds as strongly as it was the Gryphons, including me. Preds didn't have that emotional effect on each other. But we knew the demons were more powerful and that modern preds weren't immune to their influence. That Lucen had felt anything was our first proof of it. As it turned out, only the magi hadn't noticed anything, although they appeared extra nervous.

A sinister noise reverberated in the forest, and a flock of birds took to the sky. While the Gryphons and magi hurried to gather the rest of their equipment, I showed Tom the blood and the trail. His face was pale but his voice steady as we followed it. Gi found more blood on the lawn, but the trampled grass ended abruptly about ten feet from the building's heavy wood door. The entire lawn was beaten down around here so it was impossible to figure out what had happened.

"It's not important." The concern on Tom's face gave away what a concession it was for him to discount a fellow Gryphon's life as not important. "We need to get inside and get moving."

Wary of what we'd find, the p-squad threw open the main door and we entered the building. The hallway was quiet, unnervingly so when there should have been five or more Gryphons here. Evidence that they had been around and busy was everywhere, but the silence that greeted our voices when we called for them was depressing.

Those in charge of finishing the spell broke off toward the chapel area, and I hung back, waiting to see whether I was needed. Down the hallway, someone banged a piece of equipment on a wall sconce and someone else swore. It wasn't in English, but there was no mistaking the tone, nor that they weren't cursing the sconce. Following the voice, I made my way into a room on the right and then on to the kitchen where I found new blood, and this time, a body to go with it. I turned away before I could see more, but my stomach twisted.

Don't give in to anger. I curled my hands into fists and rushed to Lucen's side for emotional support.

He gave my shoulder a shake, and we headed toward the ruins. "Sounds like whoever was here succeeded in their part before they were attacked."

I let out a small breath. That wasn't much, but it did make our lives easier.

Those in charge of finishing the spell were in the middle of their work. I took a moment to observe the Gryphons and magi kneeling by the various Vessels, then my attention drifted. Whatever they were working on appeared challenging but didn't provide much to see.

The rest of the chapel was far more interesting. The ceiling had been removed, and the jagged walls jutted into the red sky like teeth. Dirt and dying vegetation decorated the perimeter, and something unseen stunk. I was familiar enough with charm ingredients to guess it probably wasn't one of them. More likely a decaying animal. I shuddered and hoped it was a small one. I didn't want to see any additional dead bodies.

Gryphons and magi buzzed about, doing whatever else was required, and the goblins huddled in a corner, checking their weapons. Puzzled by the obvious missing piece, I concentrated on the weirdness of the scene to keep from dwelling on dead Gryphons and flying monsters. When it became clear what I was searching for wasn't going to materialize, I sought out Tom.

"Where's the opening?" The same ruby haze that had been here last time remained, swirling around the floor in a fog. But aside from that, and the elaborate scrollwork of glyphs drawn on the stones, nothing appeared, well, magical. In the ensuing days, I'd expected a door or a gate or something would have made itself known. For the love of dragons, people were reporting flying demons. Didn't the demons have to walk through something to arrive in our realm?

"I think you're looking at it," Tom said.

Mitch gave Tom a bewildered glance. "I don't understand. How do they get here? How do we enter the prison?"

Tom didn't answer directly. Instead, he stepped cautiously into the fog. I held my breath, waiting for something to happen to him. One foot, then two—he paused at the edge and beckoned us over. As soon as I joined him inside the haze, I could see it. A perfectly formed oval hovered in the center of the ankle-high mist. It was devastatingly black and yet somehow bright at the same time, and it played tricks on my eyes. If I squinted, I could see through to the other side of the room. Then a breath later, it was opaque.

"I have to walk through that thing?"

"*We* have to walk through that thing?" Mitch corrected me.

Ingrid called for Tom, and we all left the area. Happily, in my case and presumably in Mitch's as well. Seeing that gate did nothing to help my nerves. Still, I spun around when both my feet touched the normal stone, and sure enough, the opening had vanished. A shiver zigzagged down my spine, too powerful to be mere fear. I assumed magic was building in the air.

"We're almost ready," Ingrid said. To Tom, she added, "Get the entry team gathered and armed."

Squaring my shoulders, I headed over to the corner where Lucen and Gi had gathered with the goblins. Taking my cue from them, I strapped on my remaining weapons. This was it. This was going to happen.

As I double-checked my cache of curse grenades, a dark shadow passed over the room. I jumped, and people murmured. The tingling magical sense I'd detected earlier grew stronger. The shadow passed a second time. In its wake, a powerful rushing noise filled the air and drowned out the shouting.

The anxiety in the room peaked, flooding my mouth with the sour taste of everyone's fear, including my own. Along with Lucen, I slid my longest blade from the sheath on my back, and a breeze lifted the hairs around my face.

I heard someone cry "There!" but the wind picked up, temporarily blinding me as my ponytail whipped my face and dead leaves went flying. Then with a thud and crashing of crumbling stone, the shadow landed atop the far wall. The wind died, and I stared into the red eyes of a demon.

TWENTY

THE DEMON'S EYES GLOWED. GLOWED LIKE SOMETHING I'D never seen before. Lots of furies had red eyes, but as this demon—this thing that had allegedly created the furies—locked my gaze, it became clear that the furies were piss-poor imitations of it.

It wore only scraps of light-colored clothing. Whether that was by choice or because the clothes it had worn before its imprisonment had disintegrated, I couldn't say. The scraps were thin and loose, but they covered the essential bits. Bits that curved and shockingly suggested the demon was female. So few furies were, and the accounts I'd read inevitably referred to the demons as its. Her face, however, was androgynous, at least to my human-ish eyes.

She squatted on the stone edge, wings settling against her back, looking like neither a dinosaur nor a dragon in my opinion. Her dark purple skin, so dark it was almost black, had an iridescent sheen, and it rippled in the fading sunlight. She might have been covered in scales or feathers. I couldn't make out details well enough to say which.

The one thing I could tell was that she was huge. Furies were always big, a trait I assumed was a combination of magic and a propensity on their part to choose tall, burly men to join their ranks. But maybe I'd been wrong, and it was all magic. The purple fiend in front of me had to be close to eight feet tall with limbs that seemed disproportionate to her torso.

"Now what?" Mitch whispered, giving voice to my own question.

We'd reached a kind of temporary stalemate. She stared, and we gawked. Even Lucen, Gi, and the magi were transfixed, as though the demon had us each locked in an epic staring contest. Only she could stare down over a dozen people at once.

The demon cocked her head to the side, and her face turned quizzical. Mannerisms just human enough to be understandable suggested she was studying us. What would her assessment be?

"We need to move," I said in a low voice, trying to break the spell. One of these creatures, possibly this very one, had killed the Gryphons who'd been stationed here. It couldn't be long before she decided to do the same to us.

I started forward, but invisible hands seemed to grasp my body. My skull felt as though it was constricting. Pressure enveloped my brain, and magic unlike any I'd felt before poked at my soul.

When furies did that, they made you angry. When satyrs did it, you were filled with lust. Whatever this creature did, it turned my mind off. I was paralyzed, stricken numb and dumb, and sensing this creature rummaging through my brain. Strange words flittered across my mind. It was speaking to me, but I couldn't understand the language, though the longer it held me in its grasp, the more of those words turned to English. It was ravaging my memories, sucking the knowledge right out of me.

I closed my eyes, willing myself to fight it, to put all that training with Claudius to use. But the demon hadn't actually initiated a bond with me. I had no power to draw on. And it laughed, threw its head back and howled with amusement at our expense.

Miserable Jessica, came a voice as sultry and strange as I'd ever heard. *What a creature you are. A failure at the only thing you ever wanted. A disgrace to your family. A feast to your lovers. A foe to your friends.*

My muscles tensed, pain rippling through my head. My thoughts turned to a memory so old I hadn't thought of it in years—the day the Gryphons had visited my elementary school. Two of them had come, a man and a woman, both regal and powerful in their black-and-gold uniforms. The teachers treated them with respect, almost reverence. That was what I was going to be. That was my calling. I had the gift, inherited from my father.

Flash. I doubled over as if smacked by an invisible hand. I struggled to remain upright, and the air weighed down my limbs. Then my sense of reality vanished once more.

In my head, it was twelve years later. I was on the subway, fleeing from school, clutching the metal rail. I was praying not to puke. The train swayed as it rounded a corner, and I clamped my mouth shut. My gift kept flaring, sending tingles of power from my head down to my fingertips. I could sense things, unnatural things, about the other passengers, and they made no sense. My gift was dying. The Gryphons said any gift that didn't mature by the time the gifted turned eighteen would vanish, and my birthday was in four hours. My face was clenched with misery. I was so stupid. It wasn't as though my life was over, after all. No, just my dreams. Just everything I'd worked and hoped for since I'd been identified as gifted at age six. The words of the three Gryphons at the Academy rang in my ears. Their faces were a practiced mask of sorrow. "While your potential is strong, there's something about it that's not quite right. I'm afraid with these doubts we can't admit you to the Gryphons' apprentice program. We're sorry. Not everyone's gift develops."

A growling noise snapped me back to the present, and I realized it was me. I clasped my hands to my head. My brain rattled with the tremor of the demon's laugher. *Get out, get out. Get out!*

Still, it gave me no threads, no power to snag. This bitch wasn't attempting to enslave me, not yet anyway. But if it could take over my brain so casually, how could I ever hope to defeat it if I did try?

Fuck. I was going to fail at this too. Why should that have been any surprise? When could I possibly ever succeed at something I wanted? I should accept my fate and move on. The universe loved screwing with me. I was a failure—a twenty-eight-year-old ex-waitress who moonlighted as some sort of vigilante; who couldn't bother to overcome her misery cravings to maintain a normal relationship; who loved a guy who could never care the same way in return; who'd spent most of her life lying to her family and friends, and yet pretended to be doing something worthwhile. Pretended her pale imitation of helping humanity was something noble, something other than illegal, immoral shit that was every bit as rotten as what preds did.

I screamed this time, punching the air in lieu of the traitorous thoughts. *Lies! All lies*, I yelled in my head.

Her voice answered back: *You think so?*

She thrust me through time again. The June sun was warm, the breeze off the Charles River cool. My cell phone rang constantly with friends and teachers frantically searching for me, and I ignored it.

"I noticed you last year," Lucen was saying to my eighteen-year-old self. It was the first time we met. A long trench coat protected his skin from the late-afternoon sun; sunglasses covered his unsettlingly lovely eyes. "I'd never seen anyone with so strong a gift be denied entry into the Gryphons, and I was curious why. So I watched you. Once it dawned on me, it was obvious. I came back this year because I knew you'd be denied again. I thought we should talk."

"Ah-ha." My throat was dry. The words came out in a croak. "So you know my name and you know why I'm a failure? Wonderful."

Lucen smiled, and my knees shook. Just that simple gesture could turn me upside down. I'd be toast if he blasted me with his real power. The thought made me ill.

"You're not a failure. Far from it." Lucen wrapped a strand of my hair around his finger. "You're extremely gifted. But, somehow, like us."

I forced out a laugh. This was ridiculous. How bad could my day get? First denial into the Gryphons. Now a satyr who'd decided to toy with me. Probably right before he knocked me on my ass and turned me into a lust addict.

Flash and I was back in the present. *Lucen saved my life, bitch. You're picking at the wrong memories.* I gritted my teeth, hand tightening around the hilt of my sword. *If you're such a badass, get off that wall and prove it.*

A stillness settled over me, and fear and anticipation mingled in my blood with the possibility that the demon would take me up on my taunt. Then she launched another blow to my soul that sent me physically staggering backward.

I sank deeper into my memories, revisiting every last scrap of a pitiful life buried in my subconscious. I gave myself over to visions of my father's funeral, to the presentation of his plaque that hung on Gryphon headquarters' wall. Thank goodness he wasn't alive to see what had become of me. I was watching from afar as Bridget and my other friends jumped and squealed for joy over their graduation from the Academy, how they'd forgotten all about me in their exuberance.

I was every failure who'd walked the Academy's grounds, every addict I was helpless to save, every ghoul lying broken and bruised in the streets. I was pushing Lucen off me in fear, feeling Steph recoil in horror as I told her the truth, hitting Andre with a chair as we succumbed to a powerful curse. I was the cause of Olef's death and the thousands of others who'd perished in the chaos since the Pit opened. I was the key to all misery and suffering everywhere—a freak of nature who never should have been and who deserved to be destroyed for her crimes.

Nausea welled inside me. Tears pricked at my eyes. And anger, oh glorious, burning, raging hatred flooded my bloodstream. This bitch couldn't define me. She was going to die.

Give in to the anger. Let her in and draw on her power.

I had just a second to comprehend that a bond was forming between us, power I could use, when it all went to hell. Spasms wracked my body. Pain, deep and blunt, pounded every nerve as the demon snatched back its power, and my guts felt like they were being ripped from my insides.

I screamed, and the sound brought me to reality. The room was alive with terrified voices. Gryphons writhed on the floor, hands on their heads. Lucen and the other preds were on their knees, seething in agony. Even the magi were hunched over, motionless.

I alone seemed capable of moving, and I raised my blade and charged the wall. The demon took off, spreading her wings and launching herself into the ruins. A popping noise echoed off the walls, and the air pressure lifted with the demon's spell. The cries of misery and fury changed to comprehensible voices. The Gryphons peeled themselves from the stones, and Tom shouted orders. Lucen and Gi appeared at my sides.

"Go, go, go!"

I could hear Tom yelling behind me as the demon swooped closer. Claw-like fingers swiped at my head and raked my hair. I raised the blade, but she was far too fast, and my moves were more self-defense than attack. I stumbled, and Lucen grabbed my arm.

An explosion rocked the area. Gunfire followed. I spun around, searching for the demon, and found the room had dissolved into chaos. Not everyone had snapped out of the demon's mental clutches. Red-eyed Gryphons were fighting goblins and each other. Equipment had toppled over. The demon beat her wings furiously, creating more wind that blew precious materials across the floor and out of the magi's grasp.

"Get in there," Tom yelled at us. "The spell is ready. Go!" He shoved a p-squad member, knocking the woman out of her stupor. She blinked a couple times, her eyes returning to brown, and raced toward me.

I was already standing in the mist, and the oval gate hovered maybe ten feet away. I sheathed my sword and ran toward it, hoping Lucen was on my heels. Above me, the demon screeched. Abandoning the magi, she stormed our way, and the wind from her wings reeked of blood and salt. I darted left then right, but she was too large. Her enormous feet touched down in front of me, blocking my way.

I reached for my knife this time, but she swung a powerful arm and sent me flying. Lucen called my name as I scrambled to my feet. More yelling. More thunder. The ground rumbled beneath my unsteady feet.

"Another one's coming," someone shouted, and I didn't dare look.

Every way I turned, however the angle, the purple demon stood between me and the gate. Her mouth opened wide in what could have been a grin, revealing rows of the pointed teeth furies favored.

My gun, where was my gun with the special bullets? I searched around my belt, but I couldn't grab it in time. Strong hands—Lucen's hands—pushed me down, and he tossed a curse grenade at the demon. The bomb sent gray smoke into the air, but the demon merely flapped her wings a few times and it dissipated.

Lucen had gotten her attention though. Snarling, she took two pounding steps our way. I reached again for my knife, and Gi burst out of nowhere and rammed right into the demon. Although she towered over him, he was no small man himself, and he held a salamander blade in his hand when they collided. Together, they crashed into the floor.

Fear for Gi, for what the demon might do to him, rushed through me.

Then Lucen and Tom were yelling, and I tore my gaze away. This was my opening, and I seized it. Without knowing who was with me and who was lost in the fray, I dashed toward the black gate. Eyes closed, I hurled myself through.

The world around me vanished. Chaos became silence, and the air was sucked from my lungs. I opened my mouth to scream, but no sound emerged. I had no voice. I had no form. Muscles and bone twisted. My guts compressed. I reached out, but my hands had vanished. I was as insubstantial as smoke.

My body reappeared just as suddenly, and painfully to boot. Palms and knees collided with the ground, and my lungs filled with air. Gasping, I lifted my head and found myself in prison.

TWENTY-ONE

Sweat beaded on my skin as I shifted to a defensive crouch, and my hand fell on the hilt of my sword. It was hot in here. Dry too. And curiously empty. Nothing stirred, not even the air.

Cautiously, I let go of the hilt and lowered my arm to my side. The ground beneath my feet wasn't ground at all, but dirt over stone. I traced a finger through the grit, examining more closely what I'd landed on. No, not dirt entirely. Mostly it was sand, and the stones beneath it were rough, unpleasant slabs. I raised my hands to my face and discovered they were bleeding. Great.

Wiping them on my pants, I circled in place. I'd expected to land among a hoard of hungry demons, but this emptiness, while probably better, was eerie. However our ancestors had created this prison, they hadn't done a perfect job. To judge by the scene, the demons had broken free of their shackles long before the Pit's door was opened. The question that remained was: if they hadn't all left yet, where had they gone?

At my back, the doorway that led here was reduced to a thin line that wobbled in midair. My heartbeat slowed to something closer to normal as I stepped away from it. I was still hoping someone friendly might follow me, and I didn't need them landing on me if so. After all, the room I was in was plenty big and hauntingly silent.

If I could even call it a room. From where I stood, the space stretched out in both directions without much variation. The Gryphons and magi had entertained a lot of speculation about what we would find in the Pit, but no one could provide useful answers. The best theory we had was that the prison would resemble whatever its creators had thought it should look like, and that could have been anything. Research about the time period and climate during its creation provided hints, but their usefulness was debatable.

It would appear that some of those hints were correct. The heat, for one. It would have been hot as hell at that latitude during the summer, and likely dry too. If that weather had been on the minds of the humans, magi, and preds who built this place, it stood to reason the prison would reflect it. But magic was malleable, as one of our own magi had reminded us. Just as the prison's creators would influence the initial design, over time the demons would alter it too with their own thoughts and desires. The only thing they couldn't do was alter themselves a door.

I was guessing the room I found myself in, however, was basically untouched. Heavy iron bars and heavier shackles, a low ceiling, and the stench of old sweat and blood all screamed grisly, ancient prison to me. There wasn't a window or a hint of natural light, but then, where would that light have come from? I was standing in a magically created bubble. One lit by millennia-old torches that were equally surreal.

The first sound I'd heard since I arrived—besides my boots scuffing the stones—came from behind. I reached for my blade again, but it quickly became clear that what I was hearing were voices. People shouting at a great distance. I recognized a couple of them and realized I was hearing the fighting back at the castle.

Before I could figure out what that meant, the gateway's thin line swelled into an oval similar to what I'd jumped through. From out of the blackness, Tom appeared. Like I had, he found the floor in an uncontrolled fall, and the bag of supplies he carried dropped from his back. I started to run over to assist, but more people were on his tail. In a heap, they landed nearby, cursing and gasping for breath and rolling out of each other's way.

The doorway snapped back to its original shape as though the newcomers had been stretching it like a rubber band. The sounds from France disappeared.

Relief flooded through me, and I grabbed one of the many stone tables in the middle of the floor for support. Lucen had made it through, along with Mitch and two other Gryphons. Both were part of World's p-squad, but neither had spoken much to me.

"What the...?" The collective comments from the group parroted my initial thoughts in three languages.

Groaning in pain, Mitch pulled himself to his knees. When he saw me, his shoulders sagged with obvious relief. The p-quad duo got to their feet first, hands on their weapons, but they faltered as they also discovered we were alone. On the floor, Tom beckoned me over as he opened his bag.

I started his way then noticed Lucen hadn't moved much. His forehead rested on the stones, his legs pulled under him. His back rose and fell, so he breathed, but he didn't get up. Was the trip through the gate affecting him differently than the rest of us? Ignoring Tom, I rushed to his side and placed a hand on his back.

He stiffened. "Please remove that." His voice was soft and vaguely pained.

I did as asked, my worry changing to confusion. "Are you hurt? What's wrong?"

Lucen didn't answer, and his breathing was loud and jagged. Although Tom called my name, I didn't move. Fear was chilling me in spite of the heat. What if Lucen had landed badly? Had Tom brought any medical supplies in that bag? What about Lucen's protective charms—were they not working in here? We'd known there was a possibility that any charms we carried in might act strangely or not at all.

Wetting my lips, I pushed a strand of stray hair from his cheek, and he grabbed my wrist. Hard. "Jess, I know you're concerned, but I meant it when I said not to touch me. Please."

"Okay, okay." He let go, and I retrieved my hand and sore wrist. Tom was glaring impatiently at me, and I scowled at him. "Just tell me if you're okay."

"Give me a minute."

That wasn't quite the same thing as "I'm fine," but I got the sense that I wasn't getting another answer. Reluctantly, I shuffled over to Tom.

He handed me a generic magic-detecting charm, similar to the ones used around Gryphon headquarters. "The magic in here is definitely interfering. I'm not sure these will be any good. They're too weak."

Indeed, the charms, which turned from green to red in response to magic, were glowing a pale pink already. Nevertheless, I strapped the one I was given around my neck, and Mitch did the same. "Will the main detector work?"

If it didn't, we had a serious problem. With no idea what the key we needed looked like or where it might be hiding, finding it could be impossible.

"It seems to be." Tom played with the dials, each of which controlled a different type of sensitive charm. It was far more powerful than the dinky single charm around my neck, but it required actual skill to use. Tom had described it to me as being like the scanners Gryphons used to detect magical residue in blood, only portable. "I'll need to calibrate so it filters out the background noise."

He wandered away, leaving Mitch and me squatting by the supply bag. Mitch's brow pinched with concern. "This is a creepy-ass place. Is he okay?"

The he in question was clearly Lucen, who was finally moving, though slowly. His hands were clenched into fists at his sides, but he was getting to his feet.

I swallowed. "I don't know."

Lucen shuffled down the length of the dungeon-like room in a controlled, deliberate motion. When he reached an open cell, he swung the door open wider. Ancient hinges creaked, and the bars shuddered. With the cell opened like a dark maw, Lucen rested his forearms along the far wall.

"I'm going to take a look around," Mitch said, climbing to his feet. "Maybe I can find that key before Tom gets his gadget ready."

While Mitch wandered away to explore, I hesitantly approached Lucen. We were all dressed in our best attempt at battle-ready clothing, seeing as we didn't know what to be ready for. For the Gryphons, Mitch and me, it was the sturdy but flexible uniform p-squad members wore into raids—some kind of magically enhanced material, both lightweight yet armored. Lucen hadn't been offered such things by the Gryphons, so he wore clothes similar to what I'd seen other preds wear when they intended to fight—pants and a form-fitting jacket made of soft dragonhide. It offered the same basic protections with the added benefit of being incredibly sexy.

The dark material also made it difficult to assess his body language in the dimly lit cell. "Are you going to tell me what's wrong, or are you going to let me worry?"

He twitched, still facing the wall. "Sorry, little siren. I don't want to worry you. I'm just trying to figure out if I'm going to be useful in here."

Shouting from behind startled me, and I spun around before I could ask why. Holding my breath, I stayed back as Tom ran over to where the other two Gryphons were agitated about something.

"Did you see that?" the woman asked in heavily accented English. "It was a dragon."

The other p-squad member shook his head. "No, it was too long, too low. A snake maybe."

"Oh, I do not like snakes," Mitch said.

"We'd better hope it's just a snake," Lucen muttered. "No telling what we might find."

Whatever it was, it had been too fast for anyone to see where it went. Turning away from the commotion, I started to ask Lucen what was going on again when the answer dawned on me—emotions.

The fear I was sensing from Mitch and the others wasn't having the effect on me I'd have expected. In fact, my magical energy reserves were not as juiced as they should be in general. Locked in here, I was cut off from the usual supply of human negativity, just as the demons had been for thousands of years. Obviously, some hint must have been seeping through the open portal to have roused them, but if so, it wasn't much. And if my magical batteries were running low, no doubt Lucen's were doing the same. Possibly his were worse seeing as we'd never figured out how much negativity I needed to be around to survive.

"You don't have the energy. Shit." I rested my shoulder against the wall next to him.

"It's not the energy. Between the five of you, I'm okay. It's everything else."

I reached for him, and he flinched. Right. For some reason, he didn't want me touching him. Damn it. "I'm not following."

"Going through the portal severed my addict bonds."

"Oh." *Oh.* Thanks to Devon, I very much understood what happened to preds—satyrs in particular—who lost their addicts. No wonder Lucen was keeping his back to the group. Now that I knew to check, I could see a telltale bulge through his dark leather pants. All the lustful magic that he usually dispersed among his addicts was building inside him. "So you have plenty of energy, you're just…"

He winced. "Having a hard time concentrating, and it's only going to get worse."

"I suppose 'think of demon jokes' isn't going to help."

"Talking to you isn't going to help."

I frowned and scooted a few inches down the wall, torn about what to suggest. I had no way to know whether Lucen's bonds would simply reform when he returned to France, and I couldn't imagine he had a clue either. Given what had been going on when we left, trying it could be even more dangerous for him. At least for the moment, no one was attacking us.

We were unlikely to remain that lucky though. It sounded as if Tom had the magic detector ready, and the others were beginning to search the vicinity. I should join them, but that would mean leaving Lucen alone to cope, and I didn't care much for that idea. This room went on and on. If I left his side, eventually we'd be separated, and he'd be vulnerable.

That settled it. There was only one thing to do. I returned to his side and discreetly—I hoped—slipped my hand over that tempting bulge in his pants. He jerked at my touch. "Addict me."

"What? Jess, no."

His tortured expression was painful to see, though I wasn't sure if it was caused by unhappiness at my suggestion or the agony of unfulfilled desire. But I knew which one I felt, and I cupped him harder. In this state, he didn't need to purposely work any power on me to rile me up. I was getting seriously damp between the legs, and it had nothing to do with the temperature.

I pressed myself against him, and he moaned quietly. Unpleasantly aware of the voices down the cell block, I lowered my voice. "I'm serious. You can offload some of your tension on me. It'll help better than sex alone, and I can handle it."

Lucen swore under his breath, and the color rose on his cheeks. "I appreciate the offer, but you alone aren't going to be enough to make this manageable. Besides, it will interfere with your ability to think straight, and we're all relying on you and Mitch if the rest of us lose our minds."

I declined to remind him what had happened to me with the purple-skinned demon, distracted by the hard edges of his body and the potent scent he was giving off. There had to be a zipper on these pants of his. Why the hell couldn't I find the zipper?

My brain had taken a turn for the lascivious, and the damned demons and their key were having a hard time competing for my attention. I wanted to lick the thin sheen of sweat from his throat. Wanted to breathe in his skin and run my tongue over the stubble on his chin. The thought of the Gryphons noticing what was going on didn't bother me half as much as it had a minute ago.

I pressed my face into the crook of his neck and nibbled on his tender skin. Lucen shoved me against the wall, releasing my hand and grabbing my backside. The heat from his erection burned through my clothes. The fabric might be resistant to salamander fire, but it was helpless against satyr flesh. "This is a bad idea," he murmured.

"I told you, I can handle it. Dump what you need to on me. I can channel and release it." I was fairly certain I could anyway. I'd been practicing how to control that sort of thing, and if I could do it with Claudius, I should be able to do it with Lucen.

His mouth slammed into mine, stealing my breath. Our tongues met, and he struggled to take all he could from the kiss. I gave it gladly, desperate for more as a moan rose in my throat. My lips were sore when he let go, but my nerves were scorching. I wasn't sure how I could be so wet when the air was so dry.

"Release is definitely in order." His grip on me tightened, and I closed my eyes in anticipation. "Are you sure about the rest of it?"

"Oh gods, yes." It occurred to me that even if the others were too busy to be aware of what was going on between us, Mitch would certainly be able to sense my lust. But Mitch had succumbed to being Lucen's addict—temporarily—for the greater good as well. Surely, he'd understand that our bad sex timing was all done in the task of saving the world.

Then Lucen freed himself from his pants, and thoughts of Mitch and the fact that I wasn't normally an exhibitionist died in my mind. I dropped to my knees and took him in my lips. As I did, I could sense Lucen's cinnamon magic swirling around me, my mind becoming heavy with the onslaught of his power.

The short burst of panic I'd always felt when Dezzi and Claudius had bonded with me never came. I trusted Lucen completely, wanted him utterly, and welcomed his power. I was so high on him already and so lost in my lust, I barely noticed a difference when the bond took hold. My nerves sizzled, begging to be blown apart by his touch.

But Lucen tensed and tugged my head away. He picked me up and carried me deeper into a rank but dark cell. "Channel it, Jess."

"I will. Soon." I gasped, not thrilled to be wasting my mouth talking, and I clasped my hand around the length of him, craving more contact. "Give me this first."

Backed against the new wall, Lucen fought the complication of dealing with my utility belt so he could unbutton my pants. "This will be temporary. You'll need to focus afterward, or I'm going to break the bond."

I wrapped my arms round his neck, entwining my fingers in his hair. "I know."

Not only was an addict's relief fleeting, it was terribly unsatisfying. I came almost as soon as Lucen thrust into me, and I buried my mouth against his shoulder to keep from crying out. All the erotic energy in me was only weakly satisfied. Lucen couldn't even pull out before I was ready for more.

"Jess?"

Damn it. Why was focusing so difficult? I could do it with Claudius's bond. *But you don't like Claudius,* the voice in my head reminded me. *Maybe it makes a difference.*

Gritting my teeth, I gave Lucen a light shove because touching him certainly wasn't making this easier. Then I pressed my hand to my bare abdomen and imagined I could feel the bond connecting us.

It showed up easily in my mind, pale blue and silky ribbons that sang with power just as they had the time I'd practiced with him. Normally, such a bond showed most of the energy flowing toward Lucen with a scant amount heading my way, but he was already helping me out as much as he was able. We weren't quite at even flow, but it was closer than I'd ever been with anyone else.

I sucked more power in, and the flow faltered in my imagination as more of the ribbons reversed course. My longing grew, but the sweet pain of the unfulfilled lust was muted under the influx of energy. My blood warmed, and I grew lightheaded.

After channeling the immense magic of a pred as strong as Claudius, Lucen's magic scarcely affected me the way it once would have. It was a good thing and indicative that my ability to contain power had grown as planned. But damn if I didn't miss the overwhelming high that I used to get.

Get moving, I told myself. I held my hand out as I'd practiced with Claudius and directed the power out through my fingers. I was careful in my aim and better with my control than I'd once been. The energy passed smoothly through me and struck the dirty floor. Grains of sand and other detritus shuddered with the impact then fell still.

I kept my hand poised for a few more seconds to make sure the channel would hold when I stopped concentrating, then I lowered my arm. My nerves continued to tingle, but that was mostly ignorable. But was it enough?

"Lucen?" I blinked a couple times to refocus my eyes.

He buttoned his pants and exhaled slowly. "You're draining me of energy, but it's not too bad."

"But is it helping?" Realizing I was pants-less myself, I pulled mine up.

"It's muted. I'm better." He paused for a moment. "It's not so much like you're taking the lust away, but you're making it easier for me to ignore it."

I didn't care what I was doing or why. Those were questions for people with a far greater understanding of magic than me. I only cared that he seemed better able to cope. It didn't hurt either that I was feeling more energetic in the process. "Then let's—"

The ground trembled, and I fell into the wall. Lucen lost his balance too, and he tumbled forward, hitting the spot next to me. Outside the cell, I could hear chains rattling and raised voices. The rumbling stopped all at once, and the silence returned.

Warily, I let go of the wall. "Earthquake?"

"In something that's not of earth?"

I had no answer to that and was spared thinking of one because Mitch appeared in the cell opening. Breathing hard, he looked us both up and down, then politely turned away. "You both all right? What did you do?"

Oops. I hadn't finished buttoning my pants before the quake, and I quickly fixed that. My cheeks flushed, making me feel like an idiot since Mitch had to be well aware of what we'd done. "I aimed the power I channeled from Lucen at the ground, but that couldn't have caused it. Could it?"

"You did destroy Purgatory's bar," Lucen said.

"Yeah, but..." I bit my lip. "I've gotten better at control." After we left Devon's apartment that night, I'd practiced with Dezzi and Claudius.

"But we're not in a normal space."

Mitch cast a cautious glance over his shoulder and seemed relieved that I'd finished buttoning up, which made two of us. "It might not have been you at all."

I didn't like that idea any better than the suggestion that my power was acting weirdly in here.

Head held high, as if emergency sex in a demon prison was totally part of the contingency plan, I strolled out of the cell. "I don't suppose you found the key yet."

Mitch retorted with a snort. "Kassin's picked up a promising reading with his gadget, and we're ready to follow."

"Let's do it." I checked to make sure my weapons were where I expected them to be, and the three of us rejoined the others.

The two p-squad members' eyebrows shot up on seeing me. In their magical senses, I appeared as just another lust addict. Tom's expression was more nuanced, but he didn't look happy. Since I was bonded with Lucen, I couldn't sense his emotions at all. That was probably for the best.

"Where are we going?" I asked, continuing to pretend nothing was up.

Tom pointed in the direction opposite of where we'd come from. "It's strongest this way, and stay alert. There's no way to tell what exactly is causing these readings."

"So you could be leading us to the rest of the demons," Mitch said.

"Theoretically not." Tom slung the pack over his shoulders. "These charms won't detect preds. It's the wrong sort of magic, but there could be other things in here."

We started walking with Tom in the lead, and I cast a glance back at the doorway. No one else had made it through. What did that suggest about what was going on the other side? Even if we found the key and Mitch or I figured out how to use it, would it matter? Were the Gryphons and magi able to finish what else needed doing to close the Pit?

These questions made me nervous, and to calm myself, I focused on sensing the magic flowing from Lucen to me. For all my former fear of becoming an addict, there was something weirdly endearing about being attached to him this way. Sharing his power was the ultimate act of trust for both of us.

Soon enough, the unsettling thoughts about what I'd left behind escaped my noticed as I became more curious about my never-changing surroundings. A fine layer of sandy dirt covered every surface, turning the world the same dusty brown. Light was provided by torches along the walls, and their flames flickered and danced unnaturally in the stagnant air. The shadows along the floor and in the cells shimmied with them. More than once, a wild shadow out of the corner of my eye made me gasp as I thought I saw a sign of life. But the strange creature the Gryphons had seen earlier didn't make a reappearance.

Interspersed with the cells and their formidable iron-barred doors were rows upon rows of metal shackles. They hung from heights that varied from shoulder-high to those barely inches off the ground, and a few had been yanked out of the wall with what must have been a frightening show of strength. Of those, some showed rusty patches that, on closer inspection, weren't rust at all but blood splotches peeking out from under the grit.

Both the cell doors and every cuff of every pair of shackles had a chunk missing, a random spot where the metal seemed to have evaporated in a clean line. The first two times I saw it, I thought the missing pieces were an anomaly or a trick of the light. But after finding the same pattern on everything, we stopped to investigate more closely.

Tom ran a thumb over the mysterious edge. "These weren't cut physically. This was a magical alteration. This was when they learned how to change their environment."

"We knew they might," Lucen pointed out. "But I didn't expect there to be so many of them."

I wasn't sure if he was referring to the cells, the shackles, or the missing pieces, but it didn't matter. So many of each suggested far too many demons. Especially if only two had escaped into the real world so far.

Mitch nudged my arm. "Look."

H wasn't pointing at the shackles but straight ahead where the corridor ended in another rough stone wall. An imposing dark wood door hung in the middle.

I shook myself. "That door wasn't there a second ago." Hell, I wasn't entirely sure it was there now. Its color and opacity seemed off, like I was staring at a cheap disguise charm.

"That entire wall wasn't there a second ago," Mitch said.

Tom studied it on his detector. "Well, it's here now, and if my readings are correct, we need to go through it."

Of course we did.

Lucen and the p-squad members took up position around the door, and I withdrew my blade. Tom did the same after attaching the detector to his belt. On his signal, one of the Gryphons flung the door open. I held my breath and waited.

TWENTY-TWO

Nothing happened.

We stood frozen in place, waiting. Any second I expected evil smoke to pour out, or whatever mysterious not-dragon creature the Gryphons had seen, or even a demon itself. With no way to mark the time, the absolute silence dragged on forever. I'd never experienced anything like it. On Earth, there was always some noise.

Finally, when the nothingness continued, we lowered our weapons and relaxed our stances in unison. The p-squad members took the lead, and we entered the next room.

"What the…?" My voice trailed away as I gaped.

The space we stood in resembled a cavern. The low ceilings, dusty walls, and sandy floor were gone, replaced by enormous arches of stone that stretched as high as any cathedral ceiling. The rocky walls glistened with water and shone with a rainbow of colors—blues of every hue, pinks, purples, and greens. The blue, a particularly stunning shade that reminded me of the sky, predominated, giving the whole area a serene glow. Where the light came from was anyone's guess. It was possible the rocks themselves were luminescent. Since the cavern wasn't real anyway, the possibilities were endless.

The air smelled damp. Not musty, but there was something unusual about it. It was a light, almost plantlike scent that was more disturbing than pleasant. With so many signs of wetness around, I expected to hear running or dripping water, but there was none.

"Enough gawking," Tom said. "Be ready."

That was easier said than done. I drew my blade, but my gaze was constantly fixating on my surroundings, and not in the watch-your-back kind of way. Nor was I the only one with an attention problem.

We traipsed along a stone floor that appeared slick and wet to the touch, but actually wasn't. Pools of water, or something resembling it, pockmarked the ground so it was impossible to walk in a straight line. Steam or smoke rose from some of them. In the light, it all had a blue hue. We left the pools alone. Though I was curious to test what the liquid was, I had nothing on me I dared lose if they were filled with some nasty curse instead of water.

"It makes sense, right?" Mitch said under his breath. He, Lucen, and I were bringing up the rear. In the humid air, his voice sounded thin. "The prison was hot and dry and dusty. They'd have been wishing the whole time they were locked in for a cool, wet place."

"Could be." Lucen motioned toward the cave wall. "Check it out."

My neck swiveled in the direction he indicated, but I saw nothing.

Tom shushed us. "We don't know what's in here."

"Living things," Lucen said. "I can see them. Watch the darkest parts of the rocks."

My stomach knotted, and I focused on a dim gap in the stone where wall met ground. I was about to tell Lucen I still couldn't see anything when I breathed sharply. The shadow hadn't moved itself, but something in it seemed to have. The darkest and lightest patch shifted.

Once I'd noticed the first hint of movement, I noticed more. "Shit. They're everywhere."

"But what are they?" Mitch asked. We all looked eerie in the strange light, but Mitch's dark skin looked paler too.

"Whatever they are," Lucen said, "I think it's wise to assume they're not friendly."

Tom's hand hovered near his gun, but he couldn't hold the magic detector and a weapon at the same time. "They either got trapped in here by accident with the demons or the demons created them."

That didn't exactly narrow it down, but I conserved my snark in case I needed it later. "So far, they're not bothering us. Let's keep going."

The p-squad guy laughed mirthlessly. "Famous last—"

One of the shadows shot out from a crevice and charged right at us. It smacked into the Gryphon's ankles, tangling them. With a cry that was cut weirdly short, he toppled over backward and into the pool behind him.

"Peter!" The female Gryphon dropped to her knees to give him a hand, but Lucen grabbed her around the waist before she could reach him.

She screamed and struggled, but Lucen was stronger. "Don't touch what's in those pools. See that? You can't help him."

See what?

I swore. Again, Lucen saw what was happening first. The Gryphon—Peter—had stopped moving. From the looks of it, he'd stopped before he'd even hit the pool. His face was contorted in fear, and his arms were spread like he'd been grappling for balance. He'd been completely paralyzed.

My heart thumped in my throat as I stared helplessly. "Maybe he's alive? We should pull him out. Do we have a rope?"

"He's not alive." Tom's voice was cold with certainty.

"Jess?" Lucen eased his grip around the other Gryphon, who was trembling and looking both sad and terrified at the same time. "Don't move."

"Why?"

"Because there's a basilisk behind you."

I swore under my breath. So this was why Tom was positive the other Gryphon was dead. Basilisks weren't native to the Americas or most of Europe, but I knew enough about magical fauna from my time at the Gryphons' Academy.

I swallowed. "Um? Ideas? Why are you looking at it? Stop looking at it!"

"They can only kill you with direct eye contact." Tom set the magical detector on the ground, his motions slow and deliberate, and retrieved the gun from his holster. "Anything else is a myth. As long as you don't lock its gaze, you're fine."

"How are we fine? Its venom is still deadly if it bites us."

Tom didn't answer in words. His draw was so fast and smooth, I barely saw it. I heard the shot, and the female Gryphon screamed. Both sounds reverberated off the walls and rattled in my blood. Then Lucen's shoulders sagged in relief.

Since nothing bit my ankles, I relaxed my muscles as much as I could under the circumstances. The air in here was cool and damp, but I'd never felt so cold with mortal fear before. I'd never felt so helpless. Lucen laid a comforting hand on me, and the warmth of his touch melted some of my terror. Along with it came the unwanted lust induced by the bond, and I had to concentrate to push the power through me and into the ground.

Turning around, I checked out the snake. It wasn't as big as I expected, no more than two feet long at most. Dark gold and black scales ran down its body, forming a winglike pattern. On its head, more gold scales circled like a crown. Most importantly, blood spilled from between its cloudy eyes. Tom's shot had been perfect.

"Thank you." I wet my lips. "I knew you were a badass before, but that was…"

"One hell of a shot," Lucen finished for me.

Tom smiled grimly. "Don't thank me yet. We've got a lot more of them in here, I'm guessing." He offered a hand to the other Gryphon. "Agent Gomes? Francisca?"

Francisca—I recalled her name as soon as Tom said it—shuddered and snapped back to herself. Taking Tom's hand, she stood. Her eyes had swollen with tears, but she blinked them away, and her face became as stony as the walls. "I'm okay. I prefer knowing what we're dealing with."

In Portuguese, Francisca whispered what I assumed was a prayer or a farewell to the fallen Gryphon. Not being religious myself, I simply and silently thanked him for his help. Then we trudged on.

As the prison had, the cavern seemed to go on forever, but the beauty of this forever was tainted with terror. Every shadow became dangerous to glance at lest a pair of glowing eyes appear in it. Every dip in the rock beneath our feet had become a possible trap. We moved silently with our weapons out. Even Tom had resorted to only sporadically checking the magic detector so he could remain armed. But if the speed of the first basilisk was any indication, we'd be damn lucky to strike another if one decided to attack.

"Up ahead." Francisca's voice was barely audible. She didn't alter the position of her sword but merely nodded to something on our right.

Afraid to glance away from where I was watching one of our flanks, I nonetheless ventured a quick peek. A bright, white light pierced the blue rock several hundred feet ahead, as though a hole had been cut in the cavern's ceiling. Leading up to it, stones rose in a series of twisting steps. A third of the way, the bottom of the cavern dropped out beneath them, creating a narrow, impossible bridge. Beneath it was more darkness.

"I don't like it," Francisca murmured. "Steep and high."

"Better than snakes," Mitch said.

My grip on my sword hilt was sweaty, and I adjusted it, imagining trying to balance with it in my hand as we climbed. Imagining what would happen if another basilisk appeared while we did. "Let's hope we make it there before we worry about falling."

I didn't understand though—not the creepy architecture nor the snakes nor the light—and I wanted to stomp my feet in frustration. This place wasn't making any sense. If the demons were molding it with their own magic, then why the cavern? Why steps that were so deadly? They had to live in here. Wouldn't they have wanted to create something hospitable? Or did they not have much control over the magic?

So many questions, and this was not the time to ponder them. Yet my mind wandered as we inched closer to the light, despite scolding myself to focus. Just because no more basilisks had attacked...

Basilisks... Venom... Suddenly, the blackness beneath the steps swarmed with them. That wasn't nothingness at all—it was a viper pit. Thousands of the creatures had gathered to strike as we approached.

I froze as if already paralyzed, certain I could see their sinewy bodies writhing in the dark. The very air seemed to hum with them too, a sinister buzz, the slippery hiss of scales sliding against scales. Beneath the stairs, the pit pulsed with life.

Lucen grabbed my hand. "We can't go near the steps."

"No. No, we definitely can't."

"The steps are going to collapse anyway," Francisca added. "They're too unsturdy."

"We should go back the way we came." Mitch too had noticed.

But Tom checked the detector. "We need to keep heading that way. You can't leave. We need you." Tom's voice was high-pitched with fear and sharp with his stressed-out twang.

Something's not right. The voice in my head felt distant and foreign, and one of the protective glyphs on my shoulder was heating up. All the protections the Gryphons and satyrs gave me had been active since the demon attack in France, but this one was going particularly wild. Something nearby must have triggered it.

Something's not right. My eyes widened with understanding. It was the panic I heard in Tom's voice that was causing this reaction. The man who'd so confidently shot that basilisk, the Gryphon who'd been so fervently preparing for this day that I'd often called him a zealot—he didn't panic. He might be afraid, but he didn't squeak with terror that we were going to desert him.

And *we* didn't desert.

Calm, I demanded of myself. *The stairs will hold, and once you're up them, the basilisks can't reach you unless you fall. You will not fall. Something is messing with your head.*

As if the something heard my thoughts, which it very well might have, the ground rumbled. I grasped Lucen's hand, my attempt at controlling my fear starting to falter with the recognition of a pattern in the sound. Footsteps. The noise echoed off the cavern walls, making it difficult to tell which direction the creature was coming from.

"Time to run," Lucen said.

I wasn't sure that was such a good idea, but hanging around didn't seem wise either. We took off as a group, five pairs of feet pounding over the rocks, splashing what I hoped was only water up our legs as we ran. Halfway to the bridge, the inky darkness below twisted and deformed. Smoky black trails with red eyes emerged from the depth, slithering over the stones—the basilisks.

"Wait, stop!" My feet faltered, and my lungs cried out in pain. The snakes were going to block the stairs. There was no way we could fight that many. No way we could avoid locking one's gaze.

I yelled again, my eyes transfixed by the teeming, slippery mass, but no one seemed to hear me. Desperate, I reached out to grab Tom's sleeve, and we both went flying. My arm and hip slammed into the ground, and I skidded over rough stone. Francisca screamed. A blinding black fear, surreal and not unlike the writhing basilisk pit, clouded my vision.

I knew then. We hadn't tripped. Something had smacked into Tom.

My sight cleared, but the cold certainty of impending death settled in my blood. I scrambled to my feet, relieved to see Tom doing the same, but not so relieved to hear a deep laugh behind me. At Tom's feet, the magic detector, which had been on his belt, lay smashed against the stones. Broken and useless. Without it, we had no chance to find the key.

What good is it now anyway? We might as well be dead.

Not dead, not yet, answered a new voice in my head, one that definitely wasn't mine. *You are a feast of fear, and I need to eat.*

I spun around, raising my blade. The demon standing before me looked much like a basilisk itself. Though not as tall as the purple one, this demon had a black tail with the same markings as the snakes. Its skin was as deep a gold and clearly scaly, and its eyes were inky. Its smile revealed two fanglike front teeth.

Tom and I hadn't been the only ones who had been knocked over. Lucen alone was standing. On my left, Francisca kneeled on one knee, her sword held in an attack position. Mitch was crouching on his toes, his hands fumbling behind his back, searching for his sword while his eyes never left the demon's face.

"Try not to be afraid," Lucen said, which of course was totally ridiculous advice. The best I could do was try not to let my fear overwhelm me.

"Got any better ideas?" Annoyance crept into my voice.

The demon sensed it and grinned wider. *You're bonded to that satyr, but not an addict. Interesting. What are you?*

I frowned. "Can you hear that?" I asked Lucen and the others.

"I can hear something, a buzzing in my head," Tom said.

Also interesting. I decided to take this conversation public. If I was obviously distracting the demon, maybe someone else could use the opportunity to attack. "I'm the abomination who was sent in here to ruin your plans."

The demon seemed to think that was incredibly funny. It tossed its head back and howled with laughter. Our opening was achieved and, no surprise, it was Tom who grasped it. As fast as he had earlier, he pulled out his gun and fired.

But the demon was no mere snake. It must have sensed Tom's intentions. That serpent tail it had whipped out, lashing Tom around the ankles. His shot went wide. Holding him by the legs, the demon flung him toward the basilisk pit.

I screamed. Francisca screamed. My fear turned to rage, and though both emotions fed the demons, such things no longer mattered to me. Rage didn't freeze me like fear did. I lost track of everyone around me, charging forward with only the thought of hacking the creature's tail off.

My sword came slicing down, but I caught only a tip of the creature's skin. Blood splattered across my face, and I was thrown backward before I could try again. Lucen shouted my name, but all I saw was the glistening rock rising up to meet me. Letting go of my sword, I braced myself for the impact. As I rolled over, I noticed Tom pulling himself to his feet by the edge of the pit. Blood trailed down his cheek, but the snakes next to him didn't attack. They were as motionless as statues.

I understood then, or thought I did. This demon wasn't yet as powerful as the ones who'd escaped. It hadn't fed as well. But somehow it had used the magic in here to create the basilisks, and they were under its control. It was all a way to prod and poke at us. To make us afraid so it—or it and others—could feed.

Yelling and the clattering of metal on stone roused me from my thoughts. Francisca and Lucen were locked in a fight with the demon, wielding their blades expertly. But even paired, the demon's tail and size gave it an advantage. Mitch had held back, and he and Tom both raised their guns, but with Lucen and Francisca fighting for their lives, they couldn't get a clear shot.

"As long as we distract it, it can't control the basilisks," I told them, not bothering to keep my voice low. Stealth was pointless if the demon could hear my thoughts.

Clutching his side, Tom stepped forward. "The detector's broken beyond repair. You're going to be on your own."

"What?"

He pulled his hand away from his side, and I gasped. More blood drenched his skin and uniform. A lot of blood. Too much blood. "I hit a rock when I landed. A sharp one. I'm not going farther. But you and Mitch —you need to finish this, so go."

"But—"

"Jess!" Lucen's voice shattered my stupor.

I turned in time to see him get off a shot right at the demon's side. That damn tail swiped him, and he crashed into the ground, but the demon screamed in fury. Francisca's voice joined it, and she ran straight at it with her blade, driving it deep into the demon's left side. A scaly arm swept around, flinging her backward, and her head slammed into the rock.

Tom fired. Mitch fired. Their shots hit their marks or close enough, but the demon was too large. It wasn't bleeding out fast enough to give up the fight, and it charged our way. I raised my blade, but Tom shoved me toward the bridge.

"Go!" he shouted again. "While you can. Let me handle this, and you do the rest."

I couldn't argue against the intensity in his eyes. Overzealous though he might have been at times, Tom had never doubted nor wavered in our mission. He would sacrifice himself to see what needed doing was finished. So, sick to my stomach, I left him and ran. If I didn't make the most of this opening, everyone was dying in vain.

I tripped on the first step because I glanced over my shoulder for Lucen, and my knee slammed into rock. Sharp, throbbing pain shot up my leg. Tom was yelling at Lucen, waving him away.

"Come on," I heard Mitch yell.

Clenching my jaw, I took off up the stairs. Footsteps pounded after me, not one set but two. Through the bond, I sensed Lucen was close by and unhappy. I couldn't think about him though, nor about Tom fighting with the demon below. I could tell he was still alive because he fired twice more, but I didn't dare look. The steps were sturdier than they appeared, but their heights and depth were uneven. If I didn't watch where I placed my feet, I'd tumble again.

I almost did anyway. The demon let out a laugh, and the entire cavern trembled. The bridge wobbled. *You think you can lock us back in here? You think you're stronger? You're so weak, so vulnerable.*

Your insults are pathetic, I told it. *A quality villain would have some better one-liners.* But it was getting under my skin, regardless. The repeated taunts didn't faze me. Its magic, however, was strengthening. When it spoke in my head, I could sense it, and I could feel the fear building once more in my blood.

We were so close now. But to what? The bright light poured in from a crevice in the rock, and I couldn't see beyond it. Fear nibbled at my mind, assuring me what was on the other side could be even worse, but I did my best to push it down. Whatever was there, it wasn't this thing behind me. That was what counted.

The bridge shook again, and the thunderous boom of the demon's footsteps echoed in my ears. I grabbed the wall for balance, hoping Mitch and Lucen could do the same. Loose stones scattered and fell into the darkness below. Then I squeezed through the crack and into the light.

TWENTY-THREE

AFTER THE DIM CAVERN, THE HARSH LIGHT MADE MY EYES tear. I stumbled a few steps forward, and my legs sloughed through some sort of fine powder that came halfway up my shins. Shielding my gaze with my free arm, I squinted at the silky, white dust.

It couldn't be.

A gust of wind almost bowled me over, and I staggered to stay upright. Hair flew into my mouth, and powder peppered my cheeks. It wasn't cold. Nor was it wet.

"Why is there snow in here?" Mitch yelled to be heard over the whistling wind.

"I don't think it is snow."

Lucen reached down and cupped a handful. It slipped through his fingers like sand but dispersed in the breeze, far too lightly. "It would be good for skiing if it were snow. It's not sand either though."

My eyes were adjusting, and I wiped the bits of whatever it was off my face. "It's more like a bad imitation of snow."

"Snow as imagined by creatures who never experienced it firsthand, perhaps." Lucen tucked his gun in his holster, gazing into the distance.

I couldn't be too upset over the lousy-imitation part. Given the landscape in here, it should have been freezing, and yet the temperature wasn't much colder than it had been in the cavern. The juxtaposition was mildly unsettling, but after what I'd just been through, unsettling was easy to ignore. Hell, anything that didn't scream *extremely poisonous snakes* wasn't worth my time. I worried worse things than strong winds waited for us, and I had no idea where to begin to search for the key.

Since there seemed to be only one way to go, however, I started the tiresome job of trudging through the non-snow. High cliff walls rose on either side of us, even taller than the walls in the cavern had been. They weren't blue, but dark rock that gleamed like polished obsidian.

Please don't let there be salamanders in here. The rest of our supplies, including nets, had been lost in the cavern. I should have grabbed the bag, but when Tom yelled at me to leave, I'd been too distraught to think things through so well. It hadn't seemed like it at the time, but I supposed my inability to keep my head on straight was an indication of panic.

I had to stop panicking. Stop feeding my enemies.

The sky was a deep, blood red. As we had in the cavern, we hiked on and on. Exhaustion, both mental and physical, ate away at me. Although I was attached to Lucen and drawing energy from him, he didn't have much to feed on either. We were down half our team, and it occurred to me that using Lucen's power might be draining him too much. I hoped the fact that he hadn't asked me to stop meant he was okay and that any drop in his energy by being bonded with me was better than the distraction of too much lust magic.

After a while it became clear that our surroundings were changing. We'd walked straight because we had no choice, but now the cliff walls were farther apart. Each time the wind gusted, blinding us with white, features moved. New cliffs and mountains would seem to spring from the not-snow. Behind us was no longer an open trail but a maze of rock formations. How were we ever going to find our way out of here?

It was a stupid question when I had no clue where the key was.

I lifted the weak magic-detecting charm from under my shirt and checked it again, but it still glowed irksomely pink. Maybe it was a shade or two darker than before, but I couldn't be certain. The red sky could be enhancing the color or a thousand other possibilities could be affecting it. I should have just been thankful nothing had attacked us yet.

Mitch glanced at his own charm, then at me, and we both shrugged. This was beyond pointless. The longer we traipsed on, the more convinced I became that we were on a fool's mission. We'd never find the key, never find our way out, and were doomed to slowly die an agonizing death of dehydration. That was, assuming exhaustion or something evil didn't get to us first.

Fuck it. I should give up. The two words repeated in my head with every painful footstep. Why did I care about saving the world anyway? What nice things had the world ever given me?

Exactly, whispered a cruel voice. *Why sacrifice yourself for the people who'd hate you? They deserve everything coming to them. You could even say they brought this on themselves.*

Not all of them. Not my family, not Steph, not Devon, not... Why was I arguing with myself? I didn't have the energy for this.

Because it wasn't myself I was arguing with. With a silent scream, I recognized that first voice as other. Another demon had crawled into my head.

The scream climbed up my throat and burst through my lips. As it did, the wind roared. I hunkered down and covered my head, and my cry lifted on the air current and was carried away. Lucen was yelling too, and so was Mitch, but their voices were distant. The wind continued to beat me with the powder, sharp grains stinging my face and hands. I couldn't open my eyes.

I was resigned to die this way when the wind calmed, and cautiously, I uncovered my head. The white stuff clung to my face, weighing down my eyelids. Freaked out, I rubbed it away and blinked as I observed my surroundings. The cliffs had shifted again. The powder had blown against the sides, leaving smooth black stone beneath my feet. Once more I was bound on both sides by high walls.

And I was alone.

"Lucen! Mitch!" I yelled my voice hoarse, and my echoes were deafening.

"Jess!" One, then both of them, returned my cries, but I was no closer to identifying where they were or getting to them. It sounded as though they'd been trapped, each on one side of the cliffs.

Wetting my lips, I yanked my sword from the sheath. Sure, getting angry was playing into the demons' games, but I was sick of being toyed with. "You want to mess with my head? You want to feed on me? You can at least have the guts to show your ugly face while you do it."

A feeling like tentacles probed my brain, and I got the sense whatever was doing it was amused by my outburst. *Asshole. Probe this.*

I closed my eyes and sought out the invisible source of the sensation. Magic was in there—in my head—somewhere. If only one of these bastards would try harder and give me some power to grab on to, maybe I'd finally get somewhere.

Then the feeling stopped, and the magic retreated. "Scared, are you?" I doubted it, but I could taunt them too.

No response came, but out of the misty white in the distance, shapes began materializing. Dark blobs initially, they grew and took on humanoid form. I brushed more powder from my eyes with one hand and pushed hair out of my face. Adopting a defensive stance, I waited.

The forms continued to darken. Shadows became substantial, and hints of color began to appear. Painfully slowly, the shapes emerged from the mist. Shadow became flesh. And as I struggled to make out what they were, their faces came into focus.

My arms fell in disbelief, and my blade clattered against the stone. I was going to retch, I was positive. Or I would have if I could breathe, but my breaths stuck to my lungs. Hundreds of figures were materializing and shuffling forward, the ones farthest in the back just faceless shadows still. But it was the figure in front, leading the mob, that horrified me the most.

It was Tom.

I took a step backward, trying to reconcile what my eyes were seeing with what my brain knew. He limped with each step, and even from this distance I could tell the side of his uniform was drenched with blood. More blood had splattered across his face, and one side of his head...

My stomach rebelled, and I clamped my lips shut tightly. One side of Tom's head appeared dented, as though something had crushed it. More blood, dark red and thick, stained his blond hair. But his eyes were open and staring right at me.

No. No, no. NO!

I took another step away, and Tom stopped. More figures congregated around him. Most didn't look as horrible as he did. They were simply strangers, though all bore the marks of various injuries. A boy with a missing arm. An older woman with a dirt-streaked face and bloody hair. A man with a ghastly green tint to his skin. Something about all of them was familiar, yet none of them had recognizable faces. And they all had the same dead expression in their eyes, the same clumsiness to their movements. A desperation and emptiness that I'd seen many times before.

They were ghouls. Every one of them, including Tom.

How they were here was another question, but stories of half-dead ghouls propelled to obey a pred's whims were well known. They were the sorts of stories you told around a campfire, stories meant to frighten. They weren't taken seriously except in studies of folklore and legend.

Preds could feed power to injured or dying addicts, sometimes enough power to keep them alive beyond what they could have survived on their own. But not this much. Not enough to overcome the injuries Tom appeared to have sustained. Preds didn't have that much power.

But I wasn't dealing with preds, was I? I was dealing with their far scarier, more powerful ancestors. Where they were getting the energy from, I didn't know. I was way out my depth, and I could only fall back on the bits of magic that made sense to me. One of those bits told me that somewhere buried inside that brain, some part of Tom existed.

I swallowed. "Tom? Tom, can you hear me?"

Tom cocked his head from side to side, but his face showed no recognition. His expression didn't even change at hearing his name.

I tried again, taking a cautious step closer and searching for a spark of life inside his pale blue eyes. Instead of showing one, Tom raised his knife and pointed the blade at me.

Dragon shit on toast. That couldn't be good.

The ghouls surrounding him lurched forward en masse. I held up my sword to block my body, but it was no shield. Cold fear spread throughout my limbs. Though I tried to fight it, the sight of hundreds of demon-controlled ghouls closing in was too much for my logical brain to handle. The fact that some of those ghouls looked more like corpses than living beings didn't help.

I hazarded a glance over my shoulder and discovered the cliff walls had moved again. I'd been blocked in on three sides. Fewer than twenty steps remained between me and the rock face, and the ghouls crept forward with frightening purpose.

"That's enough!" I yelled to the missing demons that were controlling them. I swung my sword around, grateful the closest ghouls were too far away to be hit. "I asked for you to show yourselves. Not for you to enslave a bunch of ghouls. Leave Tom alone and face me."

Predictably, I got no answer, and still the mass of people closed in. The back of my heel hit rock. I had nowhere left to go. Hands shaking, I held my sword in front of me and swung it in a light arc, but it didn't deter anyone—neither ghoul nor demon puppet master.

Worried that I was going to kill someone, I steadied my arm and stopped moving the sword, though I continued to hold it out, poised in front of me. The ghouls paused when I did, and I let out the smallest of breaths. Then the swarm parted down the center, and Tom inched toward me. He was flanked on either side by Peter and Francisca, neither of whom was in better condition.

"Tom?" My hand wavered. "Are you in there?"

My heart nagged me to lower the sword before Tom or any other innocents got hurt, but the rest of me screamed no. I was having a hard time breathing, and I feared if I lowered my blade, the crush of people would drown me.

"Tom, stop."

He was right in front of me. In front of the blade tip.

"Tom!"

I tried to move, to drop my arm before it was too late, but I couldn't. Tom walked right into the blade, and it pierced his chest with a creepy ease. Frozen in horror, I watched him take another step, driving the steel deeper into his body. He grinned as blood dribbled from his mouth.

The awful sight of it broke my stupor. Hurling a curse to the wind, I withdrew the blade from his torso, but before I could lower it, the mob was on the move once more. A hand grasped me from behind. Then two hands. Then four. Knobby fingers dug into my back and my legs. Hair ripped from my scalp. When I yelled, foul fingers were stuffed into my mouth, pulling my jaw open farther.

A cry burst through me, and though I hated myself for it, I swung out with the blade, hacking whatever was nearest to me. Clothing, flesh, and bone parted like wet clay against the steel's edge. I swung and I sliced in a wild, unthinking daze. Body after body, arms and legs and anything that dared invade my personal space fell to my sword.

The taste of ghoul fingers lingered on my tongue, and I gagged. Blood clouded my vision. I could feel it dotting my skin, and my lungs begged for fresher air. Yet the ghouls continued to come until the powder-covered rock ran with red. Someone was screaming, and it sounded like me, but I wasn't aware of making noise. I was as mindless and relentless as the ghouls.

Laughter rang in my head, deep and decidedly feminine. I cringed through it but couldn't stop. Tears pricked at my eyes. Fingers, gray and smoky, seemed to wrap around my chest.

My arms were exhausted. I'd cut a wide swath through the teeming crowd, and bodies had piled up on all sides of me. Severed legs dripping blood, torsos gashed and raw—I stood in the center of a graveyard of ghouls and carnage. It was nauseating, but not yet over. New ones plowed ahead, trampling the bodies of the dead without care. I could hear the squish of their soles as they stepped on muscles and organs.

I covered my mouth with a gore-coated hand, tasting vomit. "Haven't you had enough fun? Are you still too scared of me to show yourselves?"

The ghouls marched on, splashing puddles of blood and occasionally losing balance and falling atop the dead and dying. But that's what they got for wearing three-inch heels.

Oh, gods. I dropped my sword and sank to my knees as I gazed into the face of the one that fell. A soulless Steph looked back at me. Her arms waved to the side as she made futile attempts to stand. But how could that be? Her being here was impossible.

I spit out blood and took a good look at the newest round of bodies heading my way. The shock and horror of seeing Steph had rattled me, but now confusion crept into my head. It wasn't just Steph. I saw Bridget and Andre, Mitch and Grace. I saw my mother and my stepbrothers. There were more Gryphons who I didn't know as well, and Steph's cousins who I knew only a little better.

But they couldn't be here. None of these people could be here. I was being screwed with again, and if these people weren't here, then this was a lie. This was all some sort of magic.

I squeezed my eyes shut then opened them, trying to peer through the spell. For a second I thought I had it, everything flickered, then the moment was gone. And the ghouls inched in.

Andre's hand covered my face, and I cried out. More probing, more groping and clawing followed. Fingernails scraped my scalp, and powerful hands shoved me into the slick ground.

In spite of myself, I punched the nearest body. Andre's hand released my face as he fell off, and I struggled against the others. Scrambling to my feet, I searched my pockets for something—anything—to help me break this spell. Even a general anti-magic curse grenade was worth trying.

I found Angelia's vial instead. I'd transferred it to my pocket before we left this morning, unsure why other than that I didn't want to leave it lying around where the Gryphons could find it if I didn't come back.

For when you need a kiss, she'd said.

I didn't need a kiss. I needed a curse-breaker, but the liquid inside was drinkable. And right now, liquid of unknown taste was better than the taste of blood and skin in my mouth. As I continued to back away from the approaching ghouls, I tipped the vial back and drank.

Sweet magic broke over my tongue, filling me with the hyacinth-scent of Angelia's pheromones. My eyes closed in ecstasy, and warmth chased away my chill. My lips tingled as though brushed with the softest yet most seductive of touches, kisses that sent waves of fire down my body. The sensation passed languidly, leaving me with my lips parted for more, my nipples hard and aching.

In the moment, I forgot everything going on around me. I felt no fear and harbored no rage, only bliss. My mind was calm. But as the magic passed through, I became aware of the second presence in my head. And it was definitely not blissful but pissed off that I'd managed to ignore it, if only for a few seconds. It stood out against my peaceful state, an ugly splotch in my mind's eye.

I could see it. I could grab it. And if I could keep it like this, compartmentalized from myself, I had a chance.

I opened my eyes, and the horrific scene before me faded away. The stacks of dismembered bodies, the streams of blood, the army of ghouls who shambled toward me—they turned to ghosts then vanished. So did the fake snow, leaving me in the center of a bowl. The obsidian-black walls towered over me, smooth as glass. I was trapped, but at least the illusion was gone.

Wondering what was coming next, I examined the flawless walls. They were too perfect now to resemble rock. I circled in place, and when I finished my turn, I found I wasn't alone anymore.

TWENTY-FOUR

A NEW DEMON FACED ME, AND I RAISED AN EYEBROW BECAUSE she clearly wasn't like the others. Though she was tall, she was closer in height to a human and shaped like one too. She had no wings, no tail, no horns or claws. Her skin was a silvery white, and her facial features were alarmingly normal. A single black cloth was wrapped around her a bit like a toga, though the fabric was in appalling condition. She could have been called beautiful if not for her eyes, which were a pupil-less crimson that mirrored the color of the sky.

Under the lingering effect of Angelia's kiss, my heart was warm with courage. But when I opened my mouth to challenge this newcomer, invisible hands squeezed my skull. Gritting my teeth, I doubled over. Images flitted through my mind so quickly they were impossible to grasp, but the experience left no doubt that she was flipping through my memories like they were pages of a book. Then the hands released me.

I straightened, but she wasn't gone. Oh, no. I could detect this bitch inside my head still, a pressure under my skull.

"So you are the one who the magi prophesized could save humanity." The demon's voice was rich with an unfamiliar accent, but the voice didn't actually match her words. I got the sense she was saying one thing, and my brain was interpreting it as something else. The effect was similar to watching a dubbed movie, only dubbed movies didn't give the viewer headaches with each mismatched word.

Ignoring the disconcerting experience, I squared my shoulders, trying and probably failing to look capable of being the kickass warrior of prophecy. "I'm one of them."

"No, you are *the* one. The other like you is necessary, but he is not the one the magi saw in their visions."

"How do you know that?"

The demon's lip curled. "Because, ignorant girl, you saw it. A description of you was recorded at various times by the magi. You read the description, only you did not understand the language. Nonetheless, I do, and I have plucked the image of the words from your head."

I guess I'd been told. And didn't that just up the creepy factor a few thousand notches. She knew more about what I'd done than I did.

"Your modern expressions are very odd."

I startled. Now she was reading my thoughts too? Peachy. "I think you'll find a lot is odd about the modern world. Wouldn't you rather stay tucked in here where it's cozy and familiar?"

"Your world is our world. My people's rightful place is to rule over you as I rule over them, their queen. You are weak, and we are not. That is how life is."

"You know, that whole might-makes-right thing went out of fashion ages ago." In theory anyway, and I didn't enjoy the occasional reminders that we hadn't dumped it in history's trash bin. Still, if that was the philosophy this creature wanted to base our relationship on, then it was time to show her what might looked like these days.

My hand reached for my gun, but I got no farther than to brush the edge of my holster. A searing pain hit right behind my eyes. I froze, paralyzed with agony.

"You think I can be challenged so easily? You are no match for me, Jessica Moore. But you have a strong will, I will grant you that. I could use some human servants in the days to come. Swear your fealty, abandon your failed quest, and perhaps I will let you live."

The pressure in my head eased slightly, but the demon's magic clouded my thoughts. The last remnants of Angelia's kiss withered and died. *More,* my gift screamed at me. *Make her give you more.*

I ignored the subconscious advice, fearing the demon queen would sense my intentions. Instead, I focused on my fear, a very real terror that I wouldn't be able to defeat her. She sensed it, or her magic reacted to it naturally. Either way, I could feel her power feeding it and my heartbeat increasing. It amused her to see me cower, and that, in turn, stoked my anger.

The demon laughed, sounding delighted. "Would you like to try?"

Icy fear trickled down my spine. With absolute certainty, I could tell she knew I'd been thinking about channeling her power. But of course she did. She'd picked through my memories. She would have seen everything.

Out of ideas, I played ignorant anyway. Although whether playing was the correct word was debatable. I must have been truly foolish to think I could deceive someone who could so easily rifle through my mind. "Try what?"

"Oh, Jessica, you don't give up, do you. It's endearing, and yet tiresome and annoying."

My hands curled into fists. Fear was turning to helpless rage, and her power was forcing me to my knees. I resisted with what strength I had left, but my muscles shook, and my joints bent against my will. "Bite me, Queen Bitch. If you think I'm annoying now, just wait. I'd make a terrible slave."

"It is Beht, insolent girl."

Breathing hard through the pain, I managed to look up at her. "Bet what?"

"Beht, Silver Queen of the Night, Mother of Gods. You will address me properly if you want to live."

This time I laughed, though I cringed in pain as I did. "Beht, keeper of the world's largest ego? How about I just call you Behty for short?"

Apparently Behty didn't appreciate my sense of humor. Her pressure on me increased, finally forcing my knees to collapse and pushing me to the ground. I flailed and barely smacked the stones with my palms in time to save my chin. My already bruised knees throbbed with pain.

"I will teach you respect," Beht said. "You think you are strong enough to stand up to me and steal my magic? I will make a lesson of your people's champion. You will be my slave, and they will watch you serve me."

Try me, I thought at her.

But Behty was no fool. She'd gleaned enough about me to understand what I was capable of, and she hurled so much power my way that I couldn't withstand the blast. Shrieking in agony, I collapsed the rest of the way to the ground.

I thought I'd hurt when I'd drawn on Claudius's power the first time, but that was nothing compared to this. And unlike Claudius, when I blacked out from the pain, Beht didn't release me. She used her magic instead to drag me kicking and screaming—quite literally—back into consciousness.

I knew what I had to do. I had to channel her power, push it out of me, but I was in too much agony to focus. How was she sending me this much power and still standing? Where was it coming from after she'd been cut off from humanity for so long?

"It comes from six billion of your miserable souls," Beht replied, reading my mind. "Do you think my people fed first? I am their queen, and they've seen to my needs before their own. Save for the few envoys I've sent ahead to greet you, my people lie in wait. And now that I am strong, I will see they are cared for next. Then we will meet you, a thousand strong in number, and your billions will learn their place with you as my servant."

A thousand? I wanted to curl into a ball and weep, but I thrashed as spasms wracked my body. My muscles felt as beyond my control as my gift.

"Yield," Beht demanded. "Acknowledge that you can't defeat me, and I will stop tormenting you."

I don't yield. So said my brain, but my mouth overrode the words. Intentions didn't suffer from unbearable pain, after all, and so they didn't have the sense of self-preservation that the rest of me did. "Fine! I admit it. I can't channel all your power."

Immediately, the pain relented. My head cleared, and I ground my teeth in rage and frustration over my failure. On my hands and knees, I bent lower until my forehead touched the ground. A single, invisible hand rested on my back, holding me into this facsimile of a grovel.

Through the hair that fell around my face, I could see Beht's shoulders had sagged and her once-crimson eyes were duller. She was tired?

She was fucking tired. Understanding burned in my chest. Beht had decided the best way to defeat me was by throwing so much magic at me that I became convinced I couldn't handle it. She figured if she broke me once, she'd never need to worry I'd try to challenge her again. But her show of dominance had worn her down, possibly more than she was expecting.

My heart skipped. I had a chance. I *must* have a chance or she wouldn't have tried so hard to convince me I didn't, and possibly I only had this one chance while she was drained. Assuming, that was, that I actually could control the flow of her power.

I didn't pause to consider any more deeply or worry if I could handle another influx. Before Beht could become aware of what I was thinking, I acted. With my gift, I grabbed the hand on my back—the bond—that was holding me in place. My nerves were practically vibrating with excess power after what she did, and the visualization came easily.

I pulled, and her head snapped in my direction. Instantly, she sensed what I was doing, and she dismissed my attempt with a sneer. *Again?*

I couldn't tell if she was speaking to me or if I was only imagining her words. But I was ready for her actions, which were simple enough to predict. When the surge of power slammed into me, I met it with open arms. I flung myself wide, hurling the power in every direction, giving it no time to build inside. I sizzled from my scalp to my fingertips. Every muscle tensed and every nerve alighted, but the sensation was pure radiance. Terrible and evil, but incredible.

Inhaling deeply, I drew more power down through my legs into my feet and from my toes into the ground. I made no attempt at controlling where I sent it. Control would have been futile. I simply let the magic surge through me and fly wild. Hair rose off my neck, and I swore I couldn't feel the stones beneath my legs anymore. Fear and fury pounded me, but they weren't my emotions this time. Beht let out a strangled and animal-like cry, and the flow of energy into me dipped.

Too late for that, bitch. Squeezing my eyes closed, I grappled for more. My chest swelled. Propelled by the power, I jumped to my feet. *How about you kneel for me?*

A high, cruel laugh escaped my lips, so unlike any sound I could have tried to make on my own. I was the queen now. I could rule. Hell, I'd swear I could fly. And I would make these creatures pay for what they'd done to my friends. I would make them understand what a monster truly was.

The cliff walls flickered, and for a second I could see through them. Just darkness and a dull red glow that mimicked the fading color of Beht's eyes. The demon bared her teeth, and I felt the force of her hate as it poured into me. It was a cold, sharp power that scratched me from the inside out as it ran through. The nastiness of the sensation almost made me lose my grip, and that jolted me back to the task at hand. I was not a monster. Not one of them. It was time to end this before so much power made me forget.

Pulling Misery from my sheath, I dashed toward Beht. The demon swept out with her arm to knock me aside, but the blow glanced off me. She tried to dodge, but I was faster. With a cry of revulsion, I drove the knife blade into her chest.

Beht's howl rang in my ears, and she pounded me in the cheek with her fist. I stumbled, aware that I was hurt but unable to feel it. Growling, Beht grasped Misery's hilt and yanked the knife out of herself.

You had to be kidding me. Blood poured through her wound, and her breaths came hard and fast. *You hate me for what I've done, but you would be nothing without me,* she said in my head. *Just another weak, pathetic human. So I will take you down with me.*

She ran straight at me. It shouldn't have been possible in her state, but apparently neither of us was feeling any pain. I grabbed my gun and shot her. The first bullet went wide. The second didn't faze her.

I turned and ran, conscious of my fear returning. My sword still lay on the ground, and I could hear Beht's feet behind me, sense her connection through the bond as I reached for it. Even with all the magic coursing through my veins, I couldn't grab the hilt and run at the same time. I tripped over my feet and tumbled to the rock. Flinging myself around, I swung the blade as Beht lunged for me.

She was no illusion and didn't part as easily as the ghouls she'd sent to torment me, but part she did in a sickening display of blood. I sliced her head clean off.

TWENTY-FIVE

THE BLOODY SWORD SLIPPED FROM MY FINGERS AS THE WORLD
dissolved. In seconds, all that remained of the snowy landscape was the
red sky, only it was no longer sky. It was just there. I had no words for it or
anything else. I existed in space that was obviously not space. This was
the void without someone's magic giving it life, and it was even eerier
than the hoard of ghouls Beht had sent to torment me.

"Jess!"

Relief overwhelmed me, causing tears to prick the corners of my eyes.
"Lucen!"

Now that everything else had been stripped away, I could see him and
Mitch. High as I was on the remains of Beht's power, my feet bounced
over the ground as I raced to his side. I was completely disgusting, but
Lucen wrapped me in the best hug of my life.

"You're all right." He repeated it several times while I clung to him.
Finally, he released me and wiped blood from my cheeks. "What
happened?"

"She's dead," I whispered. Talking with an actual mouth suddenly
seemed so common, so *lesser*, and I pushed the silly thought away. Damn
this lingering power. I was neither a demon nor a god, though I felt
like one.

"Who's dead?" Lucen asked.

My head spun. Oh, right. Lucen wasn't there. He hadn't seen what happened. I needed to settle back into myself and get my head on straight, but I fucking hummed with power that I couldn't shake. "Behty, their queen. She's the one who did this." I gestured to the missing illusion as if that would explain everything.

"Um, guys." Mitch had been on the opposite side of the nothingness— if the nothingness could be said to have sides—and he jogged over. "Don't mean to cut the reunion short, but we're not done yet. We've got a missing key and *that* to deal with."

That? I followed the path of Mitch's arm, and my gaze landed on something that was genuinely unsettling, even in my current state. Demons. Hundreds of them. No, thousands. Beht had said she had thousands. They were flopped on top of one another, sprawled across the dark ground, seemingly sleeping.

Although they were drained of energy, the sheer number of them meant that the power they emanated was intense. Hot and prickly, it pressed against my skin, and I got the sense that being filled with Beht's magic was the only thing protecting me from them seeping into my head.

Neither Mitch nor Lucen had that advantage. Inexplicably, I was still Lucen's addict and, as a result, I could pick up traces of his fear traveling through our bond. Mitch, on the other hand, looked frightened enough for both of them.

"We'll just back out the way we came, right?" He gestured behind us.

"Without the key?"

Lucen took my arm and tugged me away. "We'll never find it without Kassin's detector. We'll have to figure out something else."

"No. It's here, and I'm not leaving without it. What's the point?"

"The point, little siren, is we live to try to fight another day."

I yanked my arm from Lucen's grip. He wasn't incorrect, but fighting another day wasn't enough for me. Too many people had died on this particular day to give up without trying harder. I owed it to Tom and the others who'd sacrificed their lives for us to get this far. Also, I had no desire to ever reenter this place. When I left, I wanted it locked for good, and an idea was occurring to me for how to accomplish that.

In my mind's eye, I could see glowing threads leaving my body, a whole tapestry of them in various colors. They connected me to the myriad slumbering demons. When I stole power from Beht, I must have inherited her connections to her flock, and it was these connections that explained why I continued to buzz with magic. I was still drawing on someone else's —many someone else's—energy.

Beht had used that massive power to redesign the prison. Could I use the same trick to show me the key? Better yet, could I make the prison bring it to me? It was a long shot, but—blame it on the demons' magic— I'd never been so confident in my life.

I didn't bother to explain what I was about to do because I wasn't sure if I could. I just dropped to a crouch and pressed my palms against the ground. Focusing on the magic coursing through me, I gathered what I could in my stomach then pushed it out through my palms. Above me, Lucen asked what I was up to, but I needed all my concentration and couldn't respond. The threads connecting me with the demons pulled taut as more power rushed into me.

The key. Bring me the key. Since I had no idea what it looked like, I pictured an old-fashioned one in my head. Something big, tarnished, and heavy. The prison wavered around me, and one of the men gasped. I was doing something, whatever it was.

Come on! The ground swayed and dipped between where I squatted and the demons, creating a bowl. A couple of demons stirred, and I swore silently. I must have been channeling enough magic for them to notice.

The brief distraction almost ruined any progress I'd been making. Against my will, everything shifted back to normal. I cursed again and squeezed my eyes shut, shoving away the errant thoughts. *Key. Give me the key.*

Reality buckled under me. I opened my eyes in time to see a giant brass key be burped up from the rock. It was in every way the thing I'd imagined—poorly formed and hazy on the details. Yet it radiated a power that could only be described as similar to the power generated by its magical cousins, the Vessels of Making. This had to be it. It was the real thing, its form shaped by my thoughts.

I snatched it, reveling in the heft of its weight against my hand and the tingles it shot up my arm. It was amazing, and yet I hadn't the faintest idea what to do with it.

Lucen gaped at me and ran his fingers through his hair. "You shaped the prison. How?"

"Long story. I'll explain later." Like when we were safe, if such a thing was possible.

"So that's it?" Mitch regarded the key dubiously.

"That's it."

Mitch reached for it, but the curiosity in his eyes was replaced once more by fear as he focused on something over my shoulder. "They're waking up."

I spun around, the pride at what I'd done fading as reality set in. Shadows changed among the sprawling masses as limbs and heads shifted position. Several pairs of red and golden eyes blinked. Damn it, I'd known I was waking them. I'd marveled over my accomplishment for too long.

I stuffed the key in my inner jacket pocket and grabbed the men's hands. "Time to run, I think."

Fueled by magic, I bounded across the void faster than any speed charm could have propelled me, dragging Lucen and Mitch along. Through the threads connecting me to the demons, I could sense their unrest and rage. Worse, I could sense their movement. They were underpowered but not helpless. Far in the distance, the thin white line of the gate hung in the air like a ghostly apparition. With no cliffs to block it, no cavern of basilisks to navigate, it appeared far closer than I remembered it being, and yet I feared it was still too far to reach.

The air rumbled behind us, and I tried not to think about thousands of pairs of feet stepping closer or wings taking flight. I tried not to think at all because when I did, I slowed. If I worried or wondered how I was drawing on this power, my ability to use it faltered.

I recalled something Lucen had tried explaining to me when he was teaching me about charm-breaking. *Trust the magic*, he'd said. *Don't try to second-guess it.*

It was as true in this case as it was in choosing the right anti-magic.

So I didn't run, I flew. My feet scarcely touched the ground, and holding on to Mitch and Lucen was like dragging two balloons behind me.

I didn't know how they kept up, if I was feeding them power or if their feet simply didn't touch the ground either. But I didn't dare pause to find out. The noise at our backs grew thunderous. The void shook.

Then all at once the nothing disappeared, and we were back in the prison room. A low ceiling replaced the endless sky, and flickering torches provided the light. My pace continued unbroken, the sandy stone floor as meaningless to me as the void's black nothing. Open cells whizzed past in a blur of gray iron. I could hear Lucen hollering my name and an inhuman cry of rage following. Triumph rose in my blood, and a yell of my own burst from my lips as I jumped through the gate. Instantly, all sound vanished. My insides compressed, and my voice was swallowed with no air to carry it.

I popped out the other side, yelling still. Either Lucen or Mitch fell on top of me, and I let go of their hands. Stumbling across the stones, I couldn't stop my momentum until I crashed into an object that turned out to be a very large Gryphon. He stepped away, and I fell to the ground.

"I have it! We're safe, I have it!" I gasped to get the words out, but no one was listening. When I fell silent, it was obvious why. The pounding feet I'd heard in the Pit continued to pound. Scrambling upright, I watched in horror as demons spilled out of the gate. They were slow and sluggish, but they were very much here. And without Behty hogging all the negativity, they'd be juiced in no time too.

Strong hands yanked me out of the way as a lumbering demon crashed into the floor where I'd been standing. Though I buzzed with my stolen power, my thoughts hovered somewhere above my head. Using that power to find the key was one thing. Processing mundane reality was another. I couldn't focus, and it was Lucen's turn to lead me to safety. I followed him to a sheltered alcove near the ruins' doorway and glanced around.

All hell was breaking loose, and it looked like it had been for a while. The ruins were more, well, ruined than they had been before. Walls were down, and the enormous glyph on the floor no longer glowed red but green. A few bodies lay scattered along the sides, and Gryphons, magi, and goblins alike were covered in blood. I searched for Gi, anxious about his welfare, but he was nowhere in sight. For that matter, neither was the purple demon. But more Gryphons were here than I remembered there being when I left. Helicopters too. Stealth had clearly been overridden by the need for reinforcements.

Belatedly, I looked beyond the helicopters into a sky turning pale pink in the east. Sunrise. My body didn't feel it, but it sure appeared that we'd been gone for an entire night. No wonder more Gryphons had been called.

"You have the key?" Ingrid's voice knocked me out of my daze. She darted through an opening in the chaos and knelt among the rubble with us.

I retrieved the key from my pocket, hoping Ingrid had a clue what to do with it.

You are the one, Beht had said. *But the other like you is necessary.*

Before Ingrid could take the key, I closed my fist around it. I could be making up stuff in desperation, but once again, I didn't think so. My blood still flowed with Beht's power, and it told me she'd inadvertently given me a hint about what to do. "I need Mitch."

Ingrid sat back on her heels. "What are you going to do?"

"We're going to imitate what the furies did to us to open the Pit. Only instead of draining addicts for their power, I'm going to charge this thing by draining the demons themselves." How Mitch was going to help with that, I wasn't sure. But Beht had said he was necessary, and I was certain she—and I—was correct.

While Ingrid ran to make that happen, Lucen grabbed my hands. "Do you know what you're doing? Are you sure? Because, Jess, there's power inside you—"

"It's the demons, and I need it to do this."

"It's evil. I can feel it through the bond. It's a cold darkness surrounding your heart."

I did my best to sense the energy the way Lucen described it, but I couldn't. It was simply there, stronger than any other pred power I'd fed on, but ultimately the same. "It's... Don't worry about it. I just need to use it to charge the key. Then it'll be gone."

Lucen started to say something else, but a curse grenade exploded nearby, and we shrank back. A second later, Mitch appeared, escorted by an unfamiliar Gryphon.

I let go of Lucen's hands and grabbed Mitch's, placing the key between my right palm and his left. Although I was unsure what he needed to do or how to explain my intentions, it didn't matter. Pressed between our hands, the key reacted on its own. I gasped, and Mitch swore, and in the time it took for that to happen, a circuit of magic formed among the three of us.

Instinct took over as the threads connecting me to the demons appeared before my eyes. I sucked in a breath, pulling on the collective power contained on their ends. Electricity shot through my body. Though I'd been prepared, the rush was dizzying nonetheless, and Mitch yelled an agonized and ecstatic cry as I forced the power out through me and into him.

His body exploded in light as threads appeared on him too. Now he was breathing in their power, and we were both pouring it into the key. It began to glow, the edges sharpening into focus and the color brightening. Heat seared my palm, but I couldn't let go, and I clenched my jaw. My vision blurred as hazy black shapes gathered nearby. Gryphons coming to protect us, I realized. The demons were aware of what was going on. They were trying to stop it.

But they'd been weakened by what Mitch and I were doing. We just had to last a little longer. The key felt full but not full enough. I yanked harder on the threads, and a fresh wave of dizziness wracked my head. Then the power hit a wall. My attempt to channel more into the key failed, and the backlash knocked me to the ground.

Mitch collapsed too, and the key dropped between us, glowing a dazzling golden white. He moaned, seeming to have taken the hit harder than I had, perhaps since he'd had less time to adjust. The threads that had once surrounded him vanished.

"Cover me!" I shouted to anyone nearby. Climbing to my feet, I grasped the key and charged toward the gateway, heedless of what I was running into. My threads remained, and I felt their tug on my limbs. They beckoned me toward the gate, toward the majority of the demons who were still inside.

Claws swiped at me, and wings beat down overhead. My ears rang with the sounds of gunshots and so many cries, human and not. I gasped for breath, tasting metal and not knowing whether it was my blood or the magic in the air. With my every step on the glyph, the green glow changed to white and the smoke took on an acrid scent.

Now, I yelled at myself. *Just let go.*

The glowing line hovered in front of me, and I hurled the key into it. My aim was less than perfect, but sharp strands of light shot out from the gateway, snatching the key and sucking it inside. I had a second to revel in the idea that we'd won then my ears popped. The air pressure changed, and a horrific screech reverberated off the walls.

A wing slammed me in the back, and I tumbled to the ground. As I flipped onto my back to see what hit me, my jaw dropped. The gateway hadn't merely sucked the key in. It was now sucking the demons in with it.

Afraid of another inadvertent beating, I stayed low as the furious and flailing monsters were dragged back to prison. Whoops of triumph and glee rose from the Gryphons, and I grinned. As the last of the demons disappeared into the void and the sky drained of its unnatural color, I jumped up, ready to throw my arms around Lucen.

Instead of moving forward though, I was jerked backward. The threads connecting me to the demons hadn't broken, and I was being yanked toward the Pit with them. Panic constricted my chest. I reached out, but no one and nothing solid was nearby to grab. Frantically, I struggled to run forward, but the ground slipped out from under me. Back I went, soles scraping the stone. My emotional and magical highs were gone, and I flailed helplessly.

"Lucen!"

Everywhere I turned, Gryphons were hugging and high-fiving or collapsing to the floor and weeping in relief. Everyone was too busy celebrating our victory to notice me. Everyone but him. Lucen must have noticed my distress through the bond, and he sprinted toward me.

I held out my hands as I skidded, fearing that even if he reached me, it wouldn't be enough. How could he hold me back? The magic was way too strong.

Inches separated me from the gate. His fingers grasped mine, then a hand closed around my wrist. I held on to him, my sweaty skin gliding through his grip. My throat closed, sensing this was the end. This touch would be the last I knew of him. The gate's pull was making me double over. Another second and I'd be lost, condemned to die in the void at the hands of creatures who'd kill me in nasty ways.

"I have you." Lucen's face clenched, and the bond between us flared. I'd lost track of it amidst the threads tying me to the demons, but I'd been channeling his power all this time. He hadn't been fighting me over it before since the intent had been to steal his magic, but he did now. I could sense him fighting the flow of energy between us, holding back everything he could.

Understanding that he was attempting to fight magically as well as physically, I stopped channeling his power. Pain flashed through my body as I did, but Lucen took it away. Slowly, the pressure on my back released and my feet stopped sliding, but I was being torn in two, magically yanked in both directions.

Lucen muttered under his breath and sweat beaded on his forehead. Then one of the threads snapped. Grunting in frustration, I dared another step toward Lucen. My chest heaved, and I could smell the cinnamon of his pheromones. More, I needed more.

Another thread snapped, then another. Lucen stretched forward and took a stronger hold on my arms. All at once, the rest of the threads broke. I toppled into him, shoved forward by a burst of magic at my back. It blew through me, through the bond with Lucen, and into him too.

Together, we tumbled to the ground. My head landed on his chest, then I blacked out.

TWENTY-SIX

TWO WEEKS LATER, I GAZED OUT THE WINDOW IN MY NEW office at Boston's Gryphon headquarters. My office. My office with a freaking window. It was surreal.

From this vantage point, downtown appeared back to normal. The sky was blue, and the rush-hour traffic was a nightmare, but this normality was all a trick of perspective. What I couldn't see from my window was that the world was scarred. For many people, life would never be the same. My life certainly wouldn't be, but it wasn't just the many who had died or the cities and towns picking through the pieces of their devastation that had changed.

The anti-mager protests had died down, but the sentiment behind them—the fear of the unknown—had increased. Human opinions on the Gryphons, which had once been overwhelmingly and irrationally positive, had only become more split and extreme on both sides. They were saviors and threats, and no one embodied that dichotomy in the public imagination more than I did. When the story of what happened had been told, my name had been prominently featured in it despite my best efforts to prevent it. I didn't know who was responsible for the leak this time, but my role in the events had been portrayed too positively for it to have been Xander.

On the good-news end however, the Gryphon-pred-magi alliance had sparked a grudging acknowledgment that maybe, just maybe, we would all be safer if we were willing to communicate more and in a less hostile manner. The city magical councils of the past had grown dysfunctional when they bothered to function at all. It was time for a change, and naturally heads had turned to me to implement it. The woman who didn't fit in anywhere could therefore walk among everyone as an equal. Who else had a chance to make all sides listen?

I didn't have an answer to that, but I sure did have my doubts about success. After some hard contemplation though, I'd decided taking the job the Gryphons had offered was worth a shot. They'd asked Mitch too, but he had declined. Although he was staying with the Gryphons, he was taking the opportunity to focus on becoming one of their healers. But he was doing so back in Phoenix. He'd left for home last week.

My laptop finished shutting down, and I stuffed it into my backpack. Without it, my office was pretty barren because I'd moved in just yesterday. Besides the laptop, my desk, and a mostly empty bookshelf, the only items it contained were a little red pin and a ceremonial dagger bearing the marks of *Le Confrérie de l'Aile*. They'd been Tom's, and I'd accepted them from Ingrid at his funeral.

I swallowed past the lump in my throat and lugged on my pack. I'd attended too many funerals these past weeks. Yet for all my differences with Tom, his had been the hardest emotionally.

One last time, I checked my pockets for my keys and shut the office door. Not next week, but the week after when I got back from World Headquarters, I'd have to decorate so I wasn't staring at blank walls. I did enough of that at home, and since I'd negotiated to be based out of Boston instead of Grenoble, it was time to indulge in some decorating there too. Maybe even some furniture.

After stopping by Bridget's and Andre's offices to wave goodbye for the weekend, I fought the crowds on the subway to get home. I received a few funny looks as I got off at the Shadowtown T stop. Not many people in Gryphon uniforms did that sort of thing, and I felt horribly conspicuous as I hurried to Lucen's apartment. I was being silly since most people around here already knew who and what I was, but some habits were as hard to shake as some memories.

The eighteen-year-old Academy flunky chasing after a purpose, and the twenty-eight-year-old woman who'd been framed for murder chasing after unlikely help, lingered close to the surface of my thoughts these days. I was still struck senseless sometimes by how I started there and ended up here.

The Lair was back to its usual crowded self, as were most businesses, and music poured onto the street. I cast a quick glance at the people hanging out on the patio as I climbed the steps to Lucen's apartment and let myself in. I recognized most of the faces but didn't see any friends, which wasn't too surprising. Friday was a busy night for everyone. Lucen would be working the bar, Devon would be at Purgatory, and Angelia probably would be too. I wasn't sure I'd call Gi or Melissa friends, though I'd certainly spent enough time with them over the past month, but I assumed they'd be returning to whatever they usually did when they weren't babysitting me.

I dumped my key on Lucen's kitchen table and grabbed a couple wood chips from the bag by his deck door. In his cage, Sweetpea bared his teeth at me and banged his head against the bars as I passed.

"I get it," I told the dragon. "You hate him as much as you hate me. Get used to it, you scaly rat."

I got another bang in response as I stuffed the woodchips into the mini troll's cage. Yes, that mini troll. After she'd caught him in The Feathers, Steph hadn't been able to part with him. She'd named him Marvin, but she was afraid of her landlord discovering an illegal pet. So she'd passed him to me.

I'd threatened to toss Marvin out on the street, but the bugger seemed to like me. Since no pets ever liked me, I felt guilty and couldn't do it. I couldn't keep him either though because of my impending travel, so I'd passed him to Lucen. Lucen had renamed him Potato and said he expected me to keep the cage clean.

I couldn't tolerate the thought of naming the little guy after food with Sweetpea nearby, so I'd dubbed him Sir Francis Marvin the Incorrigible and feared he was going to suffer from an identity crisis if Sweetpea didn't eat him first. But Lucen could call the mini troll whatever he wanted. The idea of sharing a pet with him made me weirdly happy.

After a shower, a change of clothes, and some food, I considered my evening's options. It had been so long since I'd had the ability to relax, I was forgetting how to do it. Obviously, going down to The Lair was a given, but I had plenty of time for that. Meanwhile, Steph had finally responded to the text I sent her before showering.

Can't do Fitzpatrick's tonight. Got plans.

I wrinkled my nose. *What plans could possibly be more important than hanging out with me?*

She wrote back a minute later. *Geez. You save the world once and your ego knows no bounds.*

Bitch. My ego is in perfect proportion to my importance.

Sticking my tongue out at her, I tossed the phone to the side. Fine, maybe I'd go to Purgatory later and mooch off Devon's goodwill after I mooched off Lucen's free booze. Or maybe I'd just stay here and read a book. But no, my books were at my apartment. I'd have to go get them and come back if I wanted to spend the night.

It was such a simple, frivolous dilemma that I indulged in angst about it for longer than it deserved. Damn, I loved non-life-threatening decisions.

I'd about decided on the book when my phone rang. Lucen had quit with the apocalyptic ringtones at last, so I was no longer cringing to "Highway to Hell" whenever someone called instead of texted.

Speaking of the horned devil, he was the one calling. "Little siren, are you coming down soon or what?"

Though I could tell he was speaking loudly, the noise in the background was defiantly louder. The Lair must be bursting at its newly repaired seams. "I was debating it."

"Stop debating it and get your perky ass down here. I have something for you."

"First, my ass might be fine but nothing about me is perky. Second, what?"

"You'll find out when you get here, and many things about you are perky. Just not your personality." He hung up.

I stuck my tongue out at him too.

Sighing, I checked that my hair hadn't frizzed too badly and went down to the bar via the back stairs that led from Lucen's apartment. As I stepped out of the kitchen and into the bar itself, a cheer went up from the room. A crowd of satyrs raised their glasses. So did Steph.

I did a double take, bewildered. I could pick Steph out easily among the crowd since she was one of the few humans and was clearly uncomfortable being here. But when she saw me, she grinned.

"You... What is this?" The bar was stuffed with those friendly faces I'd been searching for earlier. Aside from Steph, Devon was here, and Dezzi, Angelia, and many others.

Lucen stepped out from behind the bar and handed me a glass of beer. "This is called a party. We're celebrating."

"Celebrating what?"

"You're a real Gryphon now," Steph said, raising a beer of her own. "A hero living her childhood dream."

"And..." Devon worked his way forward. "We like you anyway. In fact, politically speaking, this is a brilliant move for us."

I rolled my eyes. "No more nonsense about how it's good to have a spy in enemy territory. I deliberated about accepting this job, and I'm going to take it seriously."

Lucen wrapped an arm around me, almost sloshing my beer out of the glass. "We expect nothing less of you."

"Unless, you know, you feel particularly charitable and want to tip us off before any Gryphon raids," Devon said.

Dezzi poked him in the arm and gave me an exasperated look. "We all want this new partnership to succeed. We've seen what can happen when we do not work toward a common goal."

"All right, all right." Lucen let me go. "Enough with the serious talk. Let's get back to the celebrating."

Over the next several minutes, I was surrounded by people, mainly satyrs, who wanted to wish me well, thank me for what I'd done, and—of course—proposition me. They were satyrs, after all, and apparently, I'd gone from being an interesting curiosity to a highly coveted partner. I did my best to deflect the attention and politely decline the offers, but I did kiss Angelia to a few good-natured hollers. She'd earned it for the magical kiss she'd given me.

"You'll come around to me yet." She planted an extra kiss on my cheek, making my nose tingle with her hyacinth scent. "You can't let the men have all the fun."

"Sure she can." Devon ambushed me with a delightfully clove-scented kiss. We'd already had our own celebratory reunion, at which he'd told me he was so relieved that I'd made it back alive with Lucen that he forgave me for destroying Purgatory.

When I finally made my way over to Steph, she was leaning so far over the bar that she was practically lying on it. I knew she was making her best attempt to be here for me and no doubt putting dubious trust in Lucen to protect her. Not that I thought she was in any danger. None of the people Lucen had invited were going to mess with my best friend.

Steph gestured with her beer toward Angelia. "A third satyr? I learn more about you each time I see you."

"Just getting into the spirit of things."

"Very into it."

I pretended to punch her.

Unsurprisingly, Steph didn't want to hang out at The Lair for too long, and she really did have other plans. Specifically, a date with her boyfriend who had an unexpected Friday evening off work. I watched her go, amazed at her change in attitude. Sure, she'd been anxious about coming, but she'd braved a bar full of preds for me. In her own way, Steph was making as much progress in dealing with our situation as I was.

"So." Lucen stepped up behind me and nudged me off the barstool. "We need to talk."

I followed him into the corner by the kitchen door. "This does not sound celebratory."

"Oh, don't be so sure." He slid his arms around my waist, pressing me against him. I did the same and rubbed my fingers against the smooth muscles in his back.

Our bond had shattered from the blowback when the Pit closed, and although I didn't want to be his addict, I kind of missed that magical connection. I was having a more difficult time than usual keeping my hands off him as a result. Even now, I couldn't stop myself from tugging up his shirt in the back so I could touch his skin.

"When do you fly home from France?" he asked as though he didn't notice what I was doing. It was a lie because I could tell he very much noticed.

I frowned. "Friday morning. Why?"

"Can you change it and meet me in Paris for the weekend instead?"

My curiosity was too piqued to continue removing his shirt, and I let the fabric fall back into place. "You want to meet me there?"

"It's you. It's Paris. Why is that so surprising?"

"I don't know." I let go of his back and slipped my arms between us, resting my hands against his chest. It was such a classic defensive move on my part that I couldn't avoid noticing and becoming annoyed at myself for it. "I was under the impression that it's challenging for you to travel far because you have to arrange for addict company. Unless you were thinking you'd just rebond with me when you got there?"

Lucen clasped my hands in his. "About that, there's something I need to tell you. I let go of my last addict today."

"What?" I gave him a slight push in my surprise and looked him over head to toe. He appeared quite happy to be so close to me and in no way suffering the effects he had in the Pit. "And you're calmly standing here, telling me this? How is that possible?"

"I should rephrase. I let go of my last addict today who isn't you."

Okay, we were getting somewhere. But where? I shook my head, wondering which of us had drunk too much and thinking it couldn't be me unless he'd slipped something in my beer. "You're not making sense. I'm not your addict anymore. There's no bond connecting us."

"See, I think there is. I think it's just not that kind of bond." The mischievous smile slipped from his face, and his voice turned serious. "We were bonded when that magical blast hit. I felt it travel from you into me, and I've felt different ever since. Over the past couple weeks, I've been testing things out, releasing addicts one by one, and I haven't noticed a huge change in myself. You, on the other hand, seem to be a bit more, shall we say, *amorous* than before?"

"You've always had that effect on me." But as I said it, I remembered thinking just seconds ago how much more so I'd been lately. Lucen had a point. "I don't understand."

"Neither do I. The magic involved in that spell was far beyond anything I've studied, but I'm convinced the surge had some lasting effect on me. You too, maybe. It's almost as if it transferred some of my satyrness to you. I've been spared the unquenchable lust but at your expense. It equalized us."

I opened and shut my mouth a few times, at a loss for words. But my heart hammered. "So you no longer need addicts."

It was probably the wrong thing to focus on when confronted by Lucen's information. From the point of view of a Gryphon or even other preds, the potential here was amazing if someone smarter than me could figure out this mystery. But the only part I cared about at the moment was the implication for us.

I'd been resigned to needing to share Lucen; he was worth it. But if this were true, if I no longer needed to share him… I meant, assuming he was okay with that, which was making a big leap.

Lucen could certainly figure out what was causing my tumultuous emotions. "I no longer need addicts for now. I can't promise this will last forever."

"I know, but what does it mean for you?" *What does it mean for us?* That was the question I wanted to ask, but I was doing my best not to be selfish. "Isn't your position in the domus dependent on your addicts?"

"Yes and no. My position is determined by how useful I am. Normally, usefulness depends largely on the addicts I can acquire, but they aren't the sole factor. I'm sure Dezzi and I will have lots to discuss when I tell her. But really, this probably makes me so much more awesome that Devon might have to watch his back or I'll steal his favored spot." He laughed and pulled me close again. "Now ask the question you really want to ask."

I winced at the reminder that I was so easy to read. "Fine. What does this mean for us?"

"It means I'm all yours if you want me."

"Really?"

"Really, little siren." Lucen bent down and took my lips with his, and I melted at the taste of him. A crazy, happy desire rose in me, sweet yet hot, and it wasn't going to be satisfied with this tease. I wanted to tear his clothes off and dance with joy on the bar with him.

Temporarily forgetting we were in the middle of a crowded room, I slid my hand lower down Lucen's body, chasing the length of him beneath his jeans. But a familiar laugh caught my attention, reminding me where I was and prompting more questions. Sheepishly, I pulled away and made sure to keep some distance between us. Across the room, Devon winked at me.

My love life was way too complicated, but I'd thought I'd at least been getting a handle on it. I'd had a plan. Two nights a week I stayed with Lucen, two nights with Devon, and the other three were mine to do with as I pleased, whether it was sleep alone or host a party in my bed. I kept my independence that way, and I didn't have to run into anyone's addicts because the men could damn well deal with that part of their lives on their own time.

Now though? If Lucen was willing to be monogamous, it seemed like I should be too. Except I was going to feel awful explaining this to Devon, and damn it, I'd miss him. I'd gotten used to the idea of my nontraditional relationship. Of thinking two incredibly sexy men were a good consolation prize for not being able to have a single one to myself.

Lucen followed my gaze and again guessed what I was thinking. "Why do you expect this changes anything? I'm the same person, little siren. My tastes in our naked proclivities are no different."

I snorted at the naked-proclivities euphemism but pondered his words. "Oh. So this is all good with you?"

"Well, I might want to negotiate for one more night of the week since I don't have to worry about other company. Or you could just move in and call my place your home base. That would make Potato happy, I'm sure. But we don't have to rush things. We'll figure it out."

Screw keeping my distance from him. I buried my head against his chest, laughing with confusion and amazement. "You mean it would make

Sir Francis happy, but you're right. No rush. Isn't that a nice change? If I get to keep you both, I think I'm getting the better part of this plan though."

"Oh, don't be so sure." Lucen kissed the top of my head. "Besides, this way, you have to introduce both of us to your mother one day. You're still a loser there."

I groaned, some of my giddiness draining away at the thought. "No rush there either."

I'd seen my mother once since returning, and it had been interesting. It was the first time we'd gotten together since the news about what I was broke, and much crying had been involved. Mostly, they were happy tears. Whatever I was, she was thrilled I was alive, and I was thrilled that she was as accepting of everything as she was. I suspected, however, that accepting what I was might be a touch easier than accepting my relationship choices, but who knew? Maybe she'd surprise me.

"No, no rush there either." Lucen signaled to Paulius that he was ready to return to working the bar, because the poor bartender was getting overwhelmed by the crowd. Then he turned back to me. "You deserve to be happy for a while."

I grinned. "I am happy, and you're very right. Instead of little siren, maybe you should start calling me little Miss Sunshine."

"No."

"Little Miss Positivity?"

Lucen's expression was appropriately comical, and he whipped my butt with a towel as he went back to work.

"Fine." I plopped on my favorite stool and pushed my empty beer glass his way. "Then pour me another drink. I have more celebrating to do."

Thank you for reading! Did you enjoy? Please add your review because nothing helps an author more and encourages readers to take a chance on a book than a review.

And don't miss more from Tracey Martin coming soon!

Until then read FOUL IS FAIR, by City Owl Author, Elisse Hay. Turn the page for a sneak peek!

Also be sure to sign up for the City Owl Press newsletter to receive notice of all book releases!

SNEAK PEEK OF FOUL IS FAIR

BY ELISSE HAY

Half-a-dozen heavily lined faces beamed at me. Why? Why were they *beaming*?

"You must be Aurora," the shortest, roundest one said, her words so fizzy with excitement it made my eyes water.

Oh. Shit. Me. They were excited about *me*. One of them took my arm and towed me further into the room. "Your grandmother told us all about you, dear." Hellfire. I hoped that was an exaggeration. "It's so good to see a young witch coming on board! Look, everyone, Aurora is here!"

"It's Rory." But my protest was lost beneath their effervescent welcome.

I just wanted to get to work, but apparently stage one of my induction involved a spread that could've come off a bake stand at a school fair—and, before witches were legalized, that probably would have been a common side hustle.

Scones, breakfast muffins, slices, cakes—all homemade. The tea was weaker than the water I used to wash my dishes. To top it off was a handwritten banner that read *Welcome to the East Melbourne Coven, Aurora!* It had been decorated with pressed flowers.

"Wominjeka, Rory," said a woman wearing paint-splattered pants and a somewhat wary smile. "I'm Janet."

Trust the First Nations elder to have heard my preferred name. "Hi, Janet." I caught a jar of jam as it slipped from the nicotine-stained fingers of a grinning witch. Grimly amused, I watched the way she turned the situation to her advantage, using my momentary pause as I held the jar to press a plate into my hand.

I felt like a kid while I tried to smile, remember names, respond appropriately, and not drop the scone all at the same time. *Note to self: next time I want a change, I'll get a new hair color, not a new job.*

Behind the veterans, a younger woman with awesome jet-black hair and sapphire-blue highlights sent me a look of sympathy before she quietly removed herself from the fray. Smart woman. I should've gone sapphire blue, too. And also hightailed it out of there.

Some of the cream wilted down the side of my scone to puddle on my saucer as the jam-fumbling witch planted herself beside me, blocking the nearest exit, filling the air with chatter. "Oh, and you really ought to try Suzie's blueberry bar before we get caught up on the humdrum. Suzie's grandson owns a blueberry farm out in Silvan. Brings her fresh berries, doesn't he, Suzie?" Her eyes glittered. "He's a handsome young lad, isn't he, Suzie?" she went on, patting my arm knowingly. "Great butt," she said under her breath in an aside to me. "Looks like he knows how to use his hands, too, if you know what I mean!"

I estimated the likelihood of said grandson knowing the difference between a clitoris and a haemorrhoid as slim to none.

"I should find Arthur," I said firmly, before the grandson idea could gather any momentum. "I'll be back for that slice." Gazes of a half-dozen women, who were all obviously accustomed to people submitting to their affection, swung to me. Well, curse it, if I'd wanted to be fussed over, I'd have gone to work with my own grandmother. "This is such a great welcome. But I won't feel right until I know what I'm doing."

The jar-dropping witch, who might've been Bernie or Becky or even Esmerelda, for all I knew, made a harrumph of disapproval. "Well, you won't get that from Arthur. Half the time, that boy doesn't even know what he's doing, and the other half of the time, he's pulling on his own—"

"Hush, Bernie," another said with a disapproving frown. "I'm sure Aurora knows all about wizards." She cleared her throat, and I tried very hard to smother a grin. "Well, you go on up, dear," she said, her frown melting as she gazed up at me like I was the one grandchild who hadn't spilled food on their party dress at Solstice. "And when you come on back, we'll get you all settled in. Let her go, Bernie. She's quite right. Whether we like it or not, we all have those to-do lists now."

"The old days were much simpler," said a woman whose handmade name badge read *Cici—she/her*. Cool. Pronouns. I could get in on that. "No data or performance reviews. Just you, your wand, some herbs and foci, your coven and your flock. Now there's *paperwork*."

Plus a wage, superannuation, sick leave, holiday pay, and tax deductions.

I kept that to myself, sending them all my warmest, I'm-a-good-kid-with-good-manners smile as I went past the fussily decorated table in the direction I'd been pointed.

There wasn't space to get lost. Budgets being what they were, I hadn't expected a massive, multi-story complex. "Cozy" was a nice description for the little townhouse with its high, old ceiling and narrow rooms overflowing with furniture, plants, and piles of Really Important Stuff. Still, it had character that even the governmental grey paint and grey-flecked grey flooring couldn't overwhelm, vases that overflowed, doilies, donated mismatched furniture, and candles. Of course. Put a coven in a place long enough, it'd become a home, albeit a fussy one, if it was an old-school coven. And this was a very old-school coven.

I kept my face neutral as I went up the stairs. Well, I wanted different. I wasn't going to get anything as different from my last job as this, was I?

Should've gone for the blue streaks. Or maybe purple. I'd look great with purple hair.

A thirty-something, weekend-warrior type looked up from a coffee machine that perched precariously on a hallway table. His expression was equal parts curiosity and commiseration. "Aurora?"

I put out my hand. "Rory," I said, as he took it and shook.

"Arthur. I heard the welcome party banging their drums. Forgive me for not being present, but it sounded like they had you covered." He took an extra coffee cup. Not a flower in sight. "Anyway, word on the grapevine is you're a hard arse, so I figured you'd be okay. Coffee?"

He didn't look at me to deliver any of that. I didn't care, just sighed in pleasure at his offer. "Please."

He smiled down at the coffee machine. He had dimples, and he knew how to work them.

The coffee-making ritual gave me time to look around. He mentioned a few key points of interest: a bathroom, storage, his office—which he didn't share with anyone, I noticed—a meeting room, and the tech hub of the coven, currently unstaffed.

"It's not much," he said with false humility. "But we're two blocks from the local police station, and the tram line right around the corner makes travel a breeze."

"Uh huh." I wasn't here to give a real estate appraisal.

Inside Arthur's office, I was waved towards one of the chairs across from his desk.

I glanced around. Big windows overlooking the neighbour's brickwork. A few framed landscapes. His staff mounted on brackets on the wall.

Old school.

And he definitely had the most space in the building. The rooms I'd passed showed desks and office chairs crowded in so close I'd have my knees in my ears trying to work there.

With some grim thoughts about middle managers, I settled into the chair.

"So, I thought I'd give you a quick rundown of the coven's core values before we get into the nitty gritty of your work."

I folded my hands, reached for patience, found some, and marvelled. "Sure."

"Mutual respect and equality is, of course, the foundation of this coven," he began. This from behind his big desk, sitting in his new leather chair, in the one office that didn't have seven other people crammed into it.

"Mmm." I shifted a little, wishing, not for the first time, wizards came with a *skip* button.

"I know you've heard that before," he said in a way that he probably thought was charmingly self-deprecating. "So, I won't bang on about it. You'll see it in action. Accountability is, of course, critical. Risk assessments and case notes need to be kept updated so I can manage any situation that arises. We aren't police; we're here to tend to our flock, to keep them on the straight and narrow." He nodded at his own wisdom. It was kind of like being near someone sniffing their own farts. "To engage supernaturals in our society, help smooth over any bumps, and to ensure magi use their powers wisely. We're first responders."

So he didn't know what a first responder was. He did know what paperwork was though, obviously. That was the bottom line.

He flashed his dimples again. "And, of course, we need to discuss integrity," he went on, leaning forward.

At that point, I totally zoned him out.

When he finally fell silent, I said, "Thanks, Arthur. So, about the work. I'm assuming I'll get a rundown of my caseload from one of the coven?"

He nodded his agreement. "Unfortunately, you won't be able to do a thorough hand-over due to the nature of your predecessor's departure."

Sure, sour grapes didn't give much juice. I ignored the opportunity to garner gossip. I didn't value this guy's opinion. There would be someone in the know I could talk to. Confidentiality between a coven and the world was sacrament, but I was on the inside now.

"Aurora—"

"Rory."

His smile turned apologetic. "Rory. Most of what you need to know is in the handbook." He pushed the bound manual that had been sitting exactly at right angles to his laptop toward me. *Metro Procedures for Caretaker Witches.* "This is an established coven," he went on. Just what I needed, some light bedtime reading. "Most of the witches here are very... set in their ways."

That was so obvious I had planned on letting it go without saying.

The thing was, as much as their scones and welcome poster amused me, there was a reason the traditions were what they were. We didn't always even know what those reasons were, until we messed with them.

Anyway, they were cute. In a terrifying, grandmother-level-omnipotence sort of way.

Out of nowhere, without any sort of lead-in, Arthur declared, "I'm a feminist." And then he paused.

I met his eye and bit my tongue. He just sat there as if it was my turn to say something. Perhaps dig out a gold star.

When I just waited silently, content to let the awkward pause grow even more awkward, he shuffled a little in his seat and then went on.

"I know you're from the country, and you would be used to wizards getting in your way, telling you to go back to the kitchen and cook love potions."

I had been told exactly that. Still, I wasn't giving him the satisfaction of sharing my righteous indignation.

"Love potions are a Class B substance." My words were brisk.

He grinned at me again, as if trying to get me to share a joke. "Regardless, I want you to know you have my full support." I nodded and went to stand, because surely, this was the end. "I figure a strong, independent woman like yourself wouldn't necessarily want that."

Oh, wow, there was no irony. None. Was that…even possible?

"I just hope you never need it," he said with such concern that I was taken aback.

"I think this should cover me for now, though." I added, holding up the manual. If I ever needed Arthur to bail me out, I was in very dire straits.

As shields went, it might be useful.

He stood and walked me to the door. "Part of your caseload is a local lycanthrope pack," he said with a nod. "They're considered high-risk. I'm the district expert, so you don't need to worry. We'll work that together."

My feet were lead, and ice rushed through my veins. *Sun warming my face as blood began to dry on my hands. Black cockatoos screaming their way across the sky.* I looked down at the floor beneath my feet, drew in air. I was standing on carpet. Not bridge. Not rock. Carpet.

Lycans already? Shit. Suddenly, I didn't care that I'd just been patronized.

"Who's their Alpha?"

"Beo Velvela. Police are investigating them, but we're to keep up our surveillance until charges are laid."

I ignored the clutch of anxiety in my breast. I could deal with lycans.

"Can you email me the name of the officer in charge of the investigation, information on relevant parties, and crimes they could be linked to?"

He nodded. His arm went behind me, his hand resting on the door. I stepped out of that intimate circle without thinking, but he didn't react.

"Betty—your predecessor—and I were going along to where the Alpha works as part of our surveillance. *The Playground*," he added as I opened my mouth to question him. "Mixed Martial Arts dojo and gym. Beo runs Brazilian Jiu-Jitsu classes, and his whole pack—that we've identified—attend. I've been sparring with them once a week for about two months. Betty sat and knit. She posed as my mother."

Rolling with a lycan pack as undercover surveillance? If this was normal, where the fuck was my hazard pay?

Arthur was either totally ignorant, absolutely amazing, or very brave. I highly doubted he was all three.

"I don't knit. And I don't roll with lycans." *Bones crunched, a splintering, wet sound.* My stomach rolled. Nope-ity, nope, no.

I had goals. One day, I wanted to spend a whole week eating ice cream, chips, and having amazing sex, preferably with someone else.

He shrugged. "So, you can be my girlfriend. Scroll through social media, send some snaps. You and I know you're not that sort of woman, but they'll see what they expect."

There he went again. I was tempted to hit back, but I bit my tongue.

"Is it a mixed class?"

The words popped out of my mouth while my brain held back my ample vitriol. I wondered if he heard my teeth groaning as I clenched my jaw shut.

He nodded, a faint frown appearing on his face. "The pack isn't all male, and there are some human players. It's useful for me to have someone on the sidelines. I'll need you armed and prepared if there's trouble."

On the *sidelines?* "Arthur," I said through my teeth, trying to keep hold of my last shred of patience, "if you're on a mat in the middle of a lycan pack who actually want to hurt you, there's not a damn thing anyone can do, even armed, prepared, and perfectly positioned." Okay. My vote leaned towards totally ignorant. "I'll get up to date with the information, and we'll figure out how to play it." I emphasised the *we* part, because obviously, Arthur's decision-making skills lent more towards finding opportunities to inflate his own ego rather than keeping his insides on the inside.

His frown deepened, but he nodded his agreement. "I've been going on a Tuesday. Five-thirty until seven."

"We'll keep your pattern." Although why he had a pattern for undercover surveillance, I had no idea. Tuesday night gave me a whole two days, if I counted today, which I absolutely did. Urgency drummed through my veins. *Of* course, *it's lycans. That's just great.* "Any other high-risk cases I should know about?"

"Just Beo. You've got a few moderate threats, but mostly, it's nonviolent."

Well, that was something. I went to leave, then paused; I didn't want to go off half-cocked, even if it was sort of my specialty.

"What belt are you?"

He blinked at me. "With the BJJ? White. It's just a cover."

Because anything he wasn't good at didn't matter, I suspected. Yeah, he was toast if they decided they wanted a snack. Shit. "Any combat training or hand-to-hand combat experience?"

His brows rose. "I'm a wizard, Rory."

My heart sank. Yep, that told me everything I needed to know...and confirmed my worst suspicions.

Lucky for both of us, I was a witch.

Don't stop now. Keep reading with your copy of FOUL IS FAIR, by City Owl Author, Elisse Hay, available now.

And find more from Tracey Martin at www.tracey-martin.com

Don't miss the final book, MISERY HAPPENS, coming Feb. 2023, and discover more from Tracey Martin at www.tracey-martin.com

---

I like my monsters like my coffee—strong, hot, and not trying to kill me.

I'm done with hunting down supernatural criminals. Fighting for my life everyday gets old. So, career change. Social worker for supernaturals is a way to use my skills in a no risk environment. Right?

Wrong.

It turns out the last witch in my role was slaughtered by a lycanthrope— and the prime suspect is my client who happens to be pure, forbidden deliciousness. Totally irrelevant. I get paid to support the vulnerable, not lust after them. Or assume they're guilty unless proven innocent.

But the cops are outgunned. The wizards are morally bankrupt. And the lycans are concealing information.

There's someone powerful, clever, and armed with inside knowledge who's getting rich running drugs. Someone lurking behind a network of faeries and lycanthropes. Someone corrupt enough to kill to keep their secrets.

I'm a witch. I'm not going down without a fight.

All reviews are **welcome** and **appreciated**. Please consider leaving one on your favorite social media and book buying sites.

Escape Your World. Get Lost in Ours! City Owl Press at www.cityowlpress.com.

ACKNOWLEDGMENTS

Wow, here we are at the end of the Miss Misery series. If you're reading this, thank you for sharing these stories with me. *Wicked Misery* was the first book I ever published, and I had no idea when I was writing it how far Jess's story would take her, or how far these books would take me. I hope you enjoyed the ride as much as I have.

A huge thanks to the team who gave this series a second life—Tina Moss and Yelena Casale, Danielle DeVor for edits, MiblArt for the kickass covers, Lisa Carlisle for *Misery Happens'* copy edits, and the entire crew at City Owl Press.

As always, I'd be nowhere without the support of my writing group and the wonderful community of friends I've met since I began this journey. I also can't miss thanking my family for being fantastic cheerleaders, or my husband who puts up with an awful lot in order for me to get these books written.

Finally, I need to thank the most important people of all—the readers. Books are just ink and pixels, not stories, if no one takes the time to read them. Thank you to all of you who have given some of your precious time to mine. I hope they've provided you with some fun, some humor, and some very needed escape. I'm especially grateful to the reviewers who take time to share their thoughts and feelings with others, and in some cases who have been fantastic champions of this series. I hope we get to meet again in another imaginary world.

ABOUT THE AUTHOR

TRACEY MARTIN lives in New England where she collects pen names, tattoos, and hoodies in shades of gray and black. Under the name Alanna Martin, she's the author of the *Hearts of Alaska* contemporary romance series. If you can't find her online, it's because she's lost in the woods. Send help.

www.tracey-martin.com

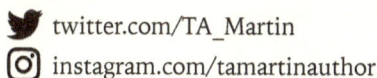 twitter.com/TA_Martin
instagram.com/tamartinauthor

ABOUT THE PUBLISHER

City Owl Press is a cutting edge indie publishing company, bringing the world of romance and speculative fiction to discerning readers.

Escape Your World. Get Lost in Ours!

www.cityowlpress.com

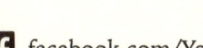 facebook.com/YourCityOwlPress
twitter.com/cityowlpress
 instagram.com/cityowlbooks
pinterest.com/cityowlpress